PRAISE FOR THE NOVELS OF
VICKI LANE

IN A DARK SEASON

*A Romantic Times Best Mystery and
Suspense Novels of 2008 Pick*

Anthony Nominee for Best Paperback Original

"The precise details and many mysteries are all skillfully drawn together at the end, and the main characters are clearly developed, complicated people who have lives outside the mystery. Elizabeth Goodweather is a perfect protagonist who shows that there can be intelligence and romance after 50."
                                                            —*Romantic Times*

"Vicki Lane is a born storyteller in the finest tradition of Sharyn McCrumb. Lane's best yet, *In a Dark Season*, is a haunting, lyrical tale of the Appalachians, as heartbreaking as it is magical. Brooding, suspenseful, and superbly written, Lane's Marshall County mysteries rank among the best regional fiction anywhere today."
                                                —Julia Spencer-Fleming

"Suspenseful, atmospheric, and beautifully written."
                                                —Sarah Graves

"Lane craftily deepens the swiftly moving plot with liberal sprinklings of Carolina folklore."   —*Publishers Weekly*

OLD WOUNDS

"Lane is very adept at creating complex, multi-faceted stories that move effortlessly from one time period to another and characters with incredible depth. She is also a master of using sensory details to make locale come alive. *Old Wounds* exemplifies these talents. Readers weary of reading too many mysteries featuring frothy amateur sleuths won't find a better antidote than *Old Wounds*." —*Mystery News*

"Vicki Lane is quite simply the best storyteller there is. Her books, like her Appalachian home, have everything: mystery, suspense, beauty, heart, and soul."
—JOHN RAMSEY MILLER

"A story so exquisitely written and perfectly paced, you will not want to put this book down. *Old Wounds* is a powerful and very personal mystery for the thoughtful Elizabeth Goodweather to solve."
—JACKIE LYNN

ART'S BLOOD

"Lane's sharp eye for detail gets put to good use in this second installment of her Appalachian series. . . . The widow Goodweather is a wonderful character: plucky, hip and wise. The dialogue sparkles with authenticity, and Lane generates suspense without sacrificing the charm and mystique of her mountain community." —*Publishers Weekly*

"Lane mixes the gentle craft of old-time quilting with the violence of a slaughtered innocent."
—Greensboro *News & Record*

SIGNS IN THE BLOOD

For Pam —
Welcome to Miss
Birdie's world!

The Day of
Small Things

A Novel

❧

Vicki Lane

[signature]

DELL BOOKS
New York

The Day of Small Things is a work of fiction. Names, characters,
places, and incidents either are the product of the author's
imagination or are used fictitiously. Any resemblance to
actual persons, living or dead, events, or locales
is entirely coincidental.

A Dell Mass Market Original

Copyright © 2010 by Vicki Lane

Published in the United States by Dell, an imprint of
The Random House Publishing Group, a division
of Random House, Inc., New York.

DELL is a registered trademark of Random House, Inc.,
and the colophon is a trademark of Random House, Inc.

978-0-385-34263-6

Cover design and digital imaging: Marietta Anastassatos
Cover illustration: Kamil Vojnar/Getty Images (girl),
Johner/Getty Images (landscape)

Printed in the United States of America

www.bantamdell.com

2 4 6 8 9 7 5 3 1

Threescore and ten I can remember well;
Within the volume of which time I have seen
Hours dreadful and things strange; but this sore night
Hath trifled former knowings.

William Shakespeare, Macbeth (II.4.1–4)

An aged man is but a paltry thing,
A tattered coat upon a stick, unless
Soul clap its hands and sing, and louder sing . . .

William Butler Yeats, "Sailing to Byzantium"

To Kate Miciak,
who wanted to let me spread my wings
and, so doing, let Birdie spread hers.

And, as always, to John.

Acknowledgments

First of all I must thank Karol Kavaya and Madelon Heatherington, members of my former critique group, who wouldn't let me kill off Miss Birdie back in the first book. Who knew how many readers (including my editor) would love this woman so much?

For all who've asked, Miss Birdie is not based on anyone I've ever known but is a composite, enhanced with a very generous dose of my own imagination. In this connection, I have to note, with sorrow, the passing of two of my friends and neighbors: Mearl Davis and Grace Henderson, two strong mountain women and great ladies who shared some DNA with Miss Birdie.

Thanks go also to Kathy Hendricks, who told me a story of a mother and a daughter that gave me an idea. Judith Arnn-Knight pointed me to useful websites. Nancy Meadows loaned me the diaries of her aunts Inez and Odessa, and their names as well; Tammy Powell shared some old-time names and ways. Thanks to Kathryn Stripling Byer, North Carolina's poet laureate, whose work is a continuing inspiration; to Mary Pat Franklin, who answered questions; and to Calvin Edney, who told me about the hatpin lady. (Sadly, there really was one.)

Thanks to Ann Collette, my wonderful agent, who always cheers me up when I begin to have doubts about my alleged career; to Deb Dwyer, the sharp-eyed copy editor who catches my mistakes and leaves lovely comments in the margins of the manuscript; and to Randall Klein, who has dealt kindly with my unusual additions to this book.

And to all the readers who send me supportive e-mails, and especially to the readers of my newsletter and (almost) daily blog, who have lived and suffered through the long, long birthing of this book: You all have kept me going through some dark moments. I hope you enjoy Miss Birdie's story.

(And now, on to the next book and the resolution of that cliff-hanger.)

꒰

PART I

Least

Dark Holler, 1922–1938

Chapter 1

A Birth

Dark Holler, 1922

On the evening of the third day of labor, the woman's screams filled the little cabin, escaping through the open door to tangle themselves in the dark hemlocks that mourned and drooped above the house. The weary midwife, returning from a visit to the privy, winced as a series of desperate shrieks tore through the still air of the lonely mountain clearing.

Pausing to readjust her loose dress and collect her strength for the battle ahead, she glanced up at the brooding trees and shook her head. "Seems like all them cries and moans is going straight up into them old low-hanging boughs—just roosting there like so many crows. And the pain and grief, it'll linger on and on till every wind that stirs'll be like to bring it back—miseries circling round the house again, beating at the air with their ugly black wings."

The country woman frowned at such an unaccustomed flight of fancy. "Law, whatever put such foolishness into my head? I'm flat wore out, and that's the truth—else how

would I come to think such quare things? But hit's a lonesome, sorrowful place fer all that and a sorrowful time fer
poor Fronie. Here's her man not yet cold in his grave and
her boy tarrying at death's door—ay, law, hit's a cruel hard
time to birth a child—iffen hit don't kill her first."

Hurrying back into the small log house, the midwife
pulled on the clean muslin apron that was the badge of her
calling. The screams broke off and the expectant mother
lay panting on the stained and stinking corn-shuck tick,
her breath coughed out in hoarse rasps. Long dark hair,
carefully combed free of tangles in vain hope of easing the
birth, fanned in damp strands around her death-pale face.
The anguish, the fear, the anger that had passed like a suc-
cession of hideous masks over the laboring woman's gaunt
countenance were replaced by an otherworldly absence of
all emotion.

Then a great ripple surged across the huge belly
swelling beneath her thin shift, and the woman's face contorted once more. Her mouth gaped but nothing more
than a strangled croak emerged. Gasping with pain and
frustration, she twisted her misshapen torso and clawed at
her heaving belly.

The midwife caught at the woman's hands and held
them till the contraction passed. "It'll be born afore sun-
down or they'll be the two of 'em to bury," she whispered
to the frightened girl standing at the bedside.

"I ain't never seen no one die." The girl's wide eyes
brimmed with tears. "My daddy, he was already gone
when they fetched him home from the logging camp. Miz
Romarie, I'm bad scared. . . ."

The midwife patted the girl's bony shoulder and then
reached for the bottle of sweet oil that stood on a nearby
stool. "We ain't got time fer that now, Fairlight. You catch

hold of yore mama's hands whilst I see kin I turn the babe and bring it on. Hold 'em tight now, honey."

Black night had come and owls called from the sighing hemlocks as the exhausted woman bent an expressionless face to her red, squalling infant. At last she spoke. "It'll allus be the least un, fer there won't be no more. Reckon that'll do fer a name—call it Least."

Chapter 2

The Peddler

Dark Holler, 1927

(Fronie)

What the Lord in His wisdom has done to me don't seem neither right nor just. To bear nine children and then to lose them as I have. And my husband Hobart gone too. They ain't none left on the place save Little Brother and the least un—and she not yet five years of age and naught but a hindrance and a worry. Brother's a good worker, I give him that, but me and him can't seem to agree—he says I'm too hard and lights out of here for ball games and singings and whatnot every chance he gets. Though he's not but sixteen, I do believe that if he would marry and bring home a stout girl, a hard worker to help here on the place, hit would settle him some.

I am plumb wore with all the work there is to do. Brother and me topped the corn by moonlight last night—laid by all them tops for cow feed come winter—and today I can't hardly go. My hands is red and cracked and the joints is swole till they look like they belong to an old, old woman.

I feel like an old, old woman too. Forty-six years of living and no more to show for it than a farm that's getting away from me, a child what ain't right, and a boy what's never happy lessen he's going down the road. Ay, law. I have heard the preacher say this life is a misery and we best think on the world to come. Ha. Reckon first we got to get through this world the best we can.

The peddler come by this evening just after dinnertime. I needed some domestic in the worst way—Least is near bout growed out of her dresses. She would just as soon run naked but it ain't fitten. I've cut up and made do with what few rags Fairlight left behind, but even those is going fast.

"What fer ye, Missus?" the peddler says, when I come out to his wagon in the road. My house is the onliest one up this way; naught but the graveyard lays beyond. Mr. Aaron, the peddler, is nigh as dark and lean as his mule. First time I seen him, I thought he might be one of them niggers I have heard tell of, but he said no, his folks was from Roosia, not Afriker. I don't know nothing of such places, having no schooling to speak of, but I figger they must be over the water somewheres.

I go catch me five young cockerels I've been fattening and trade with the peddler for a length of domestic and a paper of needles and some thread. Mr. Aaron feels of the birds and pokes out his lips.

"Not bad," says he, and pushes them into the coop he has in the back of his wagon. "What more fer ye?"

I think about it. Hit's a two-mile walk down to Tate Worley's store, and last time I traded there, Tate was plumb hateful. The peddler might be a little dearer but he wouldn't be as like to talk about my business.

"I'll take a half a pound of coffee beans and some baking powder, iffen ye got hit," I say. Then when he begins to rummage in the back of his wagon for the goods, I say, careless-like, as if I'd just remembered, "I believe I'll try a bottle or two of that Cordelia Ledbetter's Mixture. I been told hit's a right fine tonic and I am most wore to death with this hot weather."

He reaches into a crate and pulls out three bottles. "All the ladies speak highly of this nostrum," he says, solemn as can be. "It's a very popular item."

I take the bottles with their pretty lavender labels and lay them in my apron with the other things. I can hear a rustling in the big boxwoods planted along the branch. I declare I hate them things so bad, with their smell of graveyards and cat piss. I'd take an axe to them if it weren't for the trimmings man who comes ever December and buys great bundles of greenery for rich folks to stick up in their mansion-houses.

Mr. Aaron is skirmishing round in the wagon bed, setting his goods to rights, and he don't seem to notice when I flap my hand towards the house and whisper, "Least, you get yourself back inside!" I am purely shamed for anyone to see the child, dirty and quare as she is.

She wiggles out from under the boxwoods, and just as I'd feared, she has stripped down to her drawers. They are black with dirt and so is she. I flap my hand again and she takes off fer the house but just then Mr. Aaron lifts up his head.

"Little boy or little girl?" he asks. His black eyes is shining.

"Hit's a girl," I say, wishing she'd moved a mite quicker. "She took my scissors to her hair back of this . . ." but I can tell he ain't paying no mind for he's turned away and is rooting around in a big old poke. At last he brings out a piece of red and white stick candy—like what we used to give the children at Christmas.

"For your young un," he says, pointing it at me. "A present." He nods his head up and down when I don't offer to take the candy and pushes it at me. "No charge, Missus."

I wait a bit, making sure he means it, then I hold out my hand and he lays the striped candy stick across it. "Thank you kindly. That's right Christian of you," I says, wondering why he would be giving away his merchandise, but he just laughs and climbs back up to his wagon seat.

"Good day to you, Missus," Mr. Aaron says and slaps the reins on his mule's back. "Just you lay out of work a while—set on the porch and take a little of that tonic and see if it don't help your feelings."

I wait till his wagon has gone around the bend and I can't hear the *clop* of the mule's hooves on the road no more. Then I do like he said and set down on the top step. I call for Least to come get her candy but she don't show herself, so I lay it and the other things I've traded for beside me on the porch floor. I line the three bottles up and study them, then pick one and open it.

The first sip is like fire—and hit puts me in mind of the white liquor Hobart used to get from ol man Clark. Hobart never was bad to drink, but when we was first wed, now and then him and me'd both take a little sup. Hobart would fun me, saying the liquor made me frisky-like. And it did, too. But then at a brush arbor revival down by the river—hit was 1900, three years after we married—we both took the pledge and vowed never to touch ary drop again. And I never will.

I take another sup of tonic. This one goes down easier

and I begin to feel some better. I wonder if this Cordelia Ledbetter tonic can really do what all it claims. The change is awful hard on a woman what with the night sweats and the all-overs. Oh, hit seems fine not having to fool with them bloody rags every month, but on the other side, hit just means a woman don't get no rest. When a woman's period is on her, she can't make kraut or hit'll go bad, can't walk in the cucumbers or they'll mildew—oh, they's a world of things she can't do at that time. And iffen a woman feels real puny for a few days every month, why, she can slack off on her work and no one thinks the worse of her.

Least has come creeping out the door and gone back to the edge of the boxwoods. I don't say nothing but I watch as she sets herself down in the dirt and starts in a-playing with the old corncobs she calls her babies. She's made a bed for them with some of the big green leaves from the cucumber tree near the chicken house, and she's laying them ol cobs down side by each on one leaf and covering them with another. She begins to sing one of them quare little tunes of hern and the sound goes right through my head.

It is as bothersome as a circling wasper, so I call to her and hold out the candy stick. The child stares at it for the longest time before she creeps nigh. Then, without looking me in the face, she grabs hold and scuttles like a rat back into her hidey-hole.

Such a quare child. Not like the others—I think back on how it once was. Happy times long ago, like the old song says.

Me and Hobart wed in '97 and the babes begun to come, one every year at first. Little Hobe in '98, then Lemuel, then Willoree—like popping peas out of a pod.

"Two boys to help with the clearing and plowing and a girl to help you in the house," Hobart said, swelling up proud as he looked at our three strong young uns. "Hit's a good start. We'll pay off what we owe on this place and be free and clear in no time."

Ay, law, when you're young and strong, hit seems you can beat the world. Those first years we worked like dogs, not making much but always putting some by to pay off what we owed on the place. I'd spread out a quilt at the edge of the field and lay the babies on it where I could keep watch over them as I hoed. Back then I could work as hard as ary man, even when I was in the family way.

The next three to come was girls but Hobart never faulted me. "If they can work like their mama," says he, "I'll have nothing to complain of."

I take one more sup of Cordelia Ledbetter and stretch out my fingers. Seems to me the tonic has warmed them and made them feel more limber-like.

Least has come back out and is setting with her play babies and rocking to and fro, singing again, but it don't worry me so much now. I call it singing but they ain't no words what mean anything. That child still don't talk like she ought—oh, she'll say a word here or there iffen she wants a thing—and she can say No, that's for sure, but she don't string her words together. "Oh-eee-oh-iii," is what she's singing, over and over to her corncob babies.

Was a time I could line up *my* babies like that, I think, and the recollection brings hot tears to my eyes as I name them over—Little Hobe, Lemuel, and Willoree . . . Zelma, Porsha, and Fairlight. And next to last the twins, though Dexter died of the summer complaint before he was three months old, leaving Little Brother. Seven fine young uns.

And Little Hobe went off to the Great War and come back in a box; Lemuel died just a month after his daddy, the both of them killed by the fall of the same big tree— though Hobart was killed outright and Lemuel lingered, howling from the pain and mad with the fever. Then, afore I could turn about, each by each the girls married and moved off.

One thing is for sure, though, I don't aim to let it happen with Least.

᠅

Artifact: Empty Cordelia Ledbetter's Herbal Mixture bottle, ca. 1925. Found in an overgrown dump near the barn at the old house site in Dark Holler, some scratching, small chip at lip. Traces of paper label remain.

As early as 1877, Cordelia Ledbetter's herbal/alcoholic mixture was a popular nostrum for a variety of female complaints. At a time when removal of the ovaries and/or uterus was a common treatment for female reproductive disorders—and nervous disorders as well (*hysteria*—derived from the Greek word for uterus—was originally defined as "furor of the womb")—many women sought the help of Cordelia Ledbetter as a cheaper and less drastic solution to their ills.

The original recipe for Cordelia Ledbetter's Herbal Mixture:

Unicorn Root *(Aletris farinosa)* 8 oz.—This plant was used by Native Americans to treat various female complaints, from uterine prolapse to barrenness.

Life Root *(Senecio aureus)* 6 oz.—The common golden ragweed, also called Squaw Weed and Female Regulator, is a traditional uterine tonic and emmenagogue, used to produce a menstrual flow.

Black Cohosh *(Cimicifuga racemosa)* 6 oz.—Black cohosh was and continues to be a herbal specific in the treatment of menopausal symptoms.

Pleurisy Root *(Asclepias tuberosa)* 6 oz.—The orange butterfly weed that flourishes on dry pasture banks and roadsides is a carminative, used against cramps and flatulence.

Fenugreek Seed *(Trigonella foenum-graecum L.)* 12 oz.—A galactagogue, fenugreek is given to nursing mothers to increase milk production.

Alcohol (18%) to make 100 pints—The addition of alcohol as a "solvent and preservative" went a long way toward ensuring that at least some of the pain the sufferer was treating would be lessened.

Chapter 3

The Girl Who Can Read

Dark Holler, 1930

(Least)

The yard dog speaks and I look up from the peas I'm shelling. They's a woman and a girl coming up the road. Mama takes the bowl of peas from me and sets it on the floorboards of the porch, then jerks her chin at the door. "Go on," she says. "Through the house and out the back way. Git you a hoe and go to work on them beans. I'll call you when the folks is gone."

I duck my head yes ma'am and go quick-like into the house. But once I'm to where Mama can't see me, I stay near the window so's I can hear them talk. Mama don't never talk much but for when she's telling me what to do. Back when Fairlight was still living here, *she* would talk to me and read to me too. But since she run off and got herself married, they ain't no one to talk to, being as Brother's as close-jawed as Mama, and if he ain't in the field, he's gone down the road. I had wished for Fairlight to take me with her and she might have too but she was going with her man up to Detroit and Mama said I'd never stand the trip.

"Come git you uns a chair," says Mama as the woman and the girl start up the porch steps. I hear the mule-ear chair's hickory bark bottom squeak like they's mouses in it as the woman sets herself down.

"Ooo-eee!" she says, fanning her face with her handkerchief, "now it's been a time since I come up here to Dark Holler. Like to forgot what a hard climb it is. But I had in mind to git up to the burying ground and tend to my mamaw and papaw's graves, for come Decoration Day, I'll be going with Henry over to the Buckscrape where his people lie."

Mama don't say nothing and I kin hear the pop of the pea pods and the little ringing sounds as the peas fall into her enamel dishpan.

The visitor woman keeps on talking. "Fronie, tell me, was that your least un I saw just now, scooting into the house? Law, she's growed like a weed. Don't she go to school? Lilah Bel here's in Three-B now and reading like one thing. It beats all, the way that child has took to learning."

I skooch close to the window. Careful-like, I peek round the edge to look at the girl who can read. Fairlight taught me my letters and C-A-T cat and H-A-T hat but then she went off, that was the end of it. I have hid the book about Baby Ray what she give me. I look at the pictures of Baby Ray with his dog and his kitties and all and pretend that he is my little brother. Mama don't hold with me learning to read or going to school and right now she is telling the visitor, "It'll just aggravate them funny spells she takes if she gets all tired out with trying to learn more 'n she's able."

The girl who can read is taller than me and her eyes are as deep as the night. Her straight dark hair is real pretty—cut short like the girls in the wish book. She picks up my bowl of peas, sets down on the top step, and goes to shelling without no one even telling her to.

Mama looks at her and nods her head. "Now, there's a good girl. You don't know what it is, Voncel, to have a young un what ain't right."

The woman called Voncel cuts her eyes around and leans in closer to Mama. She whispers, "Well, I had heard a thing or two . . ."

And Mama leans back in her chair and draws in a deep breath. Then she lets it out *shhhhh* and says, "I tell you what's the truth, Voncel, that least un of mine has ways that are beyond my understanding. . . . Why, I'll give you a for instance—take the time she weren't yet three and I had set her on a quilt on the edge of the field where me and Brother was a-hoeing. She had her a biscuit she was gnawing on and a sugar tit to keep her happy."

Mama hitches her chair closer. "You know how it is, Voncel, you can't be with a young un ever minute and still raise a crop. So there I was, working along, chopping at the weeds and lifting my head ever so often to look and see she ain't got off the quilt. And then as I stop to catch my breath at the far end of the row, I hear Least singing. She does it all the time now, but this was the first time I heard it—a funny little high sound like the wind—and then I see they's something on the quilt beside her. I take a few steps towards her, curious to see what it could be, a branch that has fell down or—but then I see it ain't no branch. No, it is the awfullest big old copperhead you ever did see, just laying there next to her and her looking down at the ugly thing and singing that funny song."

The visitor woman makes a squealing sound like a pig. "Eee! Eee!" she says. "Fronie, whatever did you do?"

"Why, Voncel, I crept down that row of corn as quiet as ever I could creep." Mama's talking real low now, but she's told this story afore and I know the way of it. Mama goes on, spinning it out to make it last, to make the visitor woman set there with her mouth open all the while.

"Brother was in the next row over," Mama points her finger as if she could see him yet, "and he was hoeing along, not paying no mind. So when I come even with him, I spoke soft-like and pointed to the least un so's he could see for hisself that serpent laying there next to his sister. 'Don't call out,' I told him, speaking low, 'hit might startle her and was she to move sudden . . .' "

I put my fingers in my ears. I don't want to hear the rest of this story. I wait, thinking about something else. When I see the visitor woman raise her hands to her mouth and then reach over to pat Mama's shoulder, I take my fingers out and listen some more. Mama is laying back in her chair and fanning her face with her apron. The visitor woman is saying something about the school they have down the branch, but Mama cuts her off and says real sharp, "No, like I said, Voncel, Least ain't able to go to school—on account of she takes these funny spells now and again."

And then Mama says like she always does, "The child's simple and that's the truth. And seems like it worries her to be around folks. But we get on. Now tell me, Voncel, was you able to bring me them rug patterns?"

I see that the girl named Lilah Bel is looking right at the window where I'm peeking out. I stick my tongue out at her, then I jerk back out of sight and go quick and quiet out the back way. My special hoe, the light one with its blade worn down to where it looks like a piece of the moon, is leaning against the logs there on the back porch.

I grab it and take the little path through the dark whispering trees to the bean patch.

I make haste along the narrow trail so's I can get them beans hoed and Mama won't be ill with me, but I stop for a minute at the place where the Little Things stay. And then I hear the drums and see the edges of their world.

It's always like that—first the drums and the lights and then they show themselves. I step off the path and hunch down low so's I can crawl up under the drooping branches. It's under that biggest one of them old groaning trees where they have their nest. I hunker down there by the place I have fixed for them, the dancing ground with the smooth river rocks, and I listen to their sounds. Then I make a picture in my mind and begin my song and the Little Things creep out.

Chapter 4

The Quare Girl

Dark Holler, 1930

(Lilah Bel)

L ilah Bel!" Mommy calls to me from the porch and I leave my kitties and go see what it is she wants.

"Lilah Bel," she says when I get to the front steps, "I need for you to go up Dark Holler and tell Miz Fronie I got to have my rose rug pattern back. The feller at the store sent word there's a lady in Asheville wants her one of the big uns and if I can get it done afore the end of the month, I'll get paid extry."

I look down at the ground and drag my toe in the dirt. Dark Holler is where the quare girl lives, the one who takes fits and can't go to school. I don't say nothing but I make a cross in the dirt, then rub it out.

Mommy is setting in a chair with her hurt foot up on a stool. She has mended ever thing she could find to mend and has finished piecing the Dutch Girl quilt she started last winter. She can't get in the garden, not till her foot heals, and she is like to bust with being laid up this way.

She makes her voice all sad and begging, like the preacher at church giving the altar call. "Won't you do this fer me, honey? You're a big girl. And there's time aplenty fer you to get there and back afore first dark. You remember the way—down the branch past your Uncle Farnham's barn and up that next holler. I wouldn't ask you but the others is busy in the field and we could surely use the rug money long about now."

I have gone to Uncle Farnham's by myself lots of times—Mommy and Aunt Alva are always borrowing things from one another and I am the one to carry those things. So I light out but as I go, Mommy calls after me, "Dalilah Belva—you take the dog along; he'll see you safe."

I'm not scared as I walk up the road to Dark Holler with Old Drover keeping close. Me and Mommy come up this way only last month and I'm a big girl, nine years old. I'm not scared of them dark old trees nor of the quare girl who lives up there—even if she did put out her tongue at me. I'm not scared as I go past them big green bushes where it feels like someone is watching me.

Old Drover's neck fur goes up and he stops and growls real low. A skinny arm pokes out of the bush and stretches out an open hand like it was asking fer something. Old Drover drops his head and walks sideways over to the hand and puts his nose up to it. He sniffs of it real good and goes to back up a few steps. Then he circles around three times the way dogs always do and lays down there in the dirt and puts his head on his paws. He keeps his eyes on the bush like he is waiting for it to tell him what to do.

The arm pulls back and I hear someone scrabbling around in there. Then the arm shoots out again and in the open hand is a pretty rosy-orange Injun spearhead. The hand is holding it out to me and I wonder what should I do. I reckon it must be the quare girl and that maybe she wants me to look at the pretty she's found. So I come a little closer.

"That's a right fine spearhead you got," I say out loud, like it was a real person I was talking to and not just a skinny arm sticking out of a bush. "I have found me some but none of them is that big."

The bush don't say nothing but I go on talking to it. "My daddy says the Injuns used to hunt all through this country. He says they most always camped by the water and that's where you're liable to find the most of their leavings. Did you find this un nigh a branch?"

The hand kindly jerks up and down and pushes towards me, like it wants me to take the spearhead. I start to reach out for it but then I pull back right quick, suddenly a-feared that the quare girl will grab me and pull me into the bushes where she's hiding.

"I ain't gone hurt you," the bush says. "Go on, you can have it."

She is quare, that's for certain sure. But she ain't mean and she didn't take no fits whilst I was there. She showed me her play house under them big bushes, and along with the spearhead, she give me some pretty marvels. She said she had found them by the field where her brothers used to play. They's a yellow and green one and a solid blue one, what's cracked, and some others. She told me that she ain't never been away from their farm, not to school, nor church nor even down the road to Uncle Farnham's and Aunt Alva's.

"I have been *up* the road," says she, all excited and acting like that was some grand thing, such as going to Asheville on the train or such. "I been once with Mama and once with my sister Fairlight but she's gone to Detroit now. And lots of times all by myself. Visiting."

"There ain't nobody lives up there," says I. "What do you mean—visiting?"

She looks at me like I was the quare one and rolls her eyes. "Visiting the Quiet People, who'd you think? Them Quiet People up there sleeping on the hogback ridge. They like for me to set with them and tell them how the day looks and what flowers are blooming and how the sun feels. They—"

Just then there's a whistle, loud and shrill, like someone calling a dog. The quare girl freezes and shrinks down into herself like she's afraid of something. The whistle sounds again and I crawl to where they's a gap in the bush and I can see Miz Fronie standing at the open door of the house. She whistles again and then she hollers, "Least, quit your loafering and come here! I need me some more wood for the cookstove!"

I turn around to tell the quare girl that I'll help her carry in some wood, but she has vanished clean away. I see that there is a back door out of the bush, a little worn-down trail that tunnels through the thick green leaves and over the knobbly roots. It comes to me that maybe she don't want her mama to know she was talking to me.

Real quiet-like I crawl out the way I come in, then I stand behind the bush and out of sight of the house. Old

Drover is still laying there in the road but he stands up when he sees me. I brush all the dirt and dead leaves off of me. The marvels and the spear point are safe in my dress pocket and I start for the house with Old Drover at my heels.

When I come up near to the front porch, ain't no one there, so I call out, "Miz Fronie?"

Pretty quick, here she comes, red-faced and sweaty. There's a dirty apron over her housedress and I reckon her to have been busy with canning or some such work. She peers at me and bunches up her face. Then she smiles but it ain't a natural smile; to my mind, it's more like a dog baring its teeth.

"Why, you're Voncel's little girl, ain't you? What in the name of mercy are you doing up here so late? Is your mama behind you on the road?"

I come up the steps. Close to, I can smell the sweat that's making black patches under her arms. I think that when I get older and start to stink like grown-ups do, I will use Mum deodorant, the kind my mommy buys in Ransom at the drugstore. There is another smell on Miz Fronie's breath that puts me in mind of rotting fruit. This other smell worries me somehow and all at once I notice that the light is fading and dark is coming on fast.

"No'm," I say real quick, "Mommy's to home with a hurt foot."

I ask about the rug pattern and she says she's done with it. I wait on the porch while Miz Fronie goes to get the pattern and I look in the door to see if the quare girl is back in there. While I'm looking, I hear the sound of stove wood being dumped into a box and then I see the quare girl, standing in the kitchen door and pointing at me. Her blue eyes have a light to them that makes me pay attention as she brings up a finger and lays it to her lips.

I nod. *I won't tell,* I say in my mind, knowing that's what she wants.

Chapter 5

In the Barn Loft

Dark Holler, 1931

(Least)

"Wanna hear a scary story?" Lilah Bel whispers.

Me and her are up in the barn loft. She don't like my other hidey places, so we have fixed us a play house up here. Mama and Brother have gone to town and won't be back till dark, so I got all my work done early for I knew that Lilah Bel would come if she could slip away. Me and Lilah Bel have been friends for the longest time now and she knows that on the first Saturday of every month Mama and Brother go to Gudger's Stand to trade. Sometimes they even ride the train into Ransom.

"What kind of story?" I say and stretch out on the pallet that I have fixed from old quilts. Lilah Bel is sitting cross-legged at one end of the pallet and she is dividing up hard candy from the little paper poke she had in her pocket. Her shiny hair, which is darker than a horse chestnut, falls on either side of her face like blinkers on a mule. I wish my hair was pretty like hers. Mine ain't but plain old brown—and it's always braided tight. Mama braids it every Saturday night after my bath and she pulls it so hard that sometimes hit makes my eyes squinch up and water.

"Don't take on like that," she says. "Much as I got to do, I need to fix your hair so it stays fixed."

I did ask once why didn't she cut it short and I almost said *Like Lilah Bel has hers* but I stopped in time and said, "Like them girls in the wish book." Mama hadn't paid no mind; just went on pulling at my hair and fussing.

Lilah Bel has finished making two piles of the candy and she looks up. "It's a terrible story," she says, "and it really happened. Aunt Alva and Mommy was talking about it last Sunday while they washed the dishes and they didn't know I was just outside the window and could hear them, every word. It was about this lady and what happened to her babies."

"What happened to her babies?" I say and hold out a hand for my part of the candy.

Lilah Bel's eyes get real big. She takes a deep breath and tongues the piece of candy she's got in her mouth over to one side till it pokes out like she's got a chaw of baccer in there. She gives me a whole mess of lemon drops and peppermints and commences her tale.

"Well," says she, "afore Aunt Alva married Uncle Farnham and come to live over here, she lived on Twist Ankle Creek and in their church there was this lady whose babies kept dying. Not at first, for she had her a girl and four great boys, all as stout as could be. But then she had another girl and it only lived a few days. And folks all round come to the house and brought food, like folks do, and sat and visited with this lady and mourned with her. And after a time, she did seem to get to feeling some better.

"But then come another year and another baby and the

same thing happened again. And after that, every year, Aunt Alva said, there'd be a new baby and it would be as peart and healthy as anything, and then afore a week had gone by, here would come this poor lady to the neighbors, her hair flying loose and tears just a-running down her face and a dead babe wrapped in her apron."

"Had they took sick or—"

"That was what Mommy wanted to know, was it the summer complaint. Lots of babies dies that way when ever drop of milk they take just runs right through 'em, is what she said, but Aunt Alva said no, she herself had seen those dead babies and each and every one was as fat as mud. Hit just looked like they'd stopped breathing."

I suck hard on a lemon drop, letting the sour-sweet spit make a big pool in my mouth before I swallow it. Then I ask, "Why'd she want to keep having them babies iffen they was just all going to die on her like that?"

Lilah Bel looked at me funny. "Why, don't you know nothing? Married ladies just naturally have babies."

Lilah Bel is all the time letting me know that she is ten years old and goes to school, while I am only nine and ain't never been nowhere. I pick up one of last year's swiveled-up apples that's laying on the plank floor and chunk it at her.

"I don't see what's so scary about this dumb story."

"You let me finish, you'll see. Or maybe I hadn't ought to tell you the rest for it truly is the awfullest thing."

She makes like she's not going to say no more and starts turning the pages of the old wish book we have up here. Sometimes we play a game of picking out what we like best, but I know she's going to tell me the rest of the story, so I just wait and suck on my lemon drop.

Pretty soon Lilah Bel points to a picture of a baby doll

laying in a little basket. "There was three more of that lady's babies died and ever time it was the same: all the folks coming round, bringing food and making over her and folks at church praying for her on Sundays and at Wednesday night meeting too. But my Aunt Alva's mamaw suspicioned something and the next time that lady had a baby, why, Aunt Alva's mamaw she went over there and offered to stay with them and help out. She stayed there for a week and the baby was still living and she stayed for another week and the baby was still living and finally after three weeks, Aunt Alva's mamaw begun to think that the danger time was past and she could go back home.

"So she put her things back in her grip and was ready to be on her way but first she thought she'd step into the other room where the mama and baby was and take her leave. So in she went, just a-tippy-toeing in, quiet as ever she could, so as not to wake the little un. And there she seen the most dreadful thing . . ."

Lilah Bel stops and goes to looking through her candy for a peppermint drop. I poke at her with my bare foot.

"What? What did she see?"

Lilah Bel looks at me funny again and pinches her mouth together. "I'll tell you the rest but then you got to tell me something scary."

I can't think of aught scary to tell her but I nod my head and we hook our fingers together for a promise. Then she stands up and reaches for the hem of her skirt. She folds it back and I see that she has got one of her mama's great long hatpins jobbed through the cloth. She pulls it out real slow and holds it where I can see it good. Then she bends down and picks up that little apple what I had flung at her.

"Maybe you don't know it," she says, "being as you're the least un in your family and ain't been round no babies, but when they're born, new babies all have a soft spot on the top of their little heads. When Woodrow was born last year, Mommy showed me hisn and let me put my finger on it real gentle-like. I could feel the beat of his heart on that soft spot and it went up and down, up and down."

Lilah Bel is talking slow and whispery and making her eyes big. There is goose bumps coming on my arm and my mouth has gone all dry.

"You got to be very, very careful," Lilah says, staring hard at me, "that nothing don't hit that soft spot for it could kill the baby."

I sit up and swallow hard. I want to stop her from telling the rest but I can't make myself say nothing for the lights and the sounds are coming on fast. Lilah Bel has the apple in one hand and the hatpin in the other and the lights are sparking off the cruel sharp hatpin as it comes down at the baby's little head and the hatpin is going in and in and in and the mama is laughing and crying at the same time and the humming and the little drums and the lines of light are everywhere and

The cold water is in my face and some gets up my nose. I sneeze and I hear Lilah Bel hollering, "Wake up! Please, Least, you got to wake up!"

I blink my eyes and there she is, standing over me with the dipper gourd from the springhouse in her hand. She is breathing hard and I know she must have clambered down from the barn loft and run all the way to the spring to get that water. Her face is nigh as wet as mine with the tears that are running down her cheeks.

I set up and wipe my face on my skirt. "I'm all right—
that was just one of my spells. Law, you like to drownded
me."

She is still bawling as she drops down on the quilts beside me and hugs me hard. "I'm sorry, Least. I didn't
mean to . . ."

I hug her back. "I reckon you'll not need me to tell you
no scary story now—I done scared you already. But I will
tell you one thing and it's a secret—Brother's got him a
girl and he ain't telling Mama for fear of what she'll do."

∾

*Article from the "Church News" column in the Ransom
newspaper (no date)*

MANY ANGELS: THE TALE OF A MOTHER'S UNDYING LOVE

Half hidden in the hemlocks, the little family cemetery lies
at the end of a winding path trodden smooth by the daily pas-
sage of her feet. In sunshine and in rain, midst winter's snows
or 'neath Old Sol's blazing summer heat, the faithful little
mother keeps her vigil.

Of respect for her privacy and her sorrow, we shall not
name this one who has suffered such loss, but that name is
surely graven in letters of purest gold on the pages of the Ce-
lestial Record.

Nay, call her "Trueheart," she who tends the six little
graves, bringing such rustic posies as the season affords or
shaping green wreaths of box when the time of blossoming is
o'er.

In a pitiless procession, one after another these sweet
babes have been ushered to their final resting places—some
after only a few brief days of life.

But Trueheart keeps her watch, as mindful of these little ones sleeping 'neath the clay as any mother with a nursery filled with living babes. One by one she names them for us— these infants who will never grow old—and recalls for us their tiny faces, each precious and unique in her maternal memory.

How few could suffer as Trueheart has suffered, yet hold firm to a trust (cont. on p. 5)

Chapter 6

Brother's Girl

Dark Holler, 1931

(Least)

I met her a while back of this, Mama, at a ball game in Dewell Hill. She's a beauty operator at Clara's Beauty Shoppe in Ransom and she boards at Miz Jarrett's place on Hill Street."

I am on the back porch shucking the roasting ears and Mama and Brother are in the kitchen. I don't know why Brother has decided to tell Mama about this girl after keeping her a secret for so long. Whatever the reason is, I bet he wishes he had kept his big mouth shut, for Mama don't like it, not one little bit, and she is bowing up something fierce.

"A beauty operator! Lives in a boardinghouse!" Mama spits out the words like they taste bad in her mouth. "Might as well say a whore-woman from that wicked place acrost the river—and you aim to *marry* her? What kind of use is a woman like that on a farm? Who are her people? Why don't she live at home with them, like a respectable somebody?"

"Her mama's dead and her daddy's on the Southern

Railroad." Brother is talking slow and careful now, the way he does when he's trying to bring Mama around to his way of thinking. "She grew up in Hot Springs but went in to Asheville to learn her trade. She's—"

Mama snorts like a mule. "How old is this huzzy?"

Brother don't say nothing and Mama laughs, a hard ugly sound. "You don't even know, do you, son? Like as not she's someone else's leavings and she thought to catch her a man too young to know the difference betwixt spoiled—"

Brother cuts in right quick. "Don't, Mama. It ain't no use you saying any more. I aim to marry her and bring her here. Iffen that don't suit you, well, I reckon I can find another place to call home. I've worked for you since I can remember and tried to do right by you when all the others went off but, aye God, I'll please myself in my wife."

I can hear the *thockety-thock* of Mama's sharp knife against the board and I know that she is chopping up cabbage to fry with some hog jowl. She don't answer Brother for the longest time. But then at last I hear the hiss of the cabbage hitting the hot grease and she calls out, "Least, hurry up with them roasting ears; the water's a-boiling."

It is a Sunday afternoon when Brother brings his girl home to meet Mama.

"And there ain't no need for you to send Least off out of the way like you always do," he said as he made ready to go down to Gudger's Stand and meet the number eleven from Ransom. "I already told about her taking spells and why she don't go to school and all—it don't bother my girl one bit. She says she'll be tickled to have her a little sister."

At midday me and Mama don't fix no real dinner; we

just eat us an applesauce biscuit so that Mama will have time to finish up the three-egg cake she made this morning. She takes a knife and spreads the brown sugar icing acrost the top of the cake, making fancy patterns as she goes. I can tell that she has drunk some of her tonic because the end of her nose is pink and she is humming a song.

Brother was surprised when Mama told him last week that she wanted to meet his girl and that she would make a cake. But he fixed it up just as quick as he was able afore Mama could change her mind. Brother has even paid Lilah Bel's uncle to take his new truck to meet the train and bring them back to the foot of our road so's Brother's girl'll not have to make such a long walk. Mama don't know that part, and if she did, she would likely have something to say about it.

Because Brother's girl is coming, I have a new dress. Mama took some plain feed sacks and she boiled the white cloth with onion skins and roots till it come up the prettiest yellow you ever saw. And then she made a collar and little pockets out of some other feed sack cloth that had green and pink and purple flowers all over it. My new dress looks like it could have come from the wish book. I will be very careful not to spoil it.

The cake is all done and setting on the table with a piece of cheesecloth over it to keep off the flies; Mama has had me lay out four of them little green glass plates that come in the boxes of oatmeal along with forks and glasses for each of us. I set them out first one way and then another.

"Quit your fooling with them plates lest you break one," Mama says.

I am almost beside myself for this will be the first time I ever sat down with company.

"I thank you for inviting me." Brother's girl looks at Mama and smiles real sweet. Her and Brother have walked up the road and clumb the porch steps and she is out of breath a little. The fancy shoes that make her walk on tiptoe are dusty.

Mama don't get up from where she's setting with her Progressive Farmer magazine open on her lap but she nods and says, "Git you a chair and rest a spell."

Brother's girl takes the little rickety chair next to Mama. Her dress is the color of peach blossoms—the fanciest thing I ever seen. I watch how before she sets down she runs her hand behind her to smooth her skirt against her bottom. She perches there like a butterfly, looking so fluttery and so light. I see Brother watching her and I think he worries she will fly away.

Brother's girl is looking all around her and saying what a pretty place it is and how fine the weather is today. Mama answers back, "Why, yes, it is," like it surprises her.

I am setting on a little box down at the end of the porch, watching them talk and not saying nothing. Brother's girl cuts her eyes over at me. "And talk about pretty—now, I'll bet that pretty girl must be Least."

Brother crooks his finger at me and I get up and walk slow over to where they're all looking at me. Brother's girl smiles very big and takes hold of my hand. "I hope we're going to be good friends, Least. Your big brother has told me all about you."

I can't say nothing for looking at her hair. It is the color of the yellow bell flowers and it lays agin her head in big curves. I look at it the hardest, trying to figure out what makes it do like that.

"She ain't much a hand to talk," says Mama but Brother's girl just laughs and brings my hand up to touch her hair.

"I believe she's looking at my Marcel wave, aren't you, honey? How would you like me to fix your hair like that?"

I nod my head yes and now they all of them go to laughing. Their mouths are wide open and red and make me think of bad things. "Ha-ha-ha," they are saying and I pull my hand away and run back into the house and out the back door to one of my secret places. A blackberry briar snags the skirt of my new dress but I keep going till I can't hear that hateful sound no more.

Back up under the big trees it is quiet and dark. I had thought I might be about to take a spell, but they ain't no lights and the only thing I hear is the trees sighing in that lonesome talk of theirs. I stay put till I feel better and then I go to the barn.

Brother keeps the shears for the mules' manes laying between the logs, along with the doctoring ointment and hoof picks. The shears are rusty and hard to work but once I loose the plaits, my hair cuts easier.

When I come back to the house, they are all three setting at the kitchen table, eating the cake off the green glass plates. Mama is the first to see me and her fork stops halfway to her mouth. The other two look around right quick, and before Mama can say a word, Brother's girl has clapped her hands together and sung out, "Oh my goodness, looks like Miss Least is gone to be a hairdresser herself. Why, honey, I believe we can do you a

Buster Brown bob if your mama will lend me her scissors."

I am waiting for Lilah Bel. Every Saturday when Mama and Brother go to town, I put on my pretty yellow dress and wait for Lilah. It's been two Saturdays since Lilah was here and I have a lot to tell her and show her— my new dress that only got one little small tear in it and Mama mended afore she washed it. The dirt came out good and the grass stain is almost gone too.

And my hair! Brother's girl brought some special hair-washing soap with her when she come the next Sunday and she showed me how to wash my hair and tie it up in rags so it would curl pretty. Mama says it is a waste of time but being as my hair's too short to braid, then I can fix it everhow I want for she is done fooling with it.

What I want is to be like Brother's girl—all pretty and fluffy and dancing. For now I know about dancing. When Brother and his girl were here last Sunday and Mama stepped out back to visit the little house, Brother put out his hand and pulled his girl up off her chair and the two of them went to dancing right there on the porch. Brother was whistling and then they both begun to sing about being in Carolina in the morning. Which didn't make no sense for it wasn't morning a-tall, but they was jigging about and laughing like crazy folks and Brother had his arms around his girl and all the time their feet was making a song of their own, just tapping on those floorboards.

And over where I was setting and watching, my own feet begun to tap and my legs wanted to jump up and dance to the sounds they was making and the tapping and the singing was all around me till I had to close my eyes to keep from getting dizzy. At first it had seemed like a spell was coming on me but then I seen that I was being spun round by the singing, like a leaf spinning down a bold creek, and I come to see that this was a different way into that other place. I would have gone there too but just then we could hear Mama coming through the house.

Brother and his girl left off singing right quick and when Mama come out the front door, just swinging her head all around to see what all the commotion was about, they was setting on the top step, both of them looking at that Progressive Farmer magazine. I laughed inside myself to see them looking up at Mama and smiling just as calm as if they hadn't been prancing all over our front porch not a minute before.

"Now, if you haven't come back just in time to settle something!" says Brother's girl. "We was wondering—which do you prefer for laying hens—Buff Orpingtons or Rhode Island Reds?"

Brother's girl turns her head to look at me and then she closes one eye and opens it again. I know she is saying that her and Brother and me have a secret together. She is the first grown-up I have ever had a secret with and I have to wrap my arms tight around myself to keep from letting that secret bust loose. I wait till Mama has sat down and is looking at the magazine. Then I look at Brother's girl and close and open one eye, just like she done.

Chapter 7

Anointed in the Spirit

Ridley Branch, 1931

(Lilah Bel)

Ever since the revival at the brush arbor, there have been tongues of fire licking at my body. Folks say that the Holy Spirit spoke through me that night and, now that old man Beale Blankenship has got hisself run over by a train, they say that I am anointed in the spirit and have the gift of prophecy.

I don't know exactly when it happened. All I remember of that night is setting on the hard log bench and hearing the preacher call on the Lord to send down His Holy Spirit to anoint His people. I was hungry and hot and I begun to feel swimmie-headed so I whispered to Mama could I leave the brush arbor and go down by the river where it was cooler.

The next thing that I remember I was laying on the ground before the raised-up place where the elders was setting. The preacher was kneeling in the dust beside of me, just praying like one thing, and they was folks standing on the benches and waving their hands in the air.

And then Mama took me home. I asked her what had happened and she said that we'd speak of it later but we never have yet and it's been close on to two weeks now.

We did not go back to the brush arbor though the revival went on for another four days. And now Mama watches me all the time with a worried kind of a look and I heard her tell Papa that she hoped I wasn't going to begin to take fits like that poor child of Fronie's. I wonder if that's what happened to me and I think that I would like to go see Least and ask her if she feels the licking of the tongues of fire.

It isn't till three weeks have passed that I find out more about what happened at the brush arbor. Me and my sister Naomi Ruth, who is fourteen years of age and thinks she's something, are in the garden picking beans. We are working our way down the tall shady rows, me on one side, her on the other, so's not to miss a single ripe pod. The beans have done extry good this year and the seagrass strings are so thick with vines that all I can see of Naomi Ruth is her hand poking in and out of the sticky green leaves. But I can hear her plain. She is aggravated at me.

"What I think," she says in her prissy, smarty-pants voice, "is that you weren't doing nothing but putting on a show, that time at the brush arbor."

Her pink fingers are jumping in and out of the vines, pulling off the long fat pods with a sharp snapping sound.

"I wasn't putting on nothing," I say. "And I don't remember nothing either but for standing up to leave and then laying on the ground up at the front of the arbor. I don't know how I got there."

The busy fingers stop and make a peek hole in the green curtain of bean vines and Naomi Ruth puts her face up to the open spot. She looks cross and sweaty and red under her poke bonnet.

"You don't remember hollering out all them made-up words? And pointing your finger at Mr. Beale Blankenship and what you said to him?"

"No," I say, "I done told you, I don't remember nothing. What did I say?"

Naomi Ruth squinches up her face like she's trying to remember. "It was crazy talk—first you hollered out that wine is a mocker, which I have heard the preacher say back of this, and then you called out something about death coming on a black horse and the horse breathing fire and smoke and running down a silver road. And you called Mr. Beale Blankenship a drunk and a sinner, which ever one knows but it weren't fitten for you to say it, being just a little girl. And the quarest thing was that the whole time you was talking, your eyeballs was rolled back in your head till didn't nothing show but white but you was pointing right at poor ol Beale Blankenship. And he went to trembling and turning white as a ghost and then you quit talking. First you rolled your head around and then you hit the floor like someone had knocked you down." Naomi Ruth pushes her head through the hole in the bean vines and looks hard at me. "And you say you don't remember none of that?"

I look down where my basket is setting and try to make a picture out of what she has told me but I can't see nothing but the dirt and the little rocks and a devil-in-the-garden weed that we missed last time we hoed. I reach and yank it out. "No," I say one more time, "not none of that."

The hole in the green curtain closes back up and I hear Naomi Ruth making a *hmmph* sound in her throat like she don't believe me. Her pink fingers go back to yanking the beans loose and the snapping sounds come faster and faster.

It seems like there is something big pressing on me, trying to press me down into the dirt between the rows. I turn my face up to the hot blue sky and the sun that is straight overhead. And now it seems like there is a golden ray shooting right into my eye like a rock dropping down the dark well that is the narrow place between the tall bean rows. The beam of sun shoots down the bean vine well and down the well made by the brim of my poke bonnet and right into the heart of me and I know that I have been hit by the Holy Spirit and that His flame will burn in me forever.

ᴥ

Dear Sis,

Well I don't know what it is that you have herd about Dalilah Belva but yes, it is true that she was annointed by the Holy Spirit at the last revival.
Those folks who are saying ugly things about her had ougt to look to their Bibles for talking in tongues and profesizing is Scripture.
Here it is right from Acts and you can give it to Ester to read and maybe that will shut her up.
1: And when the day of Pentecost was fully come, they were all with one accord in one place.
2: And suddenly there came a sound from heaven as of a rushing mighty wind, and it filled all the house where they were sitting.

3: *And there appeared unto them cloven tongues like as of fire, and it sat upon each of them.*

4: *And they were all filled with the Holy Ghost, and began to speak with other tongues, as the Spirit gave them utterance.*

Your loving sister,
Voncel Roberts

p.s. I have canned 64 quarts of beans this week and there is more yet to come.

Chapter 8

Saved

Dark Holler, 1931

(Least)

I have waited the longest for Lilah Bel to come back. So many things has happened that I want to tell her about—starting with Brother and his girl getting married in Ransom and going off on the train and how Mama took on.

Brother come home one Sunday evening after spending the day in Ransom and as we et our supper he begun to talk about how he could make enough money in the car plants up North to send some home and we would be better off than if he stayed here on the farm. He was all worked up and talking fast and couldn't hardly set still but kept jumping up and pacing back and forth, holding his cornbread in one hand and talking between bites.

"I saw Tony Lee Warren in town—he was home for Decoration Day—and he said he knowed the feller what does the hiring at the River Rouge plant and was I to come right on, he'd guarantee I'd get a job. You'd not credit how much they're paying, even to fellers just starting."

Brother stopped and stared across the table at Mama, who was setting there all pinch-mouthed and scowling. "Mama, don't you see—there'd be money to hire the plowing done. You and Least can raise a big garden—you don't need me fer that. And it'd just be for a year or two, time to get a little ahead with some cash—"

And then Mama jumped up out of her chair and come around the table at Brother. Her glass had knocked over when she sprung up, and buttermilk begun to run across the tabletop and off of the edge. She didn't pay it no mind, though, just hauled off and fetched Brother a slap across his face so hard that his head rocked to one side.

"Hit's that painted huzzy behind this, ain't it? Got you by the pecker and now—"

"Mama!" Brother balled up his fist and pulled it back like he was going to strike. He stood there, just a-trembling all over, his nose holes all opened up like a great angry bull. "You best not say one more word iffen you want me to pass another night in this house. I swear, I'll not stay to hear such—"

But Mama wasn't paying him no mind; she was shouting out dreadful-sounding words, which I'd never heard most of them but I could tell they weren't fitten. I set still there at the table, watching the thick buttermilk dripping slow to the floor. When it had all run off and Mama and Brother were still hollering, I stood up quiet-like and went out the door.

In my secret place I could still hear their voices but I couldn't make out the hateful words. I curled up in the big smooth hollow between the roots and listened for the drums. I hoped that they would come out soon for I felt the alonest I ever had.

Up amongst the roots was the last of my corncob babies. I had wrapped her in an old cloth and put her to bed there a long time ago when Lilah laughed at me for playing with such. I reached out for the dolly and pulled her to me and held her up against my cheek. "My pretty little baby," I whispered to her, "don't you cry, your mama's here."

Lilah Bel come at last but she is all different now. She don't want to do nothing but play brush arbor revival and talk about Jesus and the Holy Spirit. Lilah says that I am a sinner and must come to church and get saved but I told her she knew Mama didn't let me go nowhere on account of my spells. Besides, Mama says that ever since my daddy died, she ain't got no use for Jesus.

But Lilah Bel says all I have to do is to say that I love Jesus and then I won't have to burn in Hell forever. Lilah tells me all about Hell and what kind of place it is and what happens to folks who go there and I cover my ears and shake my head no. Then she tells me about Jesus and what bad folks done to Him and the story is most as awful as the one about the hatpin lady but this time I don't take a spell. I just do like she says and get down on my knees and say that I love Jesus and will love Him forevermore.

"I don't know," says Lilah Bel. "By rights you had ought to be dipped in the water with the preacher saying words over you. Let's go to the deep place in the branch and do it again. But first you need to go get you unses' Bible so I can read out of it after you get saved."

"What's a Bible?" I ask her and she tells me it is a big old book with God's words wrote down in it.

"Well," says I, "there is several books on a high shelf in Mama's room where she keeps the extry lamps but don't no one ever touch them. I believe they was my daddy's."

Lilah studies on it some and decides we can get along without a Bible. So we go to the deep place in the creek and I start to take off my nice dress which she ain't said nothing about, she has been so busy saving me. She sees me start to undo my buttons and draws up her mouth.

"Oh no," she says, "you got to keep your clothes on! God don't like nekkid people."

That don't make sense to me for she has told me that God, who is really Jesus and also the Holy Spirit, made the first man and the first woman along with all the animals and everything else there is. (This was back when He was just called God—the other two names come later, Lilah says.) Anyhow, what I wonder is, if God don't like nekkid, why didn't He just make people with their clothes already on them, like He done possums and coons and birds and such?

But I hold my tongue and wade out in the cold running water in my new dress. The water is up to my knees and the hem of the dress is dragging and wet.

"Am I saved now?" I ask her, but she shakes her head and says I got to get wet all over, even my head.

"I'll come in and do like the preacher does," she says and walks right into the water like it weren't there. She stands behind me and with one hand she pinches my nose shut and with the other she pushes me under.

My eyes are open and I can see that there is a whole other world under the water—a green world with more Little Things that I had never known of—Little Things that squirm and wiggle and give off light and tiny sounds. I begin to feel quare like there is someone calling me and

I try to shake off Lilah Bel's hands so I can follow the voices that sing in my ears.

But Lilah Bel holds tight to my nose and my head and then I am back up out of the greeny dark into the light and the air. Lilah Bel lets go of me and she is praying so hard that the words all run together and don't make no sense. I leave her standing there and climb up on the bank and begin to wring the water from my new dress.

When Lilah finally gets done, I ask her am I saved. She says that I am and at last I get to tell her about Brother and his girl going off to Detroit and about the old lady who is coming to live with us.

Chapter 9

The Gifts

Dark Holler, 1931

(Granny Beck)

I knowed the first minute I seen the child Least that she had the Gifts—could read it in her eyes—though it was likewise clear she hadn't no idea of what the Gifts are and how she might use them. But she is nearing the age when they'll be at their strongest, whether for good or bad, and the most like to do her harm. Perhaps that's the reason that things has worked out this way—so that I might be here to help her through this time—to teach her of the Gifts and of the Threefold Return, as well. Lord knows I fought like one thing against coming to live with Fronie, but now that I've seen the child, I know it was meant.

Not a one of my young uns had the Gifts—folks say it often skips a generation. There was a time, though, when I thought that Fronie might—but ever when I tried to tell her about the Gifts, she'd sull up and scowl at me like I was crazy. Finally I seen she was one who could have had them, but had turned away. It may have been that her refusing the Gifts is what has soured her, making her discontent so that she is always hungering for what she's missed.

Me and Fronie never could agree. She was my oldest girl and seemed like, as the babies kept a-coming, I just didn't have the time to ever get to know her. Looking back in my memory, I see her a lap baby and then I see her when first her monthlies come on—that was when I thought I saw the signs in her face. And then I see her riding off behind that feller she married—off to his home on the other side of the county. I don't remember no in between—though reason tells me that she was in our home for sixteen year. Why I can't recall her face during all that time, I couldn't say. I know that she was there helping with each new baby—but I can't call to mind her face, except for them three times.

After she married, a year or more might go by without me seeing her or hearing aught of her and her family. I did send word that I would come help when the first babe was born and again with the rest but each time she made it clear that she didn't want me there.

And after so many years, to be dumped on her like an unwanted dog.

This morning Bevan brung me in his truck with my plunder about me and my old Delectable Mountains quilt over my legs. It is my legs that have give out on me, not my eyes or ears, and I could hear ever word Fronie and Bevan was saying. And I could see her face, so much older than I remembered and with deep furrowed lines down either side of her mouth to where I doubt she could smile if she tried. Bevan was standing on the bottom step to the porch and she on the top like she would bar him from coming up, but he had his say nonetheless.

"Fronie, you agreed to it and I told you we'd be here today. Me and Emma Ray's had the care of her ever since she got so crippled up. We never asked aught of you in all those years. But Emma Ray's mama and daddy both are in a bad way. The bank has took their farm and they got nowhere to go but to us. We can't look after three old folks. Emma Ray has done for Mama like a daughter all this time—I reckon you can take your turn now."

I knew and she knew that she would have to give in— it's just her nature to be hateful. Between them, her and Bevan managed to get me up to the porch. I can make out to hobble a little but I can't do no good with steps.

"She'll have to have Least's bed," Fronie said, looking at me like I hadn't got no sense. "I can fix the child a pallet for now."

Her and Bevan hauled my few bits and pieces into the house and I could hear them still squabbling. She hadn't spoke an actual word to me yet but finally she come out and give me a pie pan with some cornbread on it and a glass of buttermilk.

"Me and Bevan is going out to the barn. I want to see can he help me hang that stall door the bull broke down."

"Thank you, Fronie," I said, hoping that things between us might begin to improve, "I always did love cornbread and buttermilk. And I thank you for taking me in—I'm right sorry to be a burden."

Her mouth bunched up like a hen's behind and then she said, "It don't matter; I'm used to burdens."

She turned to go and then, recollecting herself, asked me did I need to use the chamber.

That's the worst of old age—coming round after so many years to where you're weak and useless as a little baby again. Fronie helped me back to the room I'm to have and pulled the pot from under the bed. She stood there waiting, tapping her foot as I did my business.

When I got done and started back for the porch, Fronie grabbed up the pot.

"I'll dash this out in the branch," she said and made for the back door, calling over her shoulder, "If Least decides to show herself, tell her I got a job for her. Tell her she's not to go wandering off till I talk to her. The child ain't got much sense but I reckon the two of you'll get along just fine."

When I got back to the porch, I went to studying the yard and what all I can see of the place where I am like to be spending the rest of my days. The road runs close to the house and I'm glad of that—it's right pleasant, when you can't do nothing but set, to watch folks in their comings and goings. Not that the road appears to me in much use, but you can't tell—someone might come up this way now and again.

I seen there was some big boxwoods over to one side and a straggly yellow bell bush but not another flower in sight. Most women would make a flower bed or maybe have some in pots on the porch but there ain't nothing of the sort here.

Oh, the pots of flowers that lined my porch railing back when I had my own house—and how proud I was of the show! Bevan's Emma Ray loves flowers—law, in springtime her thrift is a sight on earth—the way it lays like a blanket over that old stone wall—purples and pinks and a white that most burns your eyes when the sun hits it. And the peonies . . .

But ain't no use thinking on that. Emma Ray has her children to help her and Bevan does his part too. Maybe when her man was alive, Fronie had more time for flowers. Still and all, I believe she'd be a happier somebody could her eyes light on a rosebush now and again.

I wish I could help her someways—instead here I am, taking up more of her time and making things harder. Bevan has said he will try to send money every month to help out—I don't eat much; maybe the money will ease her load. And I can still snap beans and suchlike—

There was a rustling in the boxwoods and I could just make out a shape slipping along behind the leaves. At first it worried me but then I figured it must be the child— Fronie's least un and the only one still at home. Bevan told me he'd heard the poor little thing is simpleminded and bad to take fits. Another worry for Fronie.

I called out soft, "Come here, child," hoping she'd not take flight. "Come see your Granny Beck."

The sounds in the boxwoods hushed and I called again. "Come here, honey, I got a pretty for you."

She was like a half-tamed woods creature—poked her head out the bushes a little ways and looked at me with great blue eyes in the midst of a dirty sun-browned face. Her hair was a greasy snarl and the dress she had on weren't much better than a feed sack with holes in it. *I can do something about that,* I thought.

I dug into the pocket of my skirt for my charm. "Look here, honey, what I got," I said and she come out of the bushes and up the steps slow, her feet just a-dragging.

But when she got up close, her eyes went to mine before she looked to see what was in my hand and that was when I knew.

"Oh, honey," I said, feeling like I could bust out crying any minute, "there is so much I have to learn you and maybe not a lot of time left. But I'll make a beginning right now and tell you of the fairy crosses and how they come to be. Put out your hand."

When I give her the little rock charm, she studied it close and a smile started across her face, turning her from a wild thing into a pretty child. She touched the cross real gentle, running a finger all along it, tracing it up and down.

Her eyes got real big, then she whispered, "This is from the Little Things, ain't it?"

Law, they was a catch in my heart at them words. I begun to answer her but the tears come on me all to once—tears of joy that I have found her.

⁓

THE LEGEND OF THE FAIRY CROSS

Fairy crosses, also called fairy stones or fairy tears, are composed of staurolite, a combination of silica, iron, and aluminum. These minerals often crystallize into a cross-like form. Traditionally, fairy stones have been carried for good luck. They are believed to protect the wearer against witchcraft, accidents, sickness, and disaster. It is said that three U.S. presidents carried fairy crosses.

The Cherokee Indians have a legend that fairy crosses are the tears of the Little People (Yunwi Tsunsdi), tiny, reclusive creatures known for their ability to find lost people. As the story goes, the Little People were singing and dancing and drumming near the town of Brasstown when a messenger arrived with news of the Crucifixion. The terrible news made the Little People cry, and as their tears fell to the earth, the drops hardened into tiny crosses which may still be found in that locale.

An extensive collection of fairy crosses is on display at the Cherokee County Historical Museum in Murphy, phone (704) 837-6792.

Chapter 10

The Story of John Goingsnake

Dark Holler, 1931

(Least)

"Now see can you read that next part to me, honey." Granny picks up her rug machine and begins filling in the background on the bottom part of the big rug we have on the frame. I take up the book and begin.

"*He was too . . . young, this little . . . elf.* Granny, what's an elf?"

Granny Beck is helping me learn to read! It is our secret, for Mama don't hold with me learning. She says it will bring the fits on if I work my head too hard. But I have been reading and reading and reading and still not had ary fit!

We started with the Baby Ray book Fairlight gave me when she left, and I can read it all now, every word—all about Baby Ray's one little dog and two cunning kitty-cats and three white rabbits and four yellow ducks and five pretty chicks.

Baby Ray's mother sings a go-to-sleep song to him that I have learned for myself. It is this:

> *I see the moon,*
> *And the moon sees me.*
> *God bless the moon and*
> *God bless me.*

Granny Beck says that this is a pretty good song but when I am a little older she will teach me songs that will help me do things—songs of power she calls them.

"Go on, child," Granny says, "I ain't for sure but I think an elf is a right small person."

I read some more—this is a poem. Which is like a song but you just say it instead of singing. This poem is all about a little boy who wants to know when tomorrow will come. And his mama says,

> *When you wake up and it's day again,*
> *It will be tomorrow, my darling, then.*

The book I am reading out of is called *McGuffey's Fourth Eclectic Reader* and it is much harder than Baby Ray. But I go on reading the poem and now the little boy goes to bed, and when he wakes up, he kisses his mother and asks is it tomorrow. But she says no; now it is today.

Which is aggravating but I have studied on it and there ain't no way it could be any different. Another thing I have studied on is how all the mothers in these books are so loving to their children, especially at night. I would like it if Mama put me to bed. But she is too wore out, I reckon. And anyway, now I have Granny in my room and that is as nice as can be.

I have never kissed my mother.

"You read that real good," Granny Beck tells me when I am done. "But I reckon you best get back to the rug lest your mama be ill at us when she comes home. I know Fronie—she'll have it calculated to the inch how much we should've hooked today. Go on now, child; put the book back in the hidey place. And iffen you don't care, bring me a sup of water when you come back. Then I'll tell you some more stories while we work."

I do like she says but instead of water I run quick out to the springhouse and pour off some buttermilk for us. There is cornbread from breakfast and I get that too and fix us each a bowlful. Granny don't eat much, especially when Mama is watching, and she has gotten thinner since she's been here.

We have had the whole day to tell stories and practice reading, for Mama has gone with a neighbor all the way into Asheville. She has taken every one of the rugs we have made to sell for top dollar at a place called The Treasure Chest and she won't be back till after dark.

Me and Granny Beck are sitting on the porch, hooking on a big round rug that is black with red flowers called poppies all over. It is the prettiest thing—I wish we could keep it but Mama says that would be foolish with times as hard as they is—that we will need every cent we have to pay our taxes this year.

Mama is a lot happier about having Granny to live here for now Granny and me are turning out the rugs like one thing. Granny says she likes to do it but I know it hurts her hands and she sometimes has me to bring her a bowl of hot water to soak them in.

I am so glad Granny Beck is living with us. Her and me are Best Friends. Which is good, since Lilah Bel has got religion so bad, she don't hardly ever come up to play, and when she does she still won't play nothing but revival. Iffen I try to talk about the Little Things, she sulls up and says they's likely demons and I will go to the bad place if I keep on messing with them.

Granny knows about the Little Things. She don't think they's demons either. She says their real name is Yunwi Tsunsdi. She told me all about them when she gave me the little cross made from their tears—and she told me about them crying when Jesus died. I thought Lilah Bel would like that story for it had Jesus in it but she put her fingers in her ears and said she would go home if I said any more about the Little Things.

Granny Beck's papaw was full blood Cherokee and it was her papaw who told Granny Beck about Cherokee Magic, which Granny is teaching me. She says it has to be passed on by kin, knee to knee, and it can't be learned from a book.

There are lots of good stories and some scary ones— I hate the one about the Raven Mockers that eat the hearts of dead people. Another bad one is Old Spearfinger, a dreadful kind of a witch with one long finger made of bone and she will stab people with that finger and kill them and eat their liver. The worst is that, being magic, she can make herself look like someone you know and then, when you aren't paying attention, she will stab you with that finger. Sometimes I have bad dreams about Old Spearfinger and think that she is standing in our room at night, just staring at me and Granny Beck and biding her time.

But Granny says I must learn all the stories, every bit, so I will know how to use the Gifts. I had thought maybe the Gifts was things like the fairy cross she give me, but

Granny says no, the Gifts ain't things you can see. She says I will understand better later on.

I know all about the Yunwi Tsunsdi now—how they live away up on the mountains in caves or under big rocks or in the places some call laurel hells on account of how the laurel grows so close and twisted a man or dog can get hung up in it and never get out. Back when I told Granny that I had seen the Little People dancing and playing their drums, she scowled and looked at me hard.

"Best not go lookin for the Yunwi Tsunsdi, child. People who see them are like to be bumfuzzled all their lives," said she, and I wondered was it the Little People who made me take spells. I asked her but she wouldn't talk no more of them just then for, she said, night was coming on fast and it's reckoned unlucky to talk of these things after dark.

It's not all that late now but the sun is down behind the trees, so when I take Granny her bowl of buttermilk and bread I don't ask for no Cherokee Magic stories; instead I ask her to tell me the story about John Goingsnake and the Trail of Tears.

"Law, child, I reckon you could tell it to me by now, you've heard it so many times." She sops a piece of cornbread and bites into it.

"Please, Granny Beck—one more time."

Granny finishes up her cornbread. She wipes her hands good on her apron. Then she takes up her rug machine and goes to poking the black strips into the burlap backing of the rug.

"I'll tell it, honey, but we both got to work fast now, while it's yet light."

So I take up my rug machine and some of the red strips

and begin to fill in the poppy outlines while Granny Beck tells her story.

"It was almost a hundred years ago, in eighteen and thirty-eight, the army rounded up the Cherokee people who had lived in these mountains long before the white man had come. The soldiers burnt the Cherokees' houses and fields, cut down their peach trees, and said that all the Injuns would have to go west where a new home was waiting for them. The people tried to fight back but there was too many soldiers with too many guns. So the soldiers herded the Cherokee people up in a bunch to drive them like cattle to a place in Tennessee from where they would commence the long walk.

"Now, one of these Cherokees was John Goingsnake, who had been strong against the removal but when he saw it weren't no use, he give in, for he had a young wife and a baby girl and he feared what would become of them was he killed in a fight with the soldiers. So John Goingsnake and his wife and baby girl was in with them folks being marched out of Carolina into Tennessee."

"Tell the names of the wife and the baby," I say, not wanting her to leave out any part of the story. The steady sounds of our rug machines as we punch the strips into the tight burlap backing could be the sounds of the Cherokees tromping along and that thought makes the hair on my arms stand right up.

Granny Beck keeps working. But she nods and says, "Bless me, how could I leave that out? The wife's name was Nancy and the babe was called Rebekah."

"Like you," I say and she nods again.

"That's right, honey, like me. Now, the Cherokees tramped along and it was a dreadful weary time. A few of them had horses and wagons but John Goingsnake and

Nancy was afoot, leading a pack mule loaded down with all they owned and the little one riding in a basket at the side. The soldiers was all on horses and they made the whole gang step along right quick. It was terrible hard on the old folks and the little ones. And when some begun to fall sick, it was hardest of all on them. The soldiers piled the sickest ones into a wagon and it never got too full for every night when the wagon was unloaded, there would be two or three to bury. The Cherokees would dig the graves and sing over the dead, telling them they were the happy ones, to be staying forever in these green hills."

Granny falls quiet and swallows hard like there is a lump in her throat.

"And then . . ." I say to get her going again.

"And then came a day when Nancy awoke one morning, burning with a cruel fever and so weak she could hardly stand. 'Don't let them put me on the wagon,' she said to her husband, and she staggered to her feet. By holding to the mule's pack, she could just make out to stumble along. But soon she was plumb give out and John pulled half their goods off the mule—blankets and tools and anything to lighten the load so Nancy could ride. He put the baby on his back and they kept going, Nancy just barely able to hold on.

"Now, they was being marched to Tennessee along an old road called the Catawba Trail and it followed the river here in Marshall County. In time, this same trail come to be the Drovers' Road and now the railroad track sets atop it."

I have been through the woods down to the river though don't nobody know this, and I have sat and watched the train go by on the other side. And now that I know this story, I can see in my head the poor Indians tromping along so sad and it makes me like to bawl to think of it. It was by the river that they camped that night . . .

". . . and when John pulled his wife off the mule, she hardly seemed to know it but he made her a bed on their blankets and brewed a little tea with some dried pennyroyal and peppermint leaves they had brought with them. The soldiers come round with a ration of dry biscuit and water and then they set up their camps in a ring outside where the Cherokee were.

"John soaked some biscuit in water and put little soft bits in Nancy's mouth but she didn't have the strength to swaller. And before morning come, she died in his arms."

"Did John Goingsnake cry?" I ask though I know the answer. Thinking of the poor Injuns makes me want to cry.

"No, he did not, though he had loved his Nancy better than ary thing. He sat there with one hand on Nancy's cooling face, holding his sleeping baby and looking out across the river that was shining silver in the moonlight. It was the fall of the year—a dreadful dry season. He could see the rocks of the river just a-sticking up, looking most like stepping-stones all the way across the water. And that gave him an idea.

" 'Nancy,' says he, speaking low to her spirit which he knows is still about, 'I mean to stay here in the mountains with you but to do that I'll have to leave you to be buried by these others. If I get away, I vow I'll come back when it's safe and sing over your grave.'

"And with that, he picked up the babe and strapped her to his back. She stirred and whimpered but didn't wake, just drooped her head down heavy on John Goingsnake's shoulder. All round, folks was sleeping hard, wore out with the walking they'd done. Even the soldiers who was meant to be keeping guard was setting down, dozing by their campfires. Then, quiet as a hunting cat, John Goingsnake creeps to the water's edge and steps out onto a rock. The moon is making a path for him across the water and he hears a singing in his head as he steps to the second rock and then the third."

ॐ

Raven Mockers

Transcript of interview with Mary Thorn, traditional Cherokee. At Big Cove on the Qualla Boundary, 1947. Interviewer: C. L. Knight; translator: R. J. Driver.

C.K.: What about the Raven Mockers? What are they?

M.T.: They're the worst kind of witch there is. Most folks don't like to talk about them.

C.K.: How can you tell if someone's a Raven Mocker?

M.T.: No good way—they can be man or woman. One thing is, they look old because they have so many lives on top of their own. They come around when someone is sick and torment him till he dies.

C.K.: Why do they do this?

M.T.: They eat the hearts of the people they've killed. That's what keeps them alive—however many days or months or years that person would have lived if the Raven Mocker hadn't killed them, that's added to the Raven Mocker's life.

C.K.: Is there any way of stopping these witches?

M.T.: Well, when they come in a house to a sickbed, they're mostly invisible. They could be setting on the sick person's chest and doing all manner of awful things and the others in the room would just think the sick person was having trouble breathing. There are some Cherokee Doctors who know spells to stop the Raven Mockers.

C.K.: I heard the Raven Mockers can fly.

M.T.: Oh, yes, they can have big wings and when they fly at night, there are sparks flying out behind them and a wild howling like a big wind. . . .

Chapter 11

The Story of John Goingsnake (continued)

Dark Holler, 1931

(Least)

Granny stops in the middle of the story and looks to the sky where the light is starting to fade.

"Least, honey," she says, "reckon it's time for you to do the milking? I thought I heard ol Poll bawling just now."

Granny Beck always likes to do me this way but I know she is just funning. "Granny Beck," I say, "you can't leave poor John Goingsnake and his little baby in the middle of that river. You got to finish the story—there's plenty of time yet—please, Granny!"

I go over to Granny and put my arms around her. "We got to get them safe, so that baby can grow up and learn about the Cherokee Magic, ain't that so? Besides, I got three more poppies to finish." I lay my cheek next to hers and wait.

She hugs me tight. "All right, honey, we'll finish up the story afore you do your milking."

I go back to my chair and Granny opens and closes her fingers a few times, then takes her rug machine and goes back to punching in the black strips. She picks up the story and now it is almost like she is remembering something that happened to her—not just a story someone told her.

"Well now, John Goingsnake, he stood there in the middle of that broad river, wondering what to do. He could see rocks like stepping-stones to the other side but betwixt him and the next rock there was a stretch of deep rushing water. He studied the distance and knew it was too far to make a leap for. 'No telling,' thinks he, 'how deep the water is here in the middle where it runs all the year. Strong as it's running through this narrow channel, I fear was I to try to cross, the child and me could be swept away. Though,' says John Goingsnake to hisself, 'if me and the babe was took by the river, why, then we'd be with Nancy. Could be that's the best thing for us.'

"On his back, the baby stirred and made a little sound like she was a-feared, a little whining sound, and John Goingsnake stood there thinking on the meaning of that sound. A cloud passed over the moon and a hoot owl called and he studied on the meaning of them things too."

Granny looked over at me, real solemn. "That's how Injuns do; they look fer meaning in everything they see or smell, everwhat they touch or taste or hear. And being as John Goingsnake was a Cherokee wise man, he was uncommon good at knowing what the world around him was saying. But just then, standing there in the middle of the river on that long-ago night, John Goingsnake was plumb bumfuzzled.

"And then the moon come out and he looked down at that stretch of water at his feet and he was dumbstruck—

for right there in front of him, where a minute before hadn't been nothing but fast-moving water, there was a great almost flat rock with the water curling around it. Without stopping to think, John Goingsnake stepped onto the rock. And then a quare thing happened—the rock begun to move.

"John Goingsnake stood there, bending his knees and leaning this-a-way and that to keep his balance atop that swimming rock. His baby was safe on his back and John Goingsnake looked down to see the moonlight and the water rippling round the soles of his boots. It seemed to him like a long, long time in happening but at last the swimming rock brought him close enough to the other side that he could jump for it. And that's what he done—took a deep breath and leapt onto a big ledge where he fell to his knees.

"When he got to his feet, he turned round just in time to see the rock what he had rode on sink out of sight and then and there he made a special song to thank the Creator for sending the swimming rock—"

Just like I always do, I say, "Granny Beck, a rock can't swim! I bet it was one of them great big turtles I seen near the river."

And Granny reaches over and smoothes my hair down and she says, like always, "Whatever it was, honey, it was Cherokee Magic—at least that's the way I heard it. You reckon you could make a turtle carry you across the water?"

She doesn't wait for me to answer but goes on with filling in the black and I go back to punching in the red for the poppies. This is the scary part of the story, and even though I know how it comes out, I have chill bumps all up my arms as Granny Beck goes on.

"Now, John Goingsnake didn't stop to look back to see the campfires on the other side; he lit out up the riverbank and into the woods. There was a trail running along the river and turning up along a big creek but he knowed not to follow it for fear of meeting up with one of the white farmers that he knew must live up that way. Though it was nighttime, the moon was so bright that hunters and such might be traveling round."

I think of Mama walking up the road soon and hope that I can get the milking done before she gets back. But I will hear the end of this story first, even if it means a whupping.

"So John Goingsnake set off, climbing up and up into the deep woods. He reckoned maybe he could lose hisself up there for a time, till the soldiers down at the river had moved on. Then maybe, he thought, he could make his way back to his home mountains, where he knowed there was others in hiding. He figgered he could travel along the ridgetops and be back in his own country before too long.

"On and on he went, climbing through woods so steep that he was on hands and knees most of the time. It seemed to him that he'd been climbing for an hour or more when he came to a holler setting like a big bowl betwixt two ridges. A branch run down the middle and big old laurel bushes was thick and dark all above it. Just then the baby on his back stirred and begun to whimper and John Goingsnake knowed he would have to stop and feed her something and change out the moss in the rags he had wrapped around her little bottom—what we call hippens."

"How old was Baby Rebekah, Granny?" I know the answer, but this is part of the way we do the story.

"She was not yet a year of age—and still a tittie baby, getting all her nourishments from her mama. Now that her mama was gone, what would John Goingsnake do?"

I bust out with what comes next, wanting to hurry on to the good part. "John Goingsnake, he stops near a branch and gets him some water, and after he cleans the baby's bottom, he pounds up some of that dry biscuit and mixes it with the water in a drinking gourd he's carrying. And all the time, that baby's fussing and squalling and he's telling her hush. And he dips a finger in the biscuit mush and puts his finger in Baby Rebekah's mouth for her to suck on. And at first she don't like it and spits it out but then she begins to swaller some. And then . . ."

I wait, for Granny tells this part the best. She laughs a little and goes on with the story.

"And then, when the baby's swallered all she will and John Goingsnake is putting her on his back, he hears a crunching and a crackling and knows that something is climbing up the way he come. His heart begins to thump for he fears the soldiers have followed him. High above the laurel, he can see that the sky is getting lighter.

"Without waiting to see who it is coming towards him, John Goingsnake, with Baby Rebekah on his back, makes a run for the laurel and dives in.

"The laurel bushes are old and their trunks are so twisty and close-growed that in some places John Goingsnake has to get down on his belly and slip along like a real snake to get through. Behind him he can hear voices. It sounds like two men and when he looks back he sees the glitter of brass buttons in the pale morning light that is sifting down through the dark leaves."

Granny's fingers wiggle as she shows how the sun came down through the laurel leaves on that long-ago day.

She sets back in her chair, the rug machine in her lap, and stares into the past. Her voice drops down low and scary for what is to come.

"Now John Goingsnake is certain sure that it is the soldiers coming after him, and though he is in black despair, he keeps scrambling and sliding, deeper and deeper into the thickest part of that laurel hell. He moves along like only an Injun can do, making hardly a sound. But just then Baby Rebekah decides they are playing a funny game, and no matter how he tries to hush her, she keeps on laughing and babbling. And still John Goingsnake hears the voices following him . . . closer and closer and closer . . . till it seems they're at his back."

I shiver hard. The light is going fast and I can barely make out Granny's face. She is a voice coming out of the dark.

"And then, along with the baby's laughing and the growling voices coming up on him fast, John Goingsnake hears another sound. At first he thinks it is his heart, beating hard and fast in his breast, but then he realizes that the sound is coming from somewhere a little ways deeper in the laurel. And it is the sound of drums."

Chapter 12

The Story of John Goingsnake (the end)

Dark Holler, 1931

(*Least*)

"Please, Granny, tell the rest of the story. John Goingsnake heard drums way back in the laurels and then what happened?"

My last poppy is all filled in and I pick up some of the black strings and skooch over closer to Granny Beck and start to working on the background right next to her. I can't hardly see but it feels good to set so near and feel the warmth of my granny's body through her skirt and breathe in her oak leaf smell.

"Well, honey," she says like she always does, "now, you may not believe this next part. But this is how John Goingsnake told it.

"The drums was louder and louder and he followed the sound, sometimes crawling, sometimes walking crouched down, through the twisting roots and branches till he came to a kind of a clearing there in the midst of the laurels. Over to one side was a great rock cliff that reared through the green leaves and there down low was an opening—broad as two men though not but knee high—and it was from in there that the sound of the drums was coming.

"John Goingsnake had heard the stories of the Yunwi Tsunsdi and he was most certain that this was one of their dancing grounds he was in the middle of and that those drums he was hearing was their drums. But he remembered how the old folks always said that the Little People was good to help lost children. 'Well,' thinks he, looking behind him where he could hear the soldiers getting closer, 'I've got a lost child on my back and nowhere else to go.' And thinking that, John Goingsnake crawled into the opening there at the foot of the big cliff."

This is my very most favorite part.

"Tell what he saw, Granny," I beg, and I jiggle her arm to get her to hurry.

"It was only long years after," she says, "when John Goingsnake was an old, old man and wandering in his mind, that he would talk about what he saw down there. And even so, it didn't make much sense. He talked of being brought food—nuts and berries and honey—and of a red wolf suckling her cubs and Baby Rebekah nursing alongside of them. He said there was dancing and singing and sleeping and dreaming following each on each and that sometimes it was hard to tell the one from the other. He said it was always warm and dry and just light enough to see and that there was always a humming sound down there and Little Things moving around just at the edge of sight.

"Like a dream it must have been, and that was all he ever could tell of the time he and the baby Rebekah stayed with the Little People."

"How long were they there, Granny?" I can feel every hair on my arms standing up, and when I hug myself to keep from shivering, I can feel the goose bumps.

"Now, that's the quarest part of all," Granny says, her voice low and wondering, like it always is at this part of the story. "John Goingsnake always told that it was first light when he crawled into that cave with the baby on his back and the two of them curled up and went to sleep and that he woke up when he heared a rooster crow. First the rooster and then he heared a child crying and looked to see where his little Rebekah was.

"She weren't there by him and the blanket that had wrapped her was gone. John Goingsnake couldn't see nothing but the dirt floor and some shiny brown laurel leaves. And outside the crying went on and on.

"John Goingsnake grabbed the pack he'd laid his head on and the blanket he'd had around him and pulled them along with him as he crawled to the opening of the cave. His joints was as stiff as an old, old man's and his head felt like it was stuffed full of moss.

"When the daylight hit his eyes, it fair dazzled him and he blinked a time or two. There, standing in the middle of the clearing, was a little girl who looked to be about seven or eight years of age. She was naked as a jaybird, but around her shoulders was a gray blanket with a blue stripe. It was just like the one he'd wrapped around the baby when they lay down in the cave except that this one was wore most to a rag, with big holes and rips in it. And around the girl's neck was the same leather thong with the same little leather bag his own baby had worn.

" 'Who are you?' John Goingsnake called out, and his voice sounded strange to him, all rusty and creaking.

"The little girl looked at him and her crying stopped. '*Edoda*,' she said—that's Cherokee for 'papa'—'*Edoda*, I thought you'd gone away too!' And she ran to him and wrapped her little arms around him.

"Now John Goingsnake was as bumfuzzled as ever a man was. He stood there looking at this little girl who was calling him papa—this little girl who had the face of his dead wife—and he tried to make sense of what had happened. He picked up the little girl and held her to him while he turned in a slow circle to look all around. But there weren't nothing to see except right in the center of the clearing's mossy floor was a little ring of bare dirt, like the moss had been wore away by people doing a stomp dance. He didn't see no sign of the baby he'd carried to this place nor sign of the soldiers who'd been following him.

"Just then there was a loud *cock-a-doodle-doo* and a tall speckled rooster come strutting out of the laurels. He walked right up to John Goingsnake and kindly bowed before him, wiping his beak on the moss at the man's feet. The speckled rooster crowed once again then turned and paced slow and deliberate back to the laurels.

"The little girl squirmed out of John Goingsnake's arms, saying '*Edoda!* It's the guide! They said they'd be a guide!' and without another word, she fell to her hands and knees and began to crawl, following the rooster into the laurel hell.

"John Goingsnake always said that she moved like a fox, winding and twisting through those close-knit laurels. It was all he could do to keep her in sight as he fought his way through the crookedy branches that caught in his hair and snagged his shirt, tearing it easy as if the stout homespun cloth was handkerchief muslin. He reached up to pull a hank of his hair loose from a laurel twig and was surprised to find his hair was so long.

"That was when he saw it. Right there beside him was a soldier's coat, hanging from a branch like someone had put it there to air. It was all dirty and faded and the brass buttons that he remembered glittering in the morning light was tarnished and dull. John Goingsnake reached out to take one, thinking that a token from his enemy would be strong medicine for him. He pulled at the button and pulled again till it snapped off.

" 'Maybe I'll get them all,' thinks John Goingsnake and reaches for the next and gives a mighty tug.

"With that, the whole front of the coat fell open and a rib cage and two skeleton arms slid out of the coat and rattled to the mossy ground like a pile of dry sticks.

"John couldn't hardly get his breath. There he was on his hands and knees with those old dry bones falling all around him. 'Aaah! Aaah!' he said, and looking a little beyond, he saw some more bones scattered about and an old rusting musket. Off to one side, the empty eye sockets of a half-buried skull was watching him.

" 'AAAAAAH!' John Goingsnake called out and took off on his hands and knees crawling after the rooster and the little girl."

There is a creaking sound and I turn to see Mama coming up the porch steps.

"Are you both deaf and don't neither one of you hear that cow bawling?" she hollers. "If Poll takes the masticks and goes dry, I'll know who to blame."

She reaches out and catches my ear and pulls me off the stool. "Get on with that milking right now," she says. "You can take your whupping when that's done."

The barn is near dark but I manage just fine. Poll settles in with her pan of corn and for a mercy don't dance about. And when the milk is squirting into the pail, *psst psst psst,* I tell Poll how the story come out, so's not to leave John Goingsnake in that laurel hell.

I tell her how John Goingsnake caught up to the girl and the rooster just as they got to the edge of the laurels and looked down the mountain to a new-built cabin and stock corral. I tell how there was a man and woman and some children out digging taters and they looked up and seen the naked Injun girl and the long-haired Injun man behind her. I tell how the rooster weren't nowhere to be seen but the man and woman was kind and took the two Injuns into their house and cared for them.

"Then, Poll," I say as I untie her and turn her into the stall where her calf is waiting for his supper, "then John Goingsnake finally told the folks that he was a runaway from the march to the West and that if they had a mind to turn him in, they might as well go ahead and do it."

Poll steps over the log sill into the dark stall. I can hear her calf snorting and snuffling as it sucks on her and I can hear Poll's rough tongue working on the calf's fur. I stand there breathing in the smells of the warm milk and the cow dookie and the sweet scent of the hay in the loft above.

"And, Poll, when those folks asked John Goingsnake how long it had been since he'd run away from that cruel Removal march and he said he didn't rightly know— maybe a day or two—why, they looked at one another in wonder.

" 'My poor friend,' said the kind man to John Go-ingsnake, 'the last Removal march to come through these parts was in 1838—seven long years past. Where have you been all that time?' "

✌

Page from textbook with handwritten notes

Thomas the Rhymer
Part First

Ancient

True Thomas lay on Huntlie bank;
A ferlie he spied wi' his ee;
And there he saw a lady bright,
Come riding down by the Eildon Tree.

Her skirt was o' the grass-green silk,
Her mantle o' the velvet fyne,
At ilka tett of her horse's mane
Hang fifty siller bells and nine.

* * *

"Now, ye maun go wi me," she said,
"True Thomas, ye maun go wi me,
And ye maun serve me seven years,
Thro weal or woe as may chance to be."

She mounted on her milk-white steed,
She's taen True Thomas up behind,
And aye wheneer her bride rung,
The steed flew swifter than the wind.

* * *

"And see not ye that bonny road,
That winds about the fernie brae?
That is the road to Elfland,
Where thou and I this night maun gae.

"But, Thomas, ye maun hold your tongue,
Whatever ye may hear or see,
For, if you speak word in Elflyn land,
Ye'll neer get back to your ain countrie."

O they rade on, and farther on,
And they waded thro rivers aboon the knee,
And they saw neither sun nor moon,
But they heard the roaring of the sea.

It was mirk, mirk night, and there was nae stern light,
And they waded thro red blude to the knee;
For a' the blude that's shed an earth
Rins thro the springs o that countrie.

Syne they came on to a garden green,
And she pu'd an apple frae a tree:
"Take this for thy wages, True Thomas,
It will give the tongue that can never lie."

* * *

He has gotten a coat of the even cloth,
And a pair of shoes of velvet green,
And till seven years were gane and past
True Thomas on earth was never seen.

Part Second

> *When seven years were come and gane,*
> *The sun blink'd fair on pool and stream;*
> *And Thomas lay on Huntlie bank,*
> *Like one awaken'd from a dream.*

* * *

Sir Walter Scott's adaptation of a traditional Scots
ballad (1803)—story of mortal taken by faeries to
underworld common in many cultures—
Persephone—see also Keats "Belle Dame Sans
Merci"—pop quiz/essay Friday?

Chapter 13

The Yard Dog

Dark Holler, Summer 1935

(Least)

The yard dog has run off at last.

He never had no name and Mama always kept him chained to his box, there in the middle of a big patch of bare ground so that he would bark if anyone came up the road or if a strange dog was to come loafering. It was what he was there for, she said, and twice a day I would take him some cornbread and sour milk and he would eat it and then lay back down—in the shade if it was hot or in the sun if it was cool. That was all he did—that and drag his chain around so that couldn't no grass ever grow around his box.

But when Granny Beck taught me to read and when I read in the Baby Ray book about Baby Ray's little dog and how it was his friend, I thought maybe the yard dog could be *my* friend. So I saved out some scraps from my dinner, and when Mama had gone to town, I went to where he was and tried to toll him over to where I could pet him.

No matter how I tried, that old dog would get as far

away from me as his chain would reach. Or he would go in his box and not come out till I was gone, not even to eat his supper. One time when he was in there, I went to the hole at the front to see could I make friends but he just growled, low and mean-sounding, and I was afraid to put my hand out to him.

Granny Beck told me it was no good. She said being chained up all his life like that, he'd learned not to trust no one and would bite me if I fooled with him.

"The poor critter don't know nothing but his prison," she said and began to tell me of Snap, a little white dog she had once had. She told me how smart and friendly Snap was and how he would sit up and beg and would go fetch a stick and lay down and roll over and oh! all kinds of tricks.

The more she talked about Snap, the sorrier I begun to feel for the yard dog and I wondered, was I to turn him loose what would happen. I knowed Mama wouldn't hold with letting him loose but it seemed to me that he might be happier if he could go free now and again. So the next time Mama was gone, while the yard dog was sleeping I crept up and undid his chain where it was hitched to the box.

"Get up, you!" I said. "I'm turning you loose. You can run and play," I told him and I tossed the chain towards him so he could see what I had done.

He lifted his head and looked at me, then very, very slowly he got up. He begun to walk all around his patch of dirt, just a-dragging that chain after him. He must of known that he was loose, that he could go anywhere he wanted, but he never did. He circled round a few more times and went into his box.

I went into the house where Granny Beck was by the woodstove working on another rug. When I told her what I had done and how the dog wouldn't run and play, she shook her head real sad-like.

"He don't know how to be free," she said and then she frowned. "I thought he offered to bite if you come near him. How did you get the chain off him?"

"It's still on him," I said, poking some more billets into the woodstove. "I undone it at the box."

"Oh, honey," she cried, "you must run and fix it back. Don't you see? If he did run off, that chain could be the death of him was it to catch on something deep in the woods. He'd die of thirst or starve to death. Go on now, hurry!"

So I did like she said and was glad to find him in his box. "Maybe you knowed you shouldn't go off dragging that chain," I told him as I hitched it back. "But I'll find a way . . ."

It was a few days later when Granny Beck was teaching me all the uses of catnip that I had my idea.

". . . colds, to break the fever, headaches, colic—oh, there's a many a use for this," said she, sniffing at the sprig I'd brung her from the garden. "Small wonder folks brought it with them from the old country."

She put the tender leaves into her mouth and begun to chew them. "They taste of spring," she said and closed her eyes, almost like she was praying.

For a moment Granny Beck was quiet and then she said, "You can make a poultice for a sore that's slow healing and a strong tea from the leaves will help a body to sleep."

———————

I couldn't make the tea right away for the plants were not yet big enough, but when summer came and the plants grew tall and bushy with their lavender-blue flowers just a-bobbing up and down as the bees lit on them, I took a knife and cut an armful of the strong-smelling branches.

When the tea was done, I put a little honey in a cup of it and took it to Mama. Granny Beck had said it might calm Mama's nerves, but when I offered her the cupful, Mama just laughed a hateful, unhappy laugh like always.

"What do I want with that old Injun tea?" she asked and reached for her bottle of Cordelia Ledbetter. "This suits me fine; you take that cup to that old woman and let her drink it if she thinks it's so good."

That night, though, when I fed the yard dog, I mixed some of the strong catnip tea into his cornbread and milk. He sniffed at it like he knew it was different somehow but in the end he lapped it all up.

Later, when I could hear Mama snoring in her room, I crept outside and saw that the dog was snoring too. He didn't stir as I came near, and even when I laid hands on his collar, he didn't wake.

I had decided that the thing to do was to unbuckle his collar, take it off him, and buckle it back so it would look like he had slipped out of it. It was my hope that he would go run around a little, then come back and Mama would see that he didn't have to stay chained up all the time. Or maybe, I thought, he would just run away to somewhere he wouldn't have to be tied up ever.

I got up early, just before first light, and slipped outside to find out was he gone. When I peeked in his box and didn't see him, I almost laughed out loud to think of him running free. The chain and empty collar was laying there and I decided I best stretch it out tight so it would seem that he had slipped out of his collar. I caught it up and was moving slow and careful to the edge of the dirt circle when I heard a kind of whimpering sound.

There, still inside the circle, was the yard dog, crouched down and all a-tremble. When he saw that I had his collar in my hand, he begun to crawl to me, unching along on his belly till he was at my feet. Then he just lay there, making tiny little crying sounds in his throat and I seen that he wanted his collar back on.

"So he let you touch him?" Granny Beck whispered when I had told her what happened.

"I don't understand it," I said, as I helped her out of bed and to the chamber pot, "the minute I got the collar back on him, he growled at me and went back in his house."

"He's been on that chain all his life," said she. "I reckon he can't feature any other way to live."

Mama never did know what I was about with the yard dog. Every night I would let him loose—after a while, he grew used to me and I didn't have to use the catnip tea to make him sleep—and every morning I would find him still there, still laying in that old dirt circle, and I would put the collar back on. I began to grow aggravated at him for not seeing that he could be free and had almost made up my mind to give it up, when one morning I found him outside of the circle, sniffing at the grass.

I stayed just as quiet, hoping he would go on and take to the woods, but then he caught sight of me and went back and lay down, half in and half out of his box.

When I put the collar on him, I whispered to him of the woods and the mountaintop and all the things a free dog might do, but once more he just put his head between his front paws and heaved a big old sigh like he was wore out.

"It ain't no use," I told Granny Beck while Mama was up at the little house. "He'd just as soon stay tied up, I believe."

She looked at me for the longest time without a word. Then she put her head on one side. "Tell me, Least, have *you* ever thought of going away from here?"

Just then Mama come back in the house, fussing because the bees was making a nest under the step stone at the back porch.

"I hate them things," she said. "It seems likes there's more and more every year. This evening, Least, when they're all in their nest, I want you to dash some lamp oil down the hole and kill them, every one."

I did like Mama said—poured the lamp oil down the hole. I had to for she would be expecting to smell it still in the morning. But I waited till she was dozing over her tonic and then I sung the Calling Song, telling the Little Things there was danger and they must go somewhere else. They come out one by one till there was a great cloud of them hanging in the air, humming and quivering just above my head.

Go on, I told them, *it ain't safe for you here.*

It was a sight on earth, how that thick cloud of bees

begun to lengthen out and then move up towards the woods, like a great snake swimming through the air. I tried to watch to see where they went but they disappeared into the dark.

Once more I went out to let the yard dog loose, and this time, the instant I took the collar off, he made for the grass at the edge of his dirt patch and begun to roll. Well, anyway, I thought, he can have a taste of freedom, even if he don't go off. He was still sniffing around the rim of the dirt circle when I went inside, and I figured that I'd tie him back in the morning like always.

But in the morning he was gone, never to return. When I told Granny Beck, she looked at me hard and said, "He finally got off the chain that was in his head: do you see that, honey? The chain in his head was stronger than the one you undid every night. You remember that, now. It ain't only dogs that is on chains."

Mama, she didn't seem to care much. "That old dog was getting up in years anyway," said she. "It'll save me the bother of knocking him on the head."

Chapter 14

The Healing Plants

Dark Holler, Fall 1935

(Granny Beck)

I fixed a big vessel of the tea for your rheumaticks, Granny Beck. And I did it just according to how you said—gathered laurel, ivy, and dog-hobble leaves this morning and from the east side of the bushes. I put them in the pot and covered them over and as much again with water, then boiled them down good afore straining the tea."

Least is standing there by my bed, holding a gallon crock with a dishtowel wrapped round it. The steam rises and makes a wreath around her pretty head. She sets the crock down careful-like on the chair by the bed.

"Let me help you set up to where you can soak your hands in this—it's good and hot and ought to help with the aching—and while you do that, I'll wet the towel and rub the tea on your legs."

The child is so bright-eyed and hopeful that I can't bring myself to tell her that what ails me is past curing. It ain't only the rheumaticks, but there is something else amiss, something deep in my innards what ain't right.

"Mama's gone to Ransom to do some trading and she'll not be back till this evening. I've got all my chores done up. . . ."

Her blue eyes are sparkling like the sun a-dance on the water as she lays back the quilts and begins to rub my poor old limbs. Her touch does me more good even than the medicine she has brewed.

Oh, how the child has changed in these few years! That half-wild, dirty-faced little creature I first saw is as pretty a girl as ever there was. I have poured all my learning into her, and my love too, like she was an empty pitcher and me a gushing spring. No, more like she was a piece of parched earth, thirsty for the rain, for a pitcher could overflow and she has soaked up every bit of learning and love I could give her.

"That's done me a world of good, child," I tell her when the tea begins to cool, and truth is, I do feel better. I look over out the window and see that the sun is shining hard and that the wind must of laid, for them dark old trees is still for once. "If it ain't too cold, I'd like to set outside in the sunshine for a little."

It is one of those bright October days with the sky that clear endless blue and the sun setting fire to the reds and golds of the mountain trees—the sourwoods and maples and hickories. Least brings out an armchair from the house and helps me to it, then tucks my Delectable Mountains quilt around me. My eyes has grown dim to where I can't make out much more than shapes and colors but nevertheless it feels fine to be out in the air, breathing the smell of the deep woods that loom up across the way.

It seems that as my eyes has begun to give out, my nose has taken up the slack. I can travel the woods even though I can't leave the porch, and I draw in all the old friendly smells—leaf mold and rich dirt, along with a world of other scents—spice bush and the clean smell of the water in the branch over yon. There's even a smell to the sun falling on a dry rock . . . and another for that same rock when the rain first strikes it and still another when the rock is soaked and cool. So many ways of knowing . . .

If I could get around a little better . . . if I could have walked with Least through those woods, showing her all the healing plants and how they look at the different times of the year, just the way my papaw did for me . . .

She sets herself down on the porch floorboards beside me and leans against my legs. There is a healing warmth in the child's touch and I know that the Gifts are stronger in her than ever before.

"Least, honey," I say, stroking her pretty dark hair, "do you remember what the Cherokee tell about how sickness came into the world?"

She turns her face up and smiles at me. "I'll say it like you told me, Granny, so you can be sure I learned it right."

I know that she has learned it all, but the pleasure of hearing her say over the words, same as I learned from my papaw long years since, is like a crown on the beauty of this day. I sit, feeling the sun on my face, smelling the woods, and listening to Least. I am hungry for all the good things of living, hungry to know them all at once, like a greedy young un left alone at a full table afore the company comes, trying to stuff some of everything in his mouth. I am greedy for life for I have heard the black wings beating and I know that afore much longer it'll be over.

". . . and when all the animals seen how bad that people was doing them, killing them or making them slaves or harming them for no reason at all, like young uns stomping on bugs just for the fun of it, well, all the animals got together in a council and one by one, each animal thought up some manner of sickness to punish man for his heedless ways . . ."

I remember my papaw acting out the story, even down to the part where the grub worm cuts such a shine at the thought of getting back at men that he jumps up in the air and falls on his back and has to go a-wiggling along that way forever after.

". . . but then the plants felt sorry for men and so *they* got together in their council meeting and each plant said that it would be a medicine against one of those sicknesses the animals made up. . . ."

"And how did those first Injuns, those what hadn't learned from their elders, how did they know which plant would be right—"

Least jumps right in, not waiting for the rest of the question. "The plants told them. If the Injun went into the field or woods and asked polite, 'Oh, which of you Little Brothers will cure the fever my child has?' why then, if that Injun waited silent and patient, one of the plants would begin to tremble and that was the way he knowed which one to use. But, after a while, folks learned by listening to their grannies."

She rubs her head against me and goes on. "And when you collect plants like sang, you must always pass by the first three plants before you can take the fourth, and when you take a plant, you must put something good in the ground where it was—"

"They used to use red or white beads for payment," I tell her, "but if you ain't got a bead, there's other things— a flower, or, if it's sang, you must bury the shiny red seeds where you dug the plant out."

Least leaps up from the porch floor. "Granny Beck, let's us do the plant game now. You name a sickness and I'll go see can I find the plant for it."

It is a game we have played many a time. At first she would bring everwhat plants she didn't know to me and I would tell her the name and what it was good for and how to fix the medicine. Now we do it different.

I think a minute, then say, "See what you can find for the summer complaint, for the whooping cough, for a fever, and for bad monthlies."

The child fairly flies down the porch steps, making for the woods across the road. I call after her, "And chicken pox and headache too."

She laughs and it sounds like bells and she turns and waves. In the gray-brown gingham dress she has on, and with my bad eyes, she looks most like a slender sapling herself and in the next moment she disappears into the woods.

The child needs to know all these cures for when she has young uns of her own. The onliest medicines Fronie makes use of, besides that everlasting Cordelia Ledbetter tonic she is poisoning herself with, is turpentine or castor oil.

I close my eyes and let the sun warm my face. Fronie . . . ay, law . . . if Fronie has her way, Least'll never marry nor have babes. There is nothing wrong with the child but folks don't know that. Fronie has told it up and down that

Least is simple . . . fit only to stay home and care for
Fronie in her old age . . .

And the pity is that Least don't know no better herself.
I got to make her see . . .

The squeak of the wooden steps brings me back to myself. I have been wandering in a strange dream where
there is a girl who, but for her bright red hair, might be
Least. This girl is in a strange place full of fiddling
and dance music and crowds of people—a dark place
with little happiness in it though there is singing and bitter laughter. And there was a graveyard—but I have
dreamed that dream before and it don't frighten me none,
no more than dreaming of my own bed would.

I open my eyes and she is standing before me, her basket brimming with fresh-cut bark—the clean sap smells
tell me what kind they are—and knobby roots with the
dirt still clinging to them. I can make out the strong scent
of heavy clay on some and the rich, dark smell of moist
woods dirt on some other. In her hand she has a bunch of
branch mint, fresh and clean-smelling. I know she means
to make a tea for later but I reach out and take a stem.

"Granny Beck," she says, laying her basket at my feet,
"I didn't mean to wake you up. I tried to be quiet but that
old step—there just ain't no way to keep it from hollering
out."

"Hush, child," I say, biting into the mint and feeling
the wild cool nip of it in my mouth. "You've brought the
woods to me and I want to smell and taste and feel of
them. There'll be time for sleeping soon enough."

While she shows me one by one what she has brought,
half my mind is listening and adding to what she already

knows whilst the other half is puzzling how to get her loose from Fronie. How to get her free to live her own life . . .

". . . bark from white oak and black oak and from the red sugar tree and the chestnut. If I pound them and shred them and soak them in cold water, the water'll help with a woman's monthly miseries. I had to go a far piece to find the chestnut—seems like they get harder and harder to find."

"And how did you take the bark off?"

She grins real big for she likes it when I quiz her and she knows the answer. "A piece from the east side of the tree and with a downward stroke of the knife as the medicine's for down here . . ."

Least lays her hand on her belly. I have warned her what to expect when her time comes. Fronie ain't never said the first word to her about such things and the first show of blood might frighten the poor child. But now she knows it's in the natural way of things. I even made sure she has a supply of rags ready and knows what to do with them for I see signs that she is ripening . . .

". . . but if I was taking the bark so's someone could chew it for mouth sores, why then I'd just naturally make the cut going up."

"You have the right of it, child," I say. "What else have you got there?"

While she is naming them over: blackberry roots and goldenrod roots to make teas for the summer complaint, dogwood bark for headache or chicken pox . . . I am listening and nodding, for she has found all the right things, but in the back of my mind I am planning how to tackle Fronie.

༽

The Chestnut Tree by Dalilah B. Roberts—8-B

The Chestnut was once a valuable and plentiful tree in the mountains of N. Carolina, but a ~~dizeeze~~ disease has killed off almost all of them. It is said that the disease was brought in on plants from over seas, but I believe that it was God's Will because of all the sinning there is these days.

When my daddy was a little boy they would turn the hogs loose in the woods to get fat eating the Mast which is the fallen chestnuts. Daddy says that it made the sweetest pig meat. And people ate the nuts too, and roasted them in the fire, and the Indians pounded the nuts into flour to make a kind of bread.

My daddy has showed me the old hollow stumps where they cut the dead chestnuts, and how a little tree will spring up from the old roots. But that little tree will always die and it is because of the sinning.

Chapter 15

The Threefold Law

Dark Holler, December 1935

(Least)

There is blood on my drawers this morning. For a moment I just set there, out in the freezing cold little house, wondering what has happened for I don't remember hurting myself in any way. I stare the hardest at those drawers, ones that Granny Beck sewed for me out of bleached flour sacks. They are pulled down around my knees and in the middle of all that white is a big patch of brown dried blood.

What can it mean? I ask myself, and wonder am I dying. It seems hard that I should die at only thirteen years of age. There is so much more to learn—and I ain't took a spell in the longest time. Granny Beck has said that she don't see any reason I should stay at home all the time. She says that I am plenty smart.

I don't feel like I am dying or even sick but I remember what Lilah has said about how death can come in the twinkling of an eye and we must be prepared. I sit looking at the blood and hearing the tiny tapping of the sleet on the tin roof and wonder will Mama be sad when I die. I know that Granny Beck will.

What will become of Granny Beck if I die? She ain't doing no good these past months and I have to coax her to eat and help her to the chamber more and more. A few times she has had an accident in the bed and Mama has fussed to see me washing the sheets. Mama has said that if Granny Beck gets any worse and keeps me from my work, she will have to go to the county home for old people.

Maybe, I think, God will fix it so's I don't have to die and can stay here to take care of my sweet Granny Beck. I haven't never asked Him for things but I bow my head like Lilah showed me. Then I remember where I am and that it ain't a fitten place to talk to God. I know that He is everywhere but I bet He don't watch when people are doing their business.

While I am pulling up my drawers, all of a sudden I remember what Granny Beck had told me about the monthlies. And when a few seconds later there comes a wrenching, twisting feeling in my belly that is like to double me over, I know the truth—now I am a woman.

"Oh, child," says Granny Beck when I tell her. "So it's come. And you was scared, thinking there was something dreadful wrong—I mind believing the same thing when the monthlies first come on me. But I'll show you how to do so next time it don't catch you unawares."

She is laying in her bed like she does more and more these cold days. There are so many quilts piled atop her and she has lost so much flesh since fall that she don't hardly make a bump under all the covers. But her eyes are twinkling and she stretches out a hand to catch hold of me.

"Bring here the calendar, Least honey," she says and I go fetch it off the wall. Mama has marked off the days with a strong black X and we are at the first day of winter. When I show this to Granny Beck, she nods, and with the red knit cap she has on her head for warmth, she looks like some bright-eyed little bird.

"They're powerful days, them that mark the turning of the seasons. And this one is the darkest. Oh, it's full of hope and the coming of the light for this is the day the sun stops its travels to the south and turns back our way. But it's the longest night too and in this crack between the seasons, there's like to be things slipping out of the Dark into this world."

I am a little scared, sometimes, when Granny Beck talks like that, but then she laughs and shows me how to draw a little sickle moon on the day that the bleeding first begins.

"And then, beginning with that day, you count ahead twenty-eight days—and that's when you can expect your visitor again."

Her gnarly old fingers is tapping out the days that will pass and I think about how many times in her life she must have done this.

"Now, here in the beginning," Granny Beck says, "you're not likely to be right regular. But after a time your body will find its rhythm and you'll know when to be prepared."

She tells me some more things—reminding me of what herbs are best to help against the cramps and about soaking the bloody rags in cold water. Then she says a thing I had not thought of.

"You know, Least, you getting the monthlies means that your body's making ready for you to bear children."

I busy myself with straightening up the quilts and fixing her pillows more comfortable-like. They are not much good, for most of the feathers has leaked out, but by doubling them, I can help Granny to raise up a bit. Sometimes she says she feels like she is smothering, and we have tried one remedy after another but every day she is a little weaker and it ain't but very seldom she will leave her bed.

"Do you understand me, honey?" Granny Beck asks, catching my hand in hers.

"I reckon," I say, and I feel my face getting hot. Lilah Bel has told me how ladies get babies and it gives me a funny feeling to think about it. "But it don't matter about that, if I don't never get married. And I don't see how I could, for Mama says—"

"Child," Granny Beck cries out, and struggles to set up higher, "child, there ain't no reason—"

There is a sound in the doorway and I whirl around to see Mama. "There ain't no reason for Least to spend the whole morning loafering in here with you. She has got more to do than hang about waiting on you hand and foot."

Mama's face is cold and hard and in her hand hanging at her side she has the little hatchet I use on the stove wood. Her hand is just a-tremble as she lifts up the hatchet and points it at me. "Go bust up the rest of that stove wood, Least. It won't do to fall behind."

"I was aiming to do that right after I brought Granny Beck some breakfast," I say but Granny speaks up.

"Do like your mama says, Least honey. I ain't a bit hungry just now."

So I pull on an old coat that used to belong to Fairlight, then take the little hatchet from Mama and go out to the woodshed and set in on the pile of branches and trimming that is there. I can hear them quarreling back in the house and I bring the hatchet down hard, pretending that . . .

But then I remember the Threefold Law.

"Now, this ain't from my granddaddy's teaching," Granny Beck told me back when I asked couldn't she use some Cherokee Magic to stop Mama being so angry all the time. "No, this is something a granny woman I used to know told me. That old woman, for she seemed old to me at the time, me being not yet thirty and her well past the half-century mark . . ."

Granny Beck stopped in her talk and looked down at her hands. "Law, I remember how I used to wonder what it would be like to be old and how I'd think that I'd as soon die young before I went to getting all wrinkled and ugly."

"You ain't ugly, Granny Beck!" I cried and flung my arms about her and rubbed my face against her cheek. "And I like your wrinkles—they make you look all soft and . . . and loving. Not like—"

And there I'd stopped but Granny Beck hadn't seemed to notice.

"No," said she, "the Threefold Law weren't Cherokee teaching but it seems to me that it might hold for Cherokee Magic and granny woman charms and just ordinary living too."

"What is it then?" I asked, thinking it must be a mighty strong piece of magic.

"It's something like the Golden Rule that the preachers always love to talk about, and it's something like the Bible where it says an eye for an eye and a tooth for a tooth. What the Law says is that whatever you do to someone else, whether for good or for bad—that thing you did will come back to you threefold."

Chapter 16

Young David

Dark Holler, Fall 1936

(Least)

A full moon lights my path as I walk slow and careful among the Quiet People to the place where Granny Beck is. The mound they heaped over her in January has flattened out till it is just a little swelling on the hogback ridge, and when I lay down and press my face to the red dirt it still holds a mite of the sun's heat. I lay there in the silver moonlight and I pretend that it is her soft old cheek against mine.

It's a bare, mean grave, with naught to mark it but the circle of smooth rocks at the head. When the pain of my loss was still raw, I hauled them, one at a time, up the steep path from the river down below—the aching of my arms and legs not nigh the hurt in my heart.

Five rocks, one for each year I had her with me. Just a speck of time in her seventy-five years of life but for me it seemed like always and I had begun to forget the bad times afore. With her I was like a babe newborn, learning and growing under the nourishment of her love.

My Granny Beck taught me to read and she taught me

the old ways, but, more than that, she taught me how it was to be loved—and how to love someone.

There weren't never none of that with Mama. When I was little, I just took it for the way things was but after a time I begun to think there must be some bitter failing in myself. Granny Beck showed me different.

"Granny Beck," I whisper, breathing in the night smells—the fallen leaves, wood smoke drifting up from chimneys somewhere, the rank musk of a fox—"Granny Beck, it's the Hunter's Moon—a fine clear night—and I've come to visit with you again."

Her greeting brushes my face like a falling leaf and in my head I feel her welcome, soft as milkweed down. The Quiet People don't need to speak, no more than a sunrise or a tree needs words. They all have the same way of getting in amongst your thoughts so that you take their meaning. But still and all, it comforts me to talk out loud to them.

Five years was long enough for Granny Beck to pass on the things she wanted me to know—the uses of the trees and plants, the moon's ways—the paths she walks and the different names she goes by, and a world of old songs and spells, the same as Granny had learned from her own mama—Rebekah Goingsnake Godwin. And the family story with the names—the story Mama don't want known for fear of being called a half-breed.

"I tell it over every night, Granny Beck, so the names'll not be forgot and so I'll always remember where the Gifts come from."

I sit up and make myself comfortable there in the moonlight, with one hand flat on her grave. The small rustlings of the woods creatures, the soft beat of the owl's

wings as it hunts, the lonesome howl of a faraway dog—
each sound comes sharp and clear. Lifting my face to the
moon, I wrap myself in her chill light and begin the old
story once again.

"This was the way of it. Back in eighteen and thirty-
eight, John Goingsnake, son of Yellowhammer, and his
wife Nancy and their baby Rebekah was passing through
these parts along with a sight more of the Tsalagi—which
is their real name though the white men call them Cherokee—on the Long Walk to the West. When Nancy took
sick and died, John grabbed that little baby and ran and
hid so as not to have to leave these mountains that he
loved.

"John and Rebekah stayed hid for seven years until a
kind family named Godwin took them in. And when Rebekah grew up, she married Duvel Godwin and they had
a little girl and they called her Little Beck, and Little
Beck, she grew up and married Jed Thomas and they had
a baby girl and named her Sophronia—"

I hush, for of a sudden, everything has gone quiet. All
them little sounds of the night critters going about their
business has stopped and the stillness is loud in my ears. I
think that a bobcat or a fox must be lurking nigh, scaring
the others to silence, and I stand up slow to cast my eyes
around the burying ground.

Over on the far side where the big oak stands, I see
what looks like someone standing half-hid behind its
great trunk. But the shape don't move and I begin to
think it's just my eyes playing tricks on me as the moonlight sifts down through the near-bare branches of the old
tree.

In all the times I've come up this way to talk to Granny
Beck—and I come on every full moon—I ain't never seen

another living soul here at the burying ground. The first thought that hits me is that it's Mama, that she's followed me—but then I tell myself it ain't likely. Mama always drinks her tonic after supper and sleeps hard, never knowing where I go or what I do of a night.

I stand watching and squinting my eyes to see if I can make out what it is I'm seeing and all of a sudden there is a rush of soft wings and the high startled squeak of some little critter just nigh the big tree. I see the glint of metal in the moonlight and the shape jumps and says "Lorda-mercy!" all in one big breath like it was scared out of them.

"Who are you?" I call out and take a few steps towards the oak. Mama has taught me to stay hid whenever there's strangers nigh and she has told me of the terrible things that can happen to girls. But all around me I can feel the Quiet People listening and telling me not to fear.

Everwho it is stands stock-still and don't make a sound as I come closer and closer, putting one foot in front of another, slow and careful. And then I see that it ain't but a boy. He is bigger than me and has a shotgun at his side, but he's not no man, not by a long ways.

"I asked who you are," I say, pointing a finger at him, "and why for are you up here in our burying ground?"

He walls his eyes at me, showing the whites all around, and when he tries to answer, the words won't hardly come.

"S-sorry," he gets the word out at last and I see that he is all a-tremble. "I didn't mean no disrespect, ma'am." He is beginning to back away from me as he says, "I'll just slip away quiet-like and let you get back to your rest. Sorry."

I haven't never seen a boy my own age, except one time when a man and his son come to buy a heifer off of Mama. She made me stay in the house whilst they was dickering but I peeked out the window and seen them plain. That boy was spotty-faced and greasy-haired and he was all the time spitting. But this feller is as pretty a one as you could wish. He looks like the picture of Young David what was in Granny Beck's Bible—David what slew Goliath.

"Where you going?" I ask him and hold out my hand. "Why don't you stay a while and talk to me."

He draws back and I remember what Granny Beck told me once—how some folks won't walk in graveyards at night for fear of the dead people getting them. I have to stop myself from laughing as I watch his eyes getting bigger as my hand gets closer.

"You think I'm a haint, don't you?" I grab his arm and he jumps but then he looks closer at me and a big smile makes him look even prettier than the Young David.

"Naw, I was just funning with you—I can tell you ain't no ghost. But how come you to be up here?"

It is the nicest thing to be talking to someone. I have been awful lonely without Granny Beck. Lilah don't hardly ever come to see me no more and Mama keeps a close watch over me by day.

Before I know it, him and me are setting in the moonlight and talking like one thing. He tells me he is out hunting and I tell him where I live and that my mama don't let me mix with others because she says I ain't right in the head.

"You seem just as smart as anyone," says he. He smiles at me so nice and I remember back to not long afore Granny Beck died. I was outside and in the house, I heard her and Mama fussing. Then Granny Beck hollered out, "Sophronia Rushell, you had ought to be ashamed of the way you've done that young un. There ain't nary thing wrong with her but ignorance and I aim to see that she has her some kind of a life beyond staying here and doing your bidding day in and day out."

I remember puzzling over them words and trying to understand why Granny Beck was so ill at Mama. But I never got the chance to talk to her about it for that very night she took sick and went to vomicking. Mama said it might be catching and I had to sleep in Mama's room so she could stay in with Granny Beck, but in spite of Mama tending to her day and night, Granny was gone in three days. I never even got to say good-bye.

Chapter 17

Snowflower Kitty

Dark Holler, Spring 1938

(Least)

I brung you something to remember me by when I'm gone."

Young David is waiting, like always, under the big oak, and when I run to him, he holds out a honeysuckle basket with a lid on it. I shake my head no for I don't want him to leave.

"Now, listen here, Little Bird," he puts a finger under my chin and lifts my face to his, "I told you it won't be such a very long time. Working on the roads with the WPA, I can make cash money—put something by and when times is better, I'll walk up to you unses' front door and tell your mama I aim to marry up with Miss Least. But I have to go where they send me and I'll not be able to come back for our full moons."

It has been almost two years now since I first saw him, and on every full moon, except when it was bitter cold or storming, I have made the climb to the graveyard to visit with Granny Beck and he has always been here. But he won't be here no more, not for a dreadful long time.

I trace the shape of his face with my fingertips and feel the roughness of his whiskers. He has cut his hair shorter since that first time I saw him and he looks like a full-growed man now. I have learned his body and its ways as he has mine and this is why he says we must marry.

"I have done my best," says he, "to keep from getting you with child but it's awful damn hard on a feller, denying himself every time. And sooner or later . . ."

He grabs at my hand to stop it in its wandering and holds it between his. "Don't you see, Least? I want us to do this right. It won't be so very long—I promise I'll be back, time the snow flies."

Down the slope towards the river, there is a kindly scooped-out place where a wet-weather spring has made a little pond. On this warm night, the peeping love songs of the frogs fill the air, making such a commotion that it is hard to think. I throw my arms about his neck, hugging him hard as I can, and we fall together onto the thick spring grass at the edge of the woods.

Later on, when we are laying all sleepy and happy on the old quilt I always bring, I hear a kind of rustling and scratching. It is coming from the little basket which is setting over on the tree stump with our clothes.

"They's something scratching at your old basket," I say, running my bare foot up his leg, "maybe it's a mouse going after the candy."

Several times he has brung me candy from the store at Gudger's Stand—peppermints, mostly, but one time it was chocolate-covered peanuts with some kind of sweet white sticky stuff in with the nuts. That was the best thing

I ever tasted and I feel sorry that I acted so hateful when he tried to give me the basket.

"Might could be a mouse," says he, skittering his fingers along my belly. "Why don't you look and make sure?"

I get to my knees and reach for the basket, which is heavier than I expected. When I pick it up, there is a funny little crying sound and the basket tilts to one side. All of a sudden, the lid lifts off and a tiny white face with two pointy little ears looks out at me. It opens its pink mouth wide and cries *mew, mew.*

It is the prettiest pure white kitty you ever saw—prettier even than the ones in the Baby Ray book. And around its neck is a shiny red ribbon. It mews again and I hug it to me.

"Reckon she's hungry. Look over there in my overhauls' pocket—they's some sausage meat twisted up in a piece of paper. When you get her home, you might give her some milk—she ain't been off her mama but a few days."

He tells me how he traded with a neighbor—a half-day's work—for this kitty. "She ain't of the common breed—she'll have real long fluffy fur when she gets her growth," says he, stroking the kitty's little back.

He is so proud of what he's done—I can't tell him that Mama hates a cat most as bad as a snake and I will have to find some way of keeping the kitten hid.

"What will you name her?" he asks, and I feel the kitty's claws like tiny needles scratching against my breast.

I think of how long it will be before we're together again—till snow flies, he said. I look at the kitty and the moon shining on her white fur and I say, "Her name is Snowflower."

When we have loved again, he says he must go now to make it home by morning but I hang on to him till he says, "Now, Little Bird, don't you take on so. I got to do this."

He kisses me again and takes Snowflower from the basket where she has curled up to sleep some more and lays her between my breasts. He pushes me down real gentle and pulls one side of the quilt over me and the kitty.

"Just you close your eyes and lay there and think of the happy times to come, my little sweetheart," he says. "Remember, look for me at your door when the snow flies."

And he brushes my cheek with a kiss so light that it could have been one of Granny Beck's.

I listen to the sound of his steps going away until it is swallowed up by the calling of the little frogs. I know that I should dress myself and head for home to find a place to hide Snowflower, but it feels so nice here on the old quilt with the smell of him and the softness of Snowflower that I close my eyes and dream of winter.

But it ain't winter and it ain't dark no more when my eyes open. The sun is already over the ridgetop and the Snowflower kitty is licking up the last crumbs of sausage meat from the greasy piece of newspaper. I jump to my feet and pull on my clothes as fast as ever I can. I am trying to think what to tell Mama—I could say that I was out hunting branch lettuce or ramps but she will want to know why I didn't do the milking first.

And where can I hide Snowflower? I push her back in the basket and fasten down the lid. Then I grab up the quilt and make it into a loose bundle with the basket at the middle.

My mind is working hard as I hurry down the path towards home. If I can keep the kitty hid till the next time Lilah comes, maybe Lilah will take her and keep her safe. There just ain't no way—

As I come around the last bend before the barn, Mama is standing in the road, the full milk pail in her hand.

"Mama!" I say, "I was up the mountain, hunting for some ramps and . . ."

Something about the way she is looking at me chokes the lie in my throat. She sets the milk pail down real careful and takes a step forward.

The slap rocks my head back and brings the tears to my eyes. I stand still, my arms around the quilt that is hiding my Snowflower as Mama circles around me.

"And did you find you some ramps? Got a whole poke of em? So many you had to take a quilt to tote em back?"

She pokes a bony finger at the quilt and she circles and circles, poking at the quilt each time she passes. I feel her sharp black eyes seeing right into me. Her hair, which has gone all white in the past few years, is sticking out ever whichaway, and somehow she don't look like herself.

I remember the story Granny Beck used to tell about the old woman called Spearfinger and a cold feeling runs down my back.

"What's in here, you huzzy?" The finger stabs again at the quilt and she snatches it from my arms. The basket falls to the ground and the Snowflower kitty looks out but Mama don't see the kitty for she is holding up the quilt and peering close at it. She squinches up her eyes and brings the quilt up to her face. I reach down quick and push the lid of the basket shut, then pick it up and hold it

THE DAY OF SMALL THINGS

close while Mama sniffs at the quilt, like a hound looking for a trail.

All at once she makes an ugly spitting sound and flings the quilt from her.

"You nasty, lying little huzzy!" she cries. "Do you even know the name of this feller you been sneaking out of the house to lay up with?"

I tell her I call him Young David and he is coming back when snow flies to marry me but she only laughs a hateful laugh.

"You believe that, do you? That old woman filled your head with so much moonshine, you'll believe most anything. When was the last time you had your monthlies?"

When I tell her, she breathes a sigh and says well, maybe I ain't breeding. Then those sharp eyes catch sight of the basket in my arms.

"What you got there?" she says, pecking at it with that sharp bone-finger.

I say it is a kitty and that I know she can't abide them and that I will keep it away from her, but she plucks the basket from my hands.

"Well, at least this Young David business has made up my mind for me," she says, holding the basket away from her like it was a snake. "I been studying on it ever since the doctor told me about this new program they got for such as you. You ain't going to be around to care for no cat. Now take that milk in and strain it and get on with your morning's work."

I do like she says, thinking that maybe when she sees how pretty and sweet Snowflower is, she will change her mind. It ain't a bit of use to argue with her when she's like this, I tell myself. When she's some calmer, maybe after she's took her tonic in the evening, I'll talk reasonable to her.

And if she gets calmer, like she usually does, I'll ask her what is this program the doctor told her about. I wonder could it be something like school.

It's when I'm on my way to the springhouse with the strained milk that I see the Snowflower kitty.

She is laying on the trash heap out back, all limp and dirty and she don't move as I come near. There is a buzzing and a ringing in my head and I call her name but she lays still. I know that she is dead but I have to touch her to be sure. My eyes are blurring and the shapes are spinning around me as I reach for the shiny red ribbon, thinking to take it off her to have it for a keepsake.

I can't hardly see but it seems the ribbon is untied and the red of it is everywhere and my fingers are wet with it and when I pick up Snowflower Kitty, her head falls back like a red mouth opening and I scream and I scream and

ও

Newspaper article (from the **Ransom Guardian,** *5/6/2008)*

A DISGRACE TO THE STATE OF NORTH CAROLINA

by Martin Wells

They still live among us, survivors of North Carolina's almost half-century social experiment with the involuntary sterilization of poor women, otherwise known as "eugenics." Over 7,600 young lives were changed forever by this brutal program, inspired by a heartless "master race" philosophy of eugenics.

From 1929 to 1974, North Carolina was one of 33 states that allowed the forced sterilization of white and black poor women, some as young as 13 and 14, in pursuit of "the self direction of human evolution," as a newspaper editorial cartoon of the time named it.

It was none other than the U.S. Supreme Court that upheld Virginia's eugenics program in 1927 despite the fact, recently confirmed by researchers, that Virginia deliberately used forced sterilizations to "preserve white racial purity."

This so-called eugenics program was nothing more than a state-sponsored attempt to control certain parts of disadvantaged populations, using mental illness, physical maladies, anti-social behavior, sexual promiscuity, or even homosexuality as the excuse.

"There were some few who requested sterilization, not wishing to add to their families, but many of them were forced against their will," the 2004 NCDHHS Eugenics Study Committee Report noted. "In some cases, victims were children as young as 10 who had no knowledge or understanding of the procedure."

The young female victims were never told the reason or the purpose of the operations, and only years later, when they found that they were barren, did they learn from their doctors that their ability to have children had been destroyed forever.

Chapter 18

The Doctor Papers

Dark Holler, Spring 1938

(Least)

Reckon what'll become of the quare girl?" asks the fat lady who brought the plate of oatmeal cookies. She has the plate on her knees and she is eating all the cookies her own self. I watch from the front window as she picks up another one and takes a bite. She is setting there in a straight-back chair on the porch, fanning herself and dropping crumbs all down her front.

Lilah's mama is setting by her, sewing at some patchwork. She measures out a length of thread, bites it off, and threads her needle before she answers.

"Fronie did have a brother," she says, putting a blue patch face-to-face with a red one and beginning to stitch them together along one edge, "same one that brought the old lady here to live with them, but ain't no one been able to get up with him. I heared that the bank took his farm and they've all moved away looking for work."

"What about the other children? It was a good-sized family she had, weren't it? Couldn't one of them take in that poor creature—Least, ain't that her name? Hit's a scandal weren't nary a one here for the burying."

The fat lady has finished the last cookie and is picking the crumbs off her bosom and putting them in her mouth.

Lilah's mama lays her sewing in her lap and looks over at the fat lady. "I had forgot; you didn't move to Ridley Branch till after Fronie lost her man, so you never knowed her before. Yes, she did have a good many children but it seemed like after her man was took and this quare girl was born, Fronie got right quare herself. Couldn't get along with none of her girls and one by one they married and moved away. And I heard that she good as ran off the last boy when he got married."

"Still and all," says the fat lady, "kin's kin and seems like—"

"Oh, believe you me, I've searched through ever place I could look for ary sign of a letter with a return address or anything that would tell me where them children went to. I believe several moved to Detroit, but to my certain knowledge, ain't none of them ever come home, not even for Decoration Day. Not a letter nor a postcard did I find, save for one old one from the boy that was killed in the war. I asked Boaz Wagoner who carries the mail did Fronie ever get letters from away and he said he was pretty sure she never did."

The fat lady laughs and nods her head, setting her extra chins to jiggling. "Well, if anyone'd know, it'd be that feller. I declare, I've seen him setting under a tree on that old mule of his, looking through every letter and catalogue and reading all the postcards before he'd bring them to the house. You know—"

Lilah's mama ain't paying no mind and she breaks right in. "I didn't find no letters but I'll tell you what I did

find. There was some papers from a doctor that Fronie
had signed—papers about that poor girl of hers. I know
that it was always a worry—what would happen when
Least got up of an age . . . for she's a pretty thing, you
know, if she is simple. And they's some fellers . . ."

Her voice drops down to a whisper and she pulls her
chair over to talk close to the fat woman's ear. I hear her
say ". . . showed them to Sheriff Hudson and he said he'd
take care of it . . . institutionalized . . . solve the problem."

I don't wait no longer. I fling my few things into a poke
and slip out the back way. I leave them two whispering
there on the porch and light out up the hill for the burying ground. I feel a need to talk to Granny Beck and hope
that she will help me know what to do. As I climb the hill,
I look at the trees and flowers that I have known all these
years and I wonder when I will ever see them again.

Ever since Mama died, the house has been full of people, all talking a mile a minute but staying clear of me.
High Sheriff Hudson, a big fierce-looking man with a
deep-crowned black hat, asked some questions of me, but
when I ducked my head and looked away, Lilah's mama
said, "You won't do no good with Least—she's simple
and I believe she's tongue-tied as well. I ain't got the first
word out of her."

They all think that, for when I found Mama laying
there, all swole up and no breath in her, I ran down the
road like a crazy thing, looking for help. Never in my life
had I gone amongst folk, and when I came to the first
house, all that I could do was to make sounds and point
back up the hill to where Mama lay.

Ever since then, they have been in the house, poking
their noses into the dark corners, looking through Mama's
things and mine, and talking, talking, talking. If Lilah Bel

had been here, it might have been different—I could have told her what happened. But she ain't. Lilah Bel got married a little back of this and she has gone with her husband to visit his family over to Tennessee. Lilah could have told them I ain't simple.

I should have burned up them doctor papers afore I went after the neighbors. Mama had waved the papers in my face and told me what they meant—"Maybe I can't keep you from whoring around but, aye God, I can keep you from having babies. You just put this idea of going off and getting married right out of your head—you ain't fit to marry and they ain't no call for you to breed—your place is here with me."

Mama's grave is next to my daddy's—a ways off from Granny Beck's. The red dirt is still fresh and there is a canning jar with some yellow flowers in it, half-buried in the raw red dirt. I reckon Lilah's mama must have put it there for she was the only one of the folks at the burying who ever come up to the house to visit with Mama. I don't go near the grave, but the whole time I am talking to Granny Beck, I can feel Mama's angry spirit clawing against the wood of her coffin.

"I got to go away," I tell Granny Beck. "I am feared that if I stay, they will take me to that doctor and fix it where I can't have babies. And I want babies, Granny Beck, babies all little and soft like my Snowflower kitty."

The tears overtake me and I lay there on her grave, just a-blubbering. If only Young David hadn't gone away—and I remember the story of John Goingsnake and how the Little People kept him hid safe for seven years. I don't want to be away that long—just till snow flies and Young David comes back. But where can I go?

Mama's angry voice is in my head, all jagged edges and hard words but, light as a whisper on the wind, Granny tells me that I must cross the river like John Goingsnake did and there I will find a place to keep me safe. There is a picture in my head of two sisters with dark hair and I know it's them Granny Beck means.

Chapter 19

Crossing the River

Gudger's Stand, 1938

(*Least*)

I rise from Granny Beck's grave and look around, saying a good-bye to this high place where the buds is just beginning to swell on the apple trees at the edge of the woods. I say good-bye to Granny Beck and leave her and the Quiet People—quiet but for Mama, whose anger hums and buzzes in my head all the way down the road till at last I come to the river and its roaring song drowns her out.

I have but one thought—to get away from them folks and that paper from the doctor that will keep me from ever having babies. I have left a note that says GON TO MY BRUTHER. So now they will know I ain't ignorant and can take care of myself. Hard as times is, they'll be glad not to have to take me in and I don't believe none of them will try to find me.

Mama's go-to-town clothes is big on me but I put them on, hoping to look right when I am among folks, and though I am barefoot, I have a pair of slippers in my poke to wear when I come to the bridge. I have a hat too, the kind I have heard Lilah call a cloche. It comes down most over my eyes and puts me in mind of a bucket. But it should hide my face and the marks on it till I get across the river and find the place of safety Granny showed me in my mind—the house by the road where two dark-haired girls live.

I follow the path along the riverside till I come near to the bridge. There is a sight of folks on the road—wagons with horses or mules, folks afoot or riding—and I think it might be best to wait on crossing till not so many is there to take notice of me. So I find me a place to set, up in the woods above the road, where I can watch the people passing over the bridge and get accustomed to the idea of going out in the world.

Whilst I sit watching, an automobile comes just a-whirling down the twisty road on the other side, sending up a cloud of dust behind its wheels. It turns up the road to a big house that sits on a kind of bank a ways up above the railroad. In the papers and magazines Lilah sometimes brings for me to look at, I have seen pictures of automobiles with girls and young men riding in them, smoking cigarettes and laughing. Sometimes even, it would be a girl driving.

Two trains go by while I sit there, one going one way, and in a little while, another one coming the other way. Or maybe it is the same one and it got where it was going and turned around. Lilah has told me some about the trains and how you can pay money and get inside and ride on them to far-off places and I have seen them passing from across the river. Still, it is something new to watch them stop at the little gray house down by the tracks and see the people coming out or getting into the cars. Maybe someday,

after we are married, I think, me and Young David will
ride on the train together.

I lean my back against the big old tree I am setting
under and close my eyes. The stirring of the wind in the
leaves makes me think of the times Granny Beck sung to
me at night, soft and whispering so Mama wouldn't hear.
I try to make out the meaning in the sounds. Time was
that the Little Things talked to me that way but they have
been silent since the day Mama died.

The hoot of the train whistle wakes me and I open my
eyes to see the red car at the end disappearing around a
curve. It must not of stopped, for the little gray house is all
shut up and there aren't no people walking around. I don't
see no folks at all, only the red light of the setting sun
shining off the windows of the house high up on the bank.

I study on that house for a minute. It is too big for any
family I ever heard of and I wonder could it be the place
Lilah told me about—the boardinghouse she worked at
back when she was saving up for getting married. She
said it weren't far across the bridge and that she could
walk home on her afternoons off.

"There's two sisters runs it," she told me, "but one
of them got sick and had an operation so they hired me
to help with the chores—just like what I do at home—
cooking, cleaning, washing—but now I'm getting paid.
They're awful good to me. I have already bought sheets
and towels and a twenty-five-piece bride's set of Mirro
brand aluminum cookware."

Well, I think, I can cook and clean and wash. Reckon
would they hire me? And I imagine me meeting Young
David when he returns come winter, and showing him the

sheets and towels and the twenty-five-piece bride's set of Mirro brand aluminum cookware.

It is by thinking of how proud my sweetheart will be that I am able to pull the hat onto my head and push my feet into the slippers and then head for that bridge, knowing full well all that I am leaving behind. The shoes make a slapping sound on the planks of the bridge and I stay in the middle after once looking over the side down to where the water dashes against the rocks and birds come flying out from the underside of the bridge. Looking down like that makes me feel all queer and discombobulated and I don't do it a second time.

Over the railing and up the river a little ways, I see a tall gray, long-leggedy bird with a long sharp beak, standing on a rock in the river as still as if he is froze. Then all at once he gives a creaking cry, like a rusty old pump handle, spreads his great wings and flaps away, his legs trailing after him, up and up the river till my eyes can't follow him no more. I watch a little longer, wishing I could go after him.

But I can't. And I can't go back, so I turn my face to the other side of the river. At the end of the bridge there is some more houses or some such. Maybe they are the stores that Mama talked of going to for they have big windows in the front with all kindly of things setting there. The front doors is closed, though I can see a light in the upstairs of the biggest store, the one made of red bricks.

Dark is coming on and I hasten up the road to the big house, hoping that this is the place Granny Beck told me to seek. I can't hear her no more now that I'm across the bridge and it comes to me that I've left all that behind, on the other side of the river.

When I reach the end of the road, I stop to catch my

breath and look up at the house. And my heart jumps in my bosom for there, setting on the upstairs porch, is two dark-haired women. They have the reddest lips and the pinkest cheeks and their hair is hanging down in fancy curls. Both of them has on long coats of some bright shiny cloth; one is poison green and the other is bright yellow with red pictures of some kind on it. The women is smoking cigarettes and laughing, but when they catch sight of me, the one in green stands up and leans over the railing.

"Hiya, kiddo," she calls down to me and I can smell a sweet smell like honeysuckle all mixed in with the cigarette smoke. "Are you looking for someone?" She picks a speck of tobacco from her tongue and flicks it off her fingertips while she waits for me to make an answer.

"I'm looking for work," say I, keeping my face down. "Is this here place a boardinghouse?"

The two girls set in to giggling and then the green one speaks up. "I reckon you could call it that—though some don't stay very long. What kind of work can you do?"

The other one says something real quiet-like and they both go to giggling again but I don't pay no mind.

"I can cook and clean and do the wash," I tell them, "milk a cow, tend a garden . . . all them things."

They whisper back and forth and then the green one says, "You'll have to talk to the boss when he gets back, but I believe he might have work for you. Tell me, kiddo, what's your name?"

That stops me for a minute. I don't want to tell it, lest folks from the other side of the river was to come looking for me. Then I look at the one in yellow and see that the red marking on her housecoat is some kind of fancy birds and I think too of the book about Baby Ray.

"My name is Redbird," I tell them. "Redbird Ray."

PART II

Redbird Ray

Gudger's Stand, 1938

Chapter 20

Rebirth

Gudger's Stand, 1938

(Redbird)

The days and nights all run together in this place and I can't keep track of how long it is I've been here. Every time a train passes and hoots out its lonesome whistle call, I tell myself I must find a way to leave—and the trains run six and seven times a day.

But then I think I'll wait another week—the money is coming in and the dancing is like strong drink and me always wanting more. Besides, I am fearful of the questions that folk might ask if it was known who I am . . . and I am fearful of a reckoning to come. And, the boss has laid out money for my clothes and such and he'll not let me leave.

Oh, sometimes I feel like the yard dog on his chain and sometimes that I am a rabbit in a snare, here in this house that never sleeps, where the hungry eyes of the traveling men follow me and the loud wild music and the dancing of a night swirl like blackbirds in my head, confusing my thoughts and wiping away memory. I can't be Least anymore, but if Least is gone, who will meet up with Young David when the snow flies?

From the window of my room I look down to the train tracks, shining silver and curving out of sight, and watch the cars rolling by like long dusty snakes. Where they are in such a hurry to go, I can't tell, no more than I can guess where the river ends up. It don't matter for I dare not stray too far from this place—the river and the bridge and the road to Dark Holler and the burying ground. If I can hold out till winter, till Young David comes back, I'll find a way. Even now, I watch every train that stops, watch the folks alighting to see if he might be amongst them. Every now and again there's a tall man who, for a moment, makes me hold my breath in hope, but it's never him.

The smoke and cinders of the locomotive have scorched the grass to either side of the silver rails. Nothing can grow there, but beyond the tracks grassy fields stretch down to the river and far to the right are the great heaped rocks the girls call the Injun Grave. I remember the story of John Goingsnake's Nancy and I wonder if she lays there.

On the slope below my window stands a single apple tree, its branches bent low with greeny-yellow fruit. That apple tree helps me track the time—when its fruit is fallen and only a last few swiveled-up apples hang from the bare branches, I will know it's time to go.

In the room next door, Lola and Francine are waking up and getting ready for the night. I never knew there was women like them but they have been good to me, in their way, and have kept the boss from bothering me. They say they don't like the things they have to do but they don't try to leave.

"It's a bum life, kiddo," said Francine, the first time I asked her if she liked laying with all those different men, any who had the money to pay for her, "but you get used to it. Besides, times are tough—at least here I'm sure of three squares and a flop. And I can put some by—the boss don't get it all. Me and Lo are saving our tips and in another year we'll get away from Gudger's Stand and buy us a little farm in another state where no one knows how we got our money. We'll let on to be widowed sisters and we'll pick up a nice place cheap at a bank sale and go to raising chickens and teaching Sunday school."

She waved a little booklet with a tan cover at me. "This here government pamphlet explains how it works. With an initial investment of $150 and fifty White Leghorns . . ."

The evening I first come here, and told them my name was Redbird, them two women, Francine and Lola, come downstairs and talked to me a little more and Francine asked where was my home and how old was I. Some of what I told was the truth—that I didn't have no people nearby and that I needed work. But I said that I was eighteen and that was a bald-faced lie for I'll not be sixteen till October though my bosoms make me look like a woman. I told them that my sweetheart had gone off to work on the roads and that we wanted to marry but my mother was agin it.

"Are you in the family way?" Francine had asked right out, her eyes going to my belly. Francine is sharp as a tack and I was thankful I could tell her no, my period had come on me just the day before.

"But you're on the run from someone, ain't you?" and afore I could answer, she took my hand in hers. "Never you mind, Redbird; we'll help you hide till your feller comes back."

She looked at my shape again, drawing her eyebrows together till they made a V just at the top of her nose. It seemed like she was trying to make up her mind about something, but then Lola spoke up.

"No, Francie, not right off, anyway. Vergie's short-handed in the kitchen and will be glad of a girl to help. Besides, look at her face." And with that, Lola reached out and real gentle-like pulled off my hat.

Francine's mouth fell open. "Good God almighty, Redbird Ray, what the hell happened to you?"

I knowed my face was still some swole and that the bruises and cuts, though healing, was ugly, for I had heard Lilah's mama talking about how dreadful I looked. But I figured it was all to the good for hadn't none of those folks back at the house seen me except with my face so awful-looking—and I thought that maybe when it went back to the way it had been, they'd never know me at all. And I had it planned what to say, if someone asked about my face, so I was ready.

"A few days back of this," I said, "I stepped on a bee nest and fell down right hard in the middle of some rocks. I reckon I look a sight."

It's time for me to get downstairs, so I throw off my wrapper and step into the bright blue rayon dress. It is cool and sliding against my skin—almost like I was wear-ing the sky. The cracked looking-glass on the wall above the washbasin is cloudy but I can see that, though my face is long since healed up, even so, I am so changed I hardly know myself. The henna rinse that Francine put on my hair—the red suits your name, she said—has made it as bright as sumac in October and it stands out in great puffs on account of the way Lola fixed it. Them girls has had their fun, fiddling and fussing with my hair and painting my face like theirs.

At first it didn't matter what I looked like. When Francine took me to the boss and asked could he give me work in the kitchen, he took one look at my face, all bruised and scratched, and said, "She can work for her room and board. Give it a few months. Then we'll see if she's worth any more than that," and he went back to the ledger books he was writing in. He is a fine-looking, black-haired man, Mr. Revis is, and not so very old, but he seems to be of a sour disposition.

I liked working in the kitchen. Vergie is the one who does all the cooking—the big plain meals, beans and cornbread and stews and such for all us help—and the fried chicken or beefsteak or pork chops for the paying gents. She is a widow and she was glad of my help and of my company too, I believe, for she talked to me from the morning—while she rolled out the biscuit dough, her arms jiggling and white with flour, as I parched and ground the coffee—till night, when we were both kept hopping as the drummers off the trains put in their supper orders.

When I was working in the kitchen, I didn't set foot into the public room and no one ever saw me but those who belonged to Gudger's Stand. Oh, now and then a farmer would come to the kitchen door with produce to sell or more likely barter, or a blockader with some of the white liquor that Mr. Revis poured into bottles and sold by the dram after he had put something in it to give it a brown color. "Finest Scotch whisky," I heard him tell one feller, and "Mr. Jack's genuine Kentucky sourmash," he told another, though both bottles had been filled from the same fruit jar to begin with. But it was Vergie and Mr. Revis who traded with the farmers and paid the block-aders. For fear that one of them might be a neighbor who would remember me from Mama's burying, I always managed to keep busy with my head turned away whilst they were there.

Out in the public room things got right lively of a night, and when I could find a spare moment, I would watch from behind the door. There was usually some musicianers—a feller with a fiddle and another with a banjo—and Francine and Lola and the other girls, for there was seven of them in all, would dance with one an-other or with any of the fellers who would pay for a turn. Now and again a girl would take a feller upstairs but they'd both be back down in fifteen or twenty minutes, him with a foolish grin on his face and her already looking for another somebody to dance with.

The dancing . . . the dancing and the music seemed to bring back something I'd left behind. It would set my blood to rollicking beneath my skin, and as I watched the couples jigging about the floor, my foot would begin to tap and I would think of Brother and his girl dancing on the porch when Mama wasn't looking.

My favorite was the buck dancing contests they held on Saturday nights when the men and girls would dance alone, slapping their shoes on the floor in time to the music, which got louder and faster and louder and faster till one by one the dancers would drop out, fanning their faces, their clothes all sweat-soaked. "Dancing down," they called it and the music would go on and on till only one was left still dancing. If it was a customer, he would get a bottle of whichever of those fruit jar whiskies he cared to name. But mostly it was one of the girls what won or sometimes Mr. Revis himself if all the girls was busy upstairs.

I watched how they did it, and when the music was loud and all the feet pecking at the floor, raising the dust and rattling the plates and glasses on the tables, I would dance behind the kitchen door while Vergie looked on and laughed fit to kill, her big bosom shaking beneath her apron. The ringing of the banjo told my feet what to do and I danced my hopes and wants and dreams.

I lean in close to the mirror to see can I find Least but all there is looking at me is a face like the girls in the Love and Romance magazines that Lola buys whenever she can talk Francine into letting her spend a dime. Bright red lips, cheeks pink with rouge, blue on my eyelids, black on my eyelashes, and my eyebrows dark and curving like birds taking wing. I don't look like myself at all and I wonder, was Young David to see me now, would he know me.

It ain't likely, I think. For the wide-eyed, trembling woods creature that he lay down with all those times up on the hogback ridge is gone and in her place is Redbird Ray, the flat-footing floozy, the buck-dancing barmaid, the talk of the county all round. They say there has been sermons preached against me and that I have been called a snare for simple men and that my shoes are tapping on the path to Hell.

Chapter 21

Dancing

Gudger's Stand, 1938

It began in late June. I had been working in the kitchen for some months, feeling safer day by day and getting bolder too, when it happened. The dance down was bigger than usual for, with crops laid by, there was more fellers able to go loafering of a Saturday night and a good many of them come to the Stand to drink themselves silly and look at the girls. The floor had been packed with drunken fools trying for that prize of whisky but one after another had dropped out till all that was left was the boss Mr. Revis and a logger from the camp down-river. They was going at it like one thing. The musicians was picking and sawing for all they was worth and the two men still dancing hard, glaring at one another like dogs commencing to fight and throwing off sweat in spite of the cooler air coming up from the river. From the cracked kitchen door I could see the folks all clustered round and the heads of the dancers jerking up and down like a pair of limberjacks.

Like always, I had started dancing when the set begun and they was plenty of hoo-rahing to cover the sound of my shoes rapping on the kitchen floor. On and on the dance down went, and as folks dropped out, the music picked up steam till it was driving me and I could no more have quit than a waterwheel can stop while the creek flows. I was behind the door, eyes squeezed shut, dancing like it was for my life and feeling I could most take wing, when all of a sudden the music and the noise of the crowd stopped and the only sound I could hear was my own shoe soles clapping.

I pulled myself to a stop and opened my eyes to see the kitchen door standing wide and Mr. Revis there, staring like he'd never set eyes on me afore. His shirt was soaked through and a piece of his black hair was hanging over his eyes. Breathing heavy, he slicked his hair back with his fingers, never taking his gaze offen me.

"She been dancing this whole round, Vergie?" he asked, coming in and shutting the door behind him but not before I had seen all the folks in the public room looking my way.

"She started in right at the very beginning of the dance down and didn't stop—she'd likely be going yet iffen you hadn't come in. This young un's a dancing fool."

Vergie was laughing when she said that—she ain't afraid of Mr. Revis on account of she knows he couldn't never get another cook as good as her. But I hung my head, waiting to hear his anger, expecting him to curse and ask why I was wasting my time when I should have been at my work.

He just stepped closer and eyed me pretty thorough.

"Put your head up, girl," he said, and looked me in the face like he was studying on something. At last he said, "I believe it's time for you to move on to waiting tables and dancing with the customers. It'll mean cash money for you, so I reckon you don't have no objections."

Mr. Revis didn't wait for an answer but turned to leave. His hand was on the swinging door when he stopped and looked back at Vergie. "Tell the girls to do something about her clothes and show her how to wait tables before tomorrow night. If she can handle the tables and the dancing all right, I'll see about getting you some more kitchen help."

That's how it began. At first I was shy of being seen and would only carry trays and put down plates and clean off tables, but afore long, during the afternoons when we closed, Francine taught me to do partner dancing to where I could step about the floor, following her lead in a two-step or a waltz without no trouble at all. And she showed me a fancy dance called a tango.

"Ain't none of these hicks round here going to know this one," said she, dipping me backward till my new-red hair brushed against the boards, "but it'll put lead in their pencils just to watch you and me do it—I got a pin-striped gent's suit I can wear and I'll slick my hair back . . . just you wait, Redbird, there'll be some business done that night after we do our exhibition dance; most men get all worked up thinking about two women together."

As the music ended and the needle begun to skitter, Francine let loose of me and went over and turned off the Victrola. She leaned against one of the tables and lit up a cigarette.

"You know, you could make a sight more money, Redbird—fresh young thing like yourself. They'd be fighting over you."

The blue smoke come out of her nose in two great clouds and she let the cigarette hang from her lips where it wiggled as she talked.

"You're not a virgin, are you?" she asked and I had to say I didn't know what she meant by that word. When she told me, I felt my face heat up and all I could do was to look away and shake my head.

"Hmm," says she, narrowing her eyes against the smoke, "that's too bad for you'd make extra-good money for that first time. Still, I bet we could pass you off as one."

I spoke up and told her that I didn't want to do anything but wait tables and dance with the customers, and that besides, my sweetheart was coming back afore long and I'd be leaving.

"I thank you, Francine," I told her, picking my words careful-like, not wanting to seem proud or choosy, "you've already been awful good to me. Nothing against you and Lola and the other girls but I don't reckon my sweetheart would like me earning money that way."

Not another word did she say, just mashed the end of her cigarette against the wooden tabletop and left it laying there for me to clean up. She started for the stairs in the hall between the public room and Mr. Revis's quarters, but as she went through the doorway, she stopped and turned to point a finger at me.

"We don't always have our druthers in these things, Redbird. I want you to remember that."

ꝫ

Tonight at Gudger's Stand
Introducing
A Fourth of July Firecracker!
That Fiery Dancing Sensation!!
!!!LITTLE REDBIRD!!!
Dance Down at 10 P.M.
Special Prize

Chapter 22

The Attraction

Gudger's Stand, 1938

The next Saturday night was my first time as what they called an attraction. It was the second of July and a holiday feeling was everywhere. The boss had bought fireworks to shoot off and they was a great coming and going down at the depot. One of the girls had made a fancy sign on a chalkboard at the door and on it in colored chalk was my name. I must of gone and looked at it a dozen times that day.

I had been out all week, serving in the public room, waiting tables and such, and a couple of times had even stepped around the floor with a few of the regular customers. But mostly, the fellers wanted to dance with the girls that would go upstairs with them. Mr. Revis watched this for a while and that was when he got the idea for the special show with me and Francine doing the tango.

The girls ran me up the fanciest dress you ever seen. Hit was of shiny red-orange cloth and it fit as close as my own skin. It come down way low in the back and the hem was kindly jagged all around and there was a great long slit up one side. When I asked wasn't that a mistake, they just laughed.

"You really think a greenhorn like Redbird is going to put this over? Tango is for a *woman*—and a woman with some experience."

That was Lola. She was some put out that it would be me and not her dancing the tango with Francine, but Francine put an arm around her and jollied her along.

"No need to be sore, lover—it's just a dance. Besides, you know me—I like a big, fluffy girl with lots of soft flesh in my bed."

She stuck her face in between Lola's big bosoms, making a kindly gobbling sound, and we all had to laugh, even Lola. This was the way Francine did and I hardly thought a thing of it anymore.

Francine looked up and grinned. "C'mon, Lo—Redbird'll do just fine. And little as she is, I'll be able to fling her around like them Apache dancers we used to see back in the Chicago clubs."

Vergie had told me how Francine and Lola, each one lugging a big old grip, had got off the southbound train one day over a year ago and had climbed the road to the Stand in search of work. "On the run from some of them gangsters like in the movies, I make no doubt," Vergie had said. "Reckon this place looked like the end of the world to them."

Me and Francine practiced the tango over and over, till I had the hang of it. "Just think of it as fucking while you're dancing," she said, showing me how to make my body follow hers. "It's a story, see. At the beginning, you ain't sure you want to and you try to stay cold, but as the dance goes on, you warm up to the idea till you're begging for it. You'll see."

At first I couldn't take hold of the notion, being as it was a woman I was dancing with, and I stayed cold when I should have been growing warmer. I come to purely dread the sound of "La Cumparsita" on the Victrola.

Then, it must have been the third day we practiced, Francine leaned in close as we begun and whispered with her smoky, minty breath, "Pretend I'm that fella you're waiting for, why don't you?" and she nipped at my earlobe. "Remember what it was like fucking him."

It was almost as if I was back on one of them full moon nights. I had been missing him and our loving so bad and all of a sudden the touch of her hand was his touch and her long lean body, guiding me through the steps, might have been him showing me the way of love. And by the time we was done, I was in that breathless, dreaming place where everything seems just right.

"We'll knock 'em dead, kiddo," Francine told me as I followed her up the narrow box stairs to get ready for the night.

Those words caught at me. The swimmie-headed feeling swelled in my head and the buzzing began with Mama's angry voice at the back of it. I leaned against the wall to steady myself and waited for it to pass.

Francine reached the top of the stairs and looked back. "Redbird?"

"Ain't nothing." I waved her off. "Just catching my breath. It's awful close and warm here."

That night, for once, Francine and me didn't wait tables. The boss had said it would make what he called "a bigger bang" for us to come on the floor like we was new to the place. I didn't believe anyone would know us—me in that tight red dress with my painted face and my red hair falling in waves down my bare back, and Francine with her black hair slicked back except for spit curls beneath each ear. It seemed to me she was better-looking as a man, in that fancy pin-striped gentleman's suit with the black shirt and white tie, and she seemed to think so too for she strutted like a turkey gobbler before all the girls, who giggled and flirted till Lola begun to scowl and say they needed to get on downstairs.

Before they went, all the girls give me a hug and told me how fine I looked. Flo even sprayed some of her fancy perfume on me, "for luck, honey." Then off they went, clattering down the stairs, their dancing shoes making a racket that let the fellers down below know that they was on the way.

Francine reached out and squeezed my hand. "You look swell, kiddo; they're gonna eat you up." Then she put up a finger. "Listen!"

From the top of the stairs we could hear someone below hollering "Pipe down!" and then there was a shrill whistle. Everyone got quiet and the boss begun to speak in a big, important-sounding voice.

"Thank you, High Sheriff Hudson. We appreciate the assistance of the law on this busy holiday night and hasten to assure you that your efforts will not go unrewarded."

There was a big laugh from the crowd but I felt my knees go weak for the sheriff had been at the house after Mama died. He had seen me up close when he tried to ask me questions about what happened. And he was the one who had the paper about fixing it to where I couldn't have babies.

All I could think of was how I might get out of there.

The only way, apart from the stairs, was if I could some-how clamber down from the upstairs porch. I started for the little door that led out that way but Francine grabbed my hand again.

"Thirty seconds, then we're on. Excited, kiddo? Boss said he was expecting a big turnout."

I could hear feet beginning to stamp and the boss's deep voice floated up the stairs. ". . . just in time for the Glorious Fourth, the flat-footing firecracker . . . a red-hot mountain mama . . . a tango teaser . . . let's hear it for Miss Redbird Ray!!"

I had not thought I would like it so.

Francine pulled me down the stairs and, just like we had practiced, we burst into the public room like she was dragging me and I was afraid. Flo was at the Victrola and she set the needle at the beginning of "La Cumparsita" the very second Francine's foot left the bottom step. All the tables had been pushed to the walls to leave plenty of room for our dance, and men was ringing the dancing floor, two and three deep, while others was standing on the tabletops.

Like we had practiced, Francine put on a fierce scowl-ing face while she stomped all around the circle of watch-ers, pulling me like a prisoner after her as I took on like I was trying to get loose. When we had gone around once and the music had come to the right place, Francine stepped to the center of the floor, snapped me to her, and the tango began.

As we went through the steps, there at the center of all those eyes, I had a queer double feeling. First, it seemed almost like I was naked in front of this gang of men, with my bare back and the long slit in the skirt that showed my leg to above my red garter and the thinness of the dress—so thin that my nipples stood out like cherries beneath the cloth. At the same time, it come to me that all of this paint and finery had covered up the girl who was Least as good as if she was dead and buried, for wouldn't no one know me for that sad-faced somebody they had seen back in the spring.

And there was some in the crowd who *had* seen me back then, not only Sheriff Hudson, who I winked at as Francine dipped me backward right at his boot tips, but also a couple of the men who had helped to carry Mama to her grave. One of them may have been Lilah's father, but I neither knew nor cared, for suddenly Least was gone and Redbird Ray had nothing to fear.

Chapter 23

Mr. Aaron

Gudger's Stand, 1938

Night after night I danced, spinning from one man to another, for word had spread and more and more come to see the show and to have a dance with Redbird Ray. They bought tickets off a big roll that the boss kept—my tickets was red and cost twice as much as the blue ones that would buy a dance with any of the other girls. And most every one that danced with me would give me a tip for myself—nickels or dimes from the local fellers but now and again one of the big spenders off the trains would tuck a folded dollar bill in my garter.

More than one asked me to go upstairs with them, and there was several times that, drunk with the music and motion and missing Young David so bad, I thought I might as well, but the boss always shook his head.

"No, not yet," he'd say. "You're worth more to me as a dancer and a draw."

Me and Francine still did our tango dance on Friday and Saturday nights when there was a big crowd, but the other nights I helped wait tables and danced with everwho bought a ticket. It seemed a lifetime since me and Young David laid down together, and sometimes when I had danced with a good-looking, good-smelling young feller, I would find myself aching with wanting and thinking about loving.

But there was others I danced with who made me glad I didn't have to go upstairs with them—old men smelling of tobacco and rotten teeth or brash young men with too much hair oil who handled me rough when we danced and tried to put their hands up my dress. And whether they was to my liking or not, none of them ever saw beyond the shiny clothes and painted face. Which was good, for I'd not have it known who I was. But when no one knows you, it can be awful lonely.

There is one feller who comes in now and again who is somehow different from any of the others—a salesman making his rounds who likes to sit and have a whisky and watch the dancing. The only time he comes in is Saturday nights, so I reckon it's the dance downs he come for— quite a few of the customers wagers on who will be the winner and I figure him for one of these as he never goes upstairs nor even buys a dance.

He's a foreign-looking, dark-complected feller who always wears a suit and a hat too, even indoors. I couldn't say what age he is—not old, but not young neither.

"Why do you reckon that feller won't never dance with any of us? You know, Francine says he's a Jew—they's a sight of 'em where she come from—but he ain't stingy with his money—always tips good when I bring his dinner. Still, no matter how hard I tease him, he won't buy a dance. I say they's something strange about that Mr. Aaron."

Sharleen is setting on the edge of my bed, painting her toenails an ugly purple color. The tip of her tongue sticks out as she bends to finish her left little toe.

I don't know why but some devil makes me say, "I bet you a new bottle of Cutex Nail Crème *I* can get him to dance."

He is there at the same little table where he always sits. The place is crowded and I have been kept busy with the fellers and their red tickets, but I've been watching him. He has eaten his dinner and now is sipping at a glass of whisky while he watches the dancing. Lola and then Flo both has gone over to him, but each time he has just smiled and shook his head. At last, when the musicianers are taking a break, I sashay over to his table and sit down.

He surprises me by standing up and lifting his hat. "Miss . . . Redbird," he says, making a little bow, "I'm honored. What can I offer you?"

"A co-cola would go right good," I say and have to smile as he raises a finger and Sharleen comes over to take the order. She gives me a sour look but goes and gets it. The bottle still has a piece of ice clinging to it and I take and rub it on the bare skin at my throat till the heat of my body melts it and a little trickle runs between my breasts. He watches like a thirsty man.

"Right hot tonight," I say and lift the bottle to my lips. The first sip burns all the way down my parched throat.

His black eyes glitter and he takes a sup of his whisky. "As the hinges of Hell," says he. "What can I do for you?"

I ask him does he want to buy a dance with me and he says no, he don't dance. Then I tell him about my bet with Sharleen and about the Cutex Nail Crème and he laughs and says he'll buy a ticket and once again he beckons to Sharleen.

"If you'd be so kind," and he lays a greenback on the table, "I'd like to purchase five red tickets."

As you might guess, Sharleen is fit to be tied but she don't have no choice other than to take the dollar to the boss and come back with a string of my red tickets. She drops them on the table in front of Mr. Aaron and swings around to stomp off.

"Young lady, this is for you," and he holds out another greenback to her.

Sharleen is plumb flustered but she manages to make some kind of a thank-you before stuffing the bill into her stocking top and moving away.

I see the fiddler and the other musicianers coming back in and I stand up and hold out my hand. "Well, sir, reckon we best make a start on them tickets you bought so as you get your money's worth."

He draws back like he don't want to touch me and nods to my chair. "Sit back down, Miss . . . Redbird," he says. "I don't intend to dance but I've bought your time. While they battle their way through five tunes, I thought we could have a conversation."

"A conversation," I say, lowering myself back onto the chair. "What about?"

He leans towards me, his arms folded on the table. "We could begin with names. I call myself Jacob Aaron; you call yourself Redbird Ray. And then we could talk about things we have in common, people we've known, places we've been. I could ask you how your mother is—and how things are back in Dark Holler."

As the band lights into "Rye Straw," the music and Mr. Aaron's voice start to fade and get farther and farther

away. I hear the buzzing and see the lights flashing and
when I push my chair back and go to stand, I feel myself
falling and falling and falling

"She was setting with that Jew. Reckon he had anything to do with this? Maybe doctored her cold drink?"

There is voices all around me and I ain't laying on the
floor no more but on something soft. I keep my eyes
closed and try to think what to do . . . if Mr. Aaron knows
who I am . . . if he tells . . .

Someone is wiping my face with a cold wet cloth and
the voices is just a-jabbering.

"Yeah, boy, she was right with him and he bought her a
co-cola. He could of put something in it."

"I remember my daddy talking about that Jew down in
Atlanta—Leo Frank, I think the name was. Raped and
murdered a white girl. Jury convicted him all right but
then the no-good governor commuted the death sentence.
Well, sir, the good people of Georgia rose up and hung
that Jew their own selves. Reckon we ought to let Sheriff
Hudson know about this?"

"Listen to you talking about rape and murder!" It is
Francine right over me and I crack an eye to see her kneeling there with a wet rag in her hand. She is boiling mad.

"Don't any of you fools know the difference between
rape and murder and a girl fainting because of the heat?
Stand back out of the way and give Redbird some air, can't
you?"

There is some muttering and I hear the one who had
been talking about hanging say something about making
sure the Jew didn't get away before they got to the bottom
of things. For a minute I think how that would take care

of my worries—if something was to happen to Mr. Aaron.

While I am thinking those black thoughts, I feel a shadow passing between me and the light and seems like I hear the croaking cry of the Raven Mockers—the soul eaters Granny warned me of.

"No!" I holler, struggling to set up. "Mr. Aaron didn't do nothing. I was just too hot and couldn't seem to get my breath. I'll be fine."

I see that they have brought me into the boss's room. Just beyond the couch where I am is the half-open door. The dancing is going on as usual and through the jigging bodies I see that Mr. Aaron is gone.

In the back of my mind the Raven Mockers flap away, cawing and laughing at me for a fool.

～

Submitted by J. A. Aaron to the Blue Hoopoe Review (returned with form rejection)

The Eternal Scapegoat

Names, numerous beyond recall . . .
> *Ahasuerus . . .*
>> *Cartaphilus . . .*
>>> *Malchus . . .*
>>>> *Cain.*

Selves, numerous beyond recall . . .
> *Centurion, my ear lopped off and restored in the Gethsemane garden . . .*
>> *Shoemaker, on the road to Golgotha . . .*
>> *Roman keeper of the gates . . .*
>>> *Farmer, in the dawn of days.*

Sins, numerous beyond recall . . .
    It was I, killed my brother . . .
        It was I, mocked the Anointed . . .
            It was I, denied my Teacher . . .
                It was I, shot the great albatross.

Years, numerous beyond recall . . .
    Guilt, eternal . . .
        Wanderings, eternal . . .
            Sorrow, eternal . . .
                        Legacy, eternal.

> **YOUR SUBMISSION**
> **DOES NOT MEET OUR**
> **CURRENT NEEDS.**
> **THANK YOU**

Chapter 24

The Wandering Jew

Gudger's Stand, 1938

S o you saved my sorry Jew hide," he says, looking at me through his little gold-rimmed glasses. "Well, I believe in tit for tat, Miss Redbird, and I also believe you'll have need of me soon. I knew the first time I saw you—half-naked, covered with dirt and looking like a wild thing—that our paths would cross and re-cross somewhere down the road."

He leans back, studying me close. "You remember that peppermint stick? I gave it to your mama to give to you."

The next Saturday has come around and Mr. Aaron is back. He is setting at the same table as always and I see him first thing when I come downstairs. He holds up one of my red tickets and crooks his finger come here at me. Then he points to the chair across from him.

The band has just struck up a piece called "Carroll County Blues," which is a tune that just don't never want to end, and I pull out the chair and set down, feeling some aggravated for the music has got into me and my toes are tapping.

"Why don't we dance?" I make a pout face at him, like Lola does to Francine when she wants something. "And what do you mean you gave me a peppermint stick? I don't recollect no such thing. You bought me a co-cola is all."

But even as the words leave my mouth, I can taste the peppermint stick and smell the pile of dookie his mule left in the road back then. I remember how the dirt of my hidey-hole clung to my sticky hands as I played with my corncob babies. And all the while Mama sat on the front steps, weeping and then hollering meanness at me, turn and about, till she slumped down asleep. In an instant the room around me has faded to shadowy shapes, and him and that long-ago day are right there, fresh in my mind.

I rub my fingers together, almost expecting them to feel sticky. "I remember now," I say, studying his face hard. "It's been some time and you've held your age right good."

"Thank you, Redbird Ray." Mr. Aaron smiles a secret kind of smile and sips at his whisky. "And you've gone from a sorry little worm to a beautiful butterfly—or more like one of them bold, night-flying moths that burns up in the lamp flames. You want to be careful of your new wings, Redbird."

As I look at him and try to make sense of him being here, I decide that if he had wanted to tell the sheriff who I was, he would of already done it . . . or maybe he had and the sheriff didn't care. Everwhich, it seems to me there's more to Mr. Aaron than he lets on and, for good or bad, him and me is tied somehow.

"You still have that old mule?" I ask him, studying him hard to try to make out his age. There are crinkledy lines at the corners of his eyes but not no other age marks. "Still a peddler man?"

"Still a peddler but I sold my mule to an old man who I knew would treat her right and threw in the wagon for goodwill. Now I ride the train and deal in wholesale. But I've taken a notion to settle down for a spell—maybe open a department store in Asheville, which is fast growing from a town to a city. After wandering through deserts and rocky places for so long, it'll be a pleasure to rest my eyes on these green mountains."

His face has a faraway look. " 'I will lift up mine eyes unto the hills,' " he says and then raises one eyebrow. "Do you know that psalm?"

He asks the question but don't wait for an answer, just rattles on and me not understanding the half of it.

"It was one of my kin wrote that," he brags, "but, as you say, it's been some time."

Just then a hand lights on my bare shoulder and I like to jump out of my seat. I look up and it is High Sheriff Hudson standing there.

He is a tall, tall man and stout built without being fat. He's not bad-looking though his face is as wrinkled as an older man's might be. All the girls dread taking him on, for they say he is bad to be rough in bed. I know it's true for Sharleen once showed me a great angry red circle where he'd bit her on the breast. He had even broke the skin. And they all complain of how he smells—it ain't the stink of not bathing enough but something different, like there is something burned out and dead inside of him.

If it was any other of the customers, the boss wouldn't put up with such, but as it's the sheriff . . . well, who's gone arrest him? Besides, he could close the Stand down any time he took a notion. So the boss pays the girls out of his own pocket whenever they go a bout with Sheriff Hudson—the sheriff never pays for nothing, not a drink nor a dance nor a roll in the hay.

His big old hand lays heavy on my shoulder like a dead thing and I have to stop myself from flinching away. There is a bottle in his other hand and he takes a long pull on it afore saying aught. Then he sets the bottle on the table and wipes his arm across his mouth.

"You back, Aaron? Thought we'd seen the last of you." The hand begins to creep towards my neck and I shiver— someone walking on my grave, Granny would have called it.

"I got me some red tickets," the sheriff says, "and I got a mind to cut a rug with the prettiest girl in the place. I reckon you can spare her. Matter of fact, I reckon it might be time for you to move your Jew ass on."

Sheriff Hudson's hand is around my neck now. It is so big that the fingers can almost meet. And then the big hand closes and begins to pull me up.

I cast a glance at Mr. Aaron, who lifts his hands as if he was saying there weren't nothing he could do.

"Miss Redbird, I'll say goodnight now. Thank you for your company. I'll redeem my other tickets at some later date."

We both of us are standing now and the sheriff is pulling me towards the dance floor. I hold out one hand to Mr. Aaron, meaning to say I'm sorry, but he turns away and starts for the door.

It is like dancing with a great huge bear. My arms ache with holding them up so high but I know that I must keep dancing and smiling. And all the while his big old hands is traveling up and down my back, feeling and squeezing, and my face is pushed against his shirt till I know that the buttons will have left their marks.

"Oh, you pretty little thing," he whispers in my ear, his breath whisky-strong. "I got a mind to arrest you and carry you down to the jail for private questioning. Reckon I best begin by making sure you ain't packing no hidden weapons."

And with this he puts his hand right down my dress front and squeezes my titty. I try to pull away but he just yanks me closer and with his other hand brings me tight up against him to where I can feel his pecker hard under his britches.

There has been fellows get frisky with me but not like this. I feel right sure that if I make a fuss, it's like to rouse him all the more, so I just go on dancing, trying to follow his steps and keep my toes out from under his big old dusty boots.

At last the tune is over and he lets loose of me. The musicianers take a break so as the customers have time to claim a girl for the next dance. Also, now is when a fellow usually offers to buy his partner a drink. He may pay for whisky but what the girl gets is always cold tea out of a special bottle. Everyone knows this but don't no one ever raise a fuss at paying whisky prices for tea.

Sheriff Hudson don't offer to escort me to the bar, though I cast a thirsty glance in that direction. He is all worked up and he looks over to the door to upstairs where the boss is setting. Then he grabs my arm and leads me that way.

"Sheriff Hudson!" I cry, hoping to head him off rather than to have him hear a no from the boss. "I don't go upstairs," I say. "Everybody knows I just dance."

He don't pay me a bit of mind, just keeps hauling me towards the boss and the door to upstairs.

There is a fellow standing there with his arm around Lola. He is dickering with the boss and trying to get credit but he stands aside when he see the sheriff coming.

"Revis," says the sheriff, not bothering even to speak soft, "I believe I'll take a turn with Redbird."

The boss says real cool, "Don't you still have several of those red tickets I gave you? Price hasn't changed in the past half hour." Some of the men standing round start to laugh but break off quick when they see that Sheriff Hudson ain't even smiling.

He begins to speak real slow, measuring out the words, and I tremble at the anger I can feel in the way he holds me and the way he says, "I ain't speaking of dancing. I want to go upstairs and I want Redbird here to go with me."

Chapter 25

The Prize

Gudger's Stand, 1938

The sheriff's fingers are digging into my arm and he has one foot on the stairs. I pull back, and when I do, the boss looks a question at me.

"Mr. Revis," I say, my voice sounding little and shaky, "iffen you don't care, could I talk to you private for a minute?"

He considers, then, "Sheriff Hudson," he says, "I'll speak to my employee in my office." Then he hollers over to the bar, "Cooper, fix up the sheriff with a bottle from my private stock," and before the sheriff has time to say pea-turkey, the boss has taken me from him and led me back to his room.

He pulls the door to, almost shutting out the sounds of the music starting back up, and as I start to tell him that I don't want to go with the sheriff, the boss lays a finger on my lips.

"Redbird," he says, "last week you was ready to go upstairs with that good-looking brakeman off the railroad and I wasn't for it. It was my thought to save you for

something special. Being a virgin," he looked hard at me
like he was warning me not to say nothing, "being, like I
say, a virgin, that first time you should fetch a big price—
and you'd share half and half in it. Now, what we have
here is a dilemma. For as you know, Sheriff Hudson don't
pay for nothing here at the Stand. It's part of our . . ." and
the boss reaches up to smooth his mustache, the way he
does when he's studying on something, ". . . part of our
arrangement. And he ain't an easy feller to tell no—"

"Mr. Revis," I bust right in to what he's saying, "tell
him I'm on my period."

It ain't the case but it'll do till I can think how to get
away. For I see now what is in store for me and I know that
I don't want that life, not even for a little while.

The boss nods and winks and steps out the door. I put
my ear to it and hear him talking low. The sheriff's voice
is louder but I can't make out the words except that they
are angry. He rumbles along and the boss keeps talking,
just as calm. There are other men, drunk by the sound of
their voices, but I can't make out what they say.

Then I hear a woman. "Now, that's a funny thing.
Redbird was on her period two weeks ago, just like all of
us. We was laughing about how it is that we all get took
that way at once and upstairs business has to shut down.
Now if—"

It is that hateful Sharleen. She has fussed, back of this,
about me getting special billing and not doing the upstairs
work. And then the sheriff breaks in.

"Aye God, Revis, I won't stand for being put off like
this. I don't care what time of the month it is—if she's a
virgin, like you said, a little more blood won't matter, now
will it?"

There is a bang on the door and the sheriff is standing

there. Back behind him there is a ring of folks, just a-gaping, and that black-hearted Sharleen with a nasty smile on her face. The boss looks at me and jerks his thumb for me to come out and I can see he ain't going to battle with the sheriff no more.

"Redbird," he says, not quite looking at me, "you staying clear of upstairs has brought these fellers near to a boil. I reckon it's time you started and you might as well begin with Sheriff Hudson."

All them men is looking at me like they was hungry dogs and me a plate of meat. I hear muttering amongst some of them and one of the bolder ones speaks up and asks ain't there gone be an auction, like when it was Lola's first time.

Now I know that I am in a pickle, for sure. But rather than hang back and let things be decided for me by a bunch of drunken rowdies with their blood up, I step out bold as brass amongst them.

"I'll go upstairs tonight with the feller who can dance me down," says I, lifting my chin and giving a slow look round that gang of men. I let my gaze linger a spell on several of the likeliest and give each one a little bit of a smile or a wink. "Will that suit you, Mr. Revis?"

Well, there is a roaring and a hoo-rahing like you never heard, and though the sheriff tries to argue some more, the boss sees that there will be trouble iffen he don't side with the crowd. He does about the only thing he can and calls for a dance down with me as the prize. Though, he is quick to put in, it will cost two bits to enter.

The sheriff ain't happy about this turn of events but he tosses back a glass of whisky and moves away. He ain't one to take part in any contest where they might be a chance he could lose. I see him grab onto Sharleen's arm and pull her towards the stairs. She sends me another poison look but they ain't nothing she can do but go on up with him. I would feel sorry for her except for her meanness just now.

But there ain't time to worry about Sharleen for the boss has gone to talk to the musicianers—likely telling them to step out and take care of the necessary so as to be ready for a long spell of picking and fiddling. Folks is crowded round the bar getting drinks and now the boss is having some to push back the tables and make more room for the contest.

The fellers who are known to be strong dancers are talking big and making bets. I see a few right young men—just boys, really—calculating their chances, their spotty faces all grinning foolish-like. Some are turning out their pockets hoping to find two bits or are asking friends to stake them. Over by the bar a couple of old drunks who can't hardly stagger are limbering up and doing a few shaky steps. And every one of these is eyeballing me like I was already in the bed with them.

I hold up my hand so's I can say my piece and, for a wonder, they all hush as I begin to speak.

"Mr. Revis," I say, lifting my voice so's he can hear me above the scraping of the chairs and tables being moved, "now, iffen it happens that I outlast all these fine fellers . . ."

There is a burst of laughing and hooting but I keep my hand up and afore long they settle down.

"I want to get it clear," I go on. "Iffen I was to win, then there'd be no going upstairs with anyone, not tonight."

It's like all them voices come out of one throat and it makes a single sound, a big *Awww* of disappointment. But then the one voice breaks into many and they all commence to buzz again. I plow right through them, almost hollering to make myself heard.

"And I'll take part in a dance down every night till I've been bested and one of these good-looking fellers has got the prize." I give a little wink at one of the spotty-faced boys and he jerks his head back and claps his hand to his heart like he's been shot.

The boss looks at me and nods, then hollers for the musicianers to get started. I take my place in the middle of the floor and those who've paid their fee come out too and circle round me and the fiddle lights into "Sally Goodin."

The slap and thump of boots on the floor is so great you can hardly hear the music to keep in step. But soon I see that it don't matter; us dancers are marking our own time and it is the driving sound of a great locomotive CHUCK-a-chucka, CHUCK-a-chucka, CHUCK-a-chucka and all of our feet are hitting the floor at the same time till I fear we will crash right through it. We raise a knee-high cloud of dust and the everyday smell of whisky and to-bacco begins to be overtaken by the smell of sweating bodies.

At first it is hard to bear, there is so many of them—all facing me and all with the same crazy look on their faces—but directly one old drunk goes down and two fellers, what had looked like they couldn't keep going much longer anyways, stop to haul their friend up and all three of them limp off to the bar.

That makes it easier, for no one wants to be the first to quit. But now one after another of them, seeing others going strong while they themselves are winded and like to drop, these ones give it up and commence to making bets amongst themselves.

After a quarter of an hour, it is down to me, one of the

spotty faces, and four of our regular customers, strong dancers who have won whisky prizes back of this. With only five still on the floor, I can hear the music again and the tune slides from "Old Joe Clark" to "Roasted Rabbit" and the crowd sends up a laugh and they all sing together, "If you want some roasted rabbit, You can go upstairs and have it . . ." and I feel my face go bright red and I dance for all I'm worth.

And the music grabs me and it seems that my legs ain't my own, that the floor is rising and falling beneath my feet—that I am a limberjack, powered by something outside myself. And my legs rise and fall and rise and fall and I smile and smile and smile the painted smile of the limberjack.

⁓

Entry from **An Appalachian Dictionary**

Limberjack (also known as *Dancin' Dan*)—traditional Appalachian toy/percussion instrument comprised of a loose-jointed wooden figure (sometimes called a jig doll) attached to a long stick. The operator holds the doll over a thin wooden board and manipulates board and doll so that the doll's feet tap rhythmically as if clogging. Said to be of Irish origin.

Chapter 26

Redbird Flies

Gudger's Stand, 1938

I danced them down that first night, and the second and the third and the nights after that . . . and now it has come round to Saturday again and I still ain't gone upstairs with no one. The music has carried me along through the week though now my legs is sore and my feet are blistered. Last night there was blood in my slippers where some of the blisters had broke.

Every night I danced them down and every night there was fewer in the contest and more in the crowd, for the boss had raised the entry fee to half a dollar a head. But there was always some newcomers who, having heard about the contest and the prize, was eager to try their luck.

Business was awful good for midweek—plumb roaring, to tell the truth—and the boss sent for more whisky, so raw and new that he had to doctor it with all manner of things—juice from the green hulls of walnuts, tobacco, and I don't know what all. Things has been lively upstairs too and the girls is ill at me, saying the customers has been riding them extry hard, having gotten all worked up watching the dancing.

But tonight . . . I am fearful for what may happen. My feet is swole and raw and my legs have taken to cramping. I ask the boss, could we put off the dance down till Monday, but he just laughs.

"This was your idea, Redbird," he says, "and I'll not deny we're doing a land office business. But I expect there'll be more than ever here tonight, and if I try to tell them you want to cry off . . ."

He corks up another bottle he has just filled with his new-bought whisky and puts it in a crate under the bar with the others. "Was I foolish enough to do that," he says, "there's no telling what some of those fellers might get up to—the way you been teasing them." The boss leans against the bar and points a finger at me. It is all stained black from the walnut hulls and I can't take my eyes from it as he waggles it at me.

"Listen here, girl," he says. "If your feet are hurting you so bad—well, quicker you lose the dance down, the quicker you can get off your feet and on your back . . . take a load off, as you might say."

It ain't no use talking to him, so I go up the stairs to my room. It's late in the afternoon and all the girls is resting, stretched out reading romance magazines or napping. As I pass by their open doors, not one calls out to me. Sharleen is the worst; when I go by her door, she throws something my way. It falls on the floor with a soggy splat and I see that it is a used safe.

I am like to vomick but I don't let on I even saw it.

In my room I sit on my bed and watch out the window. The train has just pulled in and there is a crowd of folks getting off at the depot. Like always, I strain my eyes to see if one of them might be Young David, come back for me, but none of them is. Something in the shape of one man wearing a dark suit and toting two big old grips looks familiar but his hat hides his face from me. He is pushed aside by a gang of men from off the train. They are heading up the road towards the Stand, all laughing and talking loud. As they get nearer, I hear my name mixed in with a lot of ugly talk.

I draw back from the window and lay down on my bed. It is for certain sure that tonight I ain't got a chance of winning and I dread what is to come.

"Hey, kiddo, the boss sent me to clue you in on a few things."

Francine is standing there, leaning on the doorframe. For a minute I have a wild idea that she might help me, but even as I look at her, she reads my thoughts and shakes her head.

"Can't do it, Redbird; me and Lo ain't got our stake yet."

She comes in and sets by me on the bed, then, after a minute, she puts out her hand and pats me on the shoulder. "Sorry, kiddo," she says, sticking a cigarette in the corner of her mouth, "but remember I told you we don't always get our druthers." And she does look sorry but she strikes a match, takes a drag on the cigarette, and goes on with what she come for.

"Now," she says, all business-like. "You and me know you ain't a virgin, but whichever one of them fellers ends up with you will expect to be busting cherry. And it's up to you to make him think that's what's happening."

She reaches in her pocket and pulls out a Ponds Cold Cream jar. Only when she opens it, I see there is a little sponge all soaked with red.

"Fake blood," Francine says, like it is the most natural thing in the world. "Me and Lola got some at a special shop in Chicago and we put it to good use, traveling here. I got to be a virgin three times but she beat me by one.

"All you do," she says screwing the top back on, "is tell your feller you need to use the pot, and while you're behind the curtain, just shove the sponge up in there. Then, after you get down to business, you do your best to carry on like he's too big and he's splitting you in two. When he's done, you make a big noise about how wonderful it was and how it was worth the pain. At least, that's what you say if you're looking for any kind of tip. It's what I always do."

She stands up and goes over to the curtain that hangs across one corner of the room. "I'll leave this jar here by the pot where it'll be handy."

I am staring out the window and watching the man with two grips. He is setting under a big tree, maybe waiting for a ride somewhere. Then he takes off his hat to wipe his forehead with a big red handkerchief and I see that it is Mr. Aaron.

Francine comes back and sets down again. "Bird, it ain't nothing to worry about—it's just fucking without the loving. Same tune, different words." She throws her arm around me. "Cheer up, doll—want me to bring you a soda pop?"

"No, thank you kindly," I say, picking up her hand and putting a kiss on it. "You've been a good friend to me, Francine, and I'll not forget."

I can tell by the sound that there is a mighty big crowd gathered in the room below. All the other girls have already clattered down the stairs and there is music playing and loud talking and laughing. The dance down is set for ten and the alarm clock Francine lent me says that it is nine-thirty. I look out the window one more time and see that Mr. Aaron is still setting there.

The man's clothes Francine wore for the tango were too big for me but I had hemmed up the trousers and turned the cuffs of the jacket inside the sleeve. I hated that I was stealing from her, but I left her four dollars in the box where I'd found the suit.

I take the brown shoe polish I hooked from Sharleen's things and begin to brush it through my hair, watching in the mirror. It's hard to be sure in the dim lamplight but it looks to me as if I have covered up the red. I had cut it short a little earlier, after Francine left, and now I part it to one side and comb it till I look like a real dude. I use a little of the shoe polish on my eyebrows too.

The room below is still loud with music and, judging that my moment is near, I blow out the oil lamp and head for the stairs.

It is easier than I'd thought it would be. There is a great knot of men at the foot of the steps but they are so busy pointing out to one another which fellers will be in the dance down and making their wagers that they don't even turn to look as I shoulder past them, mumbling low that I need to take a piss.

There is a few more setting on the edge of the porch and one of them hollers at me to come have a sup of whisky.

"Thanks," I say, remembering to pitch my voice deep, "but I got to get some air," and I keep on moving down the steps and towards the big tree where the dark shape is waiting.

The smell of the big old boxwoods that line the path make me think of home and I go on walking, half expecting that there could be something inside them that will jump out and get me. But nothing stirs till I reach the big tree and speak to the man setting there.

"Mr. Aaron," I say, not bothering to lower my voice, "I hoped you'd wait."

The man in the dark clothes stands up and my heart sinks as his smell reaches me.

"And who might you be? The Jew's fancy-boy? Traveling in ladies' undergarments, if I don't miss my guess."

He laughs a fat satisfied laugh. "No point hanging around, Jewboy. I told Aaron what I'm telling you: Move on."

And he lays back one side of his suit jacket to show the sheriff star, shining silver on his vest.

Chapter 27

At the Injun Grave

Gudger's Stand, 1938

I stand there frozen with fear for what seems like half a lifetime. High Sheriff Hudson is looking down at me and laughing. He don't act as if he suspicions aught, so I mumble something and start to walk away—where to, I don't know. Just then the headlights of a vehicle coming down the road sweep across my face.

"Hold up there," the sheriff growls. "I want a closer look at you," and his big old hand wraps around my arm and pulls me back.

I try to turn away from him but he grabs my chin and pulls my face around. He leans down, staring puzzled-like, and the smell of burning and rot and whisky is strong in my nose. His eyebrows are working up and down as he studies me. The light from the vehicle passes off but he goes on staring. Then, slow and deliberate, he pulls open my suit jacket and feels of my chest.

"I be goddamn," he whispers and rips open my shirt. "Looks like the bird is trying to fly the coop. But I believe I can find a cage for you. I'll enjoy you a time and then . . ."

I know him then for a Raven Mocker like Granny Beck had told of and start to holler but my mouth is dry with fear and only a little croak come out. He laughs, and while I am trying to work up a scream, he pulls out a big old bandana handkerchief from his pocket and wads it into my mouth. Then he picks me up with one arm and begins to carry me over towards the big rocks they call the Injun Grave. I kick and struggle and try to spit out the bandana that is gagging me, but he don't pay no more mind than a daddy carrying a naughty child.

"Oh, Redbird Ray, I've got you now," he whispers, and the fingers of his free hand are busy at my clothing. "Won't do you no good to scream or get away nohow. You think any of them up there would lift a finger to help you? Your boss, him that you're trying to run out on? Or all them fellers who been spending their money in the dance downs, just in hopes of getting first chance with you? Maybe you think some of the girls—"

He stops talking and cocks his head. There is a big commotion up at the Stand and I figure they must have found that I am gone, but though the sheriff casts a glance up that way, he just keeps walking.

On the far side of the rocks, he drops me down in the grass. Holding me with one hand around my neck, he fumbles with my trouser buttons. I kick and wiggle, trying to get free, but he hits me in the face and then tightens his hold on my throat. I might as well be a mouse, held by a giant cat.

As his mouth and fingers move over my body, prying, biting, twisting, hurting, I think of trying to use the Gifts and Powers, but with the gag in my mouth I can't sing the Calling Song nor say the spells. If Granny could hear me . . . and I send my thoughts after her but I guess I am too far from her resting place.

I seek in my mind for Nancy Goingsnake—if this is her grave, might be she would help her great-great-granddaughter. My thoughts go wandering, leaving my poor body in the grass, and now I am two people. One is a helpless, naked squirming thing held down and tormented by the sheriff; the other is a spirit, wandering through a lonely spirit world, a world that is empty but for shadows that swirl and dance around me.

But if Nancy Goingsnake was ever in this place, she ain't now. With a jolt my spirit self is back in the white twisting body and I am struggling to breathe. My nose is filled with blood from when he hit me and I am choking on the gag. There is a roaring in my head and the noise up at the Stand grows louder. The sheriff stops what he was doing and puts up his head to listen.

"I believe they're feeling cheated of their prize, Redbird. Kind of the way I felt when you wouldn't go upstairs with me," he says and reaches to undo his own trouser buttons. "And now I'm gonna break you in good, you little cock tease. When I'm done, maybe I'll let those fellers up there have my leavings. Reckon you won't be so choicey after this."

And he is on me again, tearing at my breasts with his teeth and pushing my legs apart with his knees, when all at once there is a sound like an axe hitting a big log and the sheriff lets out a great *Uuhhh* and falls against me. I am most crushed with the weight of him but he just lays there, not moving. Then I feel him sliding off me to one side and I look up to see Mr. Aaron holding what must be an axe handle.

"Your face—the blood," he says and puts out a hand,

then draws it back like he don't want to touch me. "Are you hurt bad?"

I set up and pull out the gag, using it to daub at my face. I take a deep breath and the damp night air is a healing wonder to me.

"It's just a nosebleed," I tell him. "I ain't bad hurt."

Mr. Aaron turns his back on me and says, "Then get your clothes on and hurry. The sheriff isn't dead and we have to be on our way before he wakes up."

Mr. Aaron's voice is just as calm as if this ain't nothing new to him, and I make haste to do like he says. The teddy that I had on is all ripped to shreds and most of the buttons is popped loose from the shirt but I pull it closed and then get the trousers and suit coat back on.

"I thought he was you—" I start to say but, still not looking at me, Mr. Aaron raises one hand. His voice trails over his shoulder, low and steady as he sets off walking.

"No talking; my automobile is here. This way."

I follow him from behind the big rocks and across the field to where a black automobile is standing. I wonder was it the same one that shone its headlights on me and then I wonder at Mr. Aaron having such a vehicle but I stay quiet like he told me.

And when we are closer and I see a black man step out of the car and open the back door for me, I still don't say nothing, just climb in and lean back on the seat. It seems my life is changing yet again.

Mr. Aaron climbs into the front seat beside the driver. He twists around and hands me a flask over the seat. "Drink this," he says, "all of it."

Somehow I don't question; just do as he says, and the drink slides down my throat strong as fire and sweet as mountain honey. The car starts and heads up the road, past the Stand, where I can see people swarming over the porches and all around. There are folks with battery flashlights roaming around in the dark, shining them into those big boxwoods and everywhere I ain't. I see the boss on the front steps, waving his arms and hollering.

And then we are around the curve and on the road climbing above the Stand house and I look down and all the people get smaller and smaller as we move farther and farther away. The bobbing flashlights look like so many big lightning bugs and then we take another curve and they blink out.

"That should be the last you'll see of Gudger's Stand," says Mr. Aaron. "It'd not be wise for you to cross its threshold again—not for a very long time."

"Mr. Aaron," I say, with the boldness the drink has put into me, "when the snow flies, I got to go back—not to Gudger's Stand, but across the river and back up to Dark Holler. I got to—"

"You have an appointment with your young man; I know," he says, "but that's some months away. Will you trust me to arrange it for you? I can send Rafe with the auto to transport you when the time comes."

I am so wore out, with the week of dance downs and the struggle with the sheriff, that it ain't in me to argue. I lay back against the seat and watch the side of the road slide by—dark woods and fields with every now and then a sleeping house and its barns and outbuildings. There is lamplight shining at the window in one of the houses and I wonder why—a sick child? A husband not come home yet?

The driver tilts his head towards the house with the lamp, and as if he'd been asked some question, Mr. Aaron says, "After we get this child settled."

"How do you know the sheriff ain't killed?" I ask. "And even if he ain't, there's like to be trouble."

The car is turning off the main road down a narrow track to the right. Mr. Aaron swings around to face me.

"There are some useful things to be learned in a long life," says he, "and one is how to kill or not kill with a blow. Another lesson learned is the power of a strong man's vanity. High Sheriff Hudson won't be telling the story of what happened tonight. Nonetheless, you will do well to stay clear of him and the Stand and all its denizens till your appearance is very much altered. And that's why I'm leaving you here—Miss Inez and Miss Odessa will take good care of you till your appointment at snow fly."

We have stopped in the narrow road between a house on the left and a barn and some sheds on the right. In this house too an oil lamp is in the window. Mr. Aaron gets out and pulls open the door.

"This is the place," he says. "I've taken a room for you and you'll be safe here till your young man comes back."

I think of how I look, dressed in a man's suit and it all bloody and torn, my hair full of shoe polish, my nose— and I touch it careful, feeling it all swole and crusted with dried blood.

"Mr. Aaron," I say, looking towards the porch of the house. There in the pale light of the waning moon I see two women. They have long robes wrapped around them and they stand still as stone. "What will they think? And how can I pay—I have some put by but it ain't much—"

He waves his hand back and forth like he was shooing off my words. "The Misses Henderson are excellent women—they don't ask questions and they know how to keep a secret. As for payment, Miss Inez would be glad of help in the house and the kitchen. They occasionally take boarders and have just one now—a quiet-living Presbyterian who has never set foot in that place you've just left."

He beckons me out of the automobile and I hobble after him up to the porch. I am burning and aching all over and my nose, which feels like it is the size of a mushmelon, is throbbing. Every step I take hurts me. I wish I could go hide myself in the woods but it is too late, the sisters have seen me and are hurrying down to take me by the arms and help me up the steps. It is easier going with them on either side of me and for a moment I wonder why it is that, kind as he is, Mr. Aaron had never offered to take my hand, not to help me off the ground nor out of the car.

But the thought vanishes as the sisters, clucking like a pair of hens, bustle me around to a side door and into the house.

Chapter 28

Odessa and Inez

Dewell Hill, 1938

The sisters are called Odessa and Inez and I reckon it was them Granny Beck was telling me would keep me safe—not Francine and Lola. Odessa is twenty-six years of age and works at the Dewell Hill Mercantile. Inez is some younger and she will tell you that she does all the work at home. She has bad headaches some of the time and it is good that I am there to help for they is always a world of things to keep up with. But in the evenings we set on the porch and Inez picks her guitar while we sing or we all play Pollyanna which is a game the sisters have taught me. I am learning to cook all kinds of things that Mama never had time for like corn pudding and Jell-O. Jell-O is the most fun to eat and I like it almost as good as the Popsicles Odessa brings from the store.

From that very first night they have been awful kind to me—taking me in and not asking one question, not about my ripped and dirty clothes, nor why I was wearing a man's suit nor nothing.

"This young lady's name is Birdsong," Mr. Aaron said as we all went into the big kitchen on the bottom floor of the house. "And she's in need of sanctuary—as well as your dressmaking skills, Miss Inez and Miss Odessa." And he made a little bow to each of them.

The two didn't turn a hair. "They're asleep upstairs," the smaller of the two women said, "and when we heard you were coming, Inez and I waited out on the porch so as to bring you in this way. Down here we don't have to worry about waking Mama."

They pulled out a chair from the big kitchen table for me to set down. The big one studied me hard and then, without a word, went and got a dishtowel. She ran some cold water from the sink on it before she come over and handed it to me.

"Lay that against your nose," says she. "It'll help to bring the swelling down."

I knowed I was a sight on earth, my face all smeared with blood and shoe polish, and the men's clothes I had on torn and dirty. But Miss Odessa just said, "I'll get you one of my nightgowns and a robe. After Mr. Aaron leaves, you can get cleaned up a bit."

The one called Inez set a zinc tub on the floor, and after she had stirred up the coals in the woodstove, she slid a great big kettle over to where it would begin to heat. Mr. Aaron commenced to look uneasy-like and started to back towards the door.

"A bath will be the very thing, don't you agree, Miss Birdsong? And, as you are in good hands, I'll make my farewells. Ladies, Miss Odessa, Miss Inez, my respects to your mother."

He pulled a long manila envelope from a pocket inside his coat and laid it on the kitchen table. "Four months' room and board at the usual rate . . . and a bit extra for clothing and . . . ah . . . toiletries."

"Mr. Aaron," I called out as he made for the door, "where are you going?" For all at once it seemed to me that I was losing the last link to who I had been. He had called me Birdsong and it suited me fine to leave Redbird Ray behind at the river, just as I had left Least. But it worried me to see him leave.

"Where are you going?" I asked again, "And when will you be back?"

He paused at the door. "I—or if not I, my driver—will be back just before the snow flies to take you across the river. Till then, I have other obligations to fulfill. You'll be safe here, Miss Birdsong."

And he lifted his hat and was gone.

Time is like a river, Granny Beck told me, and most of us is in that river, swept along with no way of stopping or turning back. But they is some few what walks the banks of that river, up and down, stopping or going at their own pleasure. I believe that Mr. Aaron is one of these and I believe that I will see him again.

My bruises healed and Inez and Odessa fixed me up fine with some nice clothes. They taught me how to cut out a dress and how to use a sewing machine. Law, they was so much I didn't know about the ordinary way of life. Those girls stayed busy with all manner of things—games and books and picking the guitar and piecing quilts and I don't know what all.

And they both of them keep these little diaries that they write in every day, come what may, as Odessa says. They are the cutest little books with locks on them so can't no

one look at what they write. But Inez has showed me hers.
It is a little small thing and it is for five years, so there is
not room but for one or two lines for each day.

I would admire to have one of these books but there
ain't none at the store right now. Odessa says they only get
them in around Christmastime. But she has give me a
speckledy black and white composition book, with lines
ruled in it, and I am writing down things just like the sisters do.

I hated it that I couldn't go about with them—they go
to picture shows and there are entertainments up at the
school—but there is always the fear that someone or other
would know me for Redbird Ray. Or, come to that, for
Least, the quare girl. So I stay close to the house, working
in the garden and helping in the kitchen. Odessa has let
out that I am a cousin come to stay and that I am recover-
ing from an unhappy attachment and don't like going
among company. Which is true enough, in its way, I
reckon. Ha.

But months has passed, my hair has grown out, and the
henna is all gone. I can look in my mirror and see nothing
of Redbird—that firecracker dancing girl with her flam-
ing hair—nor can I see aught of the sorry little Least who
was near about feared of her own shadow.

My hair has grown long again and it is a shining dark
waterfall. When I brush it, Inez says that I look like a
princess. I have learned how to twist it up in what Odessa
calls a Grecian knot. Now the girl I see in the mirror, with
her golden skin and blue eyes and shiny hair, is a different
somebody than anyone I have been yet and I wonder how
Young David will like her.

Chapter 29

A Letter

Dewell Hill, 1938

Me and Inez is canning applesauce and there is several bushels yet to be cooked down. I am all a-sweat, though Odessa says ladies don't sweat—they glow—and I leave Inez stirring the kettle of sauce and go out for more stove wood. It is October and the air is as crisp as the apples I've been peeling. I draw in deep breaths and it feels most like I was drinking wine. The air is chill but the sky is clear blue and I know I still have a time to wait.

When I reach down to get an armful of the hot-burning locust wood, my hand touches something that moves beneath my fingers. I jump backwards, the breath most knocked out of me.

It is a great blacksnake, twined there in the warmth of the sun amongst the billets of wood. I ain't afeared of snakes but it is still the case that coming upon one all un-suspecting will give a body a start. Once I see what it is, though, I stop to watch.

He is shedding his skin, working himself free of the

dusty, worn-out old covering that even clouds his eyes. Slow and deliberate, he rubs the length of him along the sticks of wood, twisting in and out, and, as I watch, a shining new snake comes out of the mouth of the old skin and slides along the woodpile, jet bead eyes all bright and skin as glossy as Odessa's patent leather slippers. He lifts his head and looks me in the eye for a minute, then, like water going down a drain, he oozes into a rat hole there at the edge of the woodpile.

The old skin lays there, draped along the wood, and I pick it up to study on it. It is moist and supple now, and complete down to the scales that covered where his eyes was. I think how the snake is new on the outside, just like me. Twice now, I have changed from one person to another.

"Birdsong?" Inez calls. "Are you coming with that wood? The fire's most out."

Back in the kitchen, Inez is stirring at a great kettle full of apple slices. Her face is red and sweating with the heat of the stove and she pauses to wipe at it with her apron.

I drop the stove wood into the wood box and turn to go get another armload. Just then Odessa comes in the door. She is carrying a paper poke and me and Inez look at her, wondering why she is home so early from the Mercantile.

Odessa sets the poke on the table and plops down in a chair. "Ooo eee, those apples sure smell good," she says, leaning back and rolling her shoulders. "Why don't we have us each a saucer—and put some of that top milk on it?"

While we are eating our apples—hot and sweet and cinnamon-tasting with the thick cold yellow cream melting atop, Odessa tells us that her back has been acting up, and since things was slow this afternoon, they said for her to go along home.

She reaches into her poke and I hold my breath— I never know what Odessa may have brought from the store. Sometimes there are bananas, hard and green and as bad to pucker your mouth as a persimmon but they will turn sweet and soft and yellow if you let them set a few days. Another thing I like that comes from the store is Wint-O-Green Life Savers.

Today she has brought my favorite, which is Goo-Goo Clusters. They are the best thing you ever tasted, all chocolate and peanuts and marshmallow and caramel. We will save them for after supper, she says.

Then she pulls out the mail. The post office is in the store and Odessa always brings the mail home with her. She spreads out the letters on the table and pushes over a couple to Inez. Then she hands one to me.

I have never got a letter, not ever, and I don't much know what to do. I think at first maybe it is from Young David, but even as the thought rises up, I know it cannot be as this letter says on the front, *Miss Birdsong, Dewell Hill, North Carolina.*

"Go on and open it up," says Odessa. Inez is already reading one of hers and she looks up and makes a face at her sister.

"Violet says she wants to come for a short visit before it gets too cold. Ha. Last time her short visit lasted over a week."

"Now, Sis," says Odessa but I don't hear the rest for I am reading my letter.

My dear Miss Birdsong, it says. *My car and driver will be waiting for you at 11 o' clock on the night of December 16. Yours truly, J. Aaron.*

Chapter 30

When the Snow Flies

Back to Dark Holler, 1938

Just like the letter said they would be, the black car and the black man named Rafe are waiting on the dark road when I slip out the kitchen door at eleven o'clock. My bed is stripped and my bedclothes folded and I have left a note for Inez and Odessa. I puzzled over whether I should take the pretty new dresses they made for me but, remembering that Mr. Aaron had left money to pay for clothes, and knowing that the sisters was too big to wear my things, I rolled the dresses and unmentionables and such into a bundle and tied it with the sash from the cornflower blue dress.

The first flakes are falling and, as we drive the road down towards Gudger's Stand, they are like big white moths caught in the beam of the headlights. It seems a marvel that Mr. Aaron knew, over a month ago, that this would be the day it snowed. I ask the black man about this and he just says, very dignified, "We have our ways."

I had asked Rafe right off where Mr. Aaron was, having hoped to see him, if only to thank him again, but the black man shook his head. "His Friday evenings are never free—a longtime commitment prevents his being with you."

When the Stand comes in view, it is ablaze with light shining through the snow and I catch the sound of the fiddle and the banjo, the stamp of feet, and the swell of laughter. They are playing "Sherman's Burning in Hell" and I think of Fran and Lo, both Yankees, but good somebodies all the same. I hope that the money I left was enough to pay for Francine's suit I took and I hope that those girls make their stake so they can leave and set up their chicken farm soon.

The tune ends and the musicianers strike up "Under the Double Eagle." For a minute the music floods through me and takes me. I remember the drunken feel and the excitement in my blood and what it was like to be Redbird Ray, the Firecracker Dancing Girl, and for a moment my heart beats faster and my desires run back to that place on the hill.

As we pass by the turning that leads up to the Stand, an automobile is coming down the drive and its headlights sweep across the inside of our car. A fear catches at me like something bad is about to happen all over again and I start to tell Rafe to hurry, when the car pulls out fast and cuts in front of us. A flashing light goes on and the car slows, then stops in the road just ahead.

Rafe has to brake hard not to hit it and I hear him mutter, "Uh-oh." He freezes, hands on the steering wheel, as a big man carrying a flashlight gets out of the vehicle that is blocking us. The flashlight is pointing at us and the man is hid behind its dazzle but as the light moves closer and closer, I catch the heavy dead stink of a Raven Mocker and know that it is High Sheriff Hudson. In the headlights the flying snow looks like sparks around his big shape and the overcoat he has on floats out on either side of him like wings. I hear the roaring of a great wind as he gets nearer.

"Go around him, Rafe! You got to get around him and across the bridge!"

My voice don't sound like my own but Rafe throws the automobile into reverse and backs away from the Raven Mocker, which looms up before us, getting taller and taller. A great howling surrounds the evil thing and tangled up in the howling is the wail of a train whistle and the steady chug of the locomotive.

In the light of the train I see the Raven Mocker standing there all spread out in our path and the stink of its being, life upon life, surrounds us and I am choking and smothering in the foul-smelling cloud. "Rafe," I call out, "please, Rafe . . ."

Rafe's black face looks like a grinning mask, like a thing older by far than the Raven Mocker, and all at once I see that he is more than a servant. He too has the Gifts and Powers and he is making full use of them. A high wild sound comes from his lips as he shoves the car into first gear and makes for the bridge.

The Raven Mocker is howling and flapping as we brush right by him and then we are flying across the tracks without an inch to spare before the freight train roars past, its whistle blowing and its wheels singing as they slice along the metal rails.

Rafe doesn't slow down till we are across the bridge and a little ways up Ridley Branch. Over the river, I can see the dark line of freight cars flashing by like beads on a jet necklace. And then the road bends inward to where the river is out of sight and I have so many questions but Rafe answers them all with "Wait and see."

It is just now getting into my head that I am on my way back to Dark Holler—the place I fled a half a year ago. As I try to think what lays ahead, Rafe turns onto a narrow road that runs by a barn and the car is jouncing up and up into a white curtain of snow.

I only came this way once before—on the day that Mama died—and it is some time before I begin to see things I remember. There is the big flat rock in the middle of the branch and there is the crooked fence post that marks where Mama said I must not pass.

And now I see the big boxwoods that was my hidey place by the road, all white and covered with snow, and all at once I wake from this dream I'm in. Is it likely that Young David will be back this very night? What if he has come and gone, not finding me there?

Cold black fear is filling me and I cover my face with my hands, afraid of what I may see. But as the car slows and stops, I hear Rafe's deep voice saying, "You're home now, Birdsong."

I crack my fingers and look through them to the house. There is an oil lamp burning just inside the front window, the light all wavering because of the tears filling my eyes. And, as I watch and wonder, the front door opens and Young David steps out to the porch.

In an instant, I am out of the car and flying up the steps and into his arms and we are kissing and hugging and asking questions. He tells me how a black man picked him up when he was hitchhiking back home and brought him to this very place, telling him to build a fire and wait, for the girl he was expecting would be coming soon.

Later he will say that I was the most beautiful thing he ever saw—with the snow that lay on my lashes like jewels and clung to my dark hair like a wedding veil.

ॐ

Page from Inez's five-year diary

Dec 17, '38
   Cold today; more snow. Got Birdsong's room ready for the new boarder. Went to Missionary Society meeting. Hemmed brown wool skirt; cut out a dress. Artamae Brady stopped by to visit and said that High Sheriff Hudson got killed last night by the 11:20 train. Why he had got out of his car, no one knows. Violet is still here. Short visit, ha.

Chapter 31

The Taste of Joy

Dark Holler, 1938

It was a magic time, a time out of the world, those last weeks of the year in the snowbound cabin. The black man Rafe brought in boxes and boxes of groceries from the back of his automobile before he drove off into the white-swirled night. No one had disturbed the house and in the cellar there was still jars of canned garden stuff—dusty row upon row of beets and peaches, beans, corn, and kraut, gleaming soft red and orange, green and yellow when I lifted the lamp to see what was there. There was even sausage and backbone, put up last fall. We found lamp oil too, a big can of it, enough to keep the night away. The cow was gone as was the pig and the chickens, but me and Young David feasted on what there was. And we filled ourselves up with love.

I must not call him Young David no more. That was but a made-up name I gave him, along of him looking like the picture in Granny Beck's Bible. His name is Luther, a fine strong name, and when we are married, he will say *I,*

Luther, take thee—and I will be Birdsong—*Birdsong Honeycutt Gentry.*

"Seems like a big mouthful of a name for a little bitty someone like you," Luther says and he takes me in his arms and we go to loving once again. He calls me Little Bird and Birdie and sometimes Miss Birdie, and all those names sound sweet to my ear.

The snow has been falling for days but we have pulled the feather tick into the front room by the stove and piled it high with quilts. We snuggle there in the warmth and he tells me how he worked with the WPA, building roads around mountainsides over in Avery County. He has made good money and reckons that, now times is better, we might put money towards the farm that's for sale down on the branch.

For I have told him that I don't want to stay here. As long as he is by me and there is light, I can't hear Mama. But sometimes, when I wake of a night, I can hear her screaming.

I have told him most of it—how Mama killed Snowflower and about the paper that said a doctor was going to cut out some part of me so that I couldn't never have babies. I have told him how she died and that I ran away because I was afraid the neighbors would take me to that doctor.

In a way, it was hardest to tell him about Gudger's Stand and the dancing but I made a clean breast of it, though it took several days and many tears. It was midafternoon and we was under the quilts by the stove. Outside the snow was flying, beating against the windowpanes, but we was safe in our nest, finding warmth in one another.

When we was done, I begun to tell Luther something of where I'd been after crossing the river. At first he thought I was funning with him. But as I talked on, he went to shaking his head, saying, "No, no . . . you in a place like that?"

And when I come to tell him about the tango I had done with Francine, he threw off the quilts and jumped up and begun to put on his clothes.

"Luther, I didn't never go upstairs with none of them—I promise you that."

I was setting up now, a-clutching at his britchie leg with one hand and holding the quilts over my breasts with the other, but he paid me no mind, just went to pulling on his boots and his heavy coat.

The tears was beginning to come and they dripped down my face onto my bare skin. "Luther, I had to do something. I couldn't stay here and I was afraid to go far."

He shook his head and bit his lip like he was trying not to cry. Then he jammed on his old hat, pulling it down hard.

"I got to get outside," he said, his voice all choked. "I got to think."

And he was gone, slamming the door behind him. I could hear his boots crunching in the snow on the porch and the creak of the loose step and then I couldn't hear him no more.

There was naught but the crackle of the fire in the stove and the little rustling sounds of the old house around me. As I listened hard, almost holding my breath, hoping to hear the sound of his footsteps returning, I seemed to hear the tinkling voices of the Little Things beating against the windowpanes and calling to me, but then she began to speak, low and mean like she used to do, whispering that Luther'd not come back, that no one could love a crazy girl who—

I made myself as small as I could and pulled the quilts up over my head. I pretended it was Granny Beck's love wrapped around me and tried not to listen to the things that Mama was whispering.

The fire in the stove has sunk into coals when at last I hear the squeak of the front step and the sound of boots on the porch. I peek out from under the covers and see Luther as he comes in the door, stomping the snow off his boots. He looks over at me and smiles, just as sweet.

"I brung you your Santy Claus," he says and reaches into his coat pocket. Stepping over to me, he lays two oranges and a big old peppermint stick down on the quilt, then drops his coat to the floor and sets beside me.

He tells me that he decided to walk down the branch to see if the store might be open for he was of a mind to buy some meal and side meat if they had it. The rats had been at the meal in the kitchen bin and we'd not had bread all this while.

"The store was open," he says, "and there was several fellows setting by the fire and jawing. When I come in, one of them knowed me for I had done some work for him last year. He hollered out to ask what I was doing over this way."

Luther goes to peeling one of the oranges and my mouth begins to water at the sharp sweet smell. Brother used to get me an orange for Christmas.

"What did you tell him?" I ask, feeling that all the rest of my life is hanging on the next words he speaks.

He pulls the orange apart in sections and puts one to my lips.

"Well," says he, "I remembered what you said, about the note you left, saying you was gone to your brother's. So I told those fellers that we met by chance on the train, both of us coming back to Marshall County, and we found that we agreed so well that we got off and got married in Asheville."

I bite into the orange section and the taste of it is like joy in my mouth.

"So this is what we do—we give out that you've been at your brother's all this time, and you and me go into town and get married tomorrow or as soon as we can."

I throw my arms around him and kiss him with my orange-tasting mouth while he goes on talking.

"You'll likely heir this place, you and your brothers and sisters, and we'll stay here till I can fix us a new house down by the road. You've been away from folks too long."

He kisses me gentle-like and says, "All that other, we'll forget all about it and start new."

I kiss him back hard, my eyes a-swim with tears. He goes to building up the fire, still full of what all he heard at the store—that some say there is like to be another great war overseas, that there is to be a clinic with a doctor in Dewell Hill, that the old feed mill in Ransom caught fire but got put out in time.

"And the High Sheriff—that one everyone hated so bad because he helped foreclose all them farms—they said he got run over by a train a few weeks back of this—killed outright, they said, and good riddance to him."

Chapter 32

Burying Least

Dark Holler, 1939

When I learned that High Sheriff Hudson was dead, I felt like a great burden had been lifted from me. Now, I thought, there is no need to tell Luther about what happened that night by the river. I have told him about staying at Odessa and Inez's house, and about Mr. Aaron who made sure that we would find each other again. But now Luther just looks at me with a question in his eyes when I talk about that night and the black car and the black man.

For him, the story that is real is the story he told the people at the store, that we met on the train. When I remind him of the full moon nights up in the burying ground, he looks puzzled and scratches his head. "Well now, Birdie, if that's how you remember it . . ." he will say and go to tickling and teasing of me.

It stayed bitter cold through the end of December and it isn't till the first week of January in the new year of nineteen and thirty-nine that the weather moderates and we can go into Asheville and stand up before the magistrate.

There is some trouble about my age and me not having any paper to say who I am, but Luther talks to the feller real low, and when they shake hands, I see the edge of some bills sticking out between their palms before the magistrate puts his hand in his pocket and motions to me to come up to him and get married.

We walk all around the town for we have a good bit of time before the train to Ransom goes, and we eat lunch at the S & W Cafeteria, where you can get more different things to eat than I had knowed there was. You go down a long table with all the different things there in big pans and you point at what you want. I get a piece of white meat chicken and some corn and some beans and a fancy glass that has two kinds of Jell-O in it, both red and yellow, with stiff whipped cream on top. I reckon this is the way that rich people, queens and such, eat every day.

There is a black man dressed up fancy who carries our trays to a table and pulls out my chair for me to sit in. He seems very nice and I ask him does he know a feller named Rafe but he just shakes his head.

I have a ring too. Before we went to the magistrate, we went to Finkelstein's pawnshop and Luther bought me a little gold band that has leaves on it. Even while I am eating, I keep looking at my ring.

It has been a long day. I was worried both times we had to pass through the depot at Gudger's Stand that someone might see me and take me for Redbird Ray, but I kept my hat pulled down and my scarf up around my face against the cold and neither time did I see a familiar face. Another time it will be easier still, I think, as me and Luther walk across the bridge on our way back to Dark Holler.

There is a full moon rising up above the mountain and the air is not so cold as it was. I had slept most of the way back, my head on Luther's shoulder, rousing now and again to look at the gold band on my finger. Luther was dozing too and he had asked the conductor to be sure not to let us miss our stop.

Now, though it is late, I feel wide awake. Walking in the moonlight with my husband—my husband!—is as fine a thing as I can imagine. It is hardly cold at all, the weather acting like springtime to match the feeling in my heart.

"Luther," I say, catching at his hand, "let's take the road by the river and go home by way of the burying ground. I want to tell Granny Beck about us getting married."

"Little Bird, you are a sight on earth," he says. "Whoever heard of a bride spending her wedding night in a graveyard?"

But, like me, Luther is giddy with the moonlight and he gives in directly.

"Well," he says, "I reckon it'll be nice to follow the river. I like to watch the way the light plays on it. But I can see I am going to be one henpecked husband."

By the time we are climbing the path up to the burying ground, the moon is riding high. I make my way straight to Granny Beck's grave with its circle of five smooth stones and flatten out my palms on the earth above her heart. "Hey, Granny Beck," I whisper. "I'm back."

I tell her what all has happened but not out loud for Luther is setting on a nearby stone, rolling a smoke. He sets there patient, smoking his cigarette, and when I have told her all about it and felt the warmth of her happiness and love, I rise up and go to set beside him.

He puts his arm around me and we set there a minute without speaking. Then he says, "I been studying on things, Little Bird. All this that's gone before, what you told me about your mama. And then the things that granny of yours taught you—Injun charms and spells."

I start to speak but he lays a finger against my lips. "Now, all that is part of why folks called you quare. And you living up in the holler, you and your mama keeping solitary, well, it didn't much matter what you did. And I ain't saying a word against your granny for I know how much she meant to you. But we are going to go to live down on the road, amongst folks, and it seems to me that, along with forgetting about when you was living at that bawdy house, it might be as well for you to forget all them witch things your granny taught you. It don't square with scripture, Little Bird."

He kisses me sweet and gentle. "Will you make me that promise—for a wedding gift?"

And so I promise.

And in time to come I will gather up my few memories of Redbird Ray—a bracelet and a fancy pair of rhinestone hair combs—along with the first bits of writing that Granny Beck showed me, some with the words to the spells, and Luther will dig a hole up at the burying ground under the big oak and we will bury my past there—the quare girl and the dancing girl.

In later years, when he is making markers for my angels, I take a fancy to have a marker for them girls. He shakes his head, not understanding the need I feel, but wishing to lighten my sorrow, he does like I ask and fashions the marker. On the side that is buried is the name *Redbird* and on the side looking at the sky, it says *Least*.

〜

From a diary

> Today me and Luther put an end to those girls. All that was left of them is under the big oak at the yon side of the burying ground. Birdie, says Luther, it's the only way, and you must give yor solum promiss never to speak those names agin nor talk of them other things. And he give me this book to write in and said that I must burn the old ones. We got all our life ahead says he—a fine new begining and when you got a mess a young uns about the place youll fergit all this hateful bizniss. Then he showed me these words on his Bible and told me to copy them in this new book, to always remember:
>
> BLESSED IS THE MAN THAT WALKETH NOT IN THE COUNSEL OF THE UNGODLY, NOR STANDETH IN THE WAY OF SINNERS, NOR SITTETH IN THE SEAT OF THE SCORNFUL.
>
> BUT HIS DELIGHT IS IN THE LAW OF THE LORD, AND IN HIS LAW DOTH HE MEDITATE DAY AND NIGHT.
>
> AND HE SHALL BE LIKE A TREE PLANTED BY THE RIVERS OF WATER, THAT BRINGETH FORTH HIS FRUIT IN HIS SEASON; HIS LEAF ALSO SHALL NOT WITHER; AND WHATSOEVER HE DOETH SHALL PROSPER.

PART III

Miss Birdie

Ridley Branch, May 2007

Chapter 33

Looking Back

Tuesday, May 1, 2007

(Birdie)

I like the sound of that—a tree by the rivers of water bringing forth fruit. And I'll not . . .

I hold the little cardboard-backed book in my hands, feeling the covers wore soft with age and handling, and them times all come rushing back. Not but seventeen years of age, new-married and new-born into a different life, when I wrote them words.

Closing my eyes, I can see the girl I was back then, feet twisted round the legs of the kitchen chair, head bent over the page, the tip of my tongue caught betwixt my teeth, and my dark hair—"like the river by night" he called it that first time—slipping out from the pins and falling across my face. I see that girl push the hair back behind her ears and go on with her writing, printing careful as can be with her shiny yellow-painted pencil in this very book.

My printing was getting better by then, not like in them other books where it run all crooked like the words was trying to jump off the page. I surely weren't no hand to spell either—back in those days. Considering what my schooling was, it ain't no wonder. But it had come to where the pencil didn't feel all thick and clumsy in my fingers no more and I remember how I fairly marveled to see the letters springing up so quick—marching neat and straight along the thin blue lines of each page.

Reading these words wrote so long ago, it seems like hardly no time at all has passed; seems like iffen I was to look up, I'd see Luther, setting there across the table from me, his finger lining along the verses of the Bible chapter he's studying. In my mind I see the glow from the oil lamp, spreading soft across the pages of our books and touching Luther's hair with copper light.

Back then his hair was the deep dark brown of a horse chestnut, and he kept it shining clean, the prettiest hair I ever saw. Remembering back, seems like I can smell the lamp oil and hear the fluttering of the flame and the lonesome night sounds just beyond the window.

Remembering so clear the writing of these words, the careful forming of each letter the way I had learned them—the swoop of the small *f* with the little dash crossing to slow it down, the round open mouth the *O* makes, old hissing coppersnake *S*, fork-in-the-road *Y*, and big-bottom *B*—it seems I am right there, back in that time and place, and I could raise my head up from this self-same copybook and just feast my eyes upon him—Luther, young and handsome and kind as he was—and afore long he would feel my gaze and a smile would start to come across his lips. He would fight down that smile and go on studying his Bible and I would go on studying him.

He was my Bible and I read the way his thick dark eyelashes brushed down like a moth's wing on his sun-touched cheeks, the fine straight line of his nose, the softness of his lips, the set of his ears, so neat and close against his head, and the place there at his throat, where he'd undone his old blue work shirt in the evening heat to show that soft hollow where I could see the pulsing of his heart's blood. I'd watch him close, not saying a word, and at last he would look up with them fine dark eyes of hisn and say, "Well, Miss Birdie, reckon we best go to bed."

But the pages of my copybook is all yellow and brickle with age. And when I see my hand, the pointer finger, tracing along the page, just like Luther used to do, hit ain't the fine smooth hand that wrote these words, nor the hand that traced every part of Luther's body, hard and smooth and soft and rough, till I had learned it all by heart. No, this here's an old woman's hand, the joints all gnarled and swole and the skin as wrinkled and spotted as any toad frog's.

"A tree by the water, bringing forth fruit . . ." The girl what wrote them words is turned into an old, old woman, long past the three-score-and-ten mark. And the fruit that she bore, that's gone, and Luther's gone too, these twenty years. But I had Luther and I had Cletus and I had my angels. And, though tempted and tried, I have kept to my promise.

Hit weren't easy. But I read through this book ever year, just to put me in mind of those times and my vow. Those times . . . and the times before . . . and the Three-fold Law and its bitter workings.

Now I've gone and lost my place. I'm right bad to wander off in memories, good and bad alike. I reckon it's natural when you get to my age . . . where was I now?

Here 'tis . . . **bringing forth fruit and I'll not be sorry to ferget that poor crazy girl and what she done—but** . . . And there's the place where I scribbled out what I wrote—my head so full of them dark deeds that just wanted to spill out but even then, young as I was, I could bridle my hand, if not my thoughts.

There, I like to brok my solum promis alredy. So insted Ill write of the fine new house Luther is naming to build for us down near the road where the sun shines all day and ther aint all these old dark hemlocks that cries ever time the night wind stirs. Luther has already cut and hauled the timber for the house—

It's that very house I'm setting in as I read the words and I am wandering somewheres betwixt then and now and all the years between when the hateful old telephone sets in to ringing. I lay the book on top of the others I have there on the kitchen table, push back my chair, and stand up. At first I feel a little swimmie-headed, but after I steady myself, I make for the phone. I have been so far back in them long-ago times that it surprises me to find that I'm an old, old woman with arthritis that just now won't hardly let me go no faster than a snail pace.

"No, Dor'thy, I tell you I can't do it. I made a solemn promise and I've held to it, all these years. You know I have—even when Cletus . . ."

I close my eyes and pray for help, remembering the battle fought and the temptation overcome. Me and Dorothy has never even spoke of this though I had suspicioned she knew . . .

Then I take a deep breath, steady my voice, and try to speak firm and convicted. "Dor'thy, outside of that, I'll help you any way I can. Tell me, does the young un want to go back to live with her?"

Dorothy just goes on yammering—louder and faster to

where I can't get a word in edgewise. All I can do is listen and nod my head and listen some more.

They ain't no use trying to stop her—when Dorothy's got a bug in her bonnet, all a body can do is to let her run on till she gives out. She is a lot like her mama, who was Luther's aunt, and a more determined somebody there never was. But good-hearted too, like all of Luther's family.

I recollect how when at last me and Luther got married and went to tell his kin, the womenfolk questioned and worried at me like a dog with a bone till they could place who I was and how I come to be all alone in the world. There's many a family would have bowed up and made a girl like me feel unwelcome but that wasn't the way of the Gentrys.

"You be a good wife to my boy," I mind old lady Gentry saying, "and we'll every one of us be family to you."

And she kissed me on the cheek and gave me a great old book that had been her daddy's. It was called *The Royal Path of Life* and she said that if I would read it, along with my Bible and heed its lessons, I would do just fine.

I blink and in that blink of an eye the years pile back on me. I am not a new-made bride, standing in Luther's mama's house with a heavy green-backed book in my hands; I am an old woman and a widow, standing in my own living room and holding the phone with Dorothy's voice buzzing in my ear.

But I can still smell the snuff on the old lady's breath and feel the prickle of stiff hairs around her thin dry lips when she kissed me.

". . . worried sick. There's got to be some way . . . Birdie, are you listening to me?"

Dorothy has pretty well run out of things to say and at last I can get in a word.

"Dor'thy," I say, "you and me both know Prin ain't a fit mother. But if the Social Services lady ain't going to . . . Now, don't take on so. . . . We'll find us a way. . . . I'll think on it and pray on it too. . . . Yes, I'm naming to go up to the cemetery this evening long about one—soon's I have my bite of dinner. I'm a-goin' to pick up all them ol' wore-out flower arrangements and such and make the place look nice afore Bernice's boy comes to mow and weed round the stones. . . . Naw, they ain't no need fer you to come. . . ."

When we have both said our say, I hang up the phone and try to think what to do. Not what I *could* do—drawing spells, warning dreams, ill wishes, and suchlike. Though Dorothy has turned my thoughts that way, I stomp them down like I was putting out the beginnings of a brushfire.

Then I see the Bible, setting on its doily right by the telephone. I pick it up and lay it on my lap and I spread my hands on the thin black leather cover before I make my prayer. "I can't do it without You help me, Lord. . . . In Thy holy name, I ask it."

I shut my eyes and wait—and listen. Then I crack the Bible—open it and, eyes still shut, jab down my finger to see what message the Lord will send. When I un-squinch my eyes, I keep my finger on the verse, there at the bottom of the right-hand page, and straighten my spectacles. I can remember how my granny looked, doing the same thing, and figger I must look just like her.

Hit's Zechariah 4:10. *For who hath despised the day of small things?*

I look up at the living room ceiling but I'm thinking far, far beyond the beadboard and the white paint and the spider guarding the web she's just spun by the lightbulb. I'm thinking up into the clear blue sky, up to God's own heaven, and I'm seeking an answer.

Title page from **The Royal Path of Life**

THE

ROYAL PATH

OF LIFE:

OR,

Aims and Aids to Success and Happiness.

BY

T. L. HAINES, A. M.,

AND

L. W. YAGGY, M. S.,

AUTHOR OF "OUR HOME COUNSELOR."

PUBLISHED BY

WESTERN PUBLISHING HOUSE, CHICAGO.

T. K. MILLS & CO. CEDAR RAPIDS, IOWA.
DICKERSON BROS. DETROIT, MICH.
J. A. WEBSTER & CO. KANSAS CITY, MISSOURI.
SOUTHWESTERN PUBLISHING HOUSE, NASHVILLE, TENN.
SKINNER & CRAIG, ROCHESTER, N. Y.
CENTRAL PUBLISHING HOUSE, CINCINNATI, O.
EASTERN PUBLISHING HOUSE, PHILADELPHIA, PA.
UNION PUBLISHING HOUSE, SPRINGFIELD, MASS.

1878.

Chapter 34

The Burying Ground

Tuesday, May 1

(*Birdie*)

The hickory walking stick digs little holes in the hard red earth as I make my way along the path that snakes up the tree-covered slope. Black plastic garbage bags hanging over my left arm rustle and swish in time with the huffing sounds of my breath and the steady thump of my footfalls, and the lighter tap of the stick. All them different sounds working together . . . they put me in mind of the one-man band in the Fourth of July parade, away back when Luther was yet living. Me and him took Cletus in to Ransom for the rodeo and the parade and, law, he had him a time! That boy played one-man band for the rest of the summer, rigged out with an old juice harp and some of my pot lids and a cowbell he took off of old Pet. Golden memories.

This trail ain't used but seldom now and it's growed narrow with the grass and the weeds reaching out into it. Most folks heading up to the top take the road that runs by the river—twice as long but any vehicle at all can Cadillac right up to the end. Hunters comes this way now and again and I reckon deer and such use the trail. Right here it runs along a rusty barb wire fence that borders the upper edge of the old cornfield. The field's going back to the wild too, like so much of these mountains. Where once there was corn growing, thick and tall and green, food for man and beast alike, now there's young locust and poplar shooting up through the roses and blackberries. It'll all be forest afore long, though I'll not live to see it.

I spy the fire pinks in their old place by the leaning gray fence post and it lifts my heart to see them bright faces just a-smiling up at me like always at this time of year. They're good as a calendar, the wild things are. Hummingbirds coming back mid-April, raspberries bearing fruit early June, and the fire pinks blooming just afore Decoration Day. Always has been so and I pray it always will.

The trail runs into the old woods now and in the cool shade beneath the new-leafed trees, there's a world of those three-leafed flowers, the white and the pink too, making a pretty carpet over the ground. The branch is running bold after last night's rain and all along its banks big old clumps of blue and light purple flowers look like lace against the solemn gray rocks. Over beyond the tumbling water, wild iris and larkspur climb the steep slope, reaching back into the trees far as the eye can see.

It is a sight on earth and that's the truth. I stop and lean on my stick to breathe in the rich woodland smell. There's some things don't change, thank the Lord—that fine loamy smell of the dirt and the clean bite of the branch mint and how the water gurgles and sings as it goes hurrying down to the river. There's the birds calling out— sounds like one of them's saying *Sweet, sweet, sweet,* and there's the wind stirring the trees—it's all the good things of life itself and I pity the city folks who ain't never been in a mountain cove come May time.

I stand there, breathing it all in. When you come to my age, you take your time with things you value, storing them up to remember. Who can say iffen I'll still be able to climb this steep trail another spring? Thinking it could be the last time only makes it the sweeter and I mark it all down—the redbird and his mate, the hawk circling lazy overhead, the way the sun sifts through the new leaves like yellow meal through a sieve—always the same and yet, somehow, always new.

But I got to get on to the burying ground—Lord knows how much there'll be to see to—so I take leave of all my old friends and head on up the road.

When I reach the clearing—my halfway mark—things ain't much changed. The log barn's roof is rusty but it's been that way for many a year and there ain't no tin blowed loose so far as I can see. Them old dark hemlocks is still there; the breeze that's sprung up has them bending and swaying like ladies struck in grief, just a-weeping and wailing and throwing up their hands. The chimbley stands yet—the fellow who laid it knew what he was doing and that's a fact—but it's most hid by all them young locust trees. If I make it back next year, likely it'll be plumb swallowed up and I'll not see it at all.

And there's them ol' boxwoods. Taller than last year and still smelling of cat piss. Reckon how long they've been there—planted long before my time, them and the old apples beyond. I mind how me and Luther and Cletus used to come up here in the fall of the year and fill our pokes with them apples—York Imperial, the best keepers there is, though somehow they never tasted sweet to me. Law, how gnarled and twisty those old branches is. But there's fruit setting on them and there'll be apples yet another year.

I lean down to peer at the bare space beneath the boxwoods, remembering. The smell is stronger still and I wonder if there's a fox or some such denning under there. But I reckon it's just the boxwoods' own nasty smell, clinging to the greenery.

Whyever You come to make them bushes smell like an ol' tomcat's been a-spraying 'em, I do not understand, Lord. Was it me, I believe I'd a found a nicer scent. Reckon hit's just another one of them mysterious ways of Yourn like Preacher's always talking about.

I look beyond the chimbley to where there's a trace of a path into the hemlocks. I remember . . . I remember . . . and my eyes follow where my feet must not go. *The way to the Little Things, that girl called it.* And all at once I am lost in thoughts buzzing round my head like a swarm of angry bees, drowning out the birds' songs and all my fine intentions.

Then I recollect myself and turn away to follow the upward trail into the old fields. *Let it go. After all these years, can't you let it go?* The words are like a drumbeat and my steps fall into time with them, marking out the sound. *Let-it-go. Let-it-go.*

Black clouds is gathering over the old fields and the dark smell of coming rain is growing strong but still I climb, step by slow step, up to the burying ground high on the hogback ridge. The beat of the words carries me on and I am speaking them without paying them any mind. They are a wound-up clock, going of their own accord. *Let-it-go. Let-it-go.*

When I gain the ridge, I stop to catch my breath and count the familiar markers—all sorts and all ages sprinkled over the easy crest of the ridge. When I'm rested, I pass by the granite markers, from the past forty or fifty years. They are all right fancy, deep-carved with names, dates, and Bible verses. Luther and Cletus and the angels is here—one stone for me and Luther and one each for Cletus and the angels. And there's all the worn-out flowers I come to gather up, some blown and scattered by the wind across the ridgetop, some still planted in the dirt of the graves, but faded to ugly now.

I get up this way several times in the year to tend my graves—I'll clear away the Decoration Day flowers long about August and put sunflowers on each grave—big cheerful things—and though they're plastic, they look so real I've seen the birds light on them. Then, come December, I'll bring poinsettias for Christmas—red for Cletus and Luther and white for the angels. I don't let my family graves look as sorry as some of them up here. But, law, so many folks lives away now and can't get back but once a year for Decoration Day, and sometimes not even that.

The oldest ones are over here up at the top of the ridge—no fancy headstones, just homemade sand concrete markers and these white-painted slabs. The best folks could do, I reckon. Ol' Chester Honeycutt's stone is leaning way to one side; I'll ask Bernice's boy to straighten it when he comes to mow. There's many an unmarked grave here too—but those dead lie as quiet as the rest. I'll give every one of them a flower come Decoration Day.

The church people sometimes looks at me kindly funny when they sees me go to jabbing them plastic flowers all around in the grass. "Birdie honey," one asked, "don't you want me to help you find where your family lays?" Thought I was growing simple in my old age. But she didn't mean nothing by it, just trying to be helpful. She don't know how I can hear those who was laid there. Yes, even though their bodies has gone to earth and their bones has crumbled away, they still whisper to me, thankful to be remembered.

I pick my way through the unmarked graves—past Mafra Myrene and her man Josephus, William Roberts and Little Loy, Geneva—oh, my, now there's a story— and stop to pick up a Mountain Dew can someone's left right at the head of where Old Otho lay. Some folks is awful trashy but I reckon they don't know no better.

At the yon edge of the mown ground where just a narrow strip of tall grass and weeds borders the woods, the old growth begins. There's poplar, oak, and beech, their trunks thick with years but their new leaves shiny bright. What I'm seeking after lies under the biggest oak. I use my walking stick to push the long grass to one side and there it is—whitewashed concrete, set flat and almost hid by the weeds and wildflowers.

I kneel down with my old knees creaking and complaining and brush it clean. Though the date and the name are burned on my heart, it's fitting that I make sure they're still here. Beneath the dead leaves and dirt, the numbers and letters are like always: at the top * 1939 * and under that, just the single lonely word, the last letter a little lower than the rest, like as if Luther's hand had tired and let the T run down hill. Just the name—*Least*.

The tears spring up, like they always do, as I pull myself back to my feet and stand studying the marker. I lean on my stick and think of that girl and what she done . . . and all that followed. Many a year, law, yes, many a year. But it had to be done . . . it had to . . .

I am far away, back in the long ago, when I hear the sound of Dorothy's voice, chattering like a squirrel. She is somewheres down the hill where there's a place to park the vehicles but she's getting closer every second. I wipe my face on the sleeve of Cletus's old shirt that I have over my housedress, and with my stick I push the hank of grass to cover the little marker. When I'm sure it can't be seen, I make my way back amongst the graves and set in to picking up the old wore-out flowers and putting them in my garbage bag.

The sound is getting closer but I can't hear any other voice and I wonder who it is she's talking to. Maybe worried as she is, she's kept the young un out of school. I can't make out the words but it sounds like she's right upset about something. When there's something amiss, Dorothy will run on like the radio, just arguing with herself if there ain't no one else around. And even if there is, she don't leave no room for answering.

A light rain begins to fall and I stretch out my hand to catch the drops. Dorothy's voice floats up the hill, every word plain now. She is carrying on like one thing—a big long flow of words and then she stops to breathe hard and then she starts up again.

"Well, I hope to goodness she's up here . . . her truck down at the house and the door unlocked . . . what if someone's carried her off . . . I reckon I got carrying-off on my mind. . . . Course, she could of decided to walk— always has been a fool for the woods . . . With that steep climb and her eighty-five this October—and not so spry

as she once was—but will she listen? I *told* her to let me do
it—all them old wreaths and such to gather up and get
shed of and the graves to brush off to be ready for Decoration Day.

"Oh, now you're coming in stronger, the higher I
climb. Down where I parked the car, there wasn't no re-
ception at all, I reckon on account of the hills. But this is
working just fine. I can hear you real good.

"And if it isn't trying to rain! Well, I reckon it'll pass off
right quick. I swear to goodness I don't know what gets
into Birdie sometimes. . . ."

I watch and wait and here comes Dorothy, in them ugly
brown double-knit pants with the flowered loose top like
she always wears, just a-puffing and fussing as she comes
into sight. And she's talking into one of them mobile
phones she's got up to her ear, just like all the folks you see
driving their cars and yacking into their little phones like
they had something important to say or straggling round
the grocery store with that thing up against their ear
telling everwho it is on the other end, "I'm by the cereal
now . . . now I'm at the dairy case."

When she sees me, Dorothy cuts off her conversation
right quick and slips the phone into her pocket. Then
afore I can say a word, she lights into me.

"Birdie Gentry, what in the world are you doing, standing out in the rain like that? Let's us go set in my vehicle
till it stops. And why in the world didn't you bring your
truck and come by the road 'stead of walking all the long
way up that steep path and through the fields. I declare—"

Of itself, my hand reaches out and marks a protecting
sign in the rain that lays on Dorothy's plump cheek. Law,
when was the last time I done that? Seems like being up

here is bringing old times close again—the good and the bad alike.

"My granny always said that it was a fine thing to get wet in the first rain of May—that it would keep a body healthy all the year," I say and cock my head and give Dorothy a big old smile. "If I got another year."

Chapter 35

On the Path

Tuesday, May 1

(*Calven*)

The boy paused on the path and looked down the slope to the swift-running branch, then, after a moment's consideration, arched a gob of spittle toward the water. It fell short by several feet and he snorted in disgust. Pulling off his blue Carolina ball cap, Calven bent the bill into an even tighter inward curve, then settled the cap back on his head. This done, he hawked experimentally but could find nothing worth spitting. Giving it up, he glanced at his watch and grinned.

Yeah, boy! Two-fifteen and right now I'm missing English class. Too bad ol' Dor'thy didn't get the notion for me to lay out of school yesterday—then I wouldn't have had to do that stupid oral report. Ol' Prune-face Hooper like to bust a gut when I said my piece about visiting Papaw in jail. Shitfire, I just done what she told us—interview an older relative and tell what all you learnt from 'em. I reckon I learned a lot from Papaw Roy—how to make a shank and how not to let anyone—

The clattering wing beats of a pileated woodpecker near at hand startled Calven from the pleasant recollection of his latest successful challenge to authority. He turned to watch the great black and white bird rise from a pock-marked, rotting tree and flap slowly away till it was lost to sight in the forest canopy.

Son, *that is one big bird! Pile-ated peckerwood. Dor'thy showed me in that bird book she brung home. She said some calls it the Lord God Almighty bird for when it jumps up like that, making all that racket, that's what folks just naturally holler out.*

"Lord God Almighty!" the boy shouted over the sound of the rushing water. Then, with a quick glance up and down the path and in a slightly lowered tone, he added, "Shee-it *fire!*" In the distance, the woodpecker's beak sounded an answering *rat-a-tat-tat* on another tree.

Wonder could you tame one of them things? Get it to set on your shoulder, maybe teach it to attack like them hawks in that movie I saw one time? Son, them peckerwoods look near as big and mean as one of them ol' dinosaur birds, them pterydactyls we studied about in science last month.

A rich green clump of mint growing at the water's edge caught the boy's eye and he edged cautiously down the steep bank. Plucking several stems, he put one in his mouth and chewed reflectively on it as he studied the streams of water hurrying over the mossy rocks. *They might be crawdads in there. . . . Wonder what ol' Prune-face'd do was I to—*

With a reluctant shake of his head, he put the half-formed idea aside. *Naw, I better get along. I promised ol' Dor'thy I'd come right on and help with the cleanup iffen she let me walk through the woods 'stead of riding in the car with her.*

Making his way back up the slope to the path, he resumed his climb. *Dor'thy said I couldn't get lost long as I stayed to the path and kept going up—said I'd come to an old barn and a chimbley standing on an open spot about halfway to the cemetery.*

After a few more minutes of walking, he spotted them—on the left in a clearing, just as Dorothy had described. "But don't you go fooling around in that barn, you hear me, Calven? That ol' roof might fall in on you. And stay clear of that chimbley—they's bound to be copperheads hiding in the rocks."

His aunt had hesitated, evidently regretting having given her permission. "I don't know; maybe you best ride up with me . . ." Her voice trailed off, leaving room for negotiation, and she had relented when he gave his word, promising to stay away from the barn and the chimney.

Ol' Dor'thy probably thinks this place's haunted. The thought produced a small, pleasant tingle that lifted the hairs on his forearms. He stood at the edge of the path and studied the remains of the abandoned farm, wondering how near he could approach without breaking his solemn promise.

His eyes narrowed. Wasn't that a kind of a trail leading from the chimney up into those dark trees? If he followed it just a little, he could say without lying that he had stayed on the path, was she to ask him. And most likely she would.

He'd learned his Aunt Dorothy's ways pretty good—had to. That was what made it easier to live with a person—knowing their ways—as long as those ways didn't change unexpectedly—in the middle of a sentence, sometimes, like his mama when she was using crystal meth. He wondered if there'd ever been a time when Mama hadn't been kind of scary—even back when he was real little, she'd dance him around the trailer one minute, calling him dumb stuff like her little man and her love bunny, and then the next minute she'd be crying and hollering and throwing things and she'd light outta there and not come back for days.

"Wimmen!" he exclaimed, just like Mama's one-time boyfriend Bib had used to do. At least Aunt Dorothy was old—real old, seventy-something—and set in her ways. She'd not be taking up with some lowlife biker like Mama was bad to do.

Bib. Rough as a cob, that feller'd been. Two years ago when Mama had gone into the hospital, Bib had stayed at the trailer to take care of Calven—that "taking care" had meant Bib lay around watching TV and drinking beer all day, leaving it to Calven to heat up a can of beans or make some macaroni and cheese out of a box.

'Bout all he was good for was to take me to the store and give me the money to buy food—I could of made it fine without him except for that. Course, I eat a world better now I'm living with Dor'thy. She may be old but she can sure cook—and she's always making cakes or pies. Yeah, boy, I like it fine, living at her place—if there was just a little more going on. And I could get by without church twice a week.

He stood thinking, not moving from the path, as memories of what had been gave way to thoughts of time to come. A cloud moved slowly to hide the sun and somewhere in the distance a rain crow croaked its warning, but Calven was lost in his vision, oblivious to the coming shower.

When I turn sixteen and get me my driver's license—now, son! that'll change everything. Get me a job after school; not have to ride that dumb bus no more. Maybe give ol' Heather a ride to school if she wanted to.

Two years ago Heather had been a scrawny little tomboy who waited at the same clump of mailboxes as him for the lumbering yellow bus to emerge out of the morning mists. She had always been quick to take offense at any teasing and quick to pick up a rock and hurl it, accurately more often than not, at the offender. She wasn't like other girls he knew—probably because she and her family were from away—New Hampshire, he'd heard her tell her seatmate on the bus one time, where there was a big white-painted house and where she spent every summer with her grandparents while her parents traveled on business.

Last August, when the yellow buses began to roll again, he had trudged reluctantly to the mailboxes, resigned to the first day of seventh grade. He'd been surprised to see a strange kid there, waiting at the usual spot, and he'd looked for the familiar fellow inmate—the skinny little girl, always dressed in an outsize T-shirt and baggy jeans, her scrubbed face and boy-short black hair usually topped by a ball cap like his own—well, not exactly like his own; hers was red because, out of plain old backwardness as far as he could tell, Heather was for N.C. State instead of Chapel Hill.

"Where's ol' Heather at?" he had said to the new girl who was standing by the mailboxes, staring down the road and tapping her running shoe in time to the music on her earphones. "She's gone miss the bus if she don't git her butt down here."

Shifting her fancy backpack from one shoulder to the other, the new girl had turned to stare at him with eyes that were somewhere between green and brown. Black hair curled softly to just below her chin and he could see the twinkle of gold in her earlobes.

"My butt is right here, smartass. What's the matter? Don't you recognize me?"

Now he could hardly remember when Heather hadn't worn girlie clothes—tight jeans with sparkly stuff on them, tight tops in girl colors teasing him to look at the softly swelling boobies—boobies that seemed like such miracles to him that they were the first thing he looked for every morning when he went to the bus stop.

The thought of being in a car with Heather, with her sitting maybe right up next to him like he saw the high school kids doing—hell, like some of the eighth graders did in the back of the bus—made him feel a little swimmie-headed and he sobered himself by looking for a rock to fling at the old barn.

But I ain't gone be sixteen, he reminded himself, *till two years and . . .* telling the months with his fingers . . . *two years and three months and some days.*

Beneath a nearby dark green bush, he spotted an ideal throwing rock, shaped like a large flattish egg and so smooth it must have come from the river. He left the path—*only a few steps, not to say leaving*—and bent down to claim this perfect missile. In the dim cavelike space under the strong-smelling bush, he saw more of the smooth rocks laid close to one another to form an oval there beneath the pale, rough branches with their tight little leaves.

Reckon how they come there? Got to be river rocks—but why'd someone want to . . .

Noticing a worn horseshoe hanging from a nail at one end of the log barn, Calven dismissed the question in favor of throwing the perfect rock at the perfect target. He returned to the path, squinted, took aim, and hurled the rock.

Clang! The thin curve of rusted metal shivered on its

nail and fell to the ground. A crash of shattering glass followed even before the resounding ring of metal had quite
died away. Calven frowned and went to investigate.

The horseshoe had dropped straight into a patch of
stinging nettles, and the boy looked around for a stick to
retrieve it. A dead branch lying nearby caught his eye and
with it he raked through the nettles in search of his prize.
As he beat the tender, treacherous stems to one side, a glitter of glass came into view. The horseshoe was lying in the
center of a pile of identical flat glass bottles. Some were
half-buried in the black dirt; some still retained all or part
of their labels; some were jagged shards.

*Reckon they's whisky bottles some feller done hid from his old
woman. Wonder how long they've been there? Some old bottles
is worth lots of money. If it wasn't for them nettles . . .*

Renewed efforts with the branch succeeded in scraping
one of the labeled bottles toward him, through the nettles
and within reach of his cautious fingers. After wiping the
label against his jeans, he held up the bottle.

*Cordelia Ledbetter Herbal Mixture—shoot, that ain't no
whisky. Still, it's an old bottle; might be worth something. Let
me see—*

The first drops of rain caught him by surprise. He
glanced at his watch and grimaced. *I'll come back, if this
un's any good. But if I don't get moving, ol' Dor'thy's gone fuss
like one thing.*

Shoving the bottle inside the light jacket he wore, Calven took off up the path at a trot.

The uphill grade had slowed the trot to a walk by the
time the rounded hump of the graveyard was in sight.

Calven stopped in the shelter of a big poplar and leaned down, hands on his knees, to catch his breath.

On the hogback ridge above him, the two women were weaving back and forth between the graves, moving with deliberate purpose, bending, straightening. Ignoring the light rain, they circled and stooped, returning again and again to a large black rounded shape, into which they dropped the bits and pieces they had been collecting.

It was Aunt Dorothy and Miss Birdie—he knew that. And they were picking up trash and the old plastic flowers and putting them in a big garbage bag—he knew that too. So why did the sight of them make him think of that witch scene those high school kids had acted out for the seventh grade, back around Halloween?

"Double, double toil and trouble," the witches had chanted as they danced and swooped around the big black kettle, dropping in the awful ingredients for their spells.

"Fire burn and cauldron bubble." Calven whispered the words, again feeling the tingle of the hair lifting on his forearms.

Chapter 36

Morning Light

Wednesday, May 2

(*Birdie*)

I'll dance you down and when you lose
I'll take away your dancing shoes.
But if you win, my dancing girl,
I'll send you free into the world.

I wake from the old dream, my legs aching and just a-twitching to the sound of the fiddle tune ringing in my head. Rolling over slow—ain't got no other speed these days—I pull up my knees, trying to make the jittering stop. For a minute I don't move—just lay there quiet, eyes squinched shut, breathing hard as if I really had been dancing. Seems to me I can still hear the sounds of fiddle and banjo, the slap of shoes on a wooden floor—sounds that fill up the room, swelling louder and louder—till it's like a scream building in my throat.

My eyes are still closed when I stick out my arm, reaching for the bedside table and my salvation. My hand shakes as I feel around but at last I touch the soft leather,

worn smooth by years of Luther's touch, and I spread out
my fingers and flatten them on the Bible.

"Safe once more, Lord," I whisper.

I lay there like that a little longer and mouth the Lord's
Prayer. If the Bible is my refuge, then this prayer is my
strength. The words won't wear away, ever how many
times I say them. In all these long years, how many nights
has there been like this—the music and the dream and the
memories? And ever time, they're there—the Book and
the Words—the Good Book and the magic words . . .
though Luther'd not want me to name them such.

Finally the wild fiddle music fades away and I breathe
easier as the old familiar sounds of first light creep into
the room—birds chirping kindly sleepy-like, the young
rooster off in the chicken house just a-tuning up, and that
rattle the Sims boy's diesel truck makes as he heads into
Asheville to work. I lay there listening and my breathing
begins to slow down. Once again, them old night fears has
been put to flight by the Book and the Words and the
coming of the Light.

I open my eyes.

I take my time with dressing and making up my bed.
They ain't much reason for hurry, not like in the days
when I had a cow to milk and Luther and Cletus to fix
breakfast for. I can go my own pace now and that pace
gets slower every year. I wonder . . . was I to gather some
herbs and brew a tea for the aching of the arthritis, would
Luther understand . . . making tea for medicine ain't
magic . . . I saw dog hobble yesterday but didn't pick
none. I could go back . . .

In the kitchen I get a fire going in the cookstove and

stir up some biscuits, then take Pup his breakfast, walking careful on the dew-wet grass. Time was I'd of run or skipped all the way to the doghouse but this old woman's body I'm wearing slows me down and reminds me what a fall could do. I can hear Dorothy in my mind, clear as anything, "Now, Birdie, you take your stick—at your age it's awful easy to break a hip and then where would you be?"

At my age . . . no, I don't want to think about that, nor a broken hip neither, but I take my stick and I take my time.

The sun is rimming the mountaintop and I stand a minute to watch it shake loose from the trees and jump up into the clear blue sky. It puts me in mind of a young un, anxious to be up and doing, sure that the day will have some fine thing in store. And as the light floods the hills, just filling my heart and soul full of a joy I don't deserve, I think of the old hymn and find myself singing the words in my mind. *I've found the sweet haven of sunshine at last. . . .*

There's so many hymns where the sun and the Son kindly run together. What's that other one, where they sing of daylight a-dawning in your soul? And there's yet another that calls Heaven "the morning land."

I quizzed Luther about this way back when we was courting; asked if the sun was Jesus and at first he said yes, but then when I told him about singing to the sunrise, he grew kindly puzzled. Finally he said that the sun was to *remind* us of Jesus and he didn't see no harm in me singing to it, long as I was mindful that the sun was Jesus's creature just like everything else—but that it weren't Jesus Himself.

Time was . . . time was whenever the preacher spoke of Jesus, I always pictured Him to look like Luther.

The sun is climbing higher, losing color and growing smaller as he goes, and, as he goes, in my head I'm singing him on his way.

When I come back to the house and look at the clock, it is most seven-thirty and breakfast not yet cooked, so I set in to roll out the biscuits and put them in the oven. Once the biscuits is beginning to brown and fill the house with their homey smell, I lift the old iron skillet onto the stove top, slide it to the back, and lay some nice thick slices of hog jowl bacon into it. When the bacon begins to sizzle and send out that rich smell, I open the firebox door and shove in a thick billet of dry poplar.

Why is it that after all these years my mind is turning back to those very things I promised to forget—swore to put behind me? The dream . . . that dream always comes before some trial . . . the last time I had it was when Cletus—

But Cletus is gone and I got nothing more to lose. If it's me that dark fellow Death is coming after, well, let him. I've made it a good bit past my three score and ten, and was I to drop this minute, I'd not feel cheated.

I take my fork and turn the pieces of bacon. Luther showed me the best way to fry bacon—slow and low and turning it over and over. In the green glass bowl I've just pulled out of the icebox, the eggs is pretty as a picture, all smooth and pinky-brown, with just a little bloom of dew coming on them in the heat.

Looking at them eggs and smelling the coffee and bacon, feeling the friendly warmth of the woodstove and hearing the cheerful crackling of the fire, I find myself wondering if Heaven can be as nice a place as here. I remember something that my granny told me once about these misty mountains of ours they call the Smokies. Granny said God hung that haze on purpose, to hide these hills from the folks up in Heaven who was raised here, so they wouldn't look down and be homesick.

I turn back to the cookstove and fork the crisp bacon out of the skillet and onto a flattened-out paper poke. Even after I have some for breakfast, they'll be plenty more to make a bacon biscuit for my dinner. I pour off most of the grease and take up an egg to crack against the side of the skillet when the sound of a vehicle rattling over the plank bridge in front of my house stops me short.

Now, who in the world . . . ? I think, putting the egg back in the bowl and pulling the skillet to the side of the stove top away from the firebox.

I start for the living room, wondering who would be stopping by so early in the morning. The meter reader was here not a week ago and them Witnesses don't generally come except of a Saturday.

Through the window I see Dorothy's old blue Ford. She flings the door open, hops out, and hurries towards the front steps, leaving that car door wide open; run down the battery, like as not. I wonder what can it be has got her in such a state. She ain't even put up her hair, neither, just pulled it back with a rubber band. That ain't like Dorothy.

I pull open the door and wait, dreading to hear what's the matter. She has flung on her clothes any old how— shirt buttoned all crooked and she has put on one black sock and one brown. Her round face is kindly flushed like as if she's been crying or fighting or maybe both and her mouth is set in a thin line. She marches up to the porch and through the door without a word, *terrible as an army with banners,* like it says in the Book, and when I can see her close to, the look of pure hatred on her face chills my heart.

"Why, Dor'thy——" I reach out and lay a hand on her shoulder, feeling the muscles just a-quiver like a dog about to fight. "Whatever is the matter? Why, you——"

Dorothy's face begins to crumple up. "Prin's took him, Birdie!" she cries and I know right off what has happened—Calven's no-good mama has got him.

"They come by this morning afore me and Calven was even up. There was all this knocking on the door and I pulled on a housecoat and run to see who it was."

Dorothy stops and goes over to my tissue box and grabs her a handful. The tears is leaking from her eyes and she jabs at them with a big wad of tissues before she takes up her tale.

"Prin had two mean-looking fellers with her and she pushed right past me and went and woke Calven up and told him to come with her and off they went, not even waiting fer me to pack up his things.

"Birdie, you got to help me!" She is squeezing my hand right hard but I look away. It don't deter her none; she goes on squeezing and insisting. "Remember, I *know* about you, Birdie—I used to hear my mother whispering to her sisters about you and the stories that was told and how Luther turned you from all that—I know what you can *do*. It's my best chance of getting the boy back. It ain't like Cletus—it was too late for you to help him. But Calven . . . please, Birdie, you got to! "

ॐ

No. 30.   ANCHORED IN LOVE DIVINE.

JAMES ROWE.   JAMES D. VAUGHAN.

1. I've found the sweet ha-ven of sunshine at last, And Je-sus is
2. He saw me in dan-ger and lov-ing-ly came To pi-lot my
3. His love shall con-trol me in life and in death, Com-plete-ly I'll

bending a-bove; His dear arms a-round me are lov-ing-ly cast,
storm-beaten soul; Sweet "Peace" He has spo-ken and bless His dear name,
trust to the end; I praise Him each hour and my last fleet-ing breath,

CHORUS.

And sweet-ly He tells His love. The tem - - pest is
The bil - lows no lon - ger roll.
Shall sing of my soul's best friend. The dan-ger-ous tem-pest for-

o'er,...... I'm safe........ ev - er-more,.... What gladness, what
ev-er is o'er, My anchor is holding, I'm safe evermore,

rap-ture is mine; The dan - - ger is past,........ I'm
The waters are peaceful, the danger is past, My

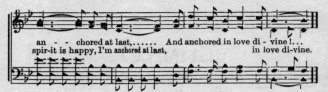

an - - chored at last,...... And anchored in love di - vine !...
spir-it is happy, I'm anchored at last, in love di-vine.

Chapter 37

Family Ties

Wednesday, May 2

(Dorothy)

". . . like a little wild thing Calven was, used to taking care of hisself. I know for certain sure he spent more time in that trailer without Prin than with her. She'd leave one of those worthless boyfriends of hers there to look after the boy while off she went to the Lord only knows where, doing the Devil probably knows what."

See how Birdie stares—reckon I sound like a crazy woman, Dorothy thought, suddenly aware of her friend's puzzled gaze. *And I'm purely trembling like a leaf. I got to calm down and make Birdie see that she must help me.*

But the words wouldn't be contained. They were flying out of her mouth in a great buzzing babble: All the dark suspicions she had hoarded, all the accusations and finger-pointings that she had restrained for the boy's sake poured out unhindered.

Her voice was rising higher and higher and the words were swarming into a dark cloud and she knew she should

stop but still she went on, clutching Birdie's arm and gab-
bling and gibbering like a tongues-talking believer.

"And why did she come back for him after all this time,
answer me that? Prin's got a use for him is why, and I
dread to think what it might be. Do you know there was
one time, and Calven not but seven years of age, Prin and
one of her boyfriends took him and they checked into a
tourist cabin so's they could use the kitchenette to cook
that old crystal meth. Calven told me about how something blew up and the feller got burned real bad—if it
hadn't been that Calven had gone outside to get Prin her
cigarettes from out of the car, who knows what might have
happened to him?"

Dorothy collapsed onto the sofa, breathing heavily. *Oh
Lord, what can I say to make Birdie see that she must help me?
And her just standing there like a carved statue while I yam-
mered on. I'll get down on my knees, if that's what it takes.*

At last Miss Birdie spoke. "So this here's the trial that's
coming," she muttered, lowering herself into the recliner
and stretching out her legs.

It took a moment for the words to register but when
they did, Dorothy sat bolt upright, exhaustion forgotten.
"You mean you knew . . ."

Birdie's face was still solemn as an undertaker's but at
least she was speaking and nodding in agreement. "Ain't
no doubt the poor little feller's had it awful rough. Never
knowed who his daddy was and then with a mother like
Prin—law, it would of been a sight better had Prin *stayed*
gone after running off like she did."

"Truer words was never spoke!" Dorothy dabbed at
her eyes but somewhere deep inside she sent up a brief
prayer of thanks. *She's coming round, I do believe.* "You

know I had just about got Calven tamed—though he's still fighting that lawless nature he was born with."

"Everybody says you've made a world of difference in that child." Birdie lay back in the recliner and closed her eyes. "When I think what he was like when first you brought him by here—not a *please* nor a *thank you* in his mouth . . ."

Much heartened, Dorothy chimed in. "His mamaw Mag *tried* when she had him, back when Prin first run off. Mag did her best, and that's the truth, but Calven's papaw—that Royal Ridder—he ain't no more fit to be around a child than them boyfriends of Prin's. And Mag won't never say no to Royal—she's a fool for that man—always has been. They might have been a chance, now that Royal's back in jail, but—"

Seeing her friend's lips tighten, Dorothy stopped mid-sentence. *Birdie never did have much use for Mag—and I can understand the why of that. But Magdalene's still my baby sister and a good somebody no matter what Birdie thinks. Mag would of done better if things had been different. . . .*

Dorothy looked down, trying to gather her thoughts, and caught sight of her uneven shirt front. "Now, will you look at that—buttoned all skee-jawed! I was in such a hurry to get over here I just throwed on my rags without paying any mind. Reckon I must look like a crazy woman, along with sounding like one."

Noticing her mismatched socks, Dorothy stuck out first one foot and then the other and gave a little laugh. "Maybe I'll set a new fashion. Leastways I managed to get out of my nightgown afore I jumped in the car to come over here."

Seeing the beginning of a smile at the corners of Birdie's lips, Dorothy went back to her pleading. Hands on her knees, she leaned toward the woman in the recliner. "But, oh, Birdie, if you could of seen them fellers Prin had with her . . . one of them was the wickedest-looking somebody I've ever seen; purely gave me chills to look at him . . . and poor little Calven, trying to act like going off with them weren't nothing out of the ordinary—"

She could hear her voice beginning to shake again. "You know how hard Calven tries to put on like he's a big tough man." Unable to sit still, she pushed herself up from the sofa, pulled off her glasses, and wiped her eyes with the back of her hand, forgetting the wadded tissues in her other.

Give me strength, Lord, to reason with Birdie and not go all distracted. Don't let her bow up on me again, Dorothy prayed as she began once more, unashamedly begging for help from the fragile-looking woman who continued to listen, eyes still shut, her expression telling nothing.

"The child looked so little and puny and scared when them two fellers got on either side of him and herded him out to that big van with the blacked-out windows—"

Dorothy felt her face begin to bunch up as she tried to keep from breaking down altogether. "I got to blow my nose," she said and stumbled like a blind thing toward the back of the house.

In the bathroom she dashed cold water on her face. *I'll just set down on the commode seat till I can feel some calmer.* Burying her face in her hands, she tried to pray but the thoughts would not be stilled. *Will Birdie help me, I wonder? Me and her ain't never talked of those things that the others whispered about, but if it's true . . .*

The smell of fresh coffee greeted her when she returned to the living room. She could smell bacon and hear the crack of an eggshell and a cheerful sizzle as the egg met the hot grease.

"Come on in here, Dor'thy, and get you a chair," Birdie called from the kitchen. "We'll have us some breakfast while we study on what to do."

Dorothy hesitated. *I must go gentle-like if I'm to get her help. Let her see that I've tried everything I can.*

In the crowded little kitchen Miss Birdie was standing at the woodstove, tending a black iron skillet in which two bright-yolked eggs were sizzling. On the table, two places were set and two moisture-beaded glasses of milk waited. Dorothy cast a guilty glance at the clock on the wall.

"Oh, Birdie! Eight o'clock already and here I've kept you from your breakfast. But my nerves are in such a state, I couldn't swallow a bite. I'll just set here with you while you have yours. I will take some of that coffee, though, if you don't care."

Taking a seat at the plastic-topped kitchen table, Dorothy added milk and sugar to her cup as Birdie lifted the eggs from the skillet and began to fix two plates. After a few sips of the hot, sweet brew, Dorothy was surprised to realize that she felt better and didn't protest when Birdie set a plate in front of her.

"Just eat what you can, Dor'thy. You got to keep up your strength."

"Oh, I . . . well, maybe just a bite." Dorothy picked up a fork and poised it over the perfectly cooked egg's swelling yolk as Birdie dropped into the opposite chair and began to butter a biscuit. This done, she set the knife back on the butter dish with a click and looked at Dorothy over the top of her wire-rimmed glasses.

"Now, I been studying on it and I think maybe the thing for you to do is to phone somebody at that place— what do you call those folks that was always coming around back when Cletus was alive, full of their quizzy questions and wanting to know did I need help with him? They're in with the Health Department—Social Services, I think it is. I recollect seeing their sign when I went for a flu shot last fall—"

"And whyever didn't I think of that myself?" Dorothy jumped to her feet, sloshing milky coffee onto the table as she clapped her cup down. "Those are the folks someone told me I would need to talk to if I wanted to be Calven's legal guardian. I'll just go give them a—"

"Set down, Dor'thy, and eat you a biscuit." Miss Birdie pointed to the clock. "It ain't but a little after eight— county offices don't never open early, and even was somebody to be there, they'll not pick up that phone till the stroke of nine."

"They've got me on hold again; every last one of them I speak to says *they* don't know but so-and-so might. . . . Hello, yes, my name is Dorothy Franklin. I'm calling about this nephew of mine that I've been taking care of. . . ."

Once more Dorothy launched into her story, ". . . his mother run off back of this and he was with his grand-mother. She's my sister but ever since she got sick she ain't able to do for the boy. . . . I'm a Certified Nurse Assistant and I've kept him in school and he's making C's now and some B's and I take him to church Sundays *and* Wednesdays. . . . No, I haven't got a lawyer; why would . . . No, I didn't know that. . . .

Almost forty-five weary minutes had limped by when

Dorothy at last set down the phone. "Lord-a-mercy but I feel like I been in a fight. Those folks . . . where'd I leave my coffee at?"

Catching sight of her half-finished cup of coffee on the table by the sofa, she grabbed it up and drained it. With a grimace of distaste, she set down the empty cup and collapsed onto the sofa, her body slumping in on itself like a deflating balloon. "I am flat wore out and that's the truth," she admitted.

Miss Birdie, who had been following the conversation from her recliner, took off her glasses and polished them on her shirt. "Sounds like things ain't much changed at that place. They used to aggravate the life out of me."

Dorothy leaned back, her eyes half-closed, and sighed. "I talked to everyone who'd listen and they all say that being as I'm not Calven's legal guardian, Prin has every right to take him back. This last woman I spoke to said that if I'd petitioned to be named guardian back when Prin run off, they could of helped me, but the way things stand right now . . ." Dorothy drew in a deep breath, opened her eyes, and fixed Miss Birdie with a stare. "The way things stand now is that the boy's gone and I've got no idea where to find him. I did hope he might call me, if they let him get to a phone. . . ."

A thought hit her and she was on her feet again and making for the door. "Which I need to get on home in case he *does* call. If I hadn't been so distracted, I'd of thought to bring my new cellphone. Calven knows that number too. Oh, Lord, why—"

"Dor'thy honey . . ." Miss Birdie was struggling to her feet, one hand outstretched, her wrinkled old face full of concern.

Dorothy stopped, one hand on the door knob. "Or

could be he's already called and left me a message. Ever-what, I'll try to get up with Mag and find out if she knows where Prin might could be. At least, if I know *where* the boy is, I'll not worry so bad."

"Dor'thy honey." Her old friend's gentle hand touched her arm and Dorothy froze, longing to hear that Birdie had changed her mind. *If only she will . . .*

"You know I'll do what I can, honey." The old woman's voice was filled with sorrow as she continued. "But what you was asking, I didn't even dare use to save my own. There's a danger in it, a danger that . . ." The words trailed away as Dorothy waited.

She didn't reply at first, then she whirled around. "Birdie," she said, and it was as though a stranger was speaking the hard cold words, "I can't be the judge of what's right and what's wrong here. All I know is, I want my boy back. You'll have to decide what's best for you."

The words seemed to be dipped in vinegar. Seeing Birdie bite her lip and hating the pain she had just caused, Dorothy reached out to take her friend's hand.

"Oh, Birdie, I don't mean to sound so harsh. My head is all a-swirl and I ain't myself. But I reckon there's one thing you *can* do for me—iffen Calven don't call and Mag don't know their whereabouts, what about that old neighbor of yours—the one who moved over to Tennessee? Didn't you tell me that she has the gift of prophecy and that she can find lost things? Well, I'm asking you to get up with her and see can she help me."

The devil in her couldn't resist adding, "Don't reckon that'll make you break no promises, will it?"

Chapter 38

Calven, Phone Home

Wednesday, May 2

(Calven)

I wonder have I been kidnapped? Can you be kidnapped if it's your own mama that has got you?

Calven stood by the door—it was locked from the outside; he'd just checked—and looked around the anonymous motel room—two double beds with brown plaid covers, a picture of a raggedy group of mailboxes hanging above his bed and the identical picture repeated above the other, a television with a lopsided antenna sitting on top of a chest of drawers, and two chairs at a small round table, where the big fellow called Darrell had left the bag from the drive-through. Calven rubbed the sore place on his shoulder and thought about the very strange day he was having.

"Calven baby, me and the boys got to go off for a while," his mama had said, ruffling his hair backward the way she always did. "There's you some lunch on the table and there's a cooler with some Pepsi and Mountain Dew in the bathroom. You stay here and watch TV and we'll be back this evening before suppertime."

Mama's looks hadn't changed much—still skinny with those big old boobs some rich boyfriend had paid for—before him and her split up—and, like always, there was bright red lipstick on her mouth and black stuff around her eyes till she looked like a raccoon. Her hair was a good bit lighter than last time he'd seen her—almost white and pulled back in a ponytail with dark roots showing all around her face. She had on tight jeans that showed her belly button and there was a new tattoo peeking out of those jeans in back, a heart-shaped design that sat right above her butt. A "tramp stamp," Heather had called that kind of tattoo one time, pointing to a picture of some rock star in the magazine they were looking at on the bus.

Calven wasn't sure how to feel about Mama coming for him the way she had. Poor ol' Dorothy like to had a fit when they took him out the door. He wished there was some way he could let Dorothy know he was all right, but the other guy—the scary-looking, weird-smelling one they called Pook—had yanked the phone right out of the wall as soon as they got in the room. Had patted Calven down too, like on the TV, just to make sure he didn't have a cellphone on him. The touch of those cold pale hands had been horrible—had made Calven want to squirm—hell, had made him want to scream. There was something bad *wrong* about this Pook guy.

And he didn't know either how to feel about being back with Mama again—he'd gotten pretty much used to the idea that she'd run off and left him and he'd told himself he didn't miss her, that she weren't no kind of a mama and he was better off at Dorothy's.

But still . . . when he had waked up this morning to see her setting there on the edge of his bed and when she had reached out and messed up his hair and said, "Rise and shine, Sunshine," like she had used to do back in the good times, he had sat up and hugged her hard as he could. He'd had to shove his face up against her bony shoulder to keep from busting out crying.

Those two fellows she had with her though—they looked like trouble. Darrell, the big one—and son, he *was* big—didn't seem like he was so mean but Calven reckoned Darrell would do whatever the other one said. And that other one . . .

"They call me Pook," he'd said, coming up real close and talking right in Calven's face. His breath stunk of cigarettes and bad teeth and his skin, even his shaved head, was the color of the belly on a dead catfish. He hadn't once taken off his sunglasses and that made it all the harder to figure him out. He moved like a young man but the dead-white skin of his face was a maze of tiny wrinkles.

This Pook wasn't real tall, maybe five foot eight—an inch or so taller than Calven, who was just now starting to get his growth—and so skinny that he looked kinda puny till you noticed the ropy muscles in his arms. And the tattoos.

Papaw Roy had tattoos something like these from his time in prison. Calven had seen them three years ago when he was staying with Mamaw and Papaw while Mama and her boyfriend went to Myrtle Beach. Papaw had been in a good mood that weekend and had told Calven a bunch of stuff he'd need to know was he ever to go to prison. Papaw had even taken a ballpoint pen and drawn a picture for Calven of the very same tattoo that was on Pook's forearm—a three-leaf clover, a Nazi swastika, and the initials A.B., all tangled together.

"Now, boy, you flat don't mess with no feller carryin' *that* ink," Papaw had warned him. "A.B. is the Aryan

Brotherhood and they're ever one of them mean as timber rattlers."

Calven had nodded his head. He had only been eleven but he had promised to stay clear of the Aryan Brotherhood.

Now Papaw Roy was back in prison, Calven was almost fourteen, and him and his mama were hooked up with a fellow wearing that very tattoo—a fellow who looked to be a sight worse than any timber rattler.

Mama had been jumpy as a cat when they all come into the motel room—couldn't sit still or even look him in the eye, but went to jittering around the room, pulling open the empty drawers and shutting them back, fluffing up the pillows on the bed he was setting on, and telling him they were locking him in to keep him safe while they went and did some business they had to do.

Calven figured they were going off to buy some reefer or crank or whatever it was they were using. He'd felt some better seeing there wasn't no kitchenette in this motel room. That meant they weren't planning to cook any meth, at least not now. He lay back against the pillows and flicked on the TV with the sound off while Mama went on spinning around the room, jabbering all kinds of stuff at him.

". . . so good to be back with my baby boy and we're gonna—"

"Sit down and shut up, Prin."

Pook's words were spoken quiet and slow—six little words in the sudden silence. They filled up the space around them and left no room for arguing. Pook hadn't even looked at Mama, nor raised his voice a lick, but her mouth had snapped shut as she dropped down onto one of the chairs at the little table and sat there without moving.

It had reminded Calven of the time Papaw shot a mourn-
ing dove out of the sky and it fell like a rock to lay there,
still and broken at their feet.

The big fella Darrell was setting on the end of the other
bed, staring at the muted TV where a cartoon cat was
chasing a cartoon dog up a tree. There was no sound at all
in the room except the dripping of the shower beyond the
open door of the bathroom and the squeak of the bed as
Pook came and sat down beside Calven.

The sunglasses and the bad breath had come up close
again, so close that Calven could see his own wide-open
eyes reflected on the shiny black lenses.

"Your mama says you're a good boy . . . and a smart
boy too. Is that so?"

Calven had squnched back against the pillows and
nodded his head.

Pook's hand shot out and grabbed Calven's shoulder,
pinching it between his thumb and fingers. "Speak up,
Good Boy, I can't hear you."

The cold fingers were jabbing into his neck in some
kind of a wrestling hold that was sending waves of pain
like an electric shock down his arm.

"Yessir," Calven had gasped. "I guess I'm pretty smart.
And I'm good . . . try to be . . ."

The iron grip relaxed but the hand stayed on his shoulder, gently massaging the area it had just punished.

"Well now, that's nice to hear. Because I've got a job for
a smart boy. And if you're good too, well, I reckon me and
you'll get along fine. The one thing you need to know
about working with me . . ." and the pincher grip of the
hand had tightened again, ". . . the one thing to keep in
mind is that when I say 'frog,' Good Boy, you had by God
better jump."

And the hand had dug into the tender place once more so that Calven had, indeed, jumped, and let out a yelp too.

Calven rubbed his shoulder again. As quick as Mama and the other two had left, he had gone into the bathroom and looked in the mirror. Just like he'd thought, there were round red marks where Pook's fingers had dug in.

"*Mother-f——*" he caught himself in mid-phrase and switched to "Son of a *bitch*!" whispering in the hollow stillness of the bathroom. He reached into the cooler, pulled out a Mountain Dew, and held the cold can against the red places for a few minutes, then popped the top and took a deep drink. He leaned against the door thinking, remembering Pook's parting words.

"You wouldn't be having any ideas about hollering for someone to let you out, would you, Good Boy?"

The sunglasses had stared at him from the door where Pook stood, one hand on the knob, the other holding to Mama's arm. Calven had started to say no, he didn't have no reason to holler, but Pook hadn't waited for an answer; he had just twisted Mama's arm behind her back and give it a jerk till the tears sprung into her eyes and she made a little sound like a hurt kitten.

"Because if I come back and you ain't here . . ." another jerk and he could see Mama bite her lips together to keep from crying out, "well, I reckon I'd have to make your mama pay for not teaching you to mind."

"I ain't gone do nothing but lay here and watch the TV," Calven had said in a hurry. "Why'd I want to go off anyhow, back to school and that ol' church twicet a week?" And he had pretended not to notice the tears running down his mama's face but had clicked the remote to surf through the various channels, keeping his eyes on the glowing screen till he heard them leave.

"*Son* of a bitch!" Calven whispered again, leaning against the locked door and brushing at his eyes. He was shaking all over. That Pook guy looked like a stone killer—and those last few minutes had made it real clear that Mama was bad scared of him. *Scared shitless, that's what Papaw would say. Pook's running things here, that's for sure. What did he mean, he had a job for a smart boy? Does that mean it was* his *idea to get me from Dor'thy . . . not just Mama wanting me back?*

The thought made his eyes water some more but he quickly wiped his forearm across them. The shaking had stopped and he could think now. *So what do I do? If I try anything, he's like to hurt Mama—maybe real bad. I reckon I just got to go along and see what happens. Keep my eyes open for a chance to get me and her away from him.*

The memory of that hand tightening its icy grip on his shoulder, the quiet, insistent voice, and the hopeless look of terror in his mama's eyes made him feel weak-kneed and swimmie-headed again. He swayed, putting a hand against the door for support.

Reckon Mama must have told him about me. The thought added to his unhappiness and he set it aside in favor of investigating the paper sack from the fast-food drive-through. He had eaten a couple of sausage biscuits earlier and they were making an uneasy lump in the pit of his stomach right now. *Still, might as well see what there is. . . .*

Two more sausage biscuits, two chicken biscuits, three containers of Tater Tots, and four fried apple pies. All cold and uninviting, but he took an exploratory bite of a fried pie anyway, then washed it down with the last of his Mountain Dew.

He glanced at his watch—8:51. First period was under way at school—Social Studies. *Wonder if ol' Heather thinks I'm sick—being as I laid out yesterday too. Wonder if any of them miss me.*

At least you ain't in school, he comforted himself. Flopping back on the bed, he clicked through the channels till he found a promising program—a rerun of an old cop show—and settling himself against the pillows his mama had fluffed up so careful, he thumbed up the volume and promptly fell asleep to the squealing of tires and the howling of sirens.

The day passed like that: dozing, watching TV, leafing through the Gideon Bible—though that quickly proved to be a bust as far as entertainment went—dozing some more. He was working his way through the Tater Tots and watching a kids' after-school show of some sort when the remote control slipped from his hand and hit the floor by the bed.

Without taking his eyes from the screen, Calven leaned over and thrust out his arm, groping blindly for the remote. His fingers swept across the gritty surface of the carpet, back and forth till they touched the little plastic box. Still watching the action on the screen, which was getting pretty stupid, he had to admit, he brought up the box, aimed it at the screen, and mashed a button.

Nothing happened.

Puzzled, he mashed it again, and then turned the device over in his hand to make sure he had the right button. His mouth dropped open.

He was holding a cellphone, one of those old kinds that didn't flip shut—a dinosaur of a cellphone no kid anywhere would want to be seen with. Paying attention now, he hung his head over the edge of the bed—there was the remote, on its side, way back almost touching the wall near the headboard. This phone had been just under the edge of the bed—here on the side close to the window.

Marveling, Calven mashed the button and the little screen lit up. He stared at it, wondering if he dared . . .

Then, out in the hallway came the sound of footsteps and low voices talking quick. Instantly, Calven slid off the bed and hurtled into the bathroom, locking the door behind him.

ॐ

Page *from* The Royal Path

~*~Mother~*~

It is true to nature, although it be expressed in a figurative form, that a mother is both the morning and evening star of life. The light of her eyes is always the first to rise, and often the last to set on a man's day of trial. . . .

Heaven has imprinted in the mother's face something beyond this world, something which claims kindred with the skies—the angelic smile, the tender look, the waking watchful eye. . . .

Mother! Ecstatic sound so twined round our hearts that they must cease to throb ere we forget it! 'tis our first love; 'tis part of religion. Nature has set the mother upon such a pinnacle, that our infant eyes and arms are first uplifted to it; we cling to it in manhood; we almost worship it in old age. . . .

Oh! there is an enduring tenderness in the love of a mother to her son that transcends all other affections of the heart. It is neither to be chilled by selfishness, nor daunted by danger, nor weakened by worthlessness, nor stifled by ingratitude. She will sacrifice every comfort to his convenience; she will sacrifice every pleasure to his enjoyment. . . .

Chapter 39

Memories

Wednesday, May 2

(*Birdie*)

I am uneasy in my mind about that child Calven. There's something don't set right about Prin coming for him like she done. I have a feeling, too, about those fellers that Dorothy said was with Prin . . . a bad feeling . . . but that won't make no nevermind to them Social Services folks Dorothy was talking to this morning. No, an old woman and her feelings don't mean dookie to young folks. They mostly stop seeing or hearing us once our hair goes to graying and our bosoms sag.

I set in to washing the breakfast dishes, and when they are in the drainer, I take the skillet and wipe it out good with the paper poke I drained the bacon on. I put the left-over biscuits and bacon on a clean plate and cover it with a dishtowel, then set it aside. Sometimes, when your mind's all distracted and running ever which way, just the doing of common everyday chores can calm a body down right good.

Poor Dorothy—that boy has come to mean the world to her. Not many women up in their seventies would take on a rank young thing like Calven and have the grit to make a decent boy of him. I have never seen her so done up—I can tell how upset she is by the way the country has crept back into her talking. All them years working in Asheville at fancy retirement homes has changed her way of talking to where she almost sounds like someone from away. "Getting above her raising," I once heard someone say of Dorothy. But it ain't so.

I am sweeping the kitchen floor when Dorothy calls to say that she's talked to her sister and that Mag didn't have no idea that Prin was back. *Or so she wants you to think,* I say to myself, not trusting Mag to speak the truth no more than I'd trust a cat with a baby bird. Nor has Dorothy heard aught from the boy, so once Dorothy has said her say, I don't wait no longer but call over to Tennessee to Belvy's house.

It is her daughter-in-law what answers, a sweet-sounding somebody, and she says that Belvy is visiting a sick neighbor. "I'll go get her long about three. Then she takes her nap, so's to be ready for church tonight . . . but I kin tell her you called. . . ."

Law, but it is welcome relief to hear they are holding church tonight. *Praise You, Lord,* I think. *Now, if You could see Your way to sending an Anointing . . .*

"Thank you kindly," I tell Belvy's daughter-in-law. "If you don't care, just tell her that Birdie is coming to church tonight and hoping for a message—she'll know who I am. Tell her I need to find a lost boy, name of Calven. And tell her . . . tell her I'm still trying to keep my promise. She'll know about that too."

I hang up the phone and think about my old friend and what I have come to see is her special Gift. When Belvy gets touched by the Spirit—what her church calls an

Anointing—she speaks prophecy and can tell where missing people or things is. Though sometimes it's like a riddle . . . or reading the Bible; you have to kindly untangle the words to get at their meaning.

If Belvy will help us, then maybe Dorothy will leave off trying to get me to go back on my promise to Luther and use the Gifts—the old ways.

I call Dorothy's number and she answers even before I hear the first ring. The eager hunger in her voice strikes to my heart and I say quick-like, "It's just me, Dor'thy. If you don't mind doing the driving, we can go over to Tennessee this very night. Belvy's church is meeting and if she gets an Anointing, maybe she can tell us where Calven is."

Dorothy don't answer right off and I think maybe she hasn't heard me. But then she says, kind of slow, "I thought maybe . . . if you just asked her, she could tell you . . . right over the telephone. Do we have to be there in the church for it to work?"

I know why she don't want to go but I just say, "I believe that we do, for good manners' sake—it's asking a lot of Belvy; whenever she receives the Spirit, it purely wears her out. The least we can do is to drive over to Tennessee and be there with her. She ain't a young woman, you know."

I hear Dorothy draw a deep breath and then she says, "It ain't the drive I'm dreading."

The whole day is before me—Dorothy has said she will come after me around five. The service don't start till seven but, even so, it's a good ways over to Cocke County and most of it on narrow winding roads. I hope we can take our time—sometimes Dorothy drives like she's hauling blockade liquor and the law is after her.

I am fidgeting like one thing and can't seem to settle down, so I call Pup and we set off for a little walk down the hard road. This time of day there's not like to be many cars passing, and after climbing up to the graveyard yesterday, I'm content to walk on the pavement where it is easy going and mostly level. Pup is cutting a shine and when he comes upon a stick laying by the side of the road, nothing will do but I must throw it for him.

I throw like the old woman that I am, not able to sail it through the air like I one time could, but Pup is happy to run after it again and again. At last he tires of the game and goes and lays in the branch to cool off.

Leaving him to waller, I walk on a little ways, then stop to rest by the mailbox at the old Ferman place. There is some nice folks from away has bought the place and are fixing up the house. They have a new mailbox with a cow painted on it and it is set in an old milk can. Law, how the memories come flooding back . . . back when me and Luther kept three cows.

That was when most everybody kept several cows and sold the extra milk. We had cans just like this one and would leave our full cans of milk at the mailboxes on Tuesdays and Fridays. Old Cameron Ridder had the contract to collect them, then haul them to the Pet Milk plant in Asheville. I remember how shocked they all was to find out that old Cam—and him a neighbor and a deacon in the church—was dipping a little milk from each can and putting it in with his—not much, but it added up to where he was getting paid for milking one more cow than he owned.

Luther took it hard, being a trusting sort of fellow. But

then him and Odus and some of the other men went and
talked to Cameron Ridder. They must have been right
persuasive for he made good on what he'd taken and
didn't try such tricks again.

I walk on a little ways, remembering the next Sunday,
after ever one knowed how he'd been stealing from his
neighbors—how old Cam, he got up and said a piece
about Jesus and the thief that was crucified with Him and
how that thief went to Heaven. And how after that didn't
no one treat Cam any different, for like the preacher said,
we are all of us lost sheep who have strayed and sinned
and we all must hope for mercy at the Day of Judgment.
And I knew that was so then, as I know it now.

We got us a new milk collector though.

I eat a bacon biscuit and some applesauce for my dinner and then I stretch out on the recliner to take a little rest
and watch my stories on the TV. There is a fellow in one
of the commercials who always puts me in mind of Cletus,
though he talks so fast you can't hardly understand him
and Cletus was slow-talking—when he talked at all.

Oh, there is still such a hole in my heart where my Cletus was! Of course I miss Luther but having a child to die
is just plumb out of the way things should go. Don't matter that I had lost so many before—Cletus was the one I
had the longest and losing him was the hardest—I won't
never get used to it.

I look in my Bible for the picture of my boy that I like
to keep by me. It was getting near wore out and my neighbor Lizzie Beth took it and made a copy and set it in plastic so's I can handle it all I want. I study it close and like
always the sight of his sweet smile revives my spirits. He

was a light in my life—a joy unlooked for after so many sorrows.

And as I think that, I think of Dorothy and how Calven has been a light for her—and now he's gone.

It ain't an easy feeling. At least I know that my boy is with Jesus and that is some consolation. I don't have to worry what will become of him. But Dorothy though . . .

The folks on the TV are fussing at one another and it looks like the wedding between Zack and Loring is put off again. I have missed what happened to cause it but I don't care. Somehow, without meaning to, I have made up my mind to see this through with Dorothy, come what may.

As I am putting Cletus's picture back in the Bible, some of the clippings I have saved between the pages fall on my lap. I look at them—there is the pieces in the paper about Cletus and there is the one about the little girl who disappeared. And there is some others I have to look at both sides and still I can't make out why I come to save them.

In amongst all these there is a faded red ticket and it most takes my breath away to see it. *Whatever is that doing in the Bible?* I think, and then I remember what Mr. Aaron said when he give it to me. *"If ever you have need for help—"*

The ring of the telephone breaks in on my thoughts and I grab it up, knowing it's Dorothy. I have a feeling all at once that she's heard from Calven.

"Birdie, he called!" She is most out of breath but she sets in a-gabbling. "He called and he was talking real fast. He didn't know where he was, a motel on the edge of some little town. He told me he'd been in the back of that big van and couldn't see nothing much but he *thought* they'd gone through Asheville and traveled east for about an hour. He said he was locked in and he'd found a cell-phone and that he'd get in trouble if they knew he'd called and we shouldn't on any account try to call him back. And then he said he was all right but he was afraid for his mama's sake and then he said . . ."

At last she stops. I can hear her drawing in a deep breath and letting it out with a little sobbing sound.

"Birdie," she says. Her voice is all a-tremble. "Calven told me he had to hang up quick because a spook was coming."

Chapter 40

With Signs Following

Wednesday, May 2

(Dorothy)

Dear Lord, what have I got myself into? I don't like snakes—never have, never will. What am I doing, going to where people pick them up and wave them around? Nasty, slimy snakes. Nasty, slimy, poisonous snakes. In church, of all places. And Birdie setting there just as calm . . .

Dorothy's Ford swung through a dizzying series of switchbacks that she negotiated almost unconsciously. Her mind was elsewhere. *Poisonous snakes. Poisonous snakes in church . . . Whyever I had to go and ask Birdie . . .*

The tires shuddered as they hit loose gravel on the shoulder, and Dorothy, averting her eyes from the steep drop-off, guided the car back onto the pavement.

"Belvy belongs to a Signs-Following Holiness Church," Miss Birdie had explained as they had set out for the drive through Hot Springs into Cocke County. "They go by a verse in the Bible . . ." and Birdie had begun to leaf through the well-worn book that rested on her lap. "Hit's in Mark . . ." The wrinkled old hands had made their familiar way through the pages. ". . . right here at the sixteenth verse. 'And these signs shall follow them that believe; In my name shall they cast out devils; they shall speak with new tongues; they shall take up serpents; and if they drink any deadly thing, it shall not hurt them.' "

Now Birdie was staring out the window, enjoying the scenery, as calm and relaxed as if she attended snakehandling services every day. Dorothy's hands gripped the steering wheel, her knuckles showing white. "So Aunt Belvy was neighbor to you at one time."

"Used to be she was." Birdie nodded in agreement. "But when their church moved over to Tennessee, Belvy and her folks went too. Hit's twenty years and more she's been over there."

Dorothy slowed to let a pickup that had been following close for miles pull around her. "I never heard of a church moving to another state. Why would they do that?"

"Well, honey," said Miss Birdie, rolling up her window to escape the cloud of black exhaust and the roar from the faulty muffler of the pickup as it strained to pass, "it was on account of they passed a law that in North Carolina, you can't handle poisonous snakes in church. So Belvy's gang packed up their serpents and moved across the line, over to Cocke County, Tennessee, where they don't have that law."

"But the snakes . . . they don't really bite, do they? Seems like I heard they pull their fangs or get rid of the poison somehow. Or dope them up . . ."

Dorothy glanced over to see Miss Birdie shaking her head. "Honey, them snakes is dangerous all right. Belvy's oldest boy died of a bite he got when he was handling in church. He'd been bit before and lived but this time . . . and Belvy's been bit several times her own self. She told me the pain was the worst she'd ever known but that the feeling of handling when she was under anointment of the Spirit was such that she'd not never turn aside when the Spirit called her, even after losing her boy that way."

The little woman paused, one hand resting on her Bible. "Yeah, buddy, Belvy's eat up with the Spirit. I just hope she gits a good dose of it tonight."

As they pulled into the crowded parking area in front of the church, Dorothy could see that the congregation was beginning to file into the modest building. *They look like regular folks,* she thought, then jumped as Birdie laid a soft hand on her arm.

"If you don't care, honey, it would be best was you to wait here till I've had a word with Belvy. These folks are a little shy of strangers at their services—there's been trouble back of this with people coming just to watch or even worse, to make fun, like their church was some kind of show."

Without waiting for a reply, Birdie stepped out of the car, almost before it came to a stop. She hurried with surprising nimbleness to intercept a tall white-haired woman being escorted to the church steps by two younger women.

Dorothy let out a long sigh. What was it Birdie had said? "Course, *I* don't believe that the Bible calls upon us to take up serpents . . . but I do believe that in a free country like America, it's only right that folks can worship how they want. And they're real careful about the children—always send them to the back before anyone so much as takes a snake out of its box."

Dorothy studied the small building. It was low and

modest, built of white-painted concrete blocks, and above its door a half-circle of plywood bore neat black lettering: *Holiness Church Of JESUS Love Anointed With Signs Following.* All the capital letters were outlined in red and the word *JESUS* was underlined twice.

At the foot of the steps, the tall woman bent down and embraced Birdie, then straightened and stood listening intently. Birdie was speaking rapidly, looking up at the imposing old woman whose impassive face wore a faraway expression.

So that's Belvy—Aunt Belvy, Birdie said the folks all call her. Will she be able to tell me where Calven is?

Birdie had said, in answer to this very question, "Yes, I believe she can. She's done it afore and she'll do it again— if the Spirit's on her. I may not worship the way these folks do but the Spirit moves on them; I've seen it happen. And when the Spirit's at work—God's at work and He can do all things."

Dorothy watched Birdie and her friend embrace again. They separated and, as Birdie came bustling back to the car, Aunt Belvy made her stately way up the concrete steps, with the solicitous aid of a dark-haired man in black trousers and a crisply white dress shirt.

As she climbed out of the car, Dorothy couldn't help saying to Birdie, who was motioning impatiently to her, "Well, they sure do treat your friend like she's the Queen of Sheba."

The minute the words were out, she was ashamed and started to say, "I didn't mean—"

Birdie lifted one finger. "Dorothy honey, don't you remember? I owe my life to that woman over yonder."

That woman over yonder . . . Dorothy studied the knot of silver-white hair and the alert set of Aunt Belvy's head. That was all she could see of the so-called prophetess who was sitting on the front row of the women's side of the church. Next to Aunt Belvy was the gray-haired woman who had welcomed them at the door and shown them to this pew at the back.

At least we're near the door, thank the Lord! Dorothy eyed the four squat plywood boxes ranged in a ragged row along the dais at the front of the room. Two had air holes arranged in the pattern of a cross on their side, a third had narrow slits, and the fourth, larger than the others, had big rectangles of hardware cloth let into the sides. Behind the metal mesh, Dorothy felt sure she could see the movement of heavy sliding shapes and she shuddered and closed her eyes. She bowed her head, praying with heart-felt fervor, *O Lord, don't let those snakes loose! I don't believe that I could stand it. Please, Lord, let that old woman tell me where Calven is. And please, Lord, keep those snakes in their boxes!*

Dorothy's prayers were interrupted as an electric guitar's earsplitting notes slid into the only slightly more annoying shrill of feedback. The musician, a teenage boy, glanced up in apology and adjusted one of the knobs on the red-painted body of his instrument. Hand-lettered in straggling capitals along the lower curve were the words AIN'T GOD GOOD?

The guitar opened the service with a foot-stomping, hands-clapping rendition of a familiar gospel song, its chorus consisting of a somewhat unsettling and often-repeated phrase suggesting that God was going to set sinners' fields on fire. Dorothy's voice was loud and true and she was happy to be singing. It took her mind off Calven for the moment . . . and off the snakers. At her side Birdie was singing more softly—evidently unsure of both words and tune. Both women were clapping, their elbows bumping now and again.

Dorothy watched intently as the dark-haired man who had helped Aunt Belvy up the steps took center stage on the dais, clapping and singing while his eyes roamed the pews.

Now, I believe that's Brother Harice, the one who brought the healing service to Birdie back when she was so sick I thought we was going to lose her. Birdie says he's a right powerful preacher. But, my, doesn't he look like he thinks he's God's gift to women! I suppose some might think he was good-looking with those sleepy eyes and poochy lips. Kind of what old Elvis might have looked like if he hadn't run to fat. No sideburns though.

She watched as Brother Harice unleashed a lazy smile, seemingly directed at a curvy young woman sitting just behind Aunt Belvy. There was the slightest suggestion of a wink as one eyelid quivered briefly, then the preacher raised a hand in the air and threw his head back, moving from side to side in time with the beat as the gospel song drew to its triumphant finish.

The last note still hung in the air when the preacher, hand pointing upward, head thrown back in rapture, called out in a voice that filled the little sanctuary.

"Rejoice and sing, brothers and sisters! It's His Holy Word moving here tonight. Do you feel it moving?"

The question brought forth a flurry of responses.

"Lift us up, O Lord!"

"Amen! Preach it, Brother!"

"Bring the Word! Hallelujah!"

The voices came from all sides—from the pew directly in front of Dorothy where a plump, grandmotherly-looking woman sat, a string of towheaded children beside her; from the men's side and a gaunt-faced man in new dark blue overalls; from one of the three heavily built men sitting on the bench to the side of the dais. Other cries of "Amen!" urged the preacher on and the guitar emitted a rapidly ascending glissando of notes, the sound climbing higher and higher to end in a shattering reverberation.

The church was ready.

"They call us ignorant hillbillies; they persecute and outlaw us believers for following the Signs!"

Now Brother Harice was pacing rapidly, back and forth on the little dais, as he exhorted the congregation. Dorothy was fascinated to see all the heads following him, *like the crowd at one of those tennis games on TV,* she thought, as she realized that her head was swiveling too.

"They say we put our children in danger every time they set foot in our church house . . ." A subtle undercurrent of no's swept through the congregation. "But I say those children are safer here . . . here with the serpents and the fire and the strychnine . . ."

"Praise Him!"

"Amen, Brother Harice!"

". . . safer here in God's House among God's people . . ."

The dark-haired preacher left the platform and strode down the aisle to lay a gentle hand on the head of a toddler, drowsing in her mother's arms. "Oh, it's a safety not of this world, brothers and sisters! It's the safety found in the loving heart of Jesus; it's the safety in the Signs and the power in the Blood . . ."

Dorothy looked past the preacher to the front of the sanctuary where a tapestry version of Leonardo's *Last Supper* shared the white-painted concrete block wall with a good-sized rectangle of varnished plywood. Here the same hand that had lettered the sign above the church door had copied down the significant verses: the lines from Mark that set this church apart as Signs Following.

> *And these signs shall follow them that believe;*
> *In my name shall they cast out devils;*
> *They shall speak with new tongues;*
> *They shall take up serpents;*
> *And if they drink any deadly thing, it shall not hurt them.*

Her gaze shifted to the snake boxes and a feeling of nausea swept over her. *I can't stay in here with them things,* she thought, and tried to stand so as to slip out the door but her legs felt as if they were made of butter. Beside her, Birdie was staring gape-mouthed at the slim-hipped, lazy-eyed Brother Harice, who was working his way down the short aisle, capping each child's head with his outspread hand.

"*Maneda sujornam,*" he called out, as his hand left the last child. "*Haremma loyavan bekoot!*"

Swinging his arms up and down as if trying to fly, the preacher turned in a slow circle, still spouting a gibberish of tongues, then hopped back down the aisle toward the dais, riding an invisible pogo stick. The congregation began to respond, at first with amens and hallelujahs, then with unknown languages as well.

The little building rocked in a Babel of tongues as Brother Harice reached the dais and picked up the largest snake box. Pitched just beneath the unintelligible phrases sounding on every side, Dorothy could hear a dry whirring.

She frowned and strained her ears to identify the

sound, then, with a sudden and involuntary shudder, realized that what she was hearing was the warning hum of several very agitated rattlesnakes.

Mesmerized, she watched as Brother Harice, his face contorted in an expression halfway between pain and rapture, undid the sturdy latch of the box. Without pausing, he pulled open the top and plunged his hand in amongst the quivering shapes that slid, coiling and uncoiling, just behind the hardware cloth screen.

Dorothy covered her eyes with one hand, praying for deliverance.

And these signs shall follow them that believe;
In my name shall they cast out devils;
They shall speak with new tongues;
They shall take up serpents;
And if they drink any deadly thing, it shall not hurt them.
Mark 16:17–18

Chapter 41

Prophecy

Wednesday, May 2

(Birdie)

Poor Dorothy! I hadn't thought how hard this might be for her. She went white as a sheet when Brother Harice picked up his serpent box, and she looks yet like she might faint. Of course, some folks is fearful of any snakes at all—like my Luther. He purely couldn't abide them, even the rat-killing blacksnakes or the pretty little ringnecks, hardly bigger than a worm. He'd go for a hoe quick as ever he saw one. But after I spoke with him some on the subject and told him I'd catch them and move them if they was harming aught, he agreed to leave them be. He never could stand to see me holding one though, always found somewhere else to be when I went after the snakes.

Now Dorothy has both hands over her face like she is praying but I know that it's on account of the serpents she don't want to look at. I hate it that she's so scared and I reach over and pat her shoulder, trying to let her know it'll be all right.

She lets out a squeak and jerks away from me, keeping them hands over her face just as tight.

"Dor'thy," I say real quiet and close to her ear, not that it's likely anyone is paying any mind to us with all that's going on up at the front of the church. "Honey, if you feel sick-like, why don't you go set in the car? Belvy'll understand and ain't none here will take it wrong."

Her voice comes out from between her hands. "I'm all right, Birdie, really I am. I'll stay here. I'll do it for Calven—anything to get my boy back. I just . . ."

I don't get the rest of what she says, what with the racket of the guitar and the rattle and ring of tambourines and a confusion of voices all around. Some folks is standing, waving their hands in testimony; others is kneeling and praying aloud. A few rows ahead of us there's a woman dancing a little two-step out in the aisle, and seeing her face, how she is lost in the music and the movement, makes me remember a time when I danced till my feet bled—with a smile on my face the whole time.

Brother Harice hands the yellow rattler he has been holding to one of those big fellers from the elders' bench who lays it across his shoulders and goes to skipping across the platform. They'll keep the snakes up there or near the front; Dorothy needn't fear that one of them'll come near her.

They's some of the Signs Followers treat the serpents awful rough—laying them down to walk on and slinging them around ever which way. I have heard of one feller who used a big rattler like a skip rope, but that was way back when Belvy and her man first took up with these folks, back when the church still met in Marshall County.

Not too long after I talked to Belvy about how them fellers was doing the snakes, she had an Anointing and prophesized that them what didn't respect the serpents as instruments of God's will would be bit. At first, didn't nothing change, but after the one who was using the rattler for a skip rope got bit and died within the hour, the handlers, in this church anyhow, begun to treat the serpents better.

Up at the front, Belvy is setting quiet in the midst of all this commotion. I can't see but the back of her head but I know she is something set apart—a calm center in this storm of worship.

Seems like long as I've knowed her, Belvy has been seeking after God. When first she was married and away from her mother, she tried one church then another till she must have got saved more times than she can remember. Made her feel good, somehow. But then it would kindly wear off and she'd find something wrong with the preacher or the teaching or the other folks in the church and she'd move on to another—mostly Baptist, of course, Hardshell, Freewill, Missionary, and I don't know what all. One time she even got mixed up with the Presbyterians—but that didn't last. Belvy likes her preachers to work up a sweat when they bring the Word.

Brother Harice has pulled out two copperheads now, one of them kindly dusty and pale looking, being just a few days from shedding his skin. Snakes is often extra touchy before they shed, as they can't hardly see, the old scales over their eyes having got all cloudy, but this one don't give the preacher no trouble. It just hangs there quiet as Brother Harice brings it up to his face and stares eye to eye with it. The second snake, its skin shiny and new, is rank and ill-tempered. It twists in the preacher's hands, thinking about escape.

The first time I saw a snake shed its skin, I thought it was a miracle—the snake looking like it was dying and then the old tired skin just shucking off and a new snake coming out the mouth of the old, leaving behind the too-small skin and crawling off to start life all over. The scales is fallen from its eyes, like Saul in the Bible, I thought to myself back then.

There is a hush falling over the congregation and now Belvy is on her feet, one hand raised high. I wonder if she's getting an Anointing, if she'll be given a message that will help us find Calven.

The other time she sought an answer for me, Belvy spoke in tongues and whirled about before she come and stood in front of me to speak the prophecy. But now she is just standing there, not moving a muscle—like she had been turned to stone. She could be one of them prophetesses of old—mighty women like Miriam or Deborah in the Bible.

She stands there like a tall tree, so straight and still, and I see how folks look at her—how they step back and give her room. Every one of them calls her *Aunt* Belvy, like they all want to claim kinship with her. She is the cornerstone of this church, no matter that being a woman, she can't preach. She can still prophesize and, buddy, when she speaks under an Anointing, they all of them perk up their ears and listen.

It was '40 or '41 when Belvy first went to a Signs-Following church; I know she had gone several times and had already made up her mind to join before she finally come by the house and told me about it. I could see right off that something was different for her face was shining like the dawn of day.

Now, Belvy was always a pretty woman and she liked to

dress up fine and fix her hair just so whenever she went out but on this day she'd left off the red lipstick and the earbobs she was so proud of. I didn't know it at the time but that's the way of the Holiness women. Vanity, they call it, to wear makeup or jewelry.

"Birdie," she said to me, taking my hands the moment she come up on the porch, and I remember thinking that even her voice sounded different, kindly *humming*, like a plucked guitar string. "Birdie," she said, "I have at long last found what I been looking for—a church so filled with the Spirit that it just naturally overflows. I have been an empty vessel all this time but now the Spirit has filled me clean to the brim."

She smiled at me then, a smile I remember just as plain—like there was light pouring out of her mouth and her eyes. And even without the lipstick and with her pretty hair slicked back from her face and pulled into a knot, at that moment she was the most beautiful woman I ever seen. Buddy, that light was just *pouring* out of her, like she was so full of the Holy Spirit that it couldn't be held back.

And that was it for her—there weren't no more shopping around for just the right preacher or church. Belvy and her man both joined with the Signs Followers and afore long it was the center of their life. Of course, she was after me to join and I did go with her a time or two. But Luther'd not put a foot in that church and it didn't set so well with him when I did. So after a time I told Belvy, as kind as I could, that her church weren't right for me.

Back then and now too, watching the Spirit move on the folks in the Holiness church, whether they're singing or testifying or taking up serpents or drinking poison or shaking tambourines or dancing before the Lord—it all puts me in mind of that time in my life that I promised

Luther to forget. But most of all, it is the dancing brings it back.

In another place I had seen people dancing till they was crazy . . . had danced that way myself till I like to run mad . . . and I knowed well how powerful that feeling could be and where it could lead. No, I was happy for Belvy but I told her then I'd not be joining her church. There was too many sleeping memories—

"Mabor abakad! Oowdutto mebavnith!"

And all at once Belvy is standing in front of me, shouting out words the Anointing has brought upon her. Her hair, still long but white as snow now, has come loose from its knot and is falling round her shoulders and down her back. Her eyes is rolled back in her head but she stands there looking at me with that blind stare and I know full well she sees me. I am on my feet now, drawn up by her power.

She is full of the Spirit again and this time it's not beauty that I see in her but Power and terrible knowledge. The Spirit clothes her like a garment and reaches out in a mighty swirling cloud—all dark blues and purples like a storm—to cover me too. I feel a stirring deep inside and the sounds in the church falls away. All I can hear is a mighty humming that crowds into my head and goes to working its way all through me. My body is trembling with the Spirit and I am held inside this spinning place of dark and light. And the humming breaks into many voices that sing and shout their different messages and then come back together, joining up to make one voice— one message. Inside the whirlwind I can hear the one voice speaking to me and I marvel to see God Himself in pieces, turning into many Gods, and not all of them human-like neither. They are whirling all around me—long white robes and naked bodies, fur and feather, fin and scale, male and female and neither and both they are—but all Gods past knowing. And then, like the voices, the Many join into One and the One is whispering inside my head.

Yes, I answer, *now I see . . . yes, I know now . . . yes, I will.*

And the whirlwind slows and becomes a cloud and the cloud melts away and it is me and Belvy standing there face-to-face, the each of us filled with a dreadful knowledge. She is speaking her words of prophecy and I . . .

And now I begin to remember . . . and now I begin to know . . .

I know that the old paths—the ones I turned away from when I made my promise to Luther—those old paths are alive with power and waiting . . . waiting for me . . . if I dare to walk them again.

"Was that a prophecy—those things she said to you?"

Dorothy is feeling right much better, now that we're in her vehicle and heading home, away from the church and the snakes. Her face was pale and sheeny with sweat all through the service and once I saw her sway like she was going to faint but she stayed in her seat.

I pat her arm and try to think of how to explain things. "Some of it was speaking in tongues—that part in the beginning that didn't make no sense at all. And then those other things she said—some was Bible verses, I'm right sure. Those words about seeing the wicked in great power and spreading like a mighty tree."

Dorothy's eyes are on the dark highway ahead. "I didn't hear in all those words nothing about where my Calven is."

"Oh, Belvy was speaking prophecy all right," I say, knowing Dorothy is disappointed not to have got a clearer message. I pat her arm again. "There was a message for you all right. What you got to remember, honey, is that verse about 'through a glass darkly.' The truth is in the words but it's up to us to puzzle it out. That's the way the Spirit does."

"Why don't you just call Aunt Belvy tomorrow and ask her what she meant?" Dorothy is holding back a yawn as she speaks, and I know that she is wore out with the battling of her hopes and her fears.

"Why, Dor'thy," I tell her, "Belvy don't ever remember a lick of what she says when the Spirit's speaking through her. You saw how she swooned, there when she'd finished, and those men caught her and helped her back to her seat. She gets plumb knocked out by the Spirit passing through her—she told me once that it was like to a great wind sweeping through a house and clearing everything out. No, honey, she don't remember nothing."

Dorothy dims her headlights as a pickup comes around the bend ahead, then, once it's gone past, puts them up high again. She travels considerably slower now that it's dark, for fear of a deer or some other animal running across the road.

"Birdie," she says after a while, "even if Aunt Belvy don't remember saying the words, maybe she could help us to understand what they mean."

I smile, thinking back to the first time I asked Belvy to explain the things she had cried out while laboring under an Anointment. "Do you ask the mail carrier to read your letters to you?" she had said, kind of surprised at my question. "That's all I am—just a mail carrier bringing messages from the Lord. I hand 'em over and it's up to you to read 'em yourself."

I start to tell Dorothy this but she is busy saying over parts of the prophecy and making guesses at what the words might mean. I put my face to the open car window and take in the rich cool night smells of the woods and the mountains—not all that much changed from times long back, not in the parts that is still wild.

Something has wakened in me since I found myself wrapped in the Spirit that fell upon Belvy. And I think . . . if this wakening come upon me in church, ain't it from God? Ain't there just the one God, however you name Him or worship Him? The God of the Cherokees and the God of the Holiness folk . . . and my Luther's Freewill Baptist God—all the same. Mighten it be that God is sending me back to all of Granny Beck's teachings, the same ones I turned from so long ago? Mighten it be this is all to His purposing?

The dark woods and slopes out there seem most as clear to my eyes as if it was day, and I yearn to be in amongst the trees. The wild places still hold their secrets and I remember . . . time was I could slip through the midnight woods, silent as any fox, hearing every leaf fall, scenting the track of the wild things, and feeling in the trunks of the old trees, the life power being pulled up from the earth beneath.

I still could, the wild girl that hides behind my wrinkly old face calls out. *Let me try . . .*

But Dorothy don't stop talking, just yammers on and on, pulling me back into now, back into the car where she is making her guesses.

"That one thing Aunt Belvy said, 'As is the mother, so is her daughter'—now I reckon that must mean Mag and

Prin." Dorothy sounds sad as she says this. Her sister Mag has been a sorry someone all her life and a great trouble to Dorothy.

"And what about that thing she said—something about a lodge in the wilderness for wayfaring men?" Dorothy goes on. "Maybe *that's* where Calven is! They's all kinds of tourist cabins and lodges all through the mountains—not so many in Marshall County as in some of the others but still . . . might be something to think about."

But even though I want to believe that Granny Beck's Powers and Gifts was from God—the one God—I am troubling over the words that Belvy said just before she swooned, words that went straight to my heart.

"There is no peace, saith the Lord, unto the wicked. Thou shalt not suffer a witch to live."

Chapter 42

Schooling

Thursday, May 3

(Calven)

There ain't nothing to it, Good Boy. I'm gonna start you at pickup, but once you get the hang of it, I believe you could make a pretty fair dip. Be better if you was smaller, but with that baby face you ought to do all right."

Pook's sunglasses looked Calven up and down and the boy felt a chill run over him as the unseen eyes studied him and foul breath surrounded him. Preserving a stony silence and what he hoped was an indifferent expression, Calven lifted his chin and stood his ground.

I got to go along with this. Play along and wait till me and Mama can get away.

They had left the motel in the early morning hours and now they were in a plain little house out in the middle of nowhere. All Calven could remember was Mama waking him and telling him they were leaving. He had managed to ask to use the bathroom before they left and had taken

care of what he needed to do. Then it was down the stairs
and out into the half-lit parking lot where he'd heard the
sound of traffic on a highway near at hand but there hadn't
been time to look for anything that would tell him where
he was.

Not that it mattered, since they were on their way
somewhere else. Pook had told him to lay down on the
back seat and go to sleep, and though Calven had thought
about trying to look for road signs when the sunglasses
weren't turned on him, he'd shut his eyes just for a
minute, so's he'd look like he was obeying, and he'd gone
and fallen deep asleep, only half-waking when they
bumped down the long dirt road that led to this little
cabin in the woods.

Then big guy Darrell, with a flashlight in one huge
hand and the other on Calven's shoulder, was pushing
him up the steps, through a front room with a brick fire-
place, and into a room where there was a cot with a thin
lumpy mattress and a musty-smelling sleeping bag.

"You stay here." Darrell had glanced at the chunky
stainless steel watch on his wrist. "Couple a hours till
sunup. You might as well get some more sleep. Pook's
meaning to start your schooling first thing after breakfast."

The big man turned to go.

"Wait a minute!" To Calven's disgust, the words had
come out high-pitched and quavering. He cleared his
throat and tried again. "They ain't no light in here."

Darrell swung the flashlight back to illuminate the little bed. "Well, git in and close your eyes. Won't matter if
it's dark—"

"Would you hold the light while I shake out the sleeping bag?" *Don't leave me in the dark by myself,* he wanted to

beg. "I just want to make sure they ain't no mice or such in there."

To Calven's surprise, the big man had done as he asked, standing patiently while Calven unzipped the sleeping bag, shook it violently, and spread it back on the cot.

"Thanks a lot." Calven nodded at Darrell, controlling his fear and trying for a man-to-man gesture. He shucked off his shoes and scrambled into the sleeping bag. " 'Preciate it. See you in the morning." He had turned on his side with his back to the door and the hulking Darrell.

"You gone sleep in your clothes?" The voice had been soft and almost motherly.

"Yeah, I mostly do." Calven pulled the sleeping bag up around his chest. "Night."

The metallic click of the bolt lock seemed to set loose all his fears, and Calven lay trembling in the suffocating darkness of the room. Trembling, *like a damn baby girl,* he jeered at himself, trying to regain his nerve.

Schooling—what had the big man meant by that? *Ol' Darrell don't seem that bad but Pook—I don't know what it is about him but I don't see how Mama can stand to be around him, much less— Shitfire, he's like something out of a horror movie—one of those bad ones me and Bib used to watch.*

For a moment Calven allowed himself to wonder about the sunglasses Pook wore, even at night, but as quickly as the thought—*What if he ain't got no eyes, just empty sockets behind those black glasses*—began to form in his mind, a wave of cold terror swept over him and he curled himself up small inside the sleeping bag.

Stop it, you big ol' baby. You ain't doing a thing but scaring yourself. You got to get real . . . make a plan . . . got to play along till you can get loose.

He yawned, exhausted by the long day and its unexpected events. *Ain't nothing gonna happen . . . just play along,* he reassured himself before sinking into deep sleep and troubled dreams.

When the first hint of morning had begun to lighten the narrow horizontal window high on the wall, Calven's eyes opened. The paralyzing fear of the night before was gone with the darkness. And now he had a plan.

He ran his fingers under the waistband of his underpants. He'd begged ol' Dorothy to buy him boxers but somehow she was convinced that boys, *active* boys, she had stressed, needed tightie whities. As he felt the cellphone there against his johnson, he had to agree.

I still got it—but will it work *way out here? Wonder how much charge it's got left. I could try calling Dorothy but . . . ain't nothing I can tell her about where we are. I'll just turn it on and make sure . . .*

Mashing the little button, he had been appalled as a tinny jingle rang out in the silence of the small room. Frantic, he had hit the button again and shoved the phone back into his briefs. Lying frozen in stark terror, Calven held his breath and listened for sounds in the rest of the house, expecting the door to fly open at any minute, expecting rough hands to seize him . . .

Shit, shit, shitfire! If ol' Pook heard that, or Darrell either, they're gone be all over me.

It had seemed to him that the thump of his heartbeat was loud enough to waken the rest of the house, but as time passed and no other sounds could be heard, he gradually grew calmer and could even hear the *rat-a-tat-tat* and raucous cry of a pileated woodpecker, as well as the soft calling of doves, and another bird somewhere that seemed to be saying *Chick weed teeeee.*

Son! That was close. But least I know the battery ain't dead.

When many minutes had passed and still there was no sound from the rest of the house, Calven folded the sleeping bag into a many-layered square, poised his finger over the cellphone's power button, and plunged the phone into the middle of the folds of padding. Taking a deep breath and breathing a desperate prayer, the boy pushed the button and waited.

. . . three, Mississippi . . . four, Mississippi . . . five, Mississippi . . . He let ten more seconds go by before withdrawing the cellphone from the muffling folds of the sleeping bag.

The light from the display panel fluttered as he deliberated. Would it be better to call 911 or Dorothy? His fingers hovered over the nine.

What would he tell 911—that his mother and her boyfriend had kidnapped him? And what then? Even if that was enough for them to send help, he had no idea where he was. No, might as well call Dorothy again—

The little square of blue light flickered and went dark.

"You set over there and pay attention, Good Boy."

With the coming of full day, Calven had been let out of his room and, after taking a whiz that must of lasted five minutes, he'd been given a box of strawberry Pop-Tarts and another Mountain Dew for breakfast. Though there were light sockets and switches, the power didn't seem to be on, and besides, there wasn't any toaster in the bare little kitchen.

Calven ripped the paper off one of the Pop-Tarts and

bit into it. *Might as well be cardboard with a little sweet stuff in it. One thing about ol' Dorothy, she likes to cook a hot breakfast.*

The thought of sausage or bacon and eggs and biscuits with jam and big glasses of milk made his mouth water. He took another tasteless bite, then lowered himself obediently onto the sagging sofa as Pook and Darrell prepared to give him his first lesson in picking pockets.

The big man took his place in the middle of the dirty linoleum floor, standing still and gazing off into space, and Pook moved to stand a little behind him.

"Now Darrell's gonna be the mark, the guy I'm trying to take a wallet off of. Darrell's too big and too slow to be any use in this game—mostly he'll just be waiting in whatever vehicle we're using, ready to get us out of there if there's trouble. But if everyone does their part right, won't be no trouble; you understand me, Good Boy? Your mama and those big tits of hers is the bait—what some call the 'stall'—"

"Where *is* my ma—where is she, anyhow?"

Pook turned the sunglasses on Calven and showed his teeth in something like a smile.

"Don't you worry none about your mama, Good Boy. Me and Prin had us a little party last night and she ain't up yet."

Pook's shaven head tilted toward a closed door on the farther wall. "Let her get her beauty sleep and we'll just pretend she's standing there in front of Darrell, rubbing them big tits against him and acting all helpless 'cause she just twisted her ankle. That's one way we do it—Prin comes sashaying along in them high heels and right when she's passing in front of the mark, she stumbles. Being he's a gentleman—and that's the only kind we bother with—he reaches to catch her and while she's batting her eyes at him and giving him a good feel—"

Pook jabbed Darrell in the ribs with his thumb. "You'd like that just fine, wouldn't you, Darrell?" and Calven was surprised to see a pink flush creep over the big man's face.

"While the mark's standing there worrying about that hard-on he's getting, the dip—and that'd be yours truly . . ."

Pook's long white fingers had hold of the lining of Darrell's back pocket. They were deftly pleating the thin material, bringing the wallet closer and closer to the top. It took only seconds and the fat brown wallet was in Pook's hand. He grinned at Calven.

"Now this is where you come in. You walk past me and I hand the wallet off to you. You drop it inside your pants."

A thought seemed to occur to Pook. "You wearing briefs, Good Boy? Or them faggot-ass boxers?"

For a moment Calven couldn't make his mouth work, than he managed to croak a reply. "I got briefs on. That's the only kind of underpants I have." The dead cellphone at his crotch seemed at least the size of a football and he had to force himself not to look down. *I got to hide that thing somewheres and do it soon.*

Pook nodded in approval. "Okay, one less thing to worry about. Now, while your mama is still doing her act, most likely the mark won't notice nothing for a while. You go this way, I go that way, and when your mama gets done, she limps off—remember, she's supposed to have a bum ankle—she goes in another direction, blowing kisses back at the mark. Hell, sometimes the mark'll try to follow her and make a date but that's when she starts going on about the big ol' jealous boyfriend that she's on her way to meet.

That kind of talk usually cools 'em down right quick. Meanwhile, you and me is going to the different places that we've set and Darrell comes and picks us up. We get down out of sight and then he picks up Prin—the big ol' jealous boyfriend, just like she said, in case the mark is watching. Slicker 'n owl shit—if everyone does their part. You reckon you can handle pickup, Good Boy?"

Without waiting for an answer, Pook moved to the small table that divided the living area from the kitchen and began to paw through the plastic grocery bags heaped in its center along with the heavy flashlight Darrell had carried the night before.

"Where's the peanut butter Nabs? I know we bought some of them. I can't eat those stinking toaster tarts or whatever the hell they are."

Calven shivered at the cold menace in Pook's voice and watched as Darrell began to sidle uneasily toward the front door. Pook's shaven head jerked around. "Did *you* eat my fucking Nabs, you greedy son of a bitch?"

The big man hung his head but didn't speak. Three quick steps and Pook was at his side, the long tube of the flashlight in his upraised hand. Without pausing, Pook swung the flashlight, burying the metal butt in Darrell's belly. The big man doubled up with a single gasp and then was silent.

Turning back to the table and pulling a bottle of Pepsi from one of the bags, Pook spoke again in a quiet, conversational tone. "Now take the van and go get me some more peanut butter Nabs. You know I don't eat no sweet shit."

Without speaking, Darrell hurried out the door, still crouched and clasping his stomach. There was the sound of dry retching, then of the van door slamming and the vehicle starting up and pulling away.

Pook twisted off the bottle cap and took a long pull of the drink, swallowing almost half the contents before stopping for a breath. Then he dropped onto the sofa beside Calven and fumbled in his shirt pocket for a pack of cigarettes.

"Want one, Good Boy?"

Calven looked at the pack in Pook's outstretched hand. "No thanks . . . wouldn't care for none . . . not now. But I was wondering . . ."

Calven frowned and studied his feet. *I got to do this right. Make him think I'm not scared of him.* "That thing you did—the way you pulled the pocket up—it wouldn't work if the guy was wearing jeans."

"The boy's paying attention—reckon he's as smart as you said he was, Prin."

Calven jerked his head up to see his mother sidling out of the door across the room. She looked pale and sick— one eye was swollen and bruised and there was a round red mark on the side of her neck. She made her shaky way to the table and grabbed a bottle of Pepsi, then shuffled back to the bedroom, glancing once toward Calven but not meeting his eyes.

"The princess ain't quite ready to be sociable, I reckon. You and me'll just have to pass the time someways."

The blank black gaze turned on him again, looking him up and down, and Calven had to fight to suppress the shiver that was threatening to sweep over him.

"How old did Prin tell me you was?"

"Fourteen . . . almost." Calven had to force the words out. There was something in the pale man's face . . . in the tone of his voice . . . a hunger, a *need*, that made this simple question terrifying.

"Fourteen . . ." Pook nodded, speaking low and to himself. ". . . a long lifetime of years ahead. That's good . . . very good."

He seemed to consider an idea that was forming, to weigh it, and then, somewhat reluctantly, to put it aside. He leaned back on the dusty cushions and lit a cigarette.

"You was asking about jeans. Now, I can snake a wallet outta a pair of tight Levi's as pretty as you ever saw. But what we're after is cash and credit cards. Reckon who's likely to have the most cash and the biggest credit line—a fella in jeans or a dude in high-class trou?"

Pook blew a stream of smoke toward the ceiling.

Act like you want to do this. Like you think this is cool. Calven leaned back, in imitation of his mentor, and yawned. "Yeah, I see what you mean. So that's what you come and got me for, to work with you uns. I can do that pickup stuff, no problem."

The colorless face was turned toward him, nodding slightly in what looked like approval.

"Maybe I will take one of them smokes now." Calven stuck out his hand. "And then whyn't you show me how to do that trick with the pocket? I bet you *I* could do that."

⌖

Part of an article from a travel magazine

Guarding Against the Professional Pickpocket

The pickpocket wants your cash . . . and your credit . . . maybe even your identity. Your ATM card, driver's license, passport, checkbook, Social Security card . . . all have value in today's criminal market, and the pickpocket is happy to relieve you of them.

A pickpocket is always on the lookout for a "mark"—someone whose attention is elsewhere and someone whose wallet or purse is easily accessible. The pickpocket sees the mark but the mark rarely notices the pickpocket—who may look like a harried suburban mom, a distracted senior, a respectable businessman—anyone who blends into a crowd. The professional pickpocket is very different from a "snatch and run" amateur; the professional pickpocket's goal is to take your possessions and vanish before you realize that you have been robbed.

The best prevention is awareness—women should never leave their purses unattended. Nor should they be left open. Shoulder bags should be worn cross-body and carried in front. A wallet in a back pocket is an open invitation to a skilled pickpocket—carry it in a front pocket or, better yet, use a hidden money clip.

Often pickpockets work as a team—one doing the actual thievery while the other acts as a . . .

Chapter 43

Witchery

Friday, May 4

(*Birdie*)

I got to wondering about witches because of something Aunt Belvy said in her prophecy, 'Thou shalt not suffer a witch to live.' "

Dorothy is pacing about my living room, looking at my pictures and fiddling with my doodads on their little bracket shelf. Every few minutes she goes and looks out the door like she was expecting someone to drive up. She says she has gotten too fidgety to sit home and wait for Calven to call again, so she has brought her new cellphone over and is spending the day with me. She also says she wants to help me with some cleaning but all that she is doing is worrying the life out of me.

Now she is looking out the window that faces the road. "That's from the Bible, those words about not suffering witches, isn't that so?"

"Why, yes, I believe it is," I tell her, and look at the Bible there on the table by my recliner, knowing I could name chapter and verse, since I'd read it over and over during the past few days. Seeking understanding, as you might say, but getting none.

The sound is turned low on the TV but I can see from their faces that Ashley is right upset with Brent—probably along of him stepping out with her best friend. She has just slapped him across that good-looking face of his and he has caught hold of her wrists and begun to kiss her but Dorothy don't seem to notice and goes right on jabbering.

"Now, the old folks always used to talk of witchy women," says she, running her finger along the slats of the venetian blinds to see if they need dusting, "but never like there was anything wrong with them. My mamaw—Uncle Luther's own mama—had charms to get shed of warts. Why, she even *called* it 'witching the warts.' "

Dorothy ain't going to leave off, I can see that. And now there's a commercial coming on anyways, so I mash the button to cut the sound all the way down.

"Well, everyone knows about water witches," I say, "the kind that can show you where to drill a well. And the thrash doctors what blows in a baby's mouth to cure the thrush and the folks who can take the fire out of a burn. But—"

Dorothy waves her hand like she is shooing flies. "I reckon those are all good witches. Or maybe not even witches at all. But what about the bad ones—the kind that Bible verse means? What about those? Have you ever heard of a kind of witch called the Raven Mocker?"

Though the day is unseasonable warm, the sound of that evil name sends a chill over me. I start to turn the TV back up, hoping not to hear more, but Dorothy has got a bug in her bonnet and just keeps going.

"I never had heard of any such, but last week Calven brought a book home from school that he has to do a book report on. He always struggles so with those reports and I've taken to reading the books myself so as to be able to help the child *and* to make sure he gets all the way through . . . otherwise he'll try to make do with reading just the first and the last chapters."

Dorothy leaves off messing with the window blinds and goes and sets on the sofa facing me, I reckon so's she can quiz me all the better. For the first time I see how tired and wrung out she looks. Her eyes is all red like she ain't been sleeping and, even setting down, she can't stop fidgeting while she talks.

"This book is all about the Cherokee Indians and their stories and what all they believed. Some of the tales is really nice and have a good little lesson at the end, almost like a Sunday school piece—but there's this one about these Raven Mockers . . ."

She trails off and don't say no more but just sets looking off into space. I don't want to talk about them old Cherokee witches, not with Dorothy nor anyone else, and I mash the button to turn up the sound on the TV.

I am just in time to hear Ashley tell Brent that her best friend is carrying Brent's baby. I can see that this is a surprise to him and he don't want to believe it, but then, at the same time, that he reckons it *could* be so. Huh! That so-called best friend is nothing but a common huzzy and, if it was me, I wouldn't give her air in a jug. And Brent ain't never—

"Birdie?"

"What is it, Dor'thy?" I cut the sound plumb off and set up in the recliner. I can see I'm going to have to give some kind of answer to all these questions.

"Do you know about the Raven Mockers?" she asks. "Great awful old things like evil birds . . ."

She looks as pale and frightened as she did back at the Tennessee church and she is doing her hands like she was washing them, rubbing them over and over without seeming to notice.

"Birdie." Her voice is low and trembly-like. "Birdie, I keep having these dreams . . . And every night I dream that it isn't Prin what's got Calven, but one of them Raven Mockers like in the book."

On the TV screen, the people in my story all of a sudden look like paper dolls moving around and I wonder why I have spent so much time worrying about their sorry doings. I point the remote control at them and watch them disappear.

"Dor'thy," I say, "let's us step outside into the sunlight. If we have to talk of such things, the daylight is the place to do it."

"The first night after Prin took Calven away, I had the dream . . . that there was this *thing* . . . well, you know how it is in dreams . . . I couldn't rightly say if it was man, woman, or a great huge bird. But it had big black wings . . . and it made a horrible laughing sound. . . ."

We have pulled our chairs to the sunny end of the porch, and though it is warm aplenty, Dorothy's words strike a chill to my bones. But I know I must hear her story and so I have brought her out into the open, where the winds can blow away the ugly words and the sun can burn off the cold dark evil.

"And in the dream, Calven is laying there and I can't tell is he dead or asleep. And this great Rav—"

"Hush, Dor'thy," I say, "there ain't no need to speak that name. I know what you're talking of."

She cuts her eyes over at me. "I had thought that you might. I heard Uncle Luther telling Mommy, oh, many and many a year ago, that you had learned a lot of Injun ways from your granny . . . and that he didn't reckon they squared with scripture."

I had figured as much. Once I made my promise to Luther, him and me never spoke of the past no more. And I know that I never spoke of it to ary soul. But from things folks in his family let slip now and again over the years, I was right sure he had told at least part of my story to some of them. And Dorothy's mother was the sister he was fondest of.

"Well, Dor'thy," I say, feeling somehow aggravated with poor, long-gone Luther, "it's been a right smart of time and I believe I've been as good a Christian as most. But go on and finish telling me about these dreams. You say you been having them every night?"

She closes her eyes. "Every night I put off going to bed because I don't want the dream. I been sitting up in the living room with the TV on, trying to stay awake, but every night, sooner or later I drop off—I can't help it.

"And then I'm back in the dark place where Calven is laying so still and this black thing is coming for him. I try to holler or to run at the thing but I can't move and I can't make a sound. And then I wake up."

"Dor'thy honey, have you—"

She looks at me and her eyes is wild. "Birdie, I have prayed and prayed. I have fallen asleep with a prayer on my lips and the Bible in my hands and still the dreams come. But the worst is that every night, in the dream, I am farther away from the boy and every night the black thing is closer to him. And in the dream I know—"

She is crying hard now and I say, "Hush, honey, it's all right; you don't need to talk about it."

But she don't pay me no mind. She is sobbing and choking but at last she says the words I had dreaded to hear.

"B-Birdie, last night it was leaning right over Calven, and its black hand or its claw, everwhat it was, was reaching down to the boy's chest." She grabs hold of my arm and she is wailing like a crazy woman now. "I know . . . I know as sure as I'm alive, if I have the dream tonight, that thing will reach in and pull out Calven's heart."

She looks around again and now her voice is naught but a whisper. "Birdie." I can't hardly make out the words but I see them on her lips.

"Birdie," she says, "the creature means to eat it."

Chapter 44

Going to Water

Friday, May 4

(Birdie)

They was a time when I had bad dreams . . . dreams of Old Spearfinger standing by my bed, and I would wake crying and shivering and crawl in bed with Granny Beck for her to hold me and comfort me with her soft words. But when I got to crying out in my sleep two and three times every night, Granny said that we must get rid of the bad dreams for once and all. That was when she showed me what the Cherokees called Going to Water.

And because I fear what will happen if Dorothy dreams that one last dream, I decide at last to break my promise to Luther.

I think I already knew I would, back at the Holiness Church when the Voice in the whirlwind told me that they is more than one way of knowing God and so, "Dor'thy," I say, "let's you and me drive down to the river. I believe that I can stop those dreams."

"This here is something my granny did for me when I was little and had real bad dreams," I tell Dorothy as we are driving along the dirt road that runs from the bridge back up to the burying place.

"It seems to me," I say, trying to convince both of us that I am right in what I purpose to do, "it seems to me that if your prayers and your Bible ain't helping against this Cherokee witch that has got into your dreams, then maybe a Cherokee spell will do the trick. Do you have a handkerchief or some such with you?"

She looks at me, kind of doubting, but I know that she is past arguing. "I have a bandana there in the glove compartment. A blue one."

"That'll do just fine," I tell her. "Now here at this wide place in the road, you can pull over and park. The riverbank ain't too growed up and it's easy to get to the water long about here."

She pulls over, cuts off the engine, and starts to get out but I say, "Now, Dor'thy, I'm trying to remember the words my granny said more than seventy years ago. So while I'm working this charm, I don't want you to speak for fear I'll get bumfuzzled and not be able to finish, do you understand?"

Dorothy is wide-eyed but she presses her lips tight together and nods, then reaches over and pulls a folded blue bandana out of the glove compartment. She offers it to me but I tell her to hold on to it. And so we make our way to the water, just as Granny and I did so many years ago.

Me and Granny couldn't get all the way down to the river, though she said that it would have been better. It was hard enough for her to hobble out the back way and to the little branch that bordered the field back of the house. But it had been a wet April and there was water enough. . . .

When we have reached the river's edge and the water is lapping around the toes of our shoes I am happy to see that long-leggety gray bird is out there. He is most always somewhere on the rocks of the river and it wouldn't seem natural not to see him.

"Now, Dor'thy," I say, "you hold the bandana in your right hand and close your eyes. I'm going to dash some water over your head. When I've done it seven times, then you open your eyes and throw the bandana in the river. As it goes to float away, I'll say the charm that'll end the bad dreams."

She nods and squinches her eyes shut. I lean on my stick and bend over to catch some water in the jelly jar I have brought for the purpose. It ain't much but it is enough that Dorothy jumps when I pour it on her head and it dribbles down her face.

"No, leave it be." I catch her hand as she is bringing the bandana to her face. "Let it work to wash away the bad memories and the fear the dreams has put into your mind."

I wonder what Dorothy would think was I to tell her how the Injuns used to do this spell. If we did it the old way, she would take off every whipstitch of her clothes but her shirt and then she would wade out and dip herself all the way under seven times. Then she would take off the shirt and let it float away.

It makes me smile to picture what folks would think was someone to pass by and see two old women, one standing naked in the river. Even as we are, I'm just as glad don't no one travel this way but very seldom.

By the time I have bent down and scooped water seven

times, my old back is about give out. But Dorothy's head is streaming wet and on her face is a little smile like she is already feeling some calmer.

"Now, Dor'thy honey, open your eyes. Take that bandana and put all them bad dreams in it, wad it up, and throw it in the water."

She does just like I say and, for a wonder, she ain't let out a peep. I believe that this is the longest I have ever been around Dorothy without her saying something.

We stand there in the sunlight, watching the water take the bandana. The river is fast-running and the blue cloth is soon out of sight, heading for the bridge and on its way to Tennessee—if it don't catch on something first.

The sparkle of the sun on the water blinds me and the steady *hurring* sound of the water busying along fills my ears. And as I let the river sounds run through my head, wiping out all that the years has put there, Granny Beck's words come back to me.

"*Oh see yoh*, listen here, Brown Beaver and White Beaver," I say, speaking strong and clear to the listening ones. "This is Dor'thy. Her soul has been released. Her soul is lifted up."

The sound of the river catches my words and carries them along but not before I can hear that it is Granny Beck's voice coming out of my mouth. Dorothy is standing stock-still, her face lifted to the sun and her eyes closed again. She has a look . . . I reckon you might could call it a look of abiding peace.

There are more words to the spell, and without even thinking on it, I open my mouth and they spill out.

"The soul has become changed. The soul has been lifted up. The evil is released."

I know that it has. I have felt its going. But I say the

last part of the spell—or Granny Beck says it . . . I can't tell no more.

"The soul has been changed. The soul, made pleasing, has been lifted up to the seventh world."

When the last words are spoke, I lean on my stick and watch the river and the gray bird wading on his queer back-jointed legs, not wanting to break into whatever has put such a smile on Dorothy's face.

Then all at once her eyes blink open. "What in the name of goodness—have I been asleep standing up?"

She gives a little shake and the water flies from her hair. She puts her hand up to it and feels of it. "Standing in the sun and sweating like a pig. Well, I never—but you were right, Birdie; a breath of fresh air was just what I needed. I feel just fine—there ain't a bit of headache left."

We drive back to the house and all the way she is chattering about how much better she feels and how she's going to go home and do some cooking for she feels it in her bones that Calven is coming back soon.

". . . one of those big chocolate pudding cakes. I can put it in the freezer and . . ."

Her chatter is like the sound of the river, running on and on. She has forgot all about the dreams and the spell.

I hope . . . I hope that it was the right thing for me to do.

As we get to the bridge and turn back onto Ridley Branch Road, I look across the river up to the old house at Gudger's Stand, all abandoned now with its windows like blind eyes. I can pick out the one that was mine and re- member how many a time I would lean out, longing to be gone from that evil place but held by my fear.

And then I hear the whistle of a train and the rumble and the rattle drawing near and I look away. There is so many things I wish that I could forget—but there ain't no one to take me to water and wash away my sins.

When I call Dorothy the next morning to ask has she heard anything from Calven, she says no. But I can tell by the sound of her voice that she is feeling a world better and I ask her how she slept.

"Oh, Birdie," says she. "You know I always sleep good—my head hits the pillow and I'm out like a light. Why, I sleep so hard I don't even dream."

ॐ

Page from the "Swimmer Manuscript": Cherokee Sacred Formulas and Medicinal Prescriptions

This Is (for) When They Have Bad Dreams

Now, then! He belongs to such-and-such a clan; he is called so-and-so. He has apportioned evil for him; where is the (one who) usually apportions evil staying?
     Now, then! Ha, now thou hast come to listen, Brown Beaver. He has apportioned evil for him. But now it has been taken; he is called so-and-so. The evil has been taken away from his body.
     Yonder where there is a crowd of human beings thou hast gone to apportion the evil. He is called so-and-so. His soul has become released. His soul has been lifted up. The soul has become changed. The soul has been lifted up.

Now, then! He belongs to such-and-such a clan; he is called so-and-so. He has apportioned evil for him; where is the (one who) usually apportions evil staying?

Now, then! Thou White Beaver, at the head (waters) of the stream thou art staying; quickly thou hast arisen, facing us. He has apportioned evil for him. But now it has been taken away. The evil (which) has been apportioned for him has been released. It has been scattered where there is a crowd of human beings (living).

Who cares what happens to it! The soul has been changed. The soul, made pleasing, has been lifted up. Up to the seventh upper (world) the soul has been raised. Sharply!

Chapter 45

Working

Saturday, May 5

(Calven)

The mark was a middle-aged man in khaki trousers and a pink knit shirt. They had watched him at the ATM machine and they were watching him now as he checked his watch and looked up and down the street. From the van's passenger seat, Calven studied him, waiting for Pook's directions.

"So, Good Boy, reckon why we're goin' after this one?"

Pook was lounging on the back seat, one arm draped around Calven's mother, who was adding a fresh layer of deep red lipstick to her mouth. Oversized sunglasses hid most of the black eye, and heavy makeup covered the rest of the bruising. Her hands were shaking and she didn't look up from the small mirror she was holding. Pook turned toward Calven, awaiting an answer.

"Well, we just saw him get a whole wad of money. And we saw him stick it in his left front pocket—not his wallet. Plus them pants he's got on—they got them loose pockets, easier to work than jeans."

Pook nodded. "Okay, so far. Now, I want you to go over there where those kids are fooling around—put yourself near to them but not in amongst them. You got that thing plugged in your ear? Fine. Make you look natural. Now get out and be ready to cross behind me soon as I've got that roll of bills. Keep going to the pickup spot—Darrell'll get you first. Let's make this slick and quick—start the day with a little bankroll. Then we'll be moving on and see how you do at something else."

Something else? Calven started to ask but a movement of Pook's hand made him reconsider. As he climbed out of the van, adjusting the iPod bud in his ear—*just like ol' Pook to give me an iPod without no music on it*—there was a tap on the back seat window and the tinted glass slid down a careful few inches.

"Like I said before, Good Boy, you get a notion to run off, it'll be your mama takes your punishment, you hear what I'm saying?"

Calven could see nothing beyond the window, but along with the cold menace of Pook's warning, he sensed his mother's fear oozing like a bad smell through the narrow opening.

"I done *told* you," he said to his reflection in the dark glass, "I know what I'm supposed to do and I ain't going nowhere."

The window slid shut and Calven, feigning a nonchalance he didn't feel, slouched across the street toward the noisy group of teenage boys milling about in front of the bus stop. Two had laid aside their knapsacks and were engaged in mock-karate combat; some were talking on cellphones; some were busily texting or playing games, thumbs flying on the tiny keypads. Not one even glanced over as Calven shambled to a spot near them, stopping to study the colorful posters affixed to a power pole at the edge of the sidewalk.

As Calven pretended to read the posters, he saw the van pull away and make a left at the next corner. Pook was on the sidewalk, hurrying in the opposite direction, a folded newspaper under his arm. He was dressed very much like the mark—pleated-front khaki slacks and a green knit shirt. A dark wig covered his shaved head and, except for the bad teeth, he looked like a hundred other guys.

Calven watched as Pook came to a corner, waited for the light, then crossed. Pook was heading his way and Calven moved around the power pole to see if the mark was still in place—yes!

In spite of his fear, Calven found himself excited by the prospect of what was to come. It was all working so far. Pook was slick—that was for sure. The mark stood there, looking at his watch. Then he moved away a few steps and Calven's heart skipped a beat—would they lose him?

No, he was looking in the window of a bookstore—and now Princess made her appearance from around the corner where the van had turned. Her skirt was long but slit high on the side and the bright orange tank top she wore could have been spray-painted on. Calven saw several men turn and stare as she went by, her high heels tapping on the sidewalk, but she ignored them, advancing on the unsuspecting mark.

As soon as Pook had passed him, also heading for the mark, Calven made his move. Pretending to pull up his pants, he retrieved the dead cellphone from his briefs and palmed it as he moved closer to the two knapsacks lying on the ground. Here he dropped to one knee and fumbled with his shoelace; when he was sure no one was looking, his hand shot out and swapped the phone in his hand for the one lying on top of the knapsack. Standing up again, Calven reached under his shirt to heist his low-riding, baggy shorts, then headed toward the mark.

He had to hustle to make the pickup. Just like Pook had said, right when his mama was next to the man in the pink shirt, she had stumbled, letting out a little *eek* of surprise and falling hard against the mark. Pink Shirt had been quick to catch her and slow to let loose of her, standing there with a foolish look on his face and asking her was she all right.

She played her part real good, holding on to the mark and jabbering a mile a minute while she held her foot up and twisted her head round to look at her shoe. The heel had broken off just like Darrell had fixed it to do. And while she was rubbing up against the mark and thanking him and all, Pink Shirt never noticed the dark-haired man next to him, the one who was reading the signs taped up on the window of the bookstore while his hand worked the lining of Pink Shirt's pocket up and up.

At the last moment, Calven made his cross—just another typical thoughtless teenager, so busy listening to his music that he bumps into responsible adults. He ricocheted off Pook, mumbled an incoherent apology, and continued on down the sidewalk *don't run, whatever you do, but keep moving* and around the corner to the waiting van. The roll of bills was riding safe at the back of his briefs— undetectable under the long, baggy shorts.

And at the front, snug against Mr. Johnson, was the little cellphone one of the karate kids had stupidly left on top of his backpack, unaware of the apprentice pickpocket who was watching.

Calven smiled. He was learning fast.

"You did okay, Good Boy."

They were back in the van, heading out of the city and north. Pook was in a good mood—which, Calven thought, was almost scarier than his usual low simmer of anger. Pink Shirt had evidently had some big plans—there was five hundred dollars in the roll of fifties. Pook had gotten Pink Shirt's wallet too and there had been almost nine hundred in there, as well as the credit cards they had already used to lay in supplies before disposing of them and the wallet in a trash can at a fast-food place.

"Use the cards first thing—before an hour's gone by—then toss 'em; that's the safest way. It'll take ol' Pink Shirt back there a while to get over cussing about his missing cash, then, when he thinks to check for his wallet, he'll spend some more time cussing and looking around for us and it'll likely be a good bit before he thinks about calling to cancel his cards. And since I lifted his cell too . . ."

Pook held up a sleek blue and silver flip phone and grinned with an unpleasant display of brown teeth. ". . . well, you know how hard it is to find a pay phone anymore. Shit, he may not have called them cards in yet. But use 'em and lose 'em in the first hour—that's my rule—and we'll stick to it."

Calven awoke from a dozing, after-lunch dream of Heather and her boobies to find that the van was parked on a dirt road. Mama and Pook were outside, pulling on white coveralls, and just then Darrell appeared by the window. He was carrying one of those magnetic signs that stick on cars and trucks and he gave Calven a friendly wink as he clicked the sign onto the door panel.

Yawning and rubbing his eyes, Calven opened the door and climbed out. "I need to whiz," he announced as Pook started to say something. Ignoring the activity around the van, Calven stepped behind a tree and reached for his zipper.

The cellphone was still there, warm and mute. At the last minute he'd remembered to turn it off before he reached the van. And he did need to pee.

"Zip it up, Good Boy; we got to get moving." Pook's voice seemed to be almost in his ear. Calven finished in a hurry and trotted back to the van.

"What's the outfits for?" he asked, noting the logo now on the side of the van—*Hurley's Cleaners—Bonded Care for Your Vacation Home.* At the rear, Darrell was unscrewing the license plate—a second one lay on the ground beside him. His mama, her face now scrubbed clean of makeup, was wrapping a scarf around her head, hiding the white-blonde hair. Pook still had the wig on but had added a yellow ball cap with the same logo as the magnetic sign. The embroidered name above his breast pocket said *Leonard.*

"We got another line of work I thought I'd see could we use you in, Good Boy. You just climb in the back of the van, and when I give the word, you get down low and throw that old blanket over you. I'll explain the rest after we get there."

Pook had taken the driver's seat with Prin riding shotgun, while Darrell and Calven climbed in back. Once the van returned to the main road, Calven had been able to pay attention to his surroundings, though aside from woods and farms, there wasn't much to see—and nothing to tell him where they were. Then he caught sight of a big billboard with a picture of a man with a fishing rod standing in a branch and wearing those chest-high rubber boots. Behind him in the picture there was a great big fancy house, all made of logs, and some fancy-looking horses grazing in a pasture beside the house. The man was flashing a shiny white smile that let you know he had lots of money and that was *his* house and *his* horses. Over his head in big gold letters it said *Wildcat Reach ~ 1.3 miles ~ You're Almost Home* . . .

His mother roused herself and reached over to tug on the sleeve of Pook's coveralls. "Pook, can we stop at the Hasty Mart up there? I need to pick up something."

Pook shrugged off her hand and, without taking his eyes from the road, shook his head. "You don't need nothing; didn't we just buy a couple hundred dollars' worth of groceries? What the hell you *need* so bad?"

"Lady stuff, Pook; I think my period's starting."

With a sigh of disgust, Pook slowed the van. "Get down and cover up now, Good Boy. And stay put till I say you can come out."

The floor space was big enough that Calven could curl up and Darrell slipped him a jacket to stick under his head like a pillow before spreading the light cotton blanket over him. Calven felt the van stop, heard the door open and slam. A few silent minutes passed, then the van's engine fired up again. Over the low rumble, he could hear Pook say, "What's that ol' boy think *he*'s looking at? I be damn if she don't turn heads everywhere she goes, even in them ugly-ass coveralls. Reckon it's long of that rack she carries."

And then the door opened and shut again and they were back on the road. There was a sharp right turn and they slowed, evidently now following a road winding up a steep incline. On and on and the hamburgers and fries he had eaten for lunch seemed to be expanding in his stomach. Cautiously, Calven lifted the blanket to let a little fresh air in with him, but when he felt the van stopping, he let it fall back and lay still as death.

Pook was talking to someone who was calling him Leonard and they were both laughing and then the van was moving again and Pook called back to him that he could sit up.

"Not many folks here now, early May. Some drive up from Atlanta or wherever for the weekend, now and again, and, come June, once school lets out, the place'll be full of rich lawyers and doctors and such. But right now it's nice and quiet, just the way we like it."

"You work here? Like the sign on the van says?" Calven pulled himself up onto the seat beside Darrell—whose coveralls said *Ronny*—and looked out the window.

They were on a narrow, newly paved, one-lane road, running through heavy woods. The roadsides showed signs of being mown and now and then there would be a clump of flowering bushes or a newly planted tree with a few giant rocks at its base. Occasionally they passed a mailbox, usually with some weird name, like *The Aerie* or *Family Folly,* and a paved driveway snaking off into the woods or following the curves of an open meadow. Once, Calven thought he glimpsed the chimneys and roof of a very large building way back in one of those fields but he couldn't be sure.

"Let's just say we're taking the place of some other folks who usually work here. Sit tight, Good Boy, and I'll show you what you got to do."

His mother had been staring silently out the window but as they turned into a drive by a big black mailbox set on a base made of a single tall stone, she roused herself. "Pook, don't you think you're maybe expecting too much? I don't mean to tell you what to do but Calven ain't never—"

"Sounds to me, Princess, like you *are* telling me what to do. You know, I believe you and me may have to have us another little talk tonight. Looks like you *still* don't understand the rules."

The even tones and low voice chilled Calven and silenced his mother, who slumped back into her seat and turned her head to gaze out the window once more. *I* got *to get us away from this feller,* Calven thought. *Mama's so scared of him, she*— And then the van lurched around a final curve and pulled up in front of the biggest log house he had ever seen—three stories high and big windows and roof peaks everywhere.

"You uns gone clean this house? Is that what you want me to help with?"

They were all climbing out of the van now and Pook put one arm around Calven's shoulders. He had to fight to keep from shuddering—it was like having a big old rattler across there. The threat of danger, even death, lay heavy on him.

Pook walked Calven around to the back of the house, the unwelcome arm still draped across the boy's shoulders. Then, motioning Calven to follow him, he dropped to his knees, and began to crawl under the vast deck that stretched across the entire back of the house.

Sunlight filtered down through the spaces in the decking, making it easy to see as they moved slowly over the bare ground along the rock foundation, Pook muttering and complaining all the while. About a third of the way in, Pook stopped, pulled a small flashlight from his pocket, and shone it on a rectangular grate.

"Right there, Good Boy, is where your part comes in. First, though, you hold this light steady . . ."

Pook pulled a screwdriver from another pocket and Calven watched, apprehension building, as the grate fell away to show an opening.

"What d'ya mean? Whatcha want me to do?"

Pook bared his ugly teeth in a demon smile and began to explain.

෨

J. Braden Holmes
6 Trinity Circle
Sag Harbor, NY 11963
(631) 725-1001
April 11, 2007

Re: Break-ins at Wildcat Reach

Melvin K. Entwhistle
President and CEO: The Holdings
Box 934
Charlotte, NC 28202

Dear Mr. Entwhistle:
   *I have on three separate occasions been in contact
with management at The Holdings at Wildcat Reach
and have, to date, received no satisfactory answer to
my inquiries.*
   *Perhaps you could advise me as to what steps are
being taken to protect my investment in this allegedly
secure gated community.*
   *The lack of regular patrols by armed security seems
an open invitation to intrusion and burglary.
Furthermore, I must suggest that employing local men
as gate guards is tantamount to no guard at all.*
   *I hope to hear that these problems are being
addressed with the speed and rigor necessary so
that property owners may enjoy the privacy and*

security implicit in the agreement signed at time of purchase.

Sincerely,

J. Braden Holmes

J. Braden Holmes
President and CEO, Holmes Investments
JBH/ls
cc. Thomas Allbright, Director,
The Holdings at Wildcat Reach
cc. Hilton Lowe, Esq., Attorney at Law

Chapter 46

The Face in the Mirror

Saturday, May 5

(Birdie)

Dor'thy . . . it's Birdie. . . . I know I already talked to you once this morning. . . . Listen here, I just had a call from Bernice and her boy saw Prin Ridder coming out of a convenience store up near Wildcat Reach. . . . Wildcat Reach . . . No, that name didn't mean nothing to me neither. Bernice says it's one of them high-priced new places fer rich folk . . . up near Yancey County . . ."

Dorothy goes to hollering all manner of questions in my ear and, quick as I try to answer one, she'll ask another.

"No, Bernice's boy, he didn't talk to her . . . said it wasn't till the vehicle had pulled out that it come to him just who that was . . . 'cording to Bernice, he said it'd been quite a while since he seen Prin and she'd changed right much. . . . Well, I asked that and Bernice asked him and he said the vehicle was heading on up the road and that there ain't nothing at all up that way 'cepting that Wildcat

Reach place. . . . Well, I reckoned you'd say that. . . . I'll be ready everwhen you want to come after me."

"Oh, Birdie, if this isn't an answer to prayer! At least we know they're still in the area. I was fearful she might have taken him who knows where. Did Bernice's boy mention if he might of seen Calven?"

Dorothy has been jabbering a mile a minute ever since she picked me up. We are headed out to that Wildcat Reach place, and if I'm not mistaken, she is going a good bit over the speed limit.

"Now, Dor'thy," I tell her, "if you're stopped for speeding, it's going to take a good bit of extra time. If it was me, I believe I'd slow down some."

She gives me a look but she slows down considerable and I answer her question.

"All Bernice's boy said was that there was this big white van with them dark windows and a sign for some kind of cleaning service on the side. He said Prin had on these tight-fitting coveralls and he saw her climb in on the passenger side. So, stands to reason they was somebody else driving. But it's not likely that was Calven, now is it? Far as I know the boy's not learned how yet, has he?"

Dorothy is staring down the road and biting her lip, trying hard not to cry but I see a tear slipping down her cheek just the same.

"He had his heart set on getting his learner's permit soon as he took this driving course at the high school but I told him he'd have to wait till he was older. I don't know if he thought I was just being hateful—I reckon it seemed so to him. But I was fearful of him getting hurt. You know boys that age ain't got no sense—"

She stops herself, and I reckon she is remembering my boy—who never could have gotten a driving license.

"Oh, Birdie," she says, and now it is a good thing she slowed down for the tears just bust loose, "I didn't mean—"

"I know you didn't mean nothing, honey." I pat her arm. "And Calven knows how much you love him—now don't take on so. Seems things is beginning to work for us—could be we'll find Prin and Calven up at that Wildcat Reach."

Dorothy sniffles some more and wipes her eyes. "I believe the turnoff is right up here. And then there ought to be a sign—according to what that feller back at the gas station said."

She slows the car some more and we go off onto a smaller road where there's another sign with gold letters. *Wildcat Reach*, it says, *1.3 miles.* There is a sorry-looking little store up ahead with a few cars out front but no white van.

Dorothy turns in to the bare-dirt parking lot where there is a beat-up old yellow Ford off to the side, a black pickup truck, and one of them little motor scooters like folks ride when their licenses have been taken away for drunk driving.

"You just stay put, Birdie," she says, "and I'll run in and see does anyone in there know of a cleaning service in the area. If we could find out the name on the van Prin was riding in . . ."

I don't want to miss nothing, so I follow Dorothy into the store. There is a tired-looking woman behind the counter, setting on a high stool and drinking a cold drink. This place has the usual line of such little stores—things like paper diapers you'd maybe run out of and not want to drive far to get, lunch food like crackers and Vienna sausage and sardines, and big old bags of livestock feed stacked over to the side. There is two fellows lounging right comfortable on them bags of feed, just loafering away the time, I reckon, and they stop their talk to look at us when we come through the door.

Dorothy marches right up to the counter and, without even a howdy, sets in to quizzing. "I wonder could you help me," she asks the woman. "I need to get up with some folks who run a cleaning service around here. They drive a big white van and I thought I had their phone number but I believe I must have copied it wrong and now I can't even remember what their name was. Law, I hate it when I can't remember things, don't you?"

Dorothy smiles real friendly at the woman, who don't answer right off but takes another swallow of the cold drink first.

"Naw," she says at last, giving her mouth a wipe with the back of her hand. "Don't nothing come to mind. You might take a look at that bulletin board over there—they's all kinds of business cards and such stuck up there."

Dorothy don't give up, just goes on smiling. "I believe they might of stopped here this morning—a white van and a woman in coveralls?"

Just then one of the loaferers calls out, "They was a woman in coveralls come in here two-three hours back of this. Good-looking little thing. Earl here follered her outside. Maybe he can help you."

Dorothy starts over to quiz Earl about this and I follow after her. Poor old Earl don't have time to get up from the sack of starter and grower crumbles he's setting on afore he finds two old women pestering him with one question after another. He kindly draws up and sends a dark look his friend's way.

"Was it a white van she was in?" Dorothy wants to know. "Was there a name on the side?"

I think she sounds awful anxious for somebody who's just looking for a phone number but I reckon Earl will just take her for another quizzy old woman, used to poking her nose into everything.

The other fellow laughs and jabs his elbow into his friend's side. "C'mon, Earl, what kind of a vehicle was that sweet thing riding in?"

Earl shifts his tobacco from one cheek to the other and says something under his breath. Then he speaks up. "Big white van—like you said. And they *was* a sign on the side . . . one of them stick-on kind . . . something about cleaning but I disremember the name." He reaches for his spit can. "Seems to me like it was to do with motor-sickles . . ."

Dorothy keeps on asking one question after another—who else was in the van and did he see a boy and all like that—but Earl can't tell her one thing we don't already know. So I go on and take a look at that bulletin board by the front door. There is all manner of notices stuck up—church singings and a cakewalk and lost hunting dogs—and I have to lift up some of the papers on the top to see the ones what's underneath.

When I see the card for the cleaning service, I pull it out from under the notice about firewood for sale and tack it on top for Dorothy to find. Then I go pick up some Nabs, and after I pay for them, I ask where is the restroom. The woman points me towards a door off to the side.

The restroom is about the size of a closet—just room

for a commode and the littlest sink you ever saw. I am washing my hands when I notice there on the side of the sink a long white hair that is dark on one end. And I can hear Dorothy saying, *Prin's hair is bleached most white. And she has those ugly dark roots. . . .*

My fingers reach out but I stop. If I pick up that hair . . . knowing full well how it could be used to give me the power over her . . . could be used to draw her to me . . .

And here, though I thought I had made up my mind already, I find I ain't sure. . . . There is a dim little mirror there over the basin and I look myself in the eye. *You made a promise.*

And the girl in the mirror whispers back. *There was an older promise. Remember.*

Her and me is facing one another down when someone taps on the door.

"Birdie honey? You all right?"

The girl is gone and the face in the mirror is the old wrinkledy one I still ain't used to, though it's looked back at me for many a year now.

"Just drying my hands, Dor'thy—I'll be right out."

I reach for a paper towel from the roll hanging there beside the sink. I think that I have made up my mind which promise I must honor, but when I go to drop the wadded-up towel in the trash, my hand brushes near the hair that lays there like a snake in the sun and the hair rises up, catching on my sleeve.

The girl is back in the mirror. She watches as I pull off another paper towel and careful pick off the hair and fold it up in the sheet. When I put the little white square into my pocket, the girl smiles at me before she fades away.

Chapter 47

Wildcat Reach

Saturday, May 5

(Birdie)

When I come out of the restroom, Dorothy is jittering around like one thing. She grabs hold of my arm and starts pulling me towards the door to outside, just jabbering away like a crazy woman.

"Birdie, I've found the name that was on the van. There was a card over there on the bulletin board for something called Hurley's Cleaners, so I asked Earl was that it and he said he believed it was. Look here—this is the number!"

Dorothy hustles me out to the parking lot and right off starts mashing buttons on that cellphone of hers. She puts it to her ear and looks over at me. "It's ringing," she says and then gets quiet.

Her eyebrows shoot up. "Is this Hurley's cleaning service?" she says, sounding like someone who's about to raise a ruckus. She listens, then goes on. "I sure hope you *can* help me . . . you see, I'm parked at this little store just outside Wildcat Reach and your big white van was right next to my car and the door was open and I believe my little

dog Sugar—she's just a tiny thing, mostly Chihuahua—
well, I believe she must of gotten into that van."

Dorothy catches my eye and swings around so's her
back is to me. I believe she's trying to keep from laughing.
And no wonder—how she can make up such a story—I
wouldn't of thought it. But she rattles on and on.

"Well, I left Sugar in my car with the window down so
she wouldn't get too hot and I went into the store to get a
cold drink, and when I came back, I like to had a heart attack. The van was gone and so was Sugar. She's done this
before—jumped into a strange car—she's the friendliest
little thing—too friendly for her own good . . . but be that
as it may, I don't reckon the folks in the van could have
gone very far. So what I was wondering, could you get in
touch with the van? Tell them—"

Dorothy breaks off sudden and stands there listening
to the quacking sound at the other end. Then she says,
and she ain't talking so brash now, "White. A big old
white van with a sign on the side that said—"

All the spunk has gone out of her voice and she says,
kinda flat-like, "Oh. I see. No, I reckon I must of made a
mistake. I thank you kindly for your trouble. . . . What?
Oh, I will; thank you."

She shuts up her little phone and puts it back in her
purse. "They say they don't have a white van—"

"Then that Earl told you wrong—must of been some
other name. I'll go ask him again and see—" I turn to go
back into the store but Dorothy catches hold of my sleeve.

"No, Birdie, he was sure of it, certain sure. He said the
name Hurley had made him think of the Harley motorcy-
cle his son had. As soon as I showed him the card, he said
that was the name. I can't make any sense of it—it had to
be the same van."

Dorothy lets go of me and just stands there, looking up and down the road. All the excitement and happiness is gone out of her face.

I reach into my pocket and touch the paper towel with that hair folded inside. I close my eyes and clear as anything I can see Prin pulling on white coveralls while a big old fellow slaps a sign onto the side of a white van. And then I see Calven come out from—

"Birdie, are you all right?" Dorothy is grabbing my arm and steering me towards the car door. "Maybe you'd best sit down."

I open my eyes and find that I do feel swimmie-headed. Seeing used to take me that way, I remember.

"Reckon it's the sun," I tell her. "I'll just clamber into the car and set. But don't you think we ought to go on to that Wildcat place? Bernice's boy said they went that way. Could be that's where they are right now."

Dorothy is all for it and we start off. She is still going on, saying that she don't understand about the name on the white van.

"Honey," I tell her, "didn't that Earl say it was a stick-on sign he saw? Well, don't you reckon that's the answer? Prin and these folks she's with is pretending to be cleaning people and they just copied the—"

"But why would they do that?"

I ain't got an answer for that and we go along in silence till we turn off the road between two big walls. They is all kinds of bushes and flowers planted in front of them and the one to the right has big gold letters saying THE HOLD-INGS AT WILDCAT REACH across it. Just inside is a little house setting smack-dab in the middle of the road with a gate like a railroad crossing to either side. The gates is

down and a man in a brown uniform comes out of the little house.

"Evening, ladies." He's real polite but he looks us over
right sharp. "Are you uns here on business or are you visiting a resident?"

"We just wanted to drive around and see the place,"
says Dorothy but the police or everwhat he is shakes his
head no.

"I'm sorry as I can be, ma'am, but this here's private
property. You can't come in unless you own property or
you have a visitor's or workman's pass."

"Now you listen here," Dorothy says and cuts off the
engine. She tells him how we are looking for her nephew
and we think he is in a white van that says *Hurley's Cleaners.* "Did that van come through here a little back of this?"

The guard don't answer but from inside the little
house, someone says, "It sure did—almost ran me over
while I was taking my walk. I told Kenny here to give
them a warning when they leave. There's a twenty-five-
mile-per-hour speed limit and that crazy fellow had to be
doing almost fifty."

When I hear the voice, I know who it is. Even though
all this time has gone by, somehow I know at once.

He'd said I might have need of him again but I'd
put it out of my mind—along with all the rest of the
past. The other day, though, when I saw that old red
ticket in my Bible, back he came into my memory, clear as
springwater—the peddler in the wagon, the traveling
salesman at the standhouse, the man who saved me all
those years ago, taking me to hide with Odessa and Inez.

I should have known *he*'d not forget.

He comes out of the little house, a good-looking man,
silver-haired now and appearing some older but not

enough. He steps up to the window of the car and I see that he is dressed like one of the rich folks. Oh, he may be wearing faded blue jeans but they've been to the laundry and have sharp creases just like suit trousers and he has on one of them knit shirts with a collar and some little animal embroideried on it. He leans down and looks in the car.

"Looking for your nephew, are you? I can understand your concern if he's riding with that crew."

He takes a look at the big watch on his wrist. "Ladies, I'm Jake Aaron and I'd be pleased to act as your guide through this gilt-edged wasp nest they call Wildcat Reach. I don't have a thing to do these days but hang around the gatehouse, talking about the old times till Kenny's sick of me. I don't believe he'll object to you taking a little tour if I go with you. That way he'll get rid of me and can have a little peace and quiet."

I can't make out why he calls this place a wasp nest but Kenny is grinning and saying, "Now, Jake, you know I like visiting with you." Dorothy is thanking him and telling him to get on in and he slides into the back seat. Kenny hands Dorothy a card to stick inside the windshield and off we go into Wildcat Reach.

"Bear right at this fork up here," Mr. Aaron tells Dorothy. "Keep following that road all the way up. As we pass the various properties maybe you'll see that van. Plenty of folks have the cleaners in on a regular basis. Of course, many of the houses are set back on their lots and you can't see them at all."

I study Mr. Aaron, remembering the last time I saw him. Still dark-complected, like he spends a lot of time in the sun, and eyes that are most black, he looks kindly foreign though he don't talk like one. He smells most like a woman, whether from his shampoo or some fancy men's toilet water, and his hands is better tended than any woman's I have seen.

Mr. Aaron catches me looking him over and puts out his hand. "Name's Jake," he says. "Are you ladies from around here?"

"Me and Dor'thy lives over near Marshall—'cross the river from Gudger's Stand," I tell him. The more I look at him, the more it all comes back to me and the nearer in time it seems.

He makes a little smile and stares hard into my eyes. "Gudger's Stand?" he says. And I nod my head and stare back.

There is a moment when he is about to say something more, then Dorothy speaks up. "You don't *sound* like a Florida person, Mr. Aaron. Have you been at Wildcat Reach long?"

He laughs. "Wildcat Reach hasn't been there long enough for a Florida person to pick up mountain talk. No, I've lived in these parts a long time—good bit of it in Asheville before I moved here—I was in retail—men's clothing, for the most part. But I know Marshall County pretty well. I've traveled its roads many a time . . ."

I look away, for the glitter of his dark eyes as he looks at me is making me swimmie-headed again, as if it was another Seeing, and I remember what Granny told me so long ago about how there is some few what lives outside of time—people who change but don't grow old like the common run. I remember how when first I learned of this I felt jealous-like, wishing that I could be one of these folks. But now that I've come this far along my own road to where I can almost catch sight of the end, I know the truth of it—those folks who must go on and on is cursed, not blessed.

In the window glass, Mr. Aaron is watching me. His dark eyes are sad now, and I think how I must look to him—how changed since the day he took me from that place. I want to make some sign, to tell him that I done good, that my life weren't for naught, but he has turned away now and I look through his shape to what's beyond.

Out the window is woods and then fields and woods again. Everything is tended just so—not the first beer can or plastic bag on the roadside—and I think about my own Ridley Branch. There are some trashy folks travels along it and every day when I go to walk, I pick up empty cans and bottles folks has tossed out. It makes me wonder if that might be the reason for the guard at the gate, to keep the trashy folks out.

All of a sudden, right in the midst of my pondering, Dorothy shouts out, "Lord have mercy!" and she swings the car hard to the right. I look round just in time to see a big white van speeding past us, going back the way we came. It is so close that I hunch up, waiting to hear the scrape of metal against metal, but then it is past and we are heading for the side of the road. There is two big bumps as the right wheels go into the ditch and the car stops, nosed into the soft dirt of the bank above the road.

We are all three of us kindly stunned—for a minute, don't no one say a word. Then Mr. Aaron asks are we all right and Dorothy begins to jabber about how that was the van we was looking for.

"We got to go after them!" she is hollering and tries to move the car but the right tires just spin in the mud of the ditch.

Mr. Aaron is pulling out his cellphone and mashing those little buttons, his thumbs just a-flying. He listens a minute and then shakes his head. "Line's busy—I was hoping to warn Kenny they were heading his way."

Dorothy puts the car into reverse and guns it but it ain't no use. We climb out of the vehicle and stand there looking at how deep the wheels is buried—most up to the hubs.

"I'll try again," Mr. Aaron says. "Maintenance has a tractor—I'll get them to pull you out . . . if Kenny'll just pick up . . ."

His thumbs skip around again, and when he holds the phone to his ear, all at once his face brightens up. "Kenny, it's Jake. Those maniacs in the white van ran us into a ditch up on Skyway Circle. Can you get maintenance to come pull us—"

And then he hushes up. His face gets real solemn and he pooches out his lips like he's thinking real hard and then nods.

"Okay, Kenny. We'll wait."

He sticks the phone back in the little holster he has on his belt. "Ladies," he says, "forgive the expression but all hell has broken loose."

Chapter 48

A Bag of Oranges

Sunday, May 6

(Calven)

The high-pitched scream brought Calven out of the bed and to his feet even before he was fully awake. It broke off just as he realized that he was standing in utter blackness with no clear idea of how he'd gotten there. Holding his breath, he listened and tried to get his bearings. An undertone of muffled thuds and stifled grunts and cries, accompanied by a steady stream of brutal words, seeped through the thin walls of the little house.

Pook didn't sound angry or excited—and that made it all the worse, Calven thought. The voice saying all those hateful things was calm and relaxed—as if Pook were enjoying himself by playing some mildly amusing game.

Calven groped his way toward the unseen door. When his hand touched the cheap paneling of the wall, he felt his way along it till he found the doorknob. Without much hope, he turned it and gave an experimental tug, but as he'd expected, the door stayed closed—still bolted on the outside.

Putting his ear to the door, Calven listened, flinching at each new thud. It was an old familiar scene being played out in the bedroom next door, but he couldn't ignore it, not when he knew that this time it was his fault.

Wasn't like it was something new; Mama's boyfriends had beat her up before. It seemed like it was just the way of things, though Calven had never understood what made her want to take up with that kind of man. And why did she make such lame excuses for them? *It was my fault,* she'd say, *I shouldn't have made him mad. He didn't mean nothing by it—he swears he'll never hit me again.*

Those boyfriends though, they'd most always been drunk or high on something when they started hitting her. Pook didn't seem to care about liquor or drugs though. *He gets high on hurting people,* Calven realized, suddenly feeling too old for his years.

After the burglar alarm in the big fancy house had gone off, right when he was opening the back door for Pook and the others, there hadn't been time for anything but hightailing it out of there. Calven had been on the floor the whole time, tossed around as the van sped down the twisting mountain road. No one had said anything. There had been one quick stop when he figured they must be changing the license plate again, but he had laid low, fearing what Pook might do.

Pook had done nothing. Not then. It had been almost dark when they arrived back at the little house and Calven was finally allowed up off the floor of the van. As he climbed out and tried to shake the stiffness out of his cramped legs, he saw Pook watching him.

"You fucked up big-time, Good Boy."

That was all. Pook had disappeared into the house,

followed by Darrell, who gave an uneasy glance back, then hurried to catch up.

"Help me carry this stuff in, baby." His mama had pulled several bulging white plastic grocery bags from the back of the van and handed them to him. She couldn't seem to look him in the eye, just loaded him up with things to carry.

They made three trips before all the supplies they had bought that morning were on the kitchen counters—crackers, cans of sardines and Vienna sausages, plastic bottles of soft drinks, beef jerky, boxes of cookies, and an unexpected bag of oranges.

When he asked for one, his mouth watering at the thought of something that wasn't fast food, Prin shook her head. "Those are Pook's. Leave them alone, you hear?"

She had laid out two flat boxes with cold pizza in them for supper. Though Calven didn't feel much like eating, he had choked down a couple of sausage-covered slices, then made for his room, hoping that his bungling the job might be forgotten by morning. *Forgotten* would be his only hope; there was no chance of forgiveness from Pook.

Pook hadn't forgotten, Calven realized, as he stood in the darkness listening to his mother's stifled cries. *He's doing like he said: Mama gets the whupping because I done screwed up. But I couldn't help it. They didn't tell me they was two alarm systems—*

The sounds were changing now. Prin was still whimpering but Calven could hear a door opening and footsteps coming near. Panicked, he stumbled blindly back toward his cot, fell onto it, and pulled the sleeping bag over his head.

The bolt slid back; the door opened; and there was a thumping of feet and a final bump as something hit against his bed. From beneath the edge of the sleeping bag, Calven could see the beam of a powerful flashlight sweep the room.

"Okay, Princess, you can spend the night in here with your sorry brat—let *him* lay awake listening to you blubber."

The light disappeared as the door slammed shut. The bolt was clicked home and a quavering voice whispered, "Calven? Baby? It's Mama."

He scooted over to make room on the narrow lumpy mattress and unzipped the sleeping bag to make a blanket that would cover them both. Prin eased herself onto the narrow bed, saying nothing but gasping slightly with the effort of each movement.

"I'm sorry, baby," she whispered as she curled up on her side with her back to him.

Calven reached out his hand and felt her back, bony through the thin T-shirt. There was a sharp intake of breath. "Don't—"

"Are you okay, Mama?" Calven flattened out his hand and laid it as gently as he could manage on her shoulder. Her fingers came up to brush against his.

"I'll be fine, baby. There'll be bruises but ain't nothing broke. That's why he uses the oranges—something he seen in a movie one time. You put oranges in a pillowcase and when you whup on someone with them, it hurts like shit. But except for the bruises, it don't do no real damage."

Prin made a sound halfway between a laugh and a sob. "I wouldn't be no good to him with broken ribs or a ruptured spleen, now would I? A few bruises don't matter on me. But you're different. Send a kid out covered in bruises and folks'll take notice."

Calven froze, black guilt flooding his mind.

"I'm sorry, Mama," he whispered. "If I hadn't of screwed up—"

Her fingers closed on his. "Hush now, baby boy. Let's talk about something else . . . something nice . . . Tell me what all you been doing while I was away."

Away was one way of saying it, he thought as she squeezed his hand. Prin had been in the hospital, trying to pull off some kind of insurance scam. At least that was what he'd overheard Dorothy and Miss Birdie clucking over. Then she had disappeared—run off without settling the big hospital bill—run off without a backward glance at her only child.

He wanted to accuse her, to tell her how he had felt when he learned that she was gone. He wanted to yell and say he hated her, that he was glad Pook had hurt her, that he wished the damage had been as deep as the wounds on his own heart. He wanted to hit her himself. He wanted her to hug him.

"C'mon, baby. We haven't had hardly any chance to talk. Tell me something nice about what you been doing since I had to go off."

Calven hesitated. *What do you care?* he thought, the words beginning to take shape in his mouth.

Mama ran a cold finger up and down the hills and valleys of his right hand. "Your Mamaw Mag said you was doing right good in school."

"School's okay," he heard himself saying, and then there was so much more to tell her—the A in math he was sure of this grading period and the special report he and Kevin had done on Hot Springs and how his science project had gotten a blue ribbon and how he was learning to play baseball and how the coach had said he had the makings of a good shortstop.

And all the time Mama's fingers kept stroking his hand and she kept saying, "That's nice, baby," or "My, but I'm proud of you!"

At last he ran down and his eyelids began to drift shut. "That's about it, I reckon. And ol' Dor'thy's been real good to me. She's some cook . . ."

Prin's hand squeezed his, harder than he would have thought she could, and she whispered real low. "Listen, son, it's good that you're happy with Dorothy. You remember that I said that . . . if anything was to happen . . . if I was to have to take off again, I want you to go back to Dorothy, you hear?"

Before he could protest, could say that he wanted her and him to get away from Pook, that he wanted to live with her again, not with Dorothy, the fingers had begun the hypnotic stroking once more and his mama had asked, "Your Mamaw Mag says you have a girlfriend. Tell me about her."

His eyes were closed and he was too sleepy to pretend not to know who she meant. He hadn't thought of Heather as a girlfriend—not yet. But it was tempting to stretch the truth just a little.

"Yeah, me and Heather does stuff together. I'm teaching her how to use a .22 and she helps me with my English homework. She's pretty hot looking too. And she's real nice even though her family is rich Yankees." Heather's dark hair and the enticing swell of her tank top came to mind and he felt Mr. Johnson stir next to the hidden cellphone.

The telephone . . . he wondered if he should tell

Mama . . . but now she was asking more about Heather
and her folks and the fingers was sliding over his hand
just as soft . . . and he was answering all her questions . . .

"Yeah, her folks are all the time going off on business
trips. They're out in California right now. . . . They got a
babysitter—some old lady from Asheville comes out and
stays with Heather when they're gone. But Heather can
sneak out any time she wants—the old lady's a sound
sleeper . . . her and me one time . . ."

On he rambled, mixing what had happened with what
he hoped might happen, till the answers to his mama's
questions merged seamlessly into a hazy, glorious dream
where he and Heather were alone on a sunlit mountainside . . .

When Calven opened his eyes, the room was filled with
morning light. Mama was gone and the door was open.
Somewhere in the house he could hear people talking.

After stepping outside to whiz, he shambled toward the
kitchen, where Mama and Pook and Darrell were sitting
around the table, eating the rest of the stale pizza. Mama's
face was pale but she looked up and gave him a kind of
sickly smile. She had on jeans and a long-sleeved shirt and
he couldn't see any sign of the bruises.

Darrell nodded at Calven, then returned to the job at
hand. Taking another slice of pizza the big man folded it
longways, and began to feed it into his mouth with steady
concentration. As he swallowed, his free hand reached for
another slice.

"Morning, Sunshine." Pook turned to look at Calven,
training the blank black stare of the sunglasses on him.
"Like I told you, Good Boy, you fucked up big yesterday.

But your mama's done paid your debt and we're gonna move on. And this time, there best be no mistakes, you hear what I'm saying?"

In the harsh morning light Pook's skin was paper white—lifeless and cold-looking. The sunlight bounced off the dark glasses and picked out the map of tiny wrinkles on his face. It took all of Calven's willpower to force himself to move toward the empty chair Pook had pulled out from the table. The pale man took a last bite of pizza and spoke as he chewed, revealing a stomach-turning confusion of brown teeth, white crust, and red sauce.

"Thanks to you, Good Boy, we can't go back to Wildcat Reach. And picking pockets may be fun but it ain't no living. What I got in mind is a one-time thing—give us enough cash to get us out of the country and set us up for a good long while. There's places a man can live like a king on five million dollars."

"I reckon you could live like a king around *here* with just a million dollars," Calven hazarded, happy to be back in Pook's good graces—the threat of danger a little farther away.

Pook leaned down to pick up something beside his chair. "Might be that one time you could. But in today's economy, a million ain't what it used to be. Now, in Mexico or maybe Costa Rica . . . and besides, after we pull off this job, it won't be healthy to stay in the country. Once the FBI get their noses in—"

"You gone rob a bank?" Calven reached for a piece of the cheese and ham and bacon pizza. Not a bad breakfast, though he was ready to eat something hot for a change.

"Bank's too much risk—no, we're gonna rob some rich Yankees—lift their precious little girl while they're away and make them pay us five million to get her back.

And you're gonna be our inside man—since you're already tight with little Miss . . . Heather? . . . is that the name you said, Prin?"

Pook's hand emerged from beneath the table, holding a battered-looking orange. Picking up the knife on the table, he sliced the orange in two and thrust half under Calven's nose. "Want some, Good Boy? Nice and juicy. Just like that little girl, I bet."

The sharp, sweet aroma rising from the glistening pulp filled Calven's nostrils and a wave of nausea swept over him. He stood, his legs feeling as if they might fold under him.

He made it outside before throwing up.

⌇

Movies This Week

THURSDAY: 9 PM
THE GRIFTERS (1991)
(Directed by Stephen Frears; screenplay, Donald Westlake; based on a novel by Jim Thompson) A small-time con artist is caught between loyalty to his feckless mother and love of his new girlfriend—both of whom are con artists themselves.

Chapter 49

Keeping Vigil

Monday, May 7

(Dorothy)

The waiting was worse than all that had gone before.

After Saturday's brief encounter with the
white van and the rapid involvement of the sheriff's department, their hopes had soared.

"They'll trace that vehicle and arrest those fellers and
I'll have Calven back; I can feel it in my bones," Dorothy
had proclaimed, her face weary but radiant. "I'll stay
home by the phone—sheriff promised they'll let me know
soon as they find Prin and those fellers."

Now, after waiting a day with no results, Dorothy had
given her cellphone number to the sheriff's office and
come back to Birdie's house for company in her vigil.

"You go ahead and watch your story," Dorothy said.
"I'll just stretch out here on the couch and finish up with
this library book of Calven's. That way, soon as he gets
back, I'll be able to help him with his report and he won't
get so behind with his class."

Kicking off her shoes, Dorothy settled herself with a

pillow at her back and opened to the page marked by the envelope her electric bill had come in.

"All right, honey," Birdie answered absently, making no attempt to pick up the remote control that lay on the table at her side. "I may just doze here a while," she added, pulling the lever to lower the chair back and shutting her eyes.

Dorothy studied the book. *Chapter Five—The Legend of the Little People.* A cartoon drawing of tiny Indians taking shelter from the rain under a wide-capped toadstool held her attention briefly, then she began to read, soundlessly attempting to pronounce the Cherokee words scattered here and there through the story.

Yunwi Tsunsdi, now there's a tongue twister of a word. I never heard such a funny name. Right funny critters too—hard to say if they're good or bad. Lead travelers astray—that's bad. But then they take care of lost children. . . .

From the corner of her eye she could see that Birdie was not napping but moving restlessly as if she couldn't get comfortable. The older woman returned the recliner to a sitting position and picked up the worn Bible from the table at her side, held it briefly, and then set it back on its doily, unopened.

Dorothy read on but each time she turned a page, she took a stealthy glance at Birdie, and again and again saw the same thing: the wrinkled hand picking up the Bible, holding it, and returning it to the table.

The old woman's lips were moving silently and now and then she nodded as if she were in conversation with herself.

Poor old Birdie. I believe she's slipping. I reckon at her age Saturday was just too much for her.

Saturday.

The helpful Mr. Aaron had been right. All hell *had* broken loose. One thing after another, going from bad to worse without letting up. Dorothy traced the events in her mind, telling them on her fingers in the order they had occurred.

One: A burglar alarm in one of the houses of the community had been tripped, sending a signal to the gatehouse, thus making the guard close the gate and call the sheriff's department.

Two: The white van had forced her car into the ditch.

Three: The guard had been on the phone with the sheriff's office as the white van barreled through the gated entrance, sideswiping a pair of joggers, one of which was now in the Asheville hospital with a concussion and a broken leg. No tractor could be sent to pull their car from the ditch till an ambulance had taken the wounded jogger away and the sheriff's men had arrived.

When at last one of the deputies had come to question them where they waited by the side of the road, Mr. Aaron had greeted him like an old friend but had remained silent as the two women told their story. Dorothy had been eager to give full particulars of the van and its occupants, happy that she had such useful and accurate information.

"A great big feller, brown hair, kindly shaggy. Looks like he could be a few bricks shy of a load, if you know what I mean. And another feller, who I take to be the boss, not near so big but wiry-like. That one has his head shaved and wears sunglasses. Looks awful mean. Couldn't say what age he might be—real white face, right wrinkled, like a smoker's sometimes gets. And Prin Ridder's with them—skinny bleached blonde with . . . well, she's got great big bosoms. I wouldn't bring it up but I reckon it's

what most men are going to notice about her. And Prin's
boy is with them—my nephew Calven. He's a good
young un and he ain't to blame if—"

The deputy, who had been scribbling in his notepad in
a vain attempt to keep pace with Dorothy's flow of information, held up his hand.

"Wait a second there, Miz . . ."

He glanced down at his notes and continued. ". . . Miz
Franklin, now let me see if I got this right. Miz . . ."
Again, the downward glance. "Miz Gentry here said you
uns were in your vehicle when a white van come around
the curve here at speed, forcing your vehicle into the
ditch; is that right?"

"Of course that's right!" she had shouted. Dorothy
blushed at the memory. *Lord, if I didn't stamp my foot like a
spoiled young un at his question.* "Birdie done told it just like
it happened! And I—"

"That's correct, Wade," Mr. Aaron had interrupted.
"That van had to have been doing around fifty."

The deputy had looked smug, flipped his notepad
shut, and tapped on its cover with his pen.

"Well now, don't you see, Jake, that's the problem. Fast
as that vehicle was traveling, how the—how the heck
could these ladies see what the suspects in the van looked
like?"

It had taken some explaining—from Prin and her
companions' early morning visit to Dorothy's house to
Bernice's boy's sighting of the van and on to Earl's information at the little store and their arrival at Wildcat
Reach. Finally, however, Mr. Aaron had smoothed things
over, leaving Wade the deputy willing to admit the possi-
bility that the descriptions he had taken down were accurate.

But by the time the fellow on the tractor came and got us out of the ditch, poor little Birdie was just about wore out. She hardly said a word coming home and she went to bed way before it even got dark. Poor little thing.

Dorothy looked at her friend—the wrinkled face, the thinning white hair, the liver-spotted hands—and remembered the vigorous woman Birdie had once been. *That night we went to the snake church . . . for a moment I thought I saw a touch of how she looked when first I knew her. But now—Lord, if she don't look plumb ancient—older than these hills.*

Almost as if she had heard the unspoken words, Birdie's blue eyes lost their confused, faraway look and focused on Dorothy.

"Dor'thy, I need to take me a little walk—this setting and waiting is getting on my nerves. You stay there and read your book—I'll not be long."

"Now, Birdie, that's a right good idea. A little fresh air'll make you feel better," Dorothy agreed.

"Fresh air . . ." Birdie's eyes were far away again as she put down the recliner's footrest and planted her shoes on the floor. "Ay, law . . . fresh air."

Once more her hand reached for the Bible and brought it to her lap. From the corner of her eye, Dorothy watched, somewhere between amusement and concern, waiting for her friend to put the book back, as before, unopened. This time, however, Birdie opened the book and took from it a small folded square of paper. Without further comment, the old woman hobbled to the door, took up her walking stick, and went out.

She oughtn't to go off alone, tired as she looks. Closing the book with a snap, Dorothy pulled on her shoes.

Watching from the door, she saw the old woman stand

in the sunshine of the front yard and raise both arms. Something in the movement brought to mind the television special she had seen once all about the Pope. Even the hickory walking stick Birdie was holding reminded her of the crook-topped stick old John Paul had carried.

Birdie stood motionless for a few moments. Then she turned toward the path that led into the woods and up the mountain.

Dorothy had her hand on the doorknob and her mouth open to call after her friend to wait, that she would come with her, when behind her the cellphone she had left on the couch began to ring.

All thoughts of Birdie disappeared and Dorothy hurried to grab up the phone, fumbling with the still-unfamiliar buttons.

"Calven? . . . Oh, the sheriff's office . . . Yes, this is Dorothy Franklin. . . . You found the white van? Was there any . . . I see, abandoned in the woods . . . in Yancey County? . . . Well, whose vehicle was it? . . . Stole down in Georgia . . . What about that sign? . . . Oh, I see what you mean . . . one of them magnet ones and they just stuck it on the side. . . . Tell me, wasn't there nothing to say where they might be now? . . . No . . . no, I understand and I thank you for letting me know. . . . Yes . . . yes, I'll do that. Thank you again."

The call ended; Dorothy heaved a sigh and stepped outside to see if Birdie might still be in sight but the little woman had disappeared. *I could go after her . . . but I got a kind of feeling she likes her time alone. Besides, this news'll keep.*

Returning to the sofa, Dorothy picked up the book but found she couldn't concentrate.

I'll get me a glass of ice tea, she thought, starting for the kitchen. *And then reckon I'll go after——*

The rumble of a vehicle rattling the planks of the bridge across the branch broke in on her thoughts and she turned to see who it was. By the time she reached the door, a dark blue compact car had come to a stop at the edge of the yard and a heavyset woman in a long-skirted house-dress was getting out. Dorothy opened the door and stepped onto the porch but the woman just nodded at her and continued on around to the passenger side.

Dorothy squinted; this visitor looked vaguely familiar but she couldn't quite put a name to her or remember where she'd seen her. Then, as the silver-headed form of Aunt Belvy emerged from the car, she knew.

The prophetess kept one hand on the car door and slowly and deliberately pulled back her head and shoulders till she stood straight as a young poplar tree. Her daughter-in-law *Marvelda, Marbella . . . something like that* waited without comment as the old woman, taller by a head, surveyed the surroundings. Aunt Belvy's haughty hawk's-beak nose lifted as she turned her face toward the path Birdie had taken and stared into the trees, evidently seeing deep, deep into the heart of the woods. Dorothy watched, fascinated, fancying for a moment a houndlike quiver and flare of the old woman's nostrils.

But now Aunt Belvy had motioned for the other's arm and the two of them were making their careful way across the grass to the low porch. Dorothy stepped outside, holding the door open, smiling and nodding at the visitors to make up for the fact that she didn't know how to address them.

"Howdy there . . . you uns come right in. Miss Birdie's just—"

"Out walking about, ain't that so?" The dark eyes in the hawk face bored into Dorothy as if daring her to contradict what was obviously a statement of fact.

"I believe she just wanted a breath of air. She'll be back directly. Now you uns come right in and get comfortable."

Aunt Belvy, supported by her daughter-in-law, paced solemnly into the house and allowed herself to be settled on the sofa, where she folded her hands, leaned back, and seemed to go to sleep. The daughter-in-law *what was her name? Marcella? Marelda?* gave the old woman a fond look before motioning Dorothy back out to the porch.

"Is she all right?" Dorothy kept her voice low as she glanced back through the door at the still figure of Aunt Belvy.

"Oh, Mamaw's just fine. She does that time and again—calls it 'gathering her powers.' Does it afore church, mostly, or if she's going to a healing. I couldn't say if she's praying or sleeping, but everwhat it is, when she opens her eyes, it'll be Katy bar the door."

The daughter-in-law raised a finger as Dorothy started to speak. "Just don't argue with her or treat her like she ain't got good sense or, buddy, she'll put you in your place right quick."

A rueful laugh accompanied a shake of the woman's head. "I learned that the hard way, believe you me."

Dorothy looked toward the path, hoping to catch sight of Birdie—Birdie, who in spite of her frail old age was better suited to deal with these people than she, Dorothy, was. But there was no sign of her friend—only the quiet rustling of an afternoon breeze stirring in the treetops and the crimson flash of a red bird disappearing into the green depths.

The gray-haired woman *Marvella, that was it* looked at

her watch. "Well, I got to scoot back home and fix supper—Mamaw said she'd be here through the night to keep vigil. Told me not to come for her till after dinnertime tomorrow. She said that, for good or for ill, her work'd be done by then."

It took a few moments for Dorothy to find her voice. When she did, she called hurriedly after the retreating figure. "Marvella, now you wait a minute! Does Miss Birdie know about this? She didn't say a word to me about it. And what do you mean, 'keep vigil'? If you don't care, I believe it'd be best for you to stay till Birdie gets back. It'll not be long; I'm sure of it."

The daughter-in-law was halfway to her car, but she turned and gave Dorothy an unreadable look. "Ain't no call for me to wait. Mamaw's set on what she's doing."

"But what *is* she doing?" Dorothy pleaded. "If she's spending the night, don't she need a toothbrush . . . a nightgown?"

A half-smile crept across Marvella's face. "No, she won't need none of that. She'll be setting up. Mamaw had a Seeing that she was going to be keeping vigil all the night long—doing battle for an immortal soul."

Marvella opened the car door and paused. The afternoon sun reflected off her glasses and danced across Dorothy's face, making her blink and shade her eyes.

"She's worried near to death about your aunt." Marvella's voice was somber and measured. "The day after you uns come to our church, Mamaw had me to call on my prayer group to pray for Miss Birdie—said Birdie's always been a quare somebody, though she has fought hard against her own nature. And then yesterday Mamaw had her Seeing—she says that on this very night Birdie will have to make her choice for once and for all, choose between God and the Devil, choose between Heaven and Hell."

Marvella ducked her head to check her watch again. "Will you look at the time! I got to get on home. My neighbor's giving a Tupperware party after supper and I promised to come buy something. But don't you worry— I'll be back tomorrow. You take care now."

౨

From Myths, Monsters, and Medicine: An Anecdotal Study of Pre-Removal Cherokee Beliefs *by J. Wyatt Somerville,* Southeastern Historical Press, 1957.

Appendix H—Demonization

Demonization occurs when a dominant religion (usually, but not invariably, **monotheistic**) labels the deity or deities of the subordinated belief system (usually, but not invariably, **polytheistic**) as demons or devils. The practice of demonization is most often linked to Christian missionaries, but demonization has been employed by other religions as well. (Cf. Exodus 34:13, "Ye shall destroy their altars, and break in pieces their pillars, and ye shall cut down their groves, and the graven images of their gods ye shall burn with fire.")

Demonizing the gods of an enemy serves the political purpose of justifying, even sanctifying, any actions against a subordinate group, be it enslavement, subjugation, internment, decimation, or genocide.
See also, **Appendix D—The Removal**

Chapter 50

Among the Quiet People

Monday, May 7

(Birdie)

Seems every time I climb it, this old road up to the burying ground gets steeper and longer. Was it only a week ago I come up here, rejoicing in the flowers and the birds and all? Today I might as well have on blinkers for all I can see is the hard path ahead nor do I hear aught but a rain crow, croaking out a warning. Law, how much has happened in so few days.

The afternoon sun is right warm for the time of year, and when I get to the shade of the woods, it's a relief to lean on my stick and rest. Would have been easier had I taken my truck and come by the river road, but that would have set Dorothy to asking questions I ain't got no answers for. Best she think I'm just a crazy old woman who's too fidgety to set still.

Which is true enough, I *am* fidgety, but the fact of the matter is I need help. I see all the deeds and doings of the past coming back around, each with its heavy burden of unpaid debt. And there's this sweet child Calven—in a sight of trouble, him and his mommy—and Dorothy begging me for help. What does that long-ago promise matter if I can do this one good thing? If I could just be sure of the power not turning on me, the way it did . . . But at my age, I can't see that there is much more I can lose.

Oh, I have turned it over and over in my mind till it made me think of the cream in a churn when the butter won't come. I have tried and tried to see a way clear . . . but all that I can figure is that I need the wisdom and the powers of the Gifts . . . those same Gifts I turned my back on so long ago.

Ain't none amongst the living I can talk to about it except for Belvy—and I already know what she would say. Belvy's right quick to call any magic that ain't Jesus-magic "witch work." She would shake her head and go to praying for me, was she to know what I'm about.

Luther was of Belvy's mind—at least while he was living. Law, how he would take on when I would come up this way to talk to my angels and to Granny Beck. "Miss Birdie," he would say, his face all sorrowful, "you know they ain't there. Every single one of them is with the Savior, the blessed little lambs."

And he would take my arm and lead me away from the graves. Sometimes he would want us to say the Lord's Prayer together, or to read a psalm or some such—as Luther got up in age, he got right churchy.

Don't matter now—I visit with him just like I do with the rest of the Quiet People and it seems to me that at last he understands. Tonight, though, it's Granny Beck I need to talk with. Oh, I'll say a word to the others and to Luther and the young uns, but it's Granny can help me decide.

My feet is just dragging and it's hard work to put one

in front of the other. I know that I am almost to the old home place and, more than usual, I dread passing it today. All that pain and hurt that I'd thought long gone is back.

When I round the bend and see the big boxwoods and the old chimbley, the smell of the smoke and the charred wood is as fresh in my mind as if it was still happening.

"We'll burn them out," Luther said, thinking to put an end to things he feared because he didn't believe in them, and he dashed the lamp oil in their hiding places and laughed to see the flames roar and leap. But when the wind come up and the fire jumped to the house, the laughing stopped. We could only watch the flames swallow the cabin up as we flew about with rake and hoe to clear a firebreak so as to keep it from spreading to the barn and the woods.

I was heavy with my first child but I worked right along with Luther till the others, who had seen the smoke, came tearing up the road with *their* implements. One of them took my rake from me and told me to go set down but I went to stomping out cinders whenever I seen one light.

By the time the house had fallen in and the wind had laid, the soles of my shoes was burned through in three places. But we had kept the fire from spreading.

I can't say that I much regretted the house; seemed like so much unhappiness and ill temper had soaked into the very walls and all through her belongings that was still there. I hadn't wanted to take none of that when we moved to our new house down on Ridley Branch. But I grieved for the Little Things and for myself that I wouldn't never see them again.

At the biggest boxwood I part the leaves and peer in. This was where their dancing ground was fixed and this was one of the first places Luther poured the lamp oil. The fire scorched the trunks and leaves, but after so many years, there ain't no sign. I push my head in a little farther and it seems I see the circle of stones, just as it used to be but that there is a gap where one stone is missing.

I puzzle over this as I walk on, past the old barn and up the road. There is a twitching and a hurry in the tall grass beside the barn, a tinkling of glass from the old dump, and a confusion of little squeals, so faint as to be more the idea of sound than sound itself. And I know they are there.

They never left me—the Little Things. I kept my promise to Luther not to sing the Calling Song, but through all the days of my life, they have stayed near at hand—a rustling in the leaves, a feather brushing my cheek, a twig snapping sudden, the humming that grows louder and louder, then stops all at once—oh, they let me know they're there.

But I never see them no more—like children with hurt feelings, they hide from me, always just at the corner of my sight. Sometimes, like now, I even see the grass move and bend as they pass, but never the Little Things themselves.

Oh-see-yoh, I say, *Hey there.* And I raise my stick in a salute like Granny showed me and I hold my breath, waiting.

For a minute, the day stops. There is no sound and nothing moves—not the water that was tumbling down the branch, nor the leaves that was a-quiver on the trees. Time ain't working right now and in the stillness I feel them trembling on the edge of coming to me.

So many years since I've seen them . . . so many years

since I've saluted them . . . and the air all round is thick with their wish to show themselves.

I stand stock-still there in the midst of the road, holding up my walking stick till the water begin to run again and the breeze to blow and time is going once more. Now my arm is shaking with weariness and I lower my walking stick and lean on it. I feel swimmie-headed and like to fall.

They ain't coming out. We ain't on the old familiar terms we once was, and if I want to see them, I will have to sing the Calling Songs and coax them that-a-way—the very thing I promised Luther I would not do. But I watch a minute longer, just to make sure, before continuing on.

At last the hogback ridge comes into sight. In all the years since I first begun coming up this way, this has been the place I can breathe free and think clear. This is where all the beginnings and endings come together.

I feel the Quiet People as they rouse from their long sleep to bid me welcome again. I brush my fingers over the gravestones of the angels and their greetings are like the tinkling of bells or the twitter of hummingbirds. Innocent lambs . . . I'll not trouble them with my worries.

Cletus is another innocent but his hello is a kind of happy chuckle, the same he would give if he had shot a groundhog or if Pup cut a shine or there was side meat for dinner. A happy boy, my Cletus. I reach in my pocket for the white arrowhead I found when I was hoeing out my cabbage and I lay it atop of his marker.

"Here's a pretty for you, son," I say and the chuckle is louder this time and I feel his rough face rub against mine.

Luther is next and he wraps me in the same loving warmth as always. I study the marker—his name with the two dates and mine with but one. Like a double bed with only one sleeper—like our bed back at the house.

"I miss you, old man," I say, setting on the tall stone to rest myself, "and I hope that you'll be glad to see me when I get there."

You know I will, Little Bird. I feel him say it, and not for the first time, I wonder what age he is now. If I had my druthers, we'd both of us be young with fine strong bodies. And what age would my angels be? Would they be babes like when I last saw them? Or would they have growed?

It's a puzzle I have thought on before this. Folks always talk of seeing their loved ones on the other side—of wanting to see their mamaws and papaws and such. But I reckon what they want is the gray-haired comfortable old mamaw they always knowed—and what if *she* wants *her* mamaw?

Sometimes I think that to give everyone their druthers, there'd have to be a sight of different heavens—in one I'd be a child with my own sweet granny, in another, me and Luther'd be young and just starting out, in another I'd be the mommy to all my babies and them alive, every one, and running and playing in the sun.

Now it's Luther's turn to chuckle. *Oh, Miss Birdie, you are a sight on earth. Stop your puzzling and get on with what you mean to do.*

I pull myself back to my feet and make my way to Granny Beck's grave.

Chapter 51

Got to Make an Escape

Monday, May 7

(Calven)

*S*he *don't care about me, not a lick. All that petting on me was just so's she could find out about Heather. Shit, that stuff last night was likely just her and Pook putting on an act—her yelling while he whupped that bag of oranges against the floor. This whole thing—them coming and taking me away from Dorothy's—I reckon it's all of it been about getting to Heather. And she let them do it. My own mother. I don't reckon she has ever cared about me at all.*

Calven buried his face in the musty sleeping bag and wiped the moisture from his eyes. His throat felt raw and, in spite of having rinsed out his mouth after throwing up, the sour taste of vomit lingered. Outside, the sound of the van faded into silence.

Pook had just laughed when Calven slunk back into the kitchen. "What's the matter, Good Boy? Don't like oranges? Or maybe the pizza ain't to your taste."

Ignoring the mocking questions, Calven had grabbed

a Mountain Dew and gone back outside. As he stood by the back steps, swilling the foul taste from his mouth, he saw that Darrell was over by the van, occupied with unloading more bags and boxes. Catching Calven's eye, he motioned him over with a jerk of his head.

"Give me a hand with the rest of this stuff, will you?" The big man handed him a tool kit and a duffel bag. "Set them under that tree yonder—we're going out and pick us up another vehicle—got to dump this one after what happened yesterday."

The van was being systematically stripped of every loose item; once the personal possessions were out, Darrell went through the interior, sweeping gum wrappers, empty chip bags, fast-food boxes, a magazine, even tiny anonymous scraps into a paper grocery bag. When this was done, he handed the bag to Calven.

"Take this over to the middle of the driveway, and burn it," he directed, digging a plastic lighter from his pocket and handing it to Calven. "Burn it all, then stomp the ashes good."

Calven had done as he was told, happy to have something that would keep him outside *away from them* a little longer. As he ground the little pile of black ashes into the dirt, he saw Darrell ripping out the carpet from the van and wadding it into big black plastic garbage bags.

"You about done, Darrell?"

Pook was standing in the doorway, looking at his watch and tapping the pointed toe of one cowboy boot.

"Yeah, that's the last of it." Darrell opened the rear hatch and slung in the bulging bags, one after another.

Prin appeared in the doorway behind Pook. Her sunglasses covered her eyes and her head was turned away from Calven.

Pook pointed to Calven and snapped his fingers. "Back in your room, Good Boy. We got some business to do and we don't need you along. You go back in there and rest up to get ready for your date with Little Miss Heather tonight."

Pook's tongue slid lasciviously around his bloodless lips. "Reckon how long it'll take her people to get the ransom together? Suit me if it's a few days—I can show you how to have some real fun with that sweet young thing."

Calven's stomach heaved again but he gritted his teeth and made for the back door, passing by his mother without a glance.

"You best take some of them cold drinks and the rest of the pizza in there with you." Pook followed him into the kitchen. "We may be gone a while."

He waited, jingling a ring thick with keys, while Calven scooped up the rest of the six-pack and the box with a forlorn few pizza slices congealing on the grease-stained cardboard.

After the key had rattled in the lock and the bolt had been slid home, Pook rapped on the door with a farewell warning. "Case you get any ideas, Good Boy, just remember you're a by-God criminal now—part of the gang and guilty of breaking and entering. Receiving stolen goods too. You think about that while we're gone."

I got to get away and warn Heather. I got to make an escape.
Calven wiped his eyes once more and sat up. He still had the phone, but the last time he'd turned it on, it had gone dead before picking up a signal. *If I could get outside, I might have better luck—if there's any charge left.*

He pulled the phone from his pants and studied it

wistfully, then put it away without trying the On key. *Don't run down the battery till you know you got a chance.*

Without much hope he went to the door and tried to open it. No luck. *Even if I was to find a wire or some such to pick the lock* and he had no idea how you did that *even was I to get the lock open, there's still that old bolt—ain't a chance there.*

Calven turned to study the window—there was a rusty screen and, beyond it, a long, narrow rectangle of dirty glass, cracked open about six inches. For lack of a better idea, he climbed up on the narrow cot. Could he get out this way?

The mattress sagged in an alarming fashion as the boy rocked from foot to foot. Though the sill was above his eye level, by straining on tiptoe, he could see a small nipple-like protrusion of toothed metal at the base of the window, evidently where the crank to open the window would go—*if there was one. They must of taken it away before they put me in here that first night.*

With a vague idea of vaulting up to the windowsill like some cartoon action hero, Calven caught the dusty ledge between fingertips and thumbs and tried a cautious bounce on the sagging mattress. *If I could just get a good hold . . . maybe it'd work better was I to grab the two ends.*

As he shifted his hands, his fingers hit something. Startled, he jerked his hand away, then returned a cautious fingertip. Metal, by the feel of it. He nudged the object toward the edge.

I be damn! It was right there all along.

Calven grabbed the window crank and, after a brief struggle, fitted it in place and began to turn.

It caught and slipped, caught and slipped, but by slow creaking fits and starts, the glass panel began to lift.

Once I get her open, I ought to be able to bust through that old screen and slide right out. It ain't so far above ground. . . .

At last the window was open as far as it would go. But it was too high—he couldn't even touch the screen, much less bust through it. And as for getting himself up there . . .

"Shee-IT!"

Calven dropped down onto the bed and lay studying the window. *How'm I gone to get up there? I got to get out.*

With a weary sigh, he stood back up on the bed. *Maybe if I was to bounce, I could catch hold—*

The first gentle attempts were disappointing. There was little bounce in the thin mattress and the wire webbing that supported it but, undeterred, Calven bent his knees and tried harder. Surely he was getting a little more height—one more and—

"NOOOO!"

One end of the cot collapsed and the mattress slid off, taking the boy to the floor, where he lay fighting back the tears of frustration that prickled at his eyes.

"Damn ol' piece of shit." He stood and kicked at the cot and to his surprise the H-shaped piece of metal that had supported the fallen end came loose and skittered across the floor.

Calven stared—first at the detached support and then, with a growing elation, at the wire grid of the cot frame.

Just like on television, he thought, as he jogged through the pine woods in what he believed to be the direction of the highway, *slicker 'n owl shit. The hero turns the old bed on end and climbs it like a ladder. Then he uses the broken-off leg thing to bust out the screen and ta-da! the fearless Calven is on his way. . . .*

Calven punched his fist into the air and paused to execute a little victory celebration, like a football player who has just crossed the goal line for a touchdown. In the midst of a high strut he stopped.

Through the pines in the distance something was moving—a flash of red—and he heard a vehicle slow, idle, and abruptly cut off.

Oh, shit! What if that's them, back already? There ain't hardly been time . . .

Moving with care now, Calven crept over the pine-needle-covered ground, silent as a wild thing. At the edge of the woods he stopped, keeping well behind a tangle of scrubby bushes while he inspected the red pickup truck and the man whose head was under the hood.

Chapter 52

A Gathering Storm

Monday, May 7

(Dorothy)

*S*he said she needed some fresh air but where in mercy's sake can she have got to?

Dorothy stepped out to the front porch and looked through the trees to the path running up the mountain. There was still no sign of Miss Birdie, not in the yard nor out on the road where she usually took her walk.

"Up in the graveyard, that's where you'll find her."

Dorothy whirled around. A moment ago Aunt Belvy had been sitting on the plastic-covered sofa, seemingly lost in a prophetic trance. Or asleep. Now she was standing, tall and imposing, in the doorway. And she was saying—no, the old woman was confused. Dorothy silently cursed Marvella for leaving this ancient, obviously crazy woman in her care as she spoke slowly and loudly into the ear of the prophetess.

"Why, you've had you a bad dream, Aunt Belvy. Birdie's not in the graveyard; she's just gone for a walk. I reckon you got a little confused—"

A bony hand grasped Dorothy's arm. "Git in your car and crank the engine, young un. I want you to take me up to the graveyard where Birdie is. She'll be talking to that old woman and I got to go protect her."

The fingers held her in a pincers grip. "And I ain't one lick confused."

Dorothy turned her car up the narrow road leading to the cemetery. Beside her sat Aunt Belvy, eyes half-closed and hands folded, her mouth curved in a small smile.

"Just don't argue with her or treat her like she ain't got good sense or, buddy, she'll put you in your place right quick." Well, Marvella got that right.

And did I ask a question or say one word? No, I did not, I just helped this old . . . this old whatever she is into my car and brought her here. There was several good reasons not to but seemed like my mouth weren't working. And now I can't remember what the reasons was anyhow.

Dorothy's tongue loosened as she brought the car to a stop, and she said to her companion, "Miz . . . Miz Belvy, if you want to set here and wait, I'll go see is Birdie up there—"

The old woman turned. Brilliant dark eyes bored into Dorothy. "What did you say your name was?"

"Dorothy . . . Dorothy Franklin . . . my mama was—"

"I know *who* you are; it was your name I disremembered." Belvy began to fumble for the door handle. "I ain't waiting here; Birdie's up there and I got to speak with her."

This time I'll not argue, thought Dorothy, hurrying around the car to open the door and help Aunt Belvy undo her seat belt and climb out, *lest she goes and turns me into a toad-frog.*

The old woman caught hold of Dorothy's arm and stood looking up the hill. Only a few gravestones at the near edge could be seen; the main part of the graveyard was hidden from view. Belvy lifted her chin and waited.

Like a hunting dog—I expect to see her nose go to wiggling any minute now. A tiny smile began to creep across Dorothy's face but she hastily rearranged her expression as the bright eyes darted sideways.

"There's some says I have a nose for evil. You best take care, Dorothy Franklin, not to be a mocker."

Dorothy's mouth fell open. "I . . . I didn't—"

"No, you didn't mean nothing." Belvy waved off Dorothy's attempts to say more and started up the path along the slope. "Don't say sorry; just arm me up this hill."

Dorothy, afraid now even to think, concentrated on helping Belvy up the trail without *seeming* to help her. The path was steep and uneven, with tree roots and rocks in plenty to trip on, but the prophetess set a brisk pace, skimming without hesitation over the rough path.

As the main part of the cemetery came into sight, the old woman stopped and held up a silencing finger. A familiar voice was speaking.

". . . stayed clear of the Gifts and Powers these many years, Granny Beck. I knowed you wouldn't have meant me to use them to do harm—but harm is what came of it back then. You know that. And you know that was why Luther made me promise . . ."

Birdie's words came and went on the little breeze that played around the hilltop. As they reached the edge of the graveyard, they could see her standing by a small white tablet and speaking, it appeared, to the ground.

". . . but this evil that has got the boy . . ." The little woman sagged against her tall stick as if exhausted and Dorothy made an involuntary move toward her, only to be stopped by the bony fingers gripping her arm.

Birdie bent slightly. She seemed to be listening intently. Half a minute dragged by and then she nodded. "I love you too, Granny Beck. I thank you and I'll do what you say."

Dorothy felt a jerk at her arm. Aunt Belvy was on the move again, coursing a zigzag path through the gravestones and calling out as she went.

"The Lord watch over thee, Birdie Gentry. The Lord preserve you from evil and Satan's snares. The Lord bless and keep you . . ."

Dorothy hastened to keep pace with her companion's steps.

Without hurry, Birdie turned toward them and Dorothy saw that her face was calm, free of the emotion that had been so strong in her words of the past few minutes.

"Thank you, Belvy, for coming. Dorothy, there's news of Calven. The boy's loose now but there's danger coming after him and we got to be there to face it for him."

Dorothy and Belvy were within arm's reach of Birdie, and Belvy, breathing hard, held out a shaking hand to her old friend. "Birdie honey, come away from this place. Just put your trust in the Lord—"

Birdie took her hand. Dorothy watched, silent as the two old women stood, fingers entwined, staring at each other. Belvy's gaunt face was drawn with anguish but Birdie's shone with a newfound peace.

"No, Belvy," she said, gazing at her friend with a be-mused affection, "my mind's made up. You've done your best with your prayers and your scripture but I can't wait no longer. For all these years I've kept faithful to the promise I made to Luther—even as my babes sickened and died, I just buried them and said, 'Thy will be done.' When they found Cletus, don't you think I wanted to call down black doom on the one who killed my poor boy?"

Birdie raised her stick high and Belvy started back as if expecting a blow.

"Don't look at me like that, Lilah Bel," Birdie's soft voice begged. "It warn't none of my doing; I stayed my hand and let that matter work itself out. Even back when I was sick unto death, I knew where I could go to find help, but because of my promise, I let you work your Bible magic with your praying and anointing and laying-on of hands. And it pulled me through that time, I give you and Him the credit. But I believe that this thing what's after Calven is an old evil that ain't susceptible to your prayers. Do you remember me telling you, all them years agone, about the Raven Mockers?"

Chapter 53

Ronnie Winemiller's Sweet Ride

Monday, May 7

(Calven)

S he's a '52 Chevy, son, in tip-top condition. Restored her myself."

Calven froze. He had been peeking through the bushes, trying to get a better look at the most beautiful truck he had ever seen. It was shaped like an old one—the kind he'd seen on those Andy Griffith reruns Dorothy was so crazy about—but it was a shiny red with a chrome bumper and hubcaps that glittered in the afternoon sun. *It looks brand-new—like something that fell through a time warp.*

Calven stepped out from the bushes, first giving a cautious look up and down the road. *Pook and them was supposed to be gone a long time but it don't hurt to be careful.*

The road, a two-lane blacktop running through gently rolling fields and woods, was empty of traffic. Calven moved closer to the truck. "How'd you know I was there?"

Still half-hidden by the hood and with his back to Calven, the man bent over the truck's engine, one hand busy in its interior.

"Saw your reflection in the air filter cover." The man straightened, wiping his hands on the rag he was holding before pointing at the shiny flat cylinder sitting atop the engine. "Good as a mirror."

He held out a hand to Calven. "Ronnie Winemiller's the name and this is my Sweet Ride. Whatcha think of her?"

Accepting the offer of a lift had cost Calven a brief struggle—Dorothy's dire injunctions against riding in cars with strangers had warred against the urgent need to get away and warn Heather. He had tried again to use the cellphone and had managed to get Dorothy's answering machine at home. But he hadn't gotten any farther than "Dor'thy, it's me, Calven, and I'm heading—" when the battery had quit, evidently for good.

Ronnie Winemiller had watched with a curious expression as Calven had jabbed at the button over and over and finally flung the useless thing into the bushes.

"You trying to get in touch with your people?" he had asked, running his fingers through his longish gray-blond hair before turning to close the hood of the red pickup.

"Yeah, but the battery's give out." Calven looked hopefully at Ronnie's belt. "You got a cell I could use maybe? It's kind of an emergency."

"One of them portable phones? Not me." Ronnie scratched his head. "I could take you to a phone booth— if we could find one. Or," he had shrugged and a smile spread across his face, "where do you live? I'm just joy-riding, letting Sweet Ride have a little exercise. How about I take you home? Is it far from here?"

If I tell him the truth, he may not believe me. Or he'll want to get the law involved and they might not believe me and there'll be time wasted. The quicker I get to Heather and get her someplace safe, the better. Then we can call the cops. And if Mama gets arrested . . .

Calven became aware that Winemiller was staring at him, waiting for an answer to his question.

"Far from here?" Calven shrugged. "Well, the thing is I don't know exactly where *here* is."

The man's eyebrows lifted but he didn't say anything. Encouraged to invention, Calven began to improvise.

"I know it sounds kinda sketchy but what happened is, some high school fellers brought me out here blindfolded and left me in the woods—kind of a club initiation, you know. And, buddy, I am flat lost. Like I said, I ain't got no idea where *here* is. I live over near Ransom, but this"—he waved one hand—"this don't look like nowhere in Marshall County that I know of."

Ronnie Winemiller shook his head. "You kids—always up to some foolishness or other. Well, son, your buddies brought you all the way to Yancey County. But that doesn't matter—it's a pretty drive over to Ransom and me and Sweet Ride'll be happy to take you there. Get in."

At least he ain't tried any funny stuff. I think it's gonna be all right, and if I get him to take me right to Heather's, Dor'thy don't have to know a thing about it.

"This is an awful nice truck, Mr. Winemiller—all this red leather and stuff. It's really sweet."

The man behind the wheel smiled like a proud father. "Did it all myself, right down to the upholstery. I'm pretty handy with all kinds of things—used to work for

Gulfstream Aerospace, fitting cabinets into private jets. Met lots of famous people too, and the things they wanted on those jets, you would not believe. Anyhow, I decided that when I retired, I'd have me a truck, and fix it every bit as nice as I fixed those jets."

He reached over to open the polished wooden door of the glove compartment, revealing an interior of specialized pigeonholes with a notepad and pen on a silver chain affixed to the door. "Pretty sharp, huh? And I'm not done yet. There's a few more nifty ideas I'm working on. But I try to take a day off now and then and just go ride around."

Ronnie Winemiller clicked the door shut and brushed a few invisible flecks off the glossy wood.

"Got an early start today. Wasn't sure which way I'd go but I had breakfast this morning at a little café over near that new place, that Wildcat Reach. Got to talking with a real nice guy sitting at the counter next to me—retired fellow like me, named Jake Aaron—he suggested I travel up this way—even drew me a map so I wouldn't miss any of the sights."

". . . and the four-speed tran. Of course, a lot of guys, they'd go the chop and channel route—turn her into a street rod, but I just wanted . . ."

Calven's eyelids drifted shut with the warmth of the sun slanting through his window, the hypnotic hum of the motor, and the soothing rise and fall of Ronnie Winemiller's voice describing the transformation of an abandoned and rusting old hulk into the sleek red beauty that was Sweet Ride. *About an hour, that's how long he said it would take to get to Ransom . . . Pook and them likely won't even be back to the house to get me by then. If things go right, I'll be waiting for Heather when the bus comes. And then I can . . .*

A big hand was on his shoulder, gently shaking him awake. "We're at the turnoff to Ransom—you got to wake up and tell me which way to go, son."

Calven blinked his eyes. Three yellow school buses were lumbering toward them, and farther down the road he could see another stopped, flag out and disgorging two small children.

Shitfire! Must of took a good bit longer than an hour. But still, we got to be ahead of Pook.

"Keep on straight, past the high school. I'll show you where to turn. And, could you hurry?"

Hurry wasn't even remotely possible. A steady stream of buses, followed by innumerable cars and trucks, was pouring out of the high school entrance. Sweet Ride was stopped by the traffic light and forced to wait as bus after bus chugged down the drive and pulled out onto the main road. Quivering with impatience, Calven watched and silently implored the buses to turn left. Every bus that made a right turn was just one more obstacle between him and Heather.

Finally, the light turned green. As they poked along the main road behind four buses and six cars, Ronnie Winemiller glanced over at him. "If she was here, my grandma would say you're acting like a wiggle-worm. You got a hot date or something?"

Calven ignored the lame adult humor and kept his face impassive. "There's this girl I need to talk to real bad before she goes home. She's probably on Bus 12 up there—the second one. If you just follow along where it goes, that's where I'm going."

"Follow that bus, eh?" Ronnie Winemiller chuckled. "Okie-dokie, me and Sweet Ride are on the case!"

After what seemed a never-ending journey of starts and stops, creeping along behind first four, then three, then two slow yellow buses, they were crossing the bridge and heading up Bear Tree Creek, directly behind Bus 12. As the bus began to empty, letting off passengers at various driveways, Calven tried to spot Heather. She wasn't in their accustomed spot—the left-hand window seat toward the back—and they weren't close enough for him to pick her out among the handful of students still aboard.

But at last he could see the familiar clump of mailboxes that was their stop just ahead.

"Right up there is where I get out, Mr. Winemiller." Calven gripped the door handle, ready to leap out as soon as the pickup stopped. "I sure do appreciate you bringing me all this way—"

The bus didn't even hesitate at the mailboxes but continued on up the road and around the next bend.

"Here?" The truck slowed and Winemiller turned a puzzled face to him. "I thought you said where the bus stopped—"

But Calven was out the door. "She must of stayed home today. I got to get on up to her house quick. Thanks for the ride!"

He slammed the door and waved, then turned to run up the black-topped drive that led to Heather's house. *Reckon he thinks I ain't got much manners. Or I'm crazy.* But he was in time—that was what mattered. He could warn

Heather and get the woman who stayed with her to take them all to Dorothy's house. Then . . .

Then what? Call the cops and tell them about Pook and what he does . . . only, then Mama'll get arrested too. He slowed, considering the situation. *But Mama's the one told Pook about Heather . . . and she don't care . . .*

A thought hit Calven . . . a doubt . . . a sudden feeling that he was maybe in over his head. He looked back down to the hard road but the red truck had vanished.

He sure got gone awful quick. Seems like . . . maybe I should of told him . . .

With a little sigh, Calven turned and started up the road, ignoring the warning bells sounding in his mind.

⌇

Newspaper article with attached note

ONE SWEET RIDE——1952 STYLE

"She's been my full-time job ever since I retired. But she was my dream for a whole lot longer than that. And every time I think I'm about done with her, I keep finding one more thing to tweak. The next project is to fit out the glove compartment with some fancy pigeonhole storage. What it is, I reckon, I don't *want* to get done. I'm having too much fun."

Amiable Ronnie Winemiller runs a chamois cloth over the already spotless hood of "Sweet Ride," his restored 1952 Chevrolet pickup truck, and he describes how he found the truck at an auction in Illinois, towed it home, and began the laborious job of restoring this classic piece of Americana.

"I kept the original 216-cubic-inch engine with Babbitt bearings—it was in good shape. The body had some rust and I sandblasted it and had it painted at a body shop. Getting the running boards loose was the biggest hassle—that and replacing the floor in the cab. It had rusted through and someone had fixed it with a combination of tar and linoleum."

Winemiller shakes his head in quiet amusement and opens the hood to reveal the (cont. page 23)

This is the article I told you about that they did on your dad right before he passed away. I hate it that he never got to finish that project he was talking about. The fancy wood he ordered is still here if you have a use for it.

Chapter 54

The Warriors

Monday, May 7

(Birdie)

Dorothy looks like a crazy woman, eyes all bugged out and hair straggling down as she comes running through the graveyard to the bench where me and Belvy are talking over what to do. I had seen her slip her cellphone from her pocket, but I already knowed who it was and what she would say. Somehow I am outside of time just now.

"Calven's come back!" she hollers.

Belvy and I swap raised-eyebrow looks. We may be old and we may have our different ways, but we both know that this battle we have been called to ain't over that easy. "Where's he at, Dor'thy honey?" I ask and I see her lips tighten up. She stands there before me and Belvy, trying to catch her breath so's she can say the rest of what I already fear.

Dorothy pushes the cellphone back in her pants pocket and takes a deep breath. "He's somewheres up the mountain looking for that little girl he thinks so much of—that Heather."

As the words leave her mouth, I feel the cold breath of a Raven Mocker stirring the air and somewhere in the back of my mind I hear the echoing of his ugly laughter.

"Who were you talking to just now, Dor'thy?" I ask and she busts into tears.

"It was that woman—Karen something—the one from Asheville who stays with Heather when her folks is away on business."

Dorothy starts in to jabbering a mile a minute. "She said it was not an hour ago, Calven come pounding on the door in a great hurry to see Heather. Karen said that Heather laid out of school today and that she took her camera up the mountaintop to get pictures of flowers and toadstools and such for some nature project she had to do. Heather told Karen she'd be up there till near dark, as she hoped to get a good picture of a sunset. So Karen told Calven all this and he lit out up the road."

Dorothy is looking back and forth from Belvy to me. Belvy has that stern look she gets when she's about to have a Seeing and I reckon my face is full of grim death and thunder and I can tell Dorothy can't make pea-turkey of none of this.

Then she finishes up and it is as bad as I thought.

"The reason this Karen called was to tell me that Calven's mama and her friends had drove up just now looking for him and Karen told them he was up the mountain with Heather.

"She said she invited them in but they said no, they'd ride on up the road and find him. So they went on up that way and then Karen got to thinking that Heather and Calven might decide to come down by way of my house and she wanted to let him know his mama was looking for him."

Oh, Lord, I am afraid when I hear these words. I turn to Belvy and she still has the Seeing look on her. I wait a minute and then she nods at me.

"We'll go together, Birdie."

"Where are you aiming to go, Birdie?" Dorothy stares at me like I have lost my mind. Belvy is already getting up and heading for the car.

"Birdie Gentry!" Dorothy cries out. "You can't— I asked you for help but I didn't mean for you to—these fellers are rough men—criminals what ought to be in jail—they like to killed that jogger—"

But I am on my feet too and making my way down the path to where Dorothy's car is parked. I can see Belvy has already got herself in and her seat belt fixed ready to go.

Dorothy is hustling after me, fumbling in her pocket for that little phone. "I'll call 911 and then we'll go over to my house and wait. There ain't no way you two—"

I know what she is thinking—what can two old women do? Me, eighty-five—and, law, how strange it seems to think that I'm that old, and Belvy older yet. But if I'm right about what we're facing, youth and strength ain't what will defeat this evil that's after Calven—no, it'll take the Gifts and the Powers that go with them.

Dorothy is still yammering and getting first on one side of me and then the other, like a dog herding a cow. She hasn't stopped fussing long enough to mash the buttons for 911.

Just then Belvy reaches out the car window and points at her. Dorothy shuts her mouth and stands stock-still.

"Dorothy." Belvy's voice is the sternest sound I ever did hear, a voice that won't never take a no. "You tell the police on the phone which way to go and then you take us to where the boy's likely to be."

I climb into the back and reach up and lay a hand on Belvy's shoulder. It's good to know that we're fighting on the same side now. She don't turn round but reaches up and pats my hand and I can feel the Power running and tingling between our fingers.

Dorothy is on the telephone now and she is explaining things to the 911.

"... it's the same ones broke in at Wildcat Reach Saturday ... and run down a feller. ... Yes, up on Bear Tree Creek. ... About three miles from the bridge ... Laurel Branch Road ... They went up the road that goes around to the top. But there's two ways up to where they are, my road and the one right before it. ... Yes, that's Godwin Holler, always has been, though the new folks there has changed the name to Goldfinch Lane. You best have a car go up each one; that way you'll have them in a trap. ... No, there ain't no houses up there ... one old barn, that's all, and some pasture, most grown up. Mainly what's up there is the worst laurel hell you ever saw ..."

Chapter 55

The Laurel Hell

Monday, May 7

(Calven)

H eatherrr!"
Hollering wasn't easy with sides aching from the exertion of trying to run up a steep path. After one more shout that trailed off into a cough, Calven put his hands on his knees and leaned over to catch his breath.

He was following the almost invisible trail that he and Heather had used many times before—a narrow footpath snaking through the woods, sometimes bending deep into the trees, sometimes paralleling the gravel road that zigzagged through overgrown fields and pastures to the mountaintop. The path was a harder climb than going by the road, but if Heather was taking pictures of flowers and such, it was likely that she had come this way.

To the right, the trees were tall, with little undergrowth, and through them he could catch a glimpse of the gravel road. To the left lay the laurel hell—a shadowy thicket of gnarled trunks and roots and dark glossy green leaves. He and Heather had argued—he called them laurel trees but she had insisted they were rhododendrons.

"And they're *bushes*, not trees, even if they're as tall as some trees. We have a book at home—I'll show you."

And she had—but in spite of the book, he still thought of the dark tangle of growth as a laurel hell. That's what Mama's old boyfriend Bib had called them and Bib had a world of stories about people who got lost in such places and never came out.

"You go deep enough into one of them hells," Bib had said, "you'll find the bones of all kinds of animals that wander in . . . or get chased in . . . and can't find their way out nohow. You'll see them old twisty trunks growing up through rib cages or out of eye sockets. . . . There's some says the laurel traps things on purpose, so as to feed off of them. . . ."

Calven looked toward the dim shadows where the trees gave way to a jungle of contorted trunks and stems, spreading out . . . lurking . . . reaching . . .

Shitfire! he admonished himself. *That was just old Bib funning with me—making hisself feel big by scaring a little kid.*

He and Heather had explored the edge of this particular laurel hell but it hadn't been all that interesting—just the maze of twisty trunks that made progress slow, the litter of brown curled-up leaves crackling underfoot, and the blue of the sky glimpsed through a lacy pattern of green above. Flowers didn't grow there and the laurel wasn't blooming yet. There wasn't any reason to think Heather would waste her time in the laurel hell—particularly now, with the sun gone behind the mountain and the shadows closing in.

Calven shivered. Then he remembered the babysitter

had said Heather was hoping to get a picture of the sunset. He smiled.

She's likely at the top or near it. With that high range to the west, the sun'll go down pretty early. I may as well go up the car road the rest of the way—be quicker.

His running shoes crunched on the gravel as he trudged past the fork in the road that led down to Dorothy's place. He could see the faded green of the painted metal roof but the rest of the house and yard were hidden by the woods in between. *Ol' Dor'thy—won't she be glad when I get back!*

As he studied the little rectangle of roof far below, Calven realized that he was about to cry. Biting his lip, he turned away and resumed his climb up the last steep switchback before the summit. *That place down there—it's more like home than anywhere I ever lived. My own room . . . regular meals . . . even ol' Dor'thy fussing at me makes it more homelike. At least she does it cause she cares. . . .*

The lump in his throat was painful now. He dragged his hand across his eyes and sniffed. *Cut that out, now. You want Heather to see you boo-hooing like a baby girl?*

A movement on the ridge above caught his attention and he stopped. Clearing his throat, he made a megaphone with his hands and called.

"*Heaaatherrr . . .*"

The figure on the ridge turned. There was a moment's hesitation and then she waved and started down the road to him, the camera around her neck bumping gently as she came.

"*Heather . . . Heather . . . Heather . . .*"

Like mocking echoes, the calls sounded below him.

Calven whirled around. Four switchbacks below, an anonymous-looking black SUV was creeping up the road.

At one open window was his mother—her head halfway out, one hand cupped at her mouth, and calling.

"*Heatherrr . . . where are you? . . . It's Calven's mom. . . . I need to talk to you about him . . .*"

On the road above, Heather stopped.

"Calven? What's going on? Where have you been, anyway? You missed—"

"We ain't got time to talk." He grabbed her hand and pulled her toward the trees. "We got to get away from them!"

The car drew closer, tires grinding on the loose gravel. Now Calven could see Darrell at the wheel and Pook beside him, dark glasses swiveling from left to right, alert for any sign of his prey. And behind Pook, still leaning out the window, still calling, Calven saw his pretty, lying, hateful mother.

"*Heather . . . don't listen to Calven . . . he's confused . . . sick in the head . . . we need to find him . . . get him help . . .*"

"Calven?"

Heather was pulling back on his hand now as he tried to drag her with him deeper into the woods. "Wait a minute! Is that really your mother? Why are you running away from her? What does she mean—"

Down below, the SUV was momentarily out of sight but the sound of its relentless progress could be heard as the engine strained and the high, sweet, false voice went on calling.

"*Heather honey, can you hear me? Be careful of him—*"

The girl's face was frightened now and she jerked her hand loose from Calven's grip. "What's going on?"

"You got to believe me, Heather." Calven forced himself not to make a grab for her hand as she moved a few paces away from him—and back toward the road. "Listen, those guys with my mom, they're real bad guys—criminals. The one with the sunglasses—"

Calven's stomach heaved at the memory of Pook's face as he talked about what he would do with Heather while waiting for the ransom. The pink, glistening tongue on the pale lips . . .

At any moment, the SUV would round the bend and Pook would spot them. "Heather, we got to run before they see us. It's not me they're after—they want to kidnap *you* and make your folks pay a big ransom. They . . . they could hurt you bad. Please, Heather, you *got* to believe me!"

"But . . . is that really your mother?"

"Yes, that's my mother. And I reckon this whole thing is her doing. She's . . . " His voice broke but he went on. "She's no good, just like those guys she's with."

Tears were streaking down Heather's sunburned face and her mouth was turned down, half-open in a silent cry. The grinding of heavy tires on gravel seemed almost deafening to Calven and he held out his hand once more.

"Please, Heather."

The girl made a tiny whimpering sound, like a small trapped animal. Then, just as the SUV nosed around the curve, she took Calven's hand and the two plunged into the woods, running for the gloom of the laurel hell.

Down on the road, the big car halted. Doors opened and slammed. There was one last call.

"Heather, honey, we're coming to get you."

And then the sound of feet, pounding through the woods after them.

~

From the second volume of Camping and Woodcraft *(1906) by*
Horace Kephart

A canebrake is bad enough, but it is not so bad as
those great tracts of rhododendron which . . . cover
mile after mile of steep mountainside where few men
have ever been. The natives call such wastes "laurel
slicks," "woolly heads," "lettuce beds," "yaller
patches," and "hells." The rhododendron is worse
than laurel, because it is more stunted and grows more
densely, so that it is quite impossible to make a way
through it without cutting, foot by foot; and the wood
is very tough. Two powerful mountaineers starting
from the Tennessee side to cross the Smokies were
misdirected and proceeded up the slope of Devil's
Court House, just east of Thunderhead. They were
two days in making the ascent, a matter of three or
four miles, notwithstanding that they could see out all
the time and pursued the shortest possible course. I
asked one of them how they had managed to crawl
through the thicket. "We couldn't crawl," he replied,
"we swum," meaning they had sprawled and
floundered over the top. These men were not lost at
all. In a "bad laurel" (heavily timbered), not far from
this, an old hunter and trapper who was born and
bred in these mountains, was lost for three days,
although the maze was not more than a mile square.
His account of it gave it the name that it bears today,
"Huggins's Hell."

Chapter 56

The Old Magic

Monday, May 7

(Birdie)

Now the path is opening afore me. Now there will be no turning back. This one last time I will sing the Calling Song and use the Powers. This one last time, if nothing don't happen, I will see the Little Things and ask their help.

As many years as it's been since I lifted my hand to the Old Magic, I don't know what's ahead—magic is a tricksy thing and the Yunwi Tsunsdi may not be forgiving of me after the way I turned away from them. And it could be that, having left it so long, my old body is too weak a vessel to hold the Powers—that they will work against me instead of doing my will.

It don't matter. Now that I have made my decision, with every breath I take the Power is pouring into me, filling my body.

Me and Belvy are both of us quiet as we gather our different strengths. Belvy's eyes is closed and her mouth is moving in prayer. I don't doubt she'll do her best, but, like I told her, she don't speak the Raven Mocker's tongue.

Dorothy, all shut-mouthed and blank-eyed, is driving the car like she was doing it in her sleep. When we came to her house, she tried to stop there, but at a word from Belvy, she went on past and took the turning that leads up the mountain. I don't know whether Belvy still has her in hand or if Dorothy has just pulled back into herself to get away from what she don't understand.

Could be she is wondering if she did the right thing, asking me to use the Powers. Every once in a while, she swivels her head around from the road ahead, back to me, then to Belvy, and again to the road. We are in sight of the top of the ridge now, and when I look behind us to the west, I see that the sun has set. I remember one of the things Granny told me, how this dim in-between time is good for magic. Things shifts and changes and Evil don't have the full power it will have once that it is black dark.

"Have you got a flashlight in this vehicle, Dorothy?" Belvy is squinting out the window at the sky. "Might be that—"

"We'll not need a flashlight." The words rise out of me without my bidding. "This matter'll be settled, for good or bad, afore dark."

It has been a long time since I spoke like that, speaking with the sure knowledge of all those people in me—John Goingsnake and Granny Beck and the girl we buried so long ago—the quare girl called Least.

The Power is flowing through me now with a great rush; from the tingling in my fingertips to the way the little fine hairs on my arms has lifted, I can feel it washing through me. And the joy of its coming blots out all the aches and pains of old age that are my familiar companions—the knee that all time wants to give way, the nagging ache of old arthritis in my hip, the stiffness of my finger joints—

they's every one of them gone or, no, not gone but covered over. I feel like I could race up the road, outpacing this car, like I could tear open the sky to bring down justice, like I could stand my ground and spit in the Raven Mocker's face.

I think of a leaf fire in fall, flaring up in one last blaze of glory before blinking out into black ashes. It may be that in the doing of this thing, I will be destroyed, but if I can save Dorothy from the hurt of losing this child she loves so much, I'll be content.

"They ain't no one up here."

The pain in Dorothy's voice stabs at my heart. The car is topping the ridgeline now and we can see in every direction but there's not the first sign of the young uns we're seeking.

Dorothy stops the car and wrenches open her door. She leaps out and opens her mouth to holler but me and Belvy both raise our hands and she falls silent. She stands there turning about and seeking with her eyes but at last she gives it up and gets back in behind the driver's wheel.

"They're somewhere down the Godwin Holler," says Belvy, "the boy, the girl, and the three evildoers. No need to let them know we're coming."

"You didn't have to—" Dorothy starts to say, then catches herself. "No, you did right; I should of known better." She points a ways along the ridge. "Want me to run the vehicle on over there?"

"That's right, Dor'thy." I lean up and pat her shoulder. "Their car is on down that other road, where the little girl's people live. You park this vehicle right where the Godwin Holler road comes out on the top and they won't be able to get by. And backing down these narrow roads ain't easy."

We creep on up the dirt track to the gravel road and Dorothy pulls her vehicle slantwise across it, blocking it good. It's a narrow road that cuts across a steep slope, and was a car to slip off, it would likely tumble over and over till it fetched up against some of the trees below.

Dorothy pulls on her parking brake and sets there, shaking her head like trying to get loose of cobwebs.

"Now, what is it you're of a mind to do up here, Birdie? Are we waiting for the police?"

I lay my hands on her shoulders, sending calm into her. This is one of the first things Granny taught me for we hoped to use it on Mama but the anger that she had carried so long was too much for such a simple spell. Oh, the calming spell gave her a night's rest now and again, but mostly she just fought against it. She never did like to be touched nohow.

Dorothy ain't so contrary and I can feel the stiffness draining out of her shoulder muscles and hear her breathing slow and sense her spirit calming.

"Dor'thy honey," I say, when she has quieted, "I'll tell you what it is we're going to do."

Chapter 57

Root and Branch

Monday, May 7

(Birdie)

Root and branch,
Tree and stone.
Two stay behind,
One goes alone.

Dorothy and Belvy take the lead down the gravel road. Belvy has Dorothy's arm to steady her and the two of them are clipping right along, their voices trailing after them.

"He is my rock and my salvation: He is my defense; I shall not be moved."

Belvy is a white-topped pillar, a warrior mighty in the Lord, marching as to war and saying scripture as she goes. And Dorothy is at her side, coming in with the *amen*'s.

"The Lord is my strength and my shield."

"Amen! Tell it."

"My trust is in the Lord."

"Hallelujah!"

They are a brave pair of Christian soldiers and I have no doubt that their faith will keep them safe. Prayers and scripture will be a help—but fight fire with fire, as the saying goes. Outsmarting this Raven Mocker witch will need all the Cherokee Magic that Granny taught me.

I take a moment to linger behind; to turn and raise my stick to each of the Four Directions and to call on all that is under heaven: fire, water, earth, air, and all living things to be with me.

The air is cooler up here and the breeze that brushes over my face seems to say *I will* and the long grass nods a promise as I start down the road after the other two. *If the Little Things are willing,* I think, *if all the Gifts are still with me* . . . and it seems that I hear the tapping of far-off drums.

I catch up with Dorothy and Belvy at the big black car parked there in the road where we knew it would be, and the scent of the Raven Mocker is strong—the smell of burnt wet wood and rotting dead things. Belvy is gazing off into the trees towards the gloom of the laurel hell and her nose is quivering like it used to do, all them years ago when we was playmates.

"In there," she points and I can't tell at first if this is her Prophesying or if she can smell them too.

Dorothy is all a-tremble with eagerness to face those three and snatch her Calven back. She has built up her own ration of Power with her love for Calven and her anger at the ones who have took him from her. It's a *kind* of a Power, that mixture of love and hate, but it ain't easy to direct.

I study on this; I want the shield of their prayers; yeah, buddy, at this pass I need every bit of help there is. But I can't have these two at my side, particularly Dorothy, who might fly out in some unconsidered way when I need to be concentrating all my strength. Besides, it's the Little Things that I am placing all my hope in and they may not come out in the face of all that prayer. As Granny Beck told me, the Jesus people treated them bad, back of this, calling then evil spirits and such, so prayers is as like to spook them as not.

I think about this as we all start into the woods. Those two'll not turn aside from danger just on my say-so but there's another way. Slowing my pace to let them go on ahead, I put up my stick and ask the trees for their help.

On the next instant, there is a squawk. A big old iron-wood has thrown out an unexpected root across the path and Dorothy has tripped and would have fell but for Belvy having ahold of her.

"Oh, my Lord," Dorothy whispers, fighting back her tears, "here I've gone and turned my ankle."

She tries to walk like it don't hurt but after a few steps she is shaking her head.

"It ain't no use," she says. "It'll be all I can do to hob-ble to the road. What shall we do? Belvy needs—"

Belvy holds up her hand. "Dorothy, we'll make our way back together. Prayer ain't weakened by distance. We'll do our part from there while Birdie carries on alone. I know that's how she wants it," and she looks me in the eye, "ain't that so, Birdie?"

As they start for the road, I hear them praying, but as soon as they are out of my hearing, I make a beeline straight for the laurel hell. It seems to me that I fly along as if I was a young girl, the branches bending out of my way and the path flattening before me.

I sing the Calling Song as I go *Oh hee, Oh hi, Oh hee,* and all around me there is the answering hum and buzz of the Little Things and the low tapping of the drums, like a thousand little beating hearts. It is as if no time has passed and I am the same girl that called them so long ago and, just as then, they are swarming to me on every side.

You came, I say and I feel their answer humming in the air.

We came.

It ain't for me, I tell them. *It's two lost children, facing the old Evil and in dreadful need of your help.* And I can feel the strength of the Little Things swelling and they are carrying me on with them towards the children and it is most like I had wings.

At the edge of the laurel hell I pause and listen. There are angry voices not far away and all at once there is the *boom* of a single gunshot. It echoes around me, but before it has died away, I am hurrying on, twisting through the web of gnarly branches, moving unhindered like in a dream.

And like in a dream I bend and wiggle and wind through the thicket of crooked stems and trunks, my old body suddenly snake-supple. The laurel twigs that catch at my hair and clothes slide away, letting go their hold as quick as they touch me. At times, I think that John Goingsnake is just behind me; at others times, it seems he is carrying me and calling me Granddaughter.

It still seems like a dream when I go a little farther and, in the middle of the laurel hell, there is a kind of a clearing, like a dancing ground. They are all of them there, posed like folks set out for a dance square, except that one of them, a big feller, is laying still on the ground. Over to the side is a rock ledge with an open place beneath and I know that more of the Little Things are waiting there.

Calven is standing with his back to me and on his right

hand is a strange bald-headed fellow. His body is young but behind his dark glasses is the wrinkled face of a Raven Mocker and he is holding a young girl by one arm and pointing a big revolver at her head.

And there, just beyond the Raven Mocker, is Prin. She looks as bad as a woman can, who is still young and what most would call pretty. Her bleached hair is like a rat's nest and there are scratches on her face where the laurel has caught her. The worst is her eyes—black-rimmed and empty as holes in the ground. I believe that she is at the end of her road, her partnering with Evil having all but eaten up her soul.

I knew that the Drawing Spell I worked up in the burying ground with Prin's hair would bring her back but I hadn't meant to call the Raven Mocker as well. Magic is tricksy, like Granny used to say, and you may get more than you bargain for when you cast a spell. Still and all, now that I've laid eyes on the Raven Mocker, it's my bounden duty to get rid of him before he does more harm.

Mr. Aaron and the black man named Rafe and the locomotive took care of the only other Raven Mocker I ever faced—and for a moment I wish that Mr. Aaron was here to help me through this one last trial. I don't doubt that he has had his finger in bringing us all to this place but now he ain't nowhere near.

Soul clap its hands and sing, and louder sing . . .

It is Mr. Aaron's voice, saying them words in my head, and I can feel him pushing me on, telling me that after all these years I must claim my Powers and stand alone.

And I know that I can.

I am singing my song silently now but the Little Things are singing back. They are massing in their nests and burrows beaneath the rock ledge, ready to help these innocent children, as has been their care and concern for all of time. When the moment is right, they will see the young uns safe.

Knowing that they are there and willing to help frees my mind considerable and I begin to pay attention to what the Raven Mocker is saying.

". . . old Darrell had just too many ideas about how to manage this. Besides, now there's one less to split the ransom with. We won't have no need for Darrell down in Mexico, will we, Princess?"

They can't see me hid away back in the laurels, and when I begin the next part of the Magic, humming low and clear, the Raven Mocker begins to swing his head around, jittering and twitching and looking behind him. The smell of his fear grows, an ugly yellow smell of rotten eggs mixing in with his usual nasty dull black scent.

"Is that you making that noise?" he hollers, pointing his gun at Prin, and she is crying now, not making a sound while the tears roll down her face. She shakes her head no and the Raven Mocker whirls around to look behind him again.

"Come out of there!" he shouts, and fires one shot, and another and another. The sound of the shots bounces around, setting the dark leaves a-tremble and waking small tinkling echoes.

The Raven Mocker waits. Then, as the sounds of the gunshots die away, the drums begin.

The beating of a thousand or more tiny drums, coming from everywhere and nowhere, and each beat trapped and repeated in your ears—it's a frightening thing and can drive a body mad in no time, especially when they don't know what it is.

The Raven Mocker opens his mouth in a great howl

and the smell of death and fear and ancient evil pours out with the cry. He begins to shake his head, like trying to fling off something that had landed there. The gun is still in his hand but it is jerking all around, and with his other hand he is brushing at that ugly bald head of his. He ain't paying no attention to the children, and I see Calven realizes this.

And now the Little Things, hundreds and thousands of them, begin to pour from their nests and burrows and swarm about the Raven Mocker, who howls and gibbers and dances like a puppet on a string. As the Little Things swirl around the evil creature, filling his ears with their song, Calven leaps right at him.

"Heather, *run!*" the boy cries and snatches her away from the Raven Mocker as the Little Things rise up in a great cloud till the children in their midst can't be seen at all.

The Raven Mocker snarls and raises his pistol, beginning to take aim at the swirling cloud that is moving away back into the laurel hell . . . moving in the direction of the road.

The words of binding are in my mouth and I am lifting my hand to destroy the weapon when the Raven Mocker turns and sees me. His mouth opens in a snarl like a rabid animal's.

"What rock did *you* crawl out from under, you damned old witch?" he growls, pointing the gun at me. "I would have thought you dead and buried long since."

Some of the Little Things are still swarming all round his ugly face and he bats at them with his free hand while he stares at me like he can't believe what's happening.

"This is your doing, ain't it?" he cries out, and I can see he is summoning up his strength. The Little Things go on humming and singing around him but he stands still in the midst of them, paying them no mind now, even as they dart at his face and hit against them old dark glasses.

They are crawling on his hands as the gun rises and comes to bear. I see them plain as I look into the black eye of the pistol barrel. I ain't scared for I know that come what may, the children are safe and I am redeemed.

The Raven Mocker puts out his tongue and runs it around his pale lips. He steadies the gun and it is pointed right at my head. "I'll kill you and eat your heart, old woman. You don't have that many years to give me but it'll be a pleasure taking them from you."

At the corner of my eye, something is moving.

Chapter 58

Valley of the Shadow

Monday, May 7

(Dorothy)

Yea, though I walk through the valley of the shadow of Death, I will fear no evil . . .' "

Like pale birds seeking roosts, the words dodged and darted through the shadows of the darkening woods as Dorothy and Belvy made their slow way toward the open slope where daylight lingered. Their faces were wan, their gait limped and faltered, but their voices, speaking the familiar words in unison, were strong.

At the end of the psalm, Dorothy halted, leaning on the crooked branch she had found to use as a cane. She wiped her face with her hand, then looked at the prophetess who stood tall and gravely serene at her side.

If I could have her faith, Dorothy thought. *Strong in the Lord . . .*

"Belvy . . ." The words were hard to say but she knew she couldn't go on till she had spoken her fears.

Taking a deep breath, she began again, "Belvy, I'm sick with worry . . . worry for Calven and for that little girl . . .

I can say I'll fear no evil but the fact is, I'm afraid for them and I'm afraid for Birdie."

Dorothy turned to gaze back into the depths of the woods, shuddering at the sight of the close-growing trees. Was it just a trick of the fading light that made the twisted trunks seem to move and crowd even closer together? *It's my nerves makes me think that,* she told herself and went on.

"You see, Belvy, it's on my account Birdie went in there. I didn't have no right to ask it of her . . . and as she marched off away from us, right into the heart of that laurel hell, I thought I saw . . . I thought there was something in her face—my uncle called it *fey*. He'd been in World War II and he said there was this kind of a look he'd seen on men before a battle . . . before they died . . ."

Aunt Belvy looked down at her. "Dorothy Gentry, Birdie is doing what she must. There was a debt owed . . . and long overdue. I believe that Birdie saw this moment as a chance to pay that old debt . . ."

Dorothy stared. "Whatever are you talking about? Birdie ain't never—"

The prophetess spoke on. ". . . and having paid at last, she's free. Safe in the arms of Jesus."

"Safe?" Dorothy clutched at the comforting word. "Is this a Seeing you're having?"

Belvy took her elbow and tugged her into reluctant movement. "Call it a Knowing—of course Birdie's safe. Come on now, let's us get out of these woods."

There were uniformed men, guns drawn, waiting by a sheriff's department SUV, as the two women limped out into the open. Dorothy, holding to Belvy's arm with one hand and wielding her crooked branch with the other, called out, "Don't shoot! It's me—Dorothy Franklin, the one what called you uns!"

The men looked at one another in astonishment, then lowered their pistols. The tallest came toward them, holstering his gun. "Miz Franklin? Are you two all right?"

"We're fine, young man, thanks to the Lord." *And no thanks to you,* Aunt Belvy's tone said. "What took you uns so long?"

Sheriff Mackenzie Blaine looked back at one of his men. "We took a wrong turn somewhere—didn't help that vandals have pulled down most of the signs along Bear Tree. Can you tell me what were those shots we heard just a little before you two came out? We—"

The questioning was interrupted by the arrival of a second patrol car, which pulled to a stop beyond the SUV. More uniformed men, guns at the ready, joined the others in helping the two old women to sit down at the side of the road. Once they were settled, the sheriff continued his questions. Where were the three criminals? Where were the children? Who had been responsible for the gunfire?

Dorothy, pale with exhaustion and pain, began to speak. "We started in, looking for Calven and Heather, but I twisted my ankle and Birdie"—Dorothy's voice cracked—"Birdie went on while Belvy and I came back."

"Birdie?" The sheriff's eyebrows shot up. "You don't mean Miss Birdie from Ridley Branch—" He turned to his deputy and Dorothy caught the words ". . . about ninety years old, God help us."

"They're every one of them back in there, Sheriff." Belvy spoke with the quiet authority of a prophetess.

"Deep in that laurel hell. But as for the gunfire . . . I couldn't say."

She paused, shut her eyes, and it seemed to Dorothy that she was consulting some inner voice. When at last she spoke, her tone was deep and oracular. "Be not afeared for the little children; they have fled the evildoers. There's one has fallen—"

Dorothy turned in amazement, her heart in her throat. "I thought you said that Birdie was safe! You said there weren't nothing could harm—"

Belvy's eyelids fluttered open. "Why, Dorothy, Birdie is just fine—"

"Well, thank the Lord!" Dorothy stared into the serene brown eyes, then, suddenly assailed by doubt, "Are you sure? I thought you hadn't seen her."

"Dead or alive," the prophetess continued, "Birdie is saved for hers is the side of the angels. She marches with the Lord of Hosts and the Hosts of the Lord are with her . . ."

The sheriff and his men exchanged skeptical glances and moved out of earshot. After a brief conference, four of the men plunged into the woods, moving quietly in the dimming light. The sheriff returned to his car and began to speak into his radio. Occasional bursts of static and garbled words broke out from the vehicle, harsh interruptions in the evening still.

Sick with apprehension, Dorothy stared after the men as the woods swallowed them. At her side, Belvy began to pray. A moment passed and Dorothy forced herself to join in. Their words rose toward the darkening sky in an overlapping series of petitions.

". . . under the shadow of Thy blessed wings, O . . ."

"Lord of hosts, strong to save, protect your servants . . ."

". . . for Thine *is* the Power . . ."

In the back of her mind, it seemed to Dorothy that somewhere in the woods, something was moving, a growing, swirling humming of a thousand tiny sounds, swelling louder and louder as it approached. She glanced at her companion. But, rapt in her prayers, Belvy seemed not to notice the oncoming sound.

I got to keep praying like Belvy. Ain't nothing else I can do to help Birdie.

Dorothy bent her head to the task and prayed—prayed with all her heart and soul—prayed till the words came of themselves. And even as the droning surrounded them, drowning out their voices, still the women prayed, lips moving silently in the whirlwind of sound.

And suddenly . . . all was quiet.

Dorothy looked up to see Calven, hand in hand with Heather, stumbling out of the woods. The children were wide-eyed and out of breath but seemed unharmed. The protecting cloud that surrounded them—

Dorothy blinked her eyes. For a moment there . . . in the fading light . . . it had looked as if there were a cloud about the pair.

She blinked her eyes again. No cloud, just two frightened children running toward her. Her vision blurred by tears of joy, she held her arms open wide to embrace the two.

"Calven! Oh, my boy! Thank you, Jesus," Dorothy cried, crushing him to her. "And little Heather! Come here, child!"

The children flung themselves down beside the weeping

woman, hugging her, rubbing their faces on her shoulders, and jabbering with excitement and relief.

"All praise to His Holy name!" Belvy raised wrinkled hands in witness. "His be the glory!"

As her eyes began to clear, Dorothy looked over Calven's head to see bobbing lights in the dark woods. The lights danced and played through the trees, slowly growing nearer.

"Sheriff!" a voice called. "We got a man and a woman dead back in here."

"She did it on purpose!" Calven's voice was cracking. "She stepped in front of his gun so we could get away."

ॐ

To Ms. Dorothy Franklin:

We are ready to execute the commission for the stone you chose (No. 35–PGp), the polished pink granite. Enclosed find suggested designs—the lamb motif seems especially appropriate.

In our recent conversation, you suggested some lines of scripture. Am I correct in assuming that these following lines are those to which you referred? I have underlined the sections that seem most suitable.

15 As the Father knoweth me, even so know I the Father: and I lay down my life for the sheep.

16 And other sheep I have, which are not of this fold: them also I must bring, and they shall hear my voice; and there shall be one fold, and one shepherd.

17 Therefore doth my Father love me, because I lay down my life, that I might take it again.

18 *No man taketh it from me, but I lay it down of
    myself. I have power to lay it down, and I have
    power to take it again. This commandment have I
    received of my Father.*

   *Trusting that one of these will prove acceptable, I
am sincerely yours,*

William O. Lupo

William O. Lupo

Marshall Monuments
Box 1054
Ransom, NC 28753

Chapter 59

I Alone

Monday, May 7

(*Birdie*)

I ain't dead yet.

I can hear them weeping and praying and carrying on as I make my slow way back through the darkened woods, and it is the strength of their prayers and love that is leading and carrying me on for the Cherokee Magic is gone from me. I am an old woman again, with an old woman's wobbling gait and weakened legs, and the steep ground and many laurel limbs make the going almost more than I can bear.

It would seem good, I think, to lay me down in the deep litter of querled brown leaves, to draw them up around me like a rustling quilt, and rest my bones. Not a bad way to depart this life, I think, on a mountainside gazing up through the leaves at the sky.

I am so tired.

Leaning on my stick, I gather my little remaining strength for what lays ahead. My task ain't over. Like the feller in the Bible who comes to Job and says *I only am escaped alone to tell thee*—I got to tell the boy and Dorothy how it was, that it might bring them some small comfort. Especially the boy. I'd not have him carry so ugly a memory of his mother throughout his life. For good or for bad, our mothers stay with us.

I close my eyes and see it all again: the Raven Mocker with his gun pointing at me, the young uns being led away by the Little Things. The Raven Mocker's face has got an unearthly greeny-white glow about it and I know that I must act quick, now while there is yet some light, for in the black dark, his powers will grow stronger.

I begin the Calling Song again, first in my mind, and then in my throat, and by the time it has reached my lips, I can hear them coming back, a mighty host of them, humming and throbbing like a single mighty heartbeat.

And the Raven Mocker whirls and goes to fire his gun into the laurel thicket, in the direction the children has just gone, and the words of the spell to jam the weapon are on my lips when there is a blur of movement and Prin hurls herself between the Raven Mocker and the children.

The gunshot rings out; there is a sharp cry; and at the same time, the cloud of the Little Things covers up the Raven Mocker and Prin. Prin, who here at the last has remembered that she is a mother and, so doing, has saved her soul.

I stand froze to the spot, watching it all unfold. I am empty of Magic. I have made use of the Gifts and Powers and now it is all beyond my control. I can only watch and hope that the Magic don't turn back on me like it has done afore.

The cloud of Little Things hangs in place like a mighty whirlwind, hiding what has happened. They make a roaring sound but somewhere within the roaring I can hear a great screeching of anger and pain from the Raven Mocker.

As I watch, the cloud begins to move again, not back to the road, the way the children were led, but across the clearing and into the deepest part of the laurel hell. The cloud is taller than a man, broader than three, and it kicks up the dead laurel leaves underfoot as it turns. It brushes past me in its going, so close that I feel the prick and sting of a few of the tiny bodies on the outside edge of the whirling mass as they hit and ping against my hands and face.

The cloud and the thing inside it are fading into the dark of the laurel hell when I look around.

And there lies Prin.

Somehow I manage to drag myself back through the half-light of the close-growing laurels though they fight me every inch of the way like they would keep me with them forever. It takes a very long time and once I hear voices near me and heavy bodies breaking through the thicket. A man calls out to tell the sheriff that there is two people dead. I start to holler to them but I am most too tired to speak. It is all I can do to put one foot in front of the other.

Then I hear the sound of Dorothy's and Belvy's voices, their separate prayers twining and twisting together, making a lifeline that leads me on and puts strength into me as I stumble through the darkening wood towards the dim light of the open mountainside.

They don't see me at first. Two lawmen are squatted down by the children, asking all manner of questions, and Dorothy's eyes are shut as she prays aloud. It is Lilah

Bel—Belvy—who spots me as I hobble out of the woods and stand there taking in deep breaths and admiring the open sky and the first twinkling stars.

And then the lawmen are upon me—quick with questions about the man with the gun. I tell them that he has gone deeper into the laurel hell and I begin to tell them that justice is being done but I stop myself in time. They'd just mark me down for the crazy old lady I know I must look like—hair a-tangle and clothes all dirt-smeared and tore.

They don't linger but set off back into the woods, leaving one behind to help us to our car. I watch the beams of their flashlights weaving through the trees and think about what they will find.

Calven comes over to me. His face don't show nothing as he says, "We thought you was the one got shot. We saw him point the gun at you when we was running away. . . . They said there was a woman dead. I reckon it's Mama got herself killed."

The hurt in his voice is like to break my heart and I put my arm through his and say, "Calven, son, help me over to Dor'thy and Belvy and let me tell how it happened."

Down at Dorothy's, we call the woman at Heather's house to let her know the young un's here and to say we will bring her back after we have a bite to eat. Once we have tended to Dorothy's ankle and made some sandwiches, they have me tell the story again, about how Prin gave her life to save her son, throwing herself in front of the pistol and dying as the bullet pierced through her heart. Calven is quiet, like he is trying to take all this in.

He had told us how those three was going to kidnap

Heather and how they couldn't have known about Heather if not for Prin. "I hated her for that," he says, "but now—"

And he stops—for fear of bawling, I reckon.

She weren't no kind of mother to this poor boy, I decide. It just weren't in her nature somehow. Running off and leaving him time after time and then putting him in the way of harm when she *was* around. But in her last deed, she gave him a greater gift even than her life. She gave him the sure and certain knowledge of her love— and he can carry that in his heart forever.

It is almost nine-thirty when we see the headlights of a car threading their way down the road from the ridge. We peek out the windows till we see the sheriff department markings on the side and we stay still as a man gets out of the car and walks towards the porch. Not till he is under the porch light and we see for ourselves that it is the sheriff do we breathe easy and open the door.

"We've found him all right," says High Sheriff Mackenzie Blaine, looking around the room at each of us. "I wanted to let you know and see if you uns were doing all right."

He glances across at Calven, who meets his eyes and nods. Heather is setting on the couch next to him and she speaks up. "Are you taking that guy to jail?"

The sheriff looks over at me. It is a long, knowing look and I give it right back. Then he says, "Well, no, we're not. The thing is . . ."

He rubs at his jaw like some folks do out of nerves. "The thing is, he got himself tangled up in the laurel somehow. Best we can figure it, he was trying to climb up one of those great big laurels, maybe trying to see over the top of all those bushes, and his foot slipped and he fell."

The sheriff looks from one to the other of us, judging how we are taking all this. "Strangest thing I ever saw. Like I said, he must of lost his footing and he fell. Of course, it wasn't much of a fall; those laurels, even the big ones, aren't that tall. But he fell and caught his neck in the fork of a big limb with his toes just inches above the ground."

The sheriff turns towards the door. "The laurels saved us the cost of a trial—just like in the old times, he was hanged by the neck until dead."

Chapter 60

The Mule

(Birdie)

They say a mule'll serve you thirty years to kill you. It weren't thirty years I served Mama but I reckon it was long enough. And who's to say—if Mama had treated me like I was a person, if she had taught me right and wrong—maybe I wouldn't have done what I did. Raise up a child in the way it should go, that's what the Book says. But it was a judgment on me, all the same.

I know that now—all them babes I bore to Luther what died so young or never drew breath—they was part of the judgment. And then for Cletus to be born simple, like what Mama had tried to make out I was. Oh, law, Mama paid for what she done to me—and I paid, time and again with each dead babe, for what I done to her.

So many times I have lived that day—in dreams, in bright sunlight, when I least expect . . .

I am back at the old home place, screaming at Mama for having cut the throat of my Snowflower kitty, hollering that I am going after Young David, and calling the Little

Things to help me. I run up towards the dark trees behind the house, singing the Calling Song. Something inside of me has broken loose and I am afraid of myself and the way I feel and would try to stop it but the something is too strong. My face is burning in the places where she hit me—first with her open hand, then with her fist, and when that didn't satisfy her, with the buckle of the belt. I can feel a thin trickle of blood, like tears creeping down my face.

Mama is right behind me. "You! Least!" she hollers, "Where do you think you're going? You run off and I'll put the High Sheriff atter you and they'll haul you off to the 'sylum, that they will. Do you hear me, Least? You stop right there!"

But I keep going and I keep singing the Calling Song. She is running hard now but I am quicker. I'll not stay here and be her servant the rest of my life, the way she has planned it from the beginning. I ask the Little Things to help me.

Bees and waspers and such has always knowed I meant them no harm. And it always is the way of it that if two folks are walking, one afore the other, the one in front who steps on the nest and riles them up won't get stung if he keeps going. It's the one coming next, the one who walks right into that great cloud of rank bees, who's like to get stung bad.

I keep hurrying on till I come to the tuft of long grass that marks the nest and I kick at it hard with my heel and keep a-going.

Mama must of put her foot right into the nest for I hear her holler and then she commences to slap at the bees. The wild song they is humming fills my ears till I can't hear the noises she is making no more.

I keep on going, thinking of my Snowflower kitty and how Mama had done her—the little head all dangling and blood a-soaking into the pretty white fur—and I circle back around the house till I am in my hidey place under the boxwood.

The little fairy cross is there in the middle of the stone circle and I pick it up and go to tapping on a stone, trying to make a pattern of sound that is different from the buzzing in my head. I tap and tap and tap till one of the arms breaks and I feel like I have done an evil thing. Then I just set and let my mind go blank.

I set there the longest time until at last my blood has cooled and I begin to think I'd best go milk ol Poll. Mama ain't in the house when I go for the pail and she has let the fire in the cookstove go most out. I build it back up and set the kettle to heating water to wash off Poll's tits. There is quiet all around me.

Mama is laying there on the path as I start for the barn with my pail of warm water. She don't move as I come up on her. I squat down beside her and look at her face, all red and swole with a thousand bites, and when I put my ear to her bosom, I can't hear no heartbeat. I rest my head there a little longer, thinking that was a thing I had never done and wishing that she had loved me, just a little.

Then I set off down the road to call the neighbors, running all the way.

Epilogue

The Sound and Smell of Joy

(Birdie)

I've had my happy times—all tumbled in together with the bad—and by God's mercy, it's them that I remember the most—them that seems the realest to me. I think back to one of those happy times—when my first babe was not but a few months old—and I nineteen years of age with my new life before me.

It is a July morning and I am on the back porch, running a wash through the wringer while little Britty Birdsong sleeps nearby in the basket we have for her. Luther is setting at the edge of the porch with the old push lawn mower he has gotten to keep things clear round the house. "With all the young uns we'll have playing about, we need us a yard, Miss Birdie," he said when he brought the contraption home that morning. "I traded two of Brownie's pups for this mower. It'll be a sight easier for keeping the grass short than that old swing blade I been using."

He sets there and sharpens the twisting blades just as careful, his file going *shhhh-shhhh-shhhh* on the steel, turning it from rust brown to shining silver. He takes his can

of 3-in-One oil and drips some real careful on the workings, then looks up at me with that sweet smile of his. My
heart swells in my bosom with love for this good man who
takes such care of me and our child. And the whisper of
the file and the scent of the oil seem like the sound and
smell of joy.

Later, when I am hanging out the clothes to dry and
Luther is pushing that mower back and forth through the
thick fescue, making a green fountain come arching out
behind, the smell of the cut grass and clean laundry is
enough to make me drunk. The mower's *rachety-rachet*
song has wakened the babe and she claps her little hands
together and crows and laughs like she is trying to sing
with it.

Another few weeks and she will sicken with the summer complaint and the mower will stay quiet, rusting in
the shed by the barn, and the laundry will be an endless
round of soiled diapers and bedclothes and her little
gowns. It will be late summer when we bury her and the
yard grass will have grown knee high.

But the joy of that perfect day, with me and Luther
young and happy, comes back to me every time I hang out
the laundry or whenever Bernice's boy comes over to cut
the grass. He uses a power mower—that rachety song is
gone forever, I reckon—but the sweet green smell of new-
mown grass don't never change.

THE END